EMBER

The Hunted Kingdom

Huntsman

EMBER

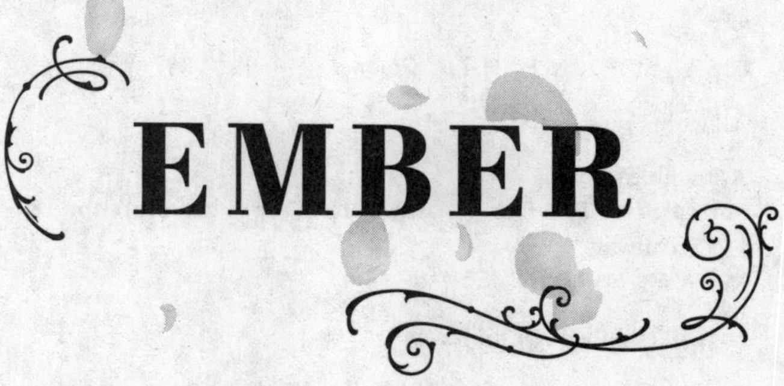

Naima Simone

BRAMBLE
Tor Publishing Group
New York

This is a work of fiction. All of the names, characters, organizations, places, and events portrayed in this work are either products of the author's imagination or used fictitiously.

EMBER

A Bramble Book
Published by Tom Doherty Associates / Tor Publishing Group
120 Broadway
New York, NY 10271

www.torpublishinggroup.com

Bramble™ is a trademark of Macmillan Publishing Group, LLC.

EU Representative: Macmillan Publishers Ireland Ltd., 1st Floor, The Liffey Trust Centre, 117–126 Sheriff Street Upper, Dublin 1, D01 YC43

The Library of Congress Cataloging-in-Publication Data is available upon request.

ISBN 978-1-250-35296-5 (trade paperback)
ISBN 978-1-250-35297-2 (ebook)

First Edition: 2026

Printed in the United States of America

10 9 8 7 6 5 4 3 2 1

To Gary. 143.

To Connie Marie Butts.
I'll miss you forever and love you longer than that.

To Rachel Brooks.
You're simply amazing, and I thank God for you.

Author's Note

From the desk of Ember Cross:

Listen, I've taken time off of work to do this, so let's make it quick. I have drugs to create and subjects to make scream. Anyway, welcome to *Ember* and the House of Cross. We're all about fashion and foul play over here. Now, before you head in and meet Asad Prince—he feasts on souls for lunch, so good luck with that shit—there are a few things we need to get out the way. I would be remiss if I didn't warn you that *Ember* is a dark romance and contains scenes that may be disturbing to some readers. So please, place your mental health and care first.

So what do I mean by *scenes*? Let me be more specific . . .

Ember includes: mentions of drug manufacturing (think Nino Brown meets Louboutin), depiction of recreational drug use (puff, puff, pass!), abuse and bullying (not shown on-page but discussed and described), scientific experiments on humans (meh, they had it coming), murder (of mostly baddies), explicit sex (filthy AF), and discussion of a mental disorder.

EMBER

CHAPTER ONE

Ember Cross

I've experienced hate before.

I hated Jennifer Myler when she slipped my crush Guillermo Braga a note during recess in the fourth grade, asking him to be her boyfriend. Served that little bitch right when she caught him kissing Kim Dixon behind the slide a week later.

I hated Anthony Warner when he pulled a Carrie and took me to prom on some bet shit, only instead of pig's blood, he humiliated me by spreading a video of him fingering me in the backseat of his car. He died right before graduation of a drug overdose. Pity. I still despise that ho though.

So yes, I've known hate.

Or I thought I did.

It isn't until this moment, staring across the ebony lid of my father's closed casket into eyes as cold and dark as the storm-darkened sky above us, that I truly understand the meaning of the word.

I *hate* Michelle Cross.

And her bitch-ass husband, too.

Yes, I do mean my father. May his soul forever do the Cupid Shuffle in hell.

One would think on the day of my father's funeral, Michelle would chip a sliver off that block of ice she calls a heart and allow me to stand with my "family." To claim one of the empty seats next to her and her sons, my stepbrothers. To at least, on *this day*, be acknowledged. To be seen. To be recognized.

But no. Even a funeral for her husband, *my father*, isn't a good enough reason to not be a cunt.

Instead, I'm exiled to the other side of the grave, relegated to one of the faceless masses of business acquaintances, employees, and nosy-ass reporters while Michelle and her sons pretend to be my father's only living relatives. Cosplay as Crosses.

After thirteen years of mental and emotional torture by Michelle and her brood, I'd built up a lot of years of loathing for my stepfamily.

And because he'd turned a willful blind eye and deaf ear to it all, anger and hate wars with love for my father as I listen to the pastor drone on about earth, ashes, and dust.

Fuck, I think I'm going to miss him a little bit.

Since I'm here and so is this pastor who supposedly has a direct line to Sky Daddy, maybe the man of God can get Him to explain how I can miss someone who's been emotionally absent for the last thirteen years. Or maybe that's one of those mysteries that we're supposed to just accept and not question God about.

Or maybe God doesn't know either.

I'm betting on the former. I mean, He still hasn't explained how He could take the only loving parent I had and leave me with a man who only acknowledged my existence to use me.

"In sure and certain hope of the resurrection to eternal life through our Lord, we commend to almighty God our brother Marcus Cross, and commit his body . . ."

A sea of people showed up today to see Marcus Cross off. Those not perched on the padded fold-up chairs stand around them in an ever-widening circle rudely encroaching on others' graves. Shit, it must break some kind of fire code, right? He would've been proud, cocky even, to witness it. Yet, even the distant cacophony of sound called Los Angeles traffic doesn't dare intrude on the cemetery's quiet as Pastor—Richter? Richard? I don't know—goes on and on. I deliberately force my mouth not to curl into a sneer. The bitch dabs at the corners of her eyes with a snow-white handkerchief, patting away imaginary tears.

I doubt she even has tear ducts, so I know the ho isn't crying for real. But the Widow Cross must put on a show for the mourners and the media allowed to film this graveside ceremony. The media forms a perimeter around the crowd of mourners, the not-so-silent shutter of cameras clicking away, providing background music like a discordant hymnal. Are their digital eyes catching the strategic angling of Michelle's body that offers a great shot of the "grieving" wife? Do they notice the lack of smeared makeup or the perfect posture that isn't slumped with sadness? Will the reporters comment on the absence of affection between mother and sons? Neither of her children comfort her, the careful distance between them an indictment rather than respect of personal space. Or maybe it's just me that isn't blinded by the mist of rain or the loamy scent of freshly turned earth.

Maybe it's just me that sees this as less of a funeral and more of a spectacle.

Nothing is sacred or private when even a funeral can be transformed into publicity and revenue for House of Cross, the successful and exclusive fashion house that was founded by my great-great-grandfather and has been run by a Cross male heir for the last four generations.

Until now.

No sons came from my father's nut sack. Just me.

And neither he nor my grandfather, may God *not* rest his soul, ever forgave me for that. As if it's my fault I was born with a pussy instead of a dick. Men. They're going to find a way to blame a woman for their shortcomings every goddamn time.

Just ask Eve.

As Pastor—shit, *what is his name*?—instructs us to bow our heads in prayer, I don't do either. Bow my head or pray. Michelle's quiet tears escalate to undignified whimpers and sobs. Good God. If there were awards for Best Performance at a Funeral . . . Instead of focusing on her, uh, display, I unwillingly shift my gaze to the man standing next to her like a golem, huge, silent, and her puppet. My childhood tormentor. My bully. My malevolent shadow.

My stepbrother Asad Prince.

I swear, when Dad decided to marry Michelle and bring her home along with her two sons, my guardian angel must've been on a binge, hitting the crack pipe and getting shit-faced, because they failed me. Epically.

Asad stands there, an imposing, stoic sentinel next to his mother, gaze fixed straight ahead, staring at nothing . . . and everything. As if he can hear my thoughts across the distance separating us, he looks at me. Those steel-gray eyes clash with mine like gladiators with raised swords, determined to fight to the death.

I return his unwavering stare, taking in his thick, dark eyebrows and smooth, peanut butter skin that make those startling smokey eyes appear almost ethereal. With lethal bone structure, a salacious yet cruelly slanted mouth surrounded by a coarse but neat, dense beard and long, curly hair pulled back into a sleek bun at the top of his head, Asad Prince stands out even among this crowd of beautiful people.

Sticks out like a fucking sore, gangrenous thumb.

It's not so surprising though. Satan had the prettiest face, after all.

The longer we engage in our visual battle, a low-grade sizzle races over the exposed skin of my face, neck, and throat. The force of that intense, unblinking gaze slides beneath the jacket of my black pinstripe pantsuit, skims the brown skin rising above the top of my vest. That damn near electrical pulse resonates with disgust, hate, maybe even a slash of fear. And underneath, fine ripples of—nope. Not even going there. Because that would make me a masochist.

And after thirteen years of unwillingly living in this man's presence, I am well versed in him being a sadist.

One of his eyebrows rises slightly, as if he's questioning why I, the cast-off Cross, would dare to maintain eye contact with him, Michelle Prince Cross's beloved oldest son? Well, fuck him. He might not consider me his equal, but I don't see him as mine either. Him, his mother, and his brother—none of them are. My veins are the only ones coursing with the DNA of the Cross family. By rights, people should be consoling me. I should be the person hovering next to that ornate casket. Yet, I've been exiled. Again. And though I should be used to it, should be resigned to this position of forced anonymity, the rank bitterness of it still tastes the same. Hasn't lost its potency.

Neither has the loneliness that skitters across my skin like a cold, whispering wind.

". . . with love, we leave you in peace. With respect, we bid you a fond farewell until we see one another again in the sure and certain hope of the Resurrection as we now commit your body to the ground."

"No." Michelle's cry rips through the air, a seemingly heartrending, brokenhearted sound to punctuate the reverend's last words of prayer. Too perfectly timed, if you ask me.

Her knees buckle, but as if choreographed, Kareem, her youngest son, catches her with a supportive arm around her shoulders and across her stomach. Her thin hand presses to her mouth, as if shuttering the rest of those plaintive sounds. A ripple of murmurs sweeps through the crowd of mourners, and the echoes of "She loved him so much" and "How is she going to go on without him?" and similar platitudes have my bullshit-o-meter pinging.

Okay, girl. Work hard for that photo op.

Moments later, Kareem guides Michelle forward to lay a red rose on top of the casket. He follows suit, as does the parade of others standing directly behind my stepfamily.

Maurice Neilson, CFO of House of Cross.

Gregory Jones, COO.

Leonard Mansfield, senior vice president.

They all march forward, flowers in hand, a dutiful, appropriately somber line of black suits and designer dresses, paying their respects with a lingering touch to the casket lid or a brief pause before moving along like a well-orchestrated performance. Well, almost everyone. Asad remains standing in front of his chair.

As do I. But not for the same reasons.

The employees and other unimportant people graciously allowed to attend the graveside service must wait until the family and executives file out before they can move forward with their flowers and final words. The press continues to snap away, eager to catch every moment that transpires. If they only suspected the truth, that Marcus Cross's only child is in attendance and relegated to stand with the employees instead of family, this quiet buzz would transform into a feeding frenzy. But they don't know. Barely anyone does, and that's just the way Marcus wanted it. In life and now in death. Especially in death.

Michelle and Asad will make sure of that.

Why should today be different from any other though?

The truth is I haven't been considered or treated like a daughter or sister in thirteen long, torturous years. Not since Dad showed up to the house with Michelle and her two sons.

"You okay, Em?" Perla Emory, my friend and co-worker, gently taps the back of my hand and peers up at me from her five-feet-even height.

A gust of wind ruffles her signature purple pixie cut and she blinks at me, concern bright from behind her blue-and-gold-frame glasses. She crosses her arms over her chest, casting a glance over her shoulder. She isn't exactly a people person, and her discomfort with being around a sizable crowd like this practically bleeds from her pores. Despite being an employee of HoC, she's here for me, and I appreciate that more than words can express. While most people would look at Perla and call her mousey, I see the opposite. To me, she's unique, sweet, and adorable. And can't forget brilliant.

Though smiling is the very last thing I feel like doing, I scrounge one up for Perla.

"I'm good."

She squints at me, but after several seconds, sucks her teeth.

"Okay. I know you're lying, but I'ma let you have that." This time my smile at her is a little more genuine. "I'm going to head out. Do you want to ride to the repast with me, Gus, and Jaq? We have room—"

"No, she's riding in the family car." A strong hand wraps around my upper arm in an implacable, don't-start-no-shit grip seconds after the interruption.

For a moment, I close my eyes and clench my jaw. Even if I didn't recognize that low, sin-gift-wrapped-in-nightmares voice, the rush of fight or flight roaring through my blood and pounding in my ears would've clued me in. Only one person incites this particular blend of rage, adrenaline, and dread.

And heat. Pure, unadulterated heat.

Asad.

I inhale a low, deep breath and open my eyes, meeting Perla's wide gaze. The instinctual urge to tell Asad where he and his family can go by way of that fucking car burns my tongue. But the anxiety and fear saturating Perla's expression bank the irritated words.

I get it . . . I do. My stepbrother is evil incarnate. And honestly that's an insult to Satan, who's probably sitting on his throne of lies right now, saying, "Bitch, don't do me like that." And having those gunmetal-gray eyes fixed on you would have anyone with half the sense God gave a gnat silently reciting the Lord's Prayer. So no, I don't blame Perla, and since I care for her—and she's one of the few people in this world who cares for me—I step in the line of fire for her.

Because apparently me and that gnat are congenital twins.

"A-are y-you sure, Em?" Perla stutters, still having my back even though her fear permeates the air like the dark earth they're about to lower my father into. She even releases a small whimper when Asad switches his narrowed focus to her.

My heart pinches at the courage Perla displays on my behalf, as misplaced as it is.

Hell no dances on my tongue. I drove myself here since I wasn't invited to ride in the family limo. Since I wasn't considered good enough, important enough, to join them. Keep that same fucking energy. Not that I would've consented to joining Michelle, Asad, and Kareem anyway. That would've been like volunteering to ride shotgun with a cackle of hyenas. Still . . .

"Yes, I'm good," I assure her, not removing my stare from my stepbrother. Only a fool diverts their attention from the biggest threat in the room. A fool who's not particularly fond of their throat. It takes everything in me not to snatch my attention or arm away from him. From his touch that burns through my clothes, straight through to my skin and beneath like a fiery brand. I detest that his implacable grip makes me feel both trapped . . . and grounded. Shit. "You can go ahead. I'll see you at the repast."

"Okay." I drag my gaze away from Asad and glance at Perla in time to not miss her soft sigh of relief or the softening of her expression. With a final nod, she hightails it away from us.

A few people still linger, gathered in small clumps, voices never rising above a level that's respectful of the dead. Like they give a fuck. Seems to me, they'd probably enjoy the noise. Liven up this place some. Must be boring as fuck being, well . . . dead.

Most of the press has dissipated, with a few sticking around like barnacles, hungry for that last shot. Several reporters trail after Michelle and Kareem as they make their way across the cemetery toward the main road and line of vehicles idling there.

"Give your last respects to your father, and let's go," Asad orders, and in spite of the nerves tripping over themselves in my belly, I arch an eyebrow at him.

Another thing only a fool does—show fear. Like most predators, Asad would smell that shit and go in for the kill.

I should know.

In the thirteen years he's been in my life, I've died a thousand times.

"Thank you for the offer of a lift, but no thank you," I say, voice even, void of the hate swarming inside my chest, saturating my bones. *Now* he wants me to be included with the "family"? Why the switch up? Because that better-late-than-never bullshit is a bone thrown to desperate losers. So why—*nope*. Don't care. I don't want any part of it. Besides, anything that comes from Asad cannot bode well for me. "I planned on staying here until they finish burying Marcus."

He cocks his head, studying me like I'm one of the worms that will eventually crawl into the coffin with my father and make him food. *Don't you fidget, bitch,* I silently hiss to myself. Yes, that intense, scalpel-sharp gaze might send a flood of anxiety and heat rushing through me, but damn if he knows.

Anxiety, because Asad Prince can be called many things—brilliant, ruthless, lethal, sociopath—but predictable isn't one of them. He's capable of anything.

Heat, because looking at this man is like staring into the face of the sun. Blinding, painful if you do it for too long. It scorches.

His beauty is a Venus flytrap. He uses it to lure a person in, and before they're aware of the real danger they're in, it's too late. They're eaten alive.

"That could take hours," he finally says.

I shrug a shoulder, finally . . . finally tearing my gaze from him and looking over at the glossy black coffin and flowers gathered on top and nearly spilling over the sides like a waterfall of color.

"I'll wait as long as it takes." Glancing back at him, I smile.

His gaze drops to my mouth, and I clench my fingers around my black Hermès clutch. Anything to prevent me from lifting my fingers to my lips and scrubbing away my plum lipstick along with the unnerving, phantom touch of his eyes. An electrified current crackles across my skin, jumping down my spine and wrapping around my waist. His fingers, still gripping my arm, singe through skin to bone beneath. Marking me. Igniting something hated, something . . . dark and needy underneath.

Once more, I shift my attention to the casket. I have no problem admitting this time it's from cowardice. Or self-preservation.

That same sense of desperate self-defense urges me to pull away from him, free myself. Insert as much distance as possible between us because that grasping, electric pulse surging through me is as dangerous as the monster before me.

"What the fuck for?" Asad demands, impatience humming in that dark, roughened-silk voice.

"Because." I force my lips to curl higher, and I wonder if the smile appears as ugly as it feels. As hungry as the rage and grief churning and mating inside me. "One man managed to rise from the dead. I want to make sure Marcus doesn't make it two for two."

If my callous explanation surprised him, he doesn't betray it. Yet his silence hangs over us like a condemnation. Like I give a fuck. He doesn't know what it feels like to be ignored, neglected, and deemed unworthy. Not the great Asad Prince. Marcus treated him more like his child than he ever did me.

So fuck both of them.

"You have two choices, Ember." I pretend like my name uttered in *that* voice doesn't send a trickle of resentment and anticipation through my veins. "A, you can walk over to the G Wagon waiting on us and get in. Or B, I throw your li'l ass over my shoulder and carry you over to that G Wagon. Either way, you're leaving this fucking cemetery."

"What about C? There's no third option?" The trepidation and healthy dose of "what the fuck?" having its way with me aren't reflected in my voice. *Show no fear.* A mantra I've learned and exhibited since childhood. Still . . . Asad has always been a show-versus-tell kind of man, so I have zero doubts he would carry through on his threat. And nobody would dare stop him. So why am I goading this man? I don't know. Must be temporary delirium from no breakfast.

A beat of silence, and then he shifts closer to me. My gaze is still focused on the casket, but like a fucking Police song, I'm very aware of every move he makes, every breath he takes. Living with him for over a decade has taught me it's in my best interest to keep careful track of him.

"C, I can pry that casket open, toss you on top of your father's stinking corpse, and bury you right along with him. See if you and him will make that rising-from-the-dead shit a three-peat."

The shiver that rips through me should be fear. Hell, if it was fear, I could try and convince myself I have even a splinter of morality left. But while I have no problem lying to other people, I refuse to do it with myself. That shiver is all sharp hope and eagerness. For all the torment Asad inflicted on me, he's never physically touched me. The same can't be said for his ho of a mother, but Michelle's touch never had something akin to a fever simmering beneath my skin. Never had me anticipating glimpsing bruises darkening my body. Never had me longing for my breath to be cut off by strong, absurdly elegant fingers wrapped around my throat.

Like I said. No morality left.

Because only a sick-ass bitch would lust after the bully and monster that made her childhood a nightmare she couldn't wake up from.

"A it is."

This wasn't a battle I could win, and over the years, I've learned how to wisely choose them. Asad and Michelle might think they've won every skirmish we've engaged in, but I plan on claiming the war as my prize.

With Marcus gone, all they see is House of Cross. Claiming the whole empire. Me? The only thing in my front view is freedom.

Autonomy.

And getting the fuck away from them.

Turning, I tug my arm free from his grip, but it isn't lost on me that if he truly willed it, I would have him clamped around me like a Pandora bracelet. I slowly walk over to the casket, stopping right on the edge of the open grave. The fragrance from the fresh flowers tickles my nose, smelling like death and final goodbyes. I inhale, dragging the scent deep into my lungs and holding it there. This is what I'll carry with me, not the Cool Water cologne that was his signature scent. The familiar anger rises within me, and the pain swimming underneath doesn't temper it.

"I'm not going to stand here and give you some sentimental farewell. We both know it would be bullshit. We barely spoke to each other in the thirteen years since Mommy died; I won't be a hypocrite and eulogize you now. One thing I can thank you for—you've been consistent. You abandoned me in life and you're doing it again in death. See? You never switched up. Goodbye, Marcus."

I open my clutch and remove the item I'd stolen from the safe in his office late last night. Comical how he didn't think I knew of its existence, much less the combination to open it. Slowly, I lift my arm and tuck a ring bearing the Cross family crest among the flowers, hiding it from sight. Since the line of male heirs to the House of Cross and its empire died with Marcus, I think it's fitting the heirloom passed down from son to son goes into the ground with him. He's taking a secret with him, too. Call it my parting gift to the father who didn't give a fuck about me unless he could use me. Even then, he didn't care about me as much as what I could do for him.

Briefly closing my eyes, I give him both middle fingers, then shoulders drawn back, I walk away without a backward glance.

I head in the direction of the path that leads to the cemetery's private street, currently lined with all models of luxury vehicles. By now, only stragglers litter the freshly mown grass. Most people have either left or are waiting in their cars to exit the gated property.

"Mr. Prince, we offer our condolences on the passing of your father . . ." A tall, slim, and either brave or disturbingly reckless reporter with a short, dark red bob and black shirt and skirt, slightly too short and inappropriate for the occasion, approaches Asad.

He barely pauses in his long stride to address her, but I don't wait for him, continuing toward the Hummer he pointed out. Marcus made it his lifelong ambition to hide my existence from the general public's knowledge, and old habits die hard. I can't lie though. A rebellious, furious, and petty part of me wants to barge over there and introduce myself as Marcus Cross's only daughter. Kind of like Edward Rochester's only wife, both hidden unwanted and scurried away. Both hiding a killing rage.

But no. I keep walking. Even after Marcus's death, I'm keeping the status quo, toeing the line.

Moments later, he reappears at my side, his long-legged stride easily catching up with me. Must've been a very short conversation. At damn near six feet, five inches, Asad towers over me by nearly a foot, and his muscled bulk far outweighs me. And I'm not a small woman. My family runs a fashion house, but my frame—all breasts, hips, ass, and thighs—isn't the "ideal" model-thin or tall. Another black mark against me.

Ask me if I give a fuck.

We silently advance on the waiting gleaming, black-on-black Hummer, and I deliberately inhale a breath and allow my mask in place and drop the barricaded shield around my heart. All necessary and learned precautions when coming in contact with my stepmother. Do I want to analyze why I'm just now erecting these barriers and not when Asad first approached me?

No, I'll pass.

The driver opens his door and climbs out of the vehicle, but Asad holds a hand up to him and stretches his other arm across me, opening the rear door. The heat and the scent of his Creed cologne mingled with an undertone of cedarwood and musk that even I couldn't duplicate in my lab reach out to me.

Shoring up my protective walls, I reluctantly slide into the waiting vehicle and sink down onto the long, black leather seat across from Michelle and Kareem. The sound of teeth being sucked greets me, and I meet my stepmother's glare. Her mouth curls as if a rancid odor followed me in, and though a lava-hot hate tries to melt the ice around my emotions, I simply cross my legs and clasp my hands together, resting them on my lap without flinching or dropping my gaze. Unlike her son, she doesn't put fear into my heart. No matter how many times she laid a belt over my back and legs, yanked my hair until I swore my scalp bled, or put her cigarettes out on my skin, she could never break me.

For a moment, my eyes clash with Kareem's and the warm, weighty sympathy there barely registers. Not because I don't think it's genuine. Kareem Prince is nothing if not . . . genuine. Genuinely polite. Genuinely nice. Genuinely weak.

At one very brief time, I almost considered him a safe space. A space who didn't belittle, threaten, or punish. But very quickly, I learned Kareem wasn't Switzerland. Kareem, with his pretty brown eyes, handsome face, and lean, wiry build, was more like a country that puts up a brief fight, then caves to the bigger power.

He's the least dangerous of the three. But that's only because his malice wouldn't be intentional, just apologetic.

Asad enters right behind me; his big body settles on the same seat as mine, and I inch over, again placing much-needed space between us. And I still feel crowded. Almost like I'm suffocating, though the vehicle could fit about ten more people.

"What is this? What are you doing here?" Michelle snaps, distaste dripping from the question. A stunning woman with long, dark hair, piercing eyes, elegant, almost elfin features, and a willowy, toned frame that could easily grace one of HoC's catwalks, even the sneer on her face can't take away from her beauty. That lump of calcified shit in her chest does though. "This is for family only."

That dig is lightweight compared to all the other shit she's said to me over the years. Must be the stress of the day getting to her.

Yet . . . the reminder that my last name might be Cross but I'm unwanted and unloved still hits its target.

I hate that for me. Hate that she can still manage to hurt me after all these years. Maybe Marcus's death and my imminent emancipation will trigger the beginning of some kind of healing.

Or fuck healing.

I'll just take Teflon-esque skin.

"Ask your son," I say with a small shrug.

She leans forward, hate glistening in her eyes instead of tears for her dearly departed husband. "Bitch, I'm asking you. Get your sad, ugly ass out of—"

"Mom, please." Kareem, ever the peacemaker, sets a hand on his mother's shoulder, attempting to . . . what? Calm her? Stop the caustic, foul words streaming from her lips like acid?

A little too late to save me from that.

Thirteen years too late. As he well knows.

"Oh, stop it, Kareem." Michelle swats his hand away, sucking her teeth at him. "You're always playing Captain Save-a-Ho with this *thing*." She scans me from the top of my head down to the pointed toes of my special edition House of Cross stilettoes—the last design my mother created before she died. Anger flashes in her dark eyes, and her mouth tightens until it's little more than a ruby-red thin line. "I repeat, what are you doing here? This is reserved for family only."

I reach for the handle on the door next to me. "Fine with me." It's not like I want to be here. And I never claimed these muthafuckas anyway.

"Touch that door if you want to." The silken yet hard-as-armor warning halts my movement, my fingers hovering just above the handle.

A latent bratty part of me itches to brush my fingers over the door, defying him. Pushing him. Just to see what the consequences would be. Though Asad was my biggest childhood tormentor next to his mother, the urge to needle him is as familiar, as prevalent, as the disgust and unrelenting curiosity. I glance at him, that big body with its broad, strong shoulders and thick thighs spread wide, knees slightly bent, and his aloof, almost bored expression that gives away nothing. Except for those eyes. A flicker in those silver depths promises retribution.

My belly twists, tautens. Flutters.

And I lower my arm.

"I told her to ride with us," he says to his mother as he removes his cell phone from the inside pocket of his black suit jacket. He switches his attention to whatever is on the screen. Knowing him, it's either destroying someone's life or arranging a fuck. Y'know. Tuesday.

Something as inconsequential as his stepfather dying wouldn't stop business as usual.

I'm envious.

I'd rather be in my lab or studio, working. Anywhere but here.

"Why, Prince?" Michelle demands.

That's right. She calls her son "Prince," as if it's a title instead of his last name. Not far off since Marcus treated him like the son he never had—the son he wished I was. Asad was his second-in-command and not to be questioned.

He doesn't immediately answer his mother, instead continues to scroll through his phone, and even type out something on it. A couple minutes of silence pass before he finally raises his head and fixes his unblinking gaze on his mother. He's not even looking at me, and a small shiver trips down my spine.

But hell, I want to know the answer to her question as well.

"Because I wanted to." His flat tone has Michelle straightening and leaning against the seat back. After a moment, she dips her chin and smiles, but the three blind mice could see that shit is forced. "And the gossip about the circumstances involving Marcus's death has already started."

Acidic bile races for the back of my throat at that reminder. I know about the nature of gossip and rumors.

The whispers of murder.

A man who attains Marcus's level of influence and power can't do so without amassing enemies. But murder? A part of my mind refuses to accept it. Maybe because of a latent remnant of naïveté that can't believe someone would actually resort to that? Definitely not because Marcus wouldn't incite someone to take that drastic action. On more than one occasion, I've wanted to commit a li'l bit of patricide myself. But those were just that—words, daydreams, fanciful thoughts.

"I'm not sure what this has to do with me," I point out.

"For once, she says something I agree with," Michelle snaps.

Bite me, bitch.

"I'd prefer not to give anyone else something to put in their mouths," Asad continues. "When we walk into that repast, we're going to at least appear like a family unit. Since everyone in this muthafucka is an expert at faking shit, that shouldn't be a big ask."

Appear like a family unit? Not a big ask?

The fuck?

I wasn't even allowed to sit with them during my father's funeral or graveside service, but he's concerned about a united front now? Granted, not many people outside of House of Cross's board and a handful of employees knew I existed. Still, *they* knew. And no matter how . . . complicated my relationship was with Marcus, these bitches could've allowed me that. But they didn't. And *now* he wants to include me?

Michelle and Asad have treated me like curated shit from the day they darkened the foyer of my childhood home. Kareem was . . . the lesser of two evils. Not evil like his mother and older brother, just . . . timid. When it came to standing up to them, well, he never did. And nothing has changed in thirteen years.

And Asad actually thinks requesting I pretend this trio of sociopaths is family isn't a *big ask*?

Why not ask Nick Cannon to get a vasectomy, too?

"Yes, it is, Prince," Michelle hisses. "I don't understand—"

"Hold that thought, Michelle," I interrupt, lifting up a finger. She leans forward, eyes glittering, body damn near vibrating with rage at my disrespect, and her hand slightly rises as if she's about to slap fire out of me. I wish a muthafucka would. She'd find I'm not the same teenager who had to live and breathe that "turn the other cheek" shit. Try that, and she would find out I'm more of the "flip a fucking table" scripture follower. "You're going to have to explain to me like I'm three because I still don't understand what this has to do with me. I'm just a scientist in the cog of the machine," I say, trying and failing to keep the faint taunt from my voice. "Why would a nameless, faceless employee walk into the newly deceased's celebration of life with his family? I was good with making my way there, eating dry-ass finger foods, and leaving all incognito and under my own power. This"—I wave a hand around the interior, encompassing the three of them—"isn't necessary."

It could be my imagination, but a blast of frigid air drifts over my skin, and I stiffen against the shiver ready and willing to overtake my body. Asad's head slowly turns my way, and a burst of nerves trembles in my belly as I wait, wait, wait for that narrowed scrutiny to land on me. Nerves and, *fuck*, anticipation.

"It's necessary because I said it is," he states, tone flat, ominous. "Everyone will be on their best behavior. I don't give a fuck how we truly feel about each other. When we walk up in there, the media better report we look like the Black Partridge Family or they gon' see the other fucking side of me. Understand?"

Michelle nods, though anger burns in her gaze, and Kareem murmurs an agreement, still obsequious to the authority he wears like the delicious scent that clings to him.

I stare straight ahead, not uttering a word. He can take my silence any—

A hard, ruthless grip pinches my chin, turning my head to face Asad. I'm seconds away from jerking his hand off me; I even lift my own hand from my lap to do just that. But the slight narrowing of his eyes makes me rethink that course of action right quick. That *don't get fucked-up in here* glance and the tightening of his fingers on me until it feels like a vise is steadily twisting, bruising me. The tender flesh inside of my mouth presses into the edge of my teeth, but I don't drop my gaze from his. I'm not that grieving, pitiful twelve-year-old desperate for his attention but scared of the pain it inevitably brings.

Asad has never broken me.

Not him or his old bitch of a mother or his pussy of a brother.

So even though the tinge of blood hits my tongue, I still silently order him to go fuck himself. As if he can read my mind or see the message in my stare, his lips curl in the barest definition of a smile. And it's not a nice one. No, it's downright mean.

My stomach knots again, and this time my heart joins the circus.

Trepidation and a little bit of panic, yes. But, Jesus, take me to the cross, I wish that's all it was.

"I asked you a question, Ember. It wasn't rhetorical. Do you understand what I just said? Nod if you do."

Fuck you. I hate you. I wish you'd choke on that rancid pussy you're always deep diving into and die.

I nod.

"Good."

He releases me with a slight shove, and while I want to massage my aching jaws, I don't give him the satisfaction. Returning my focus straight ahead, I don't miss the damn near feral gleam of satisfaction and perverse pride in Michelle's eyes. Yeah, her horned and hoofed spawn has done her proud.

Kareem's gaze softens with sympathy, pity—I can't tell and don't care to decipher it. Both have greasy humiliation sliding through my chest.

"Also, there's certain business I'd rather discuss here in private than in a roomful of people with the eyes and ears as open wide as their mouths. Sam called. Marcus left instructions to have his will read the day of his funeral. I've scheduled it for directly after the repast at seven p.m. Everyone must be there."

Asad doesn't glance my way, but I know that last sentence was directed toward me. After all, I'm the only person in this asylum who would dare defy him.

The rest of the ride to the House of Cross building downtown is passed in silence from me and Asad and quiet conversation between Michelle and Kareem. The car turns onto Olympic Boulevard and the steel-and-glass monolith also known as House of Cross headquarters broods against the cloud-heavy sky. The Castle, HoC employees call it. And with its peaked, regal roof, it does resemble that fairy-tale architecture. My great-grandfather had the building constructed in the seventies, moving the offices from the original location on Santee Alley in the fashion district.

As if of its own volition, my gaze traces the imposing figure with the gilded HoC cresting the roof. And as always, the vestiges of awe and pride whisper and brush over my sternum. This is my birthright. This—the building, the business, the empire—was germinated, built, and expanded by my family's dreams, hands, blood. Michelle and her sons might have infiltrated my family and plotted, planned, and played the sycophants to claim it and its legacy as their own, but they're not Cross born. In this they're imposters, and I'm the only true heir.

They've stripped me of so much, but *that* they can't touch. No matter how much they hunger to. No matter how much Marcus resented me for it.

Stubbornness, a misguided sense of loyalty, and ill-placed love have kept me here all this time. In truth, I should've been walked, taken my work with me. But try as I might—try as *he* fucking might—I couldn't eradicate that little girl who remembered her mother whispering that despite the neglect, her father loved her and was a good man. Couldn't completely squelch the dregs of love and hope that one day, one day he would finally see me, appreciate me.

The thing I learned about hope? It, too, is for losers.

Yet . . . I stayed.

That hope and the man centered around it are gone forever, and so is my tenure here with House of Cross. I'm done.

They just don't know it yet.

I hold the warmth of that knowledge close as the driver steers the Hummer into the underground parking deck reserved for executives and officers of the company. Goes without saying, I have to park with everyone else in the public deck a block down the street.

In minutes, we've exited the vehicle and entered the elevator that will carry us to the main level. Asad stands in the front, his tall frame and broad shoulders nearly blocking out my view of the steel doors. Michelle posts up next to him, and Kareem is a step behind his mother and older sibling. That leaves me in the rear. It doesn't escape me that our positions in the elevator are a direct reflection of the hierarchy in our "family."

What does the Good Book say though?

The last will be first and the first, last.

If Jesus said it, then I'm not arguing.

Soon enough, we exit the lift and head down the long, empty back hallway with its decorative sconces and thick, oatmeal carpet. We tread past the strip of ornately framed floor plans mounted on the walls, each displaying the timeline and growth of the Castle. They pay silent witness to our hypocritical march toward the ballroom on the other side of the building. Yes, a ballroom, because a conference room just won't do.

As we approach the open, large double doors, Asad stops just short of the entrance. And like good little soldiers, we stop behind him. Noise from the cavernous room beyond trickles out to greet us, tempting us to enter. Or in my case, warning me away. The melodious, nearly quiet music provides a bassline to the low laughter and chatter pouring out of the open doors. Floors above us, HoC staff work away. And beneath them, in the ballroom just feet in front of me, the rarefied elite already drink and feast in honor of a man who would slit their throats as easily as blink if it meant fattening his bottom line.

Maybe I do belong here, then.

I find myself staring at the short, soft whorls of hair almost brushing Asad's collar. They defy the sleek bun he's gathered his hair into, and I'm torn between congratulating them for their rebellion and scrubbing my fingers down my side to stifle the tingle urging me in a suicidal mission to touch those strands.

I blink. God, I need a drink or a blunt. Maybe both.

Asad doesn't pivot to face us, but he does turn his head until his thick beard nearly glances his shoulder. His sharp, unforgiving, and perfect profile is in stark view.

"No fuckups in here."

And with that dire warning, he strides forward, entering the ballroom. Inhaling a deep breath, I follow him.

And enter into hell.

CHAPTER TWO

Asad Prince

"Do you know the woman that walked in behind them?"

I stiffen slightly at the attempted whisper from a woman behind me. Making an appropriate but noncommittal response to the congressman currently trying to low-key beg for a campaign donation, I tune in to the not-so-quiet conversation. Out of the corners of my eyes, I glimpse two women, a tall brunette and a petite blond, both barely covered in dresses that wouldn't have been out of place at 4Play instead of a funeral for a world-renowned fashion house.

Neither the instrumental music pouring into the ballroom through the discreet surround sound nor the rising flow of chatter and laughter can conceal the women's voices. Not that they're trying to be unobtrusive. Foolish bitches. This is my playground, my territory. This room might be the size of two fucking football fields, but nothing happens here that I'm not aware of. Including this inappropriate, rude-as-fuck conversation about something that's not their gotdamn business. I shift, angling my body so I have a clearer view of the two women while still giving the congressman the impression that I give a damn about the words steadily tumbling out of his mouth without any semblance of a break.

"I don't know. I saw her at the funeral, but she wasn't sitting with the family on the first pew. Maybe she's their assistant." The brunette lifts a glass, taking a sip. "There's one thing I'm certain of though. She definitely doesn't belong to Prince or Kareem for that matter. Truth be told, I'm not sure if she's a man or woman."

Not-so-quiet snickers follow that petty bullshit. I briefly survey the immediate area. Michelle, in her element as a social hostess, holds court across the room near one of the ridiculous dove-shaped ice sculptures. And Kareem . . . I grind my teeth, a flare of pain blooming along my jaw. Kareem hovers near Ember, two glasses of wine in hand. As he extends one toward her and Ember gifts him a smile, I battle to smother the searing burst of anger sliding through my chest. Always solicitous, my brother. Always the good son, the kind sibling.

Nothing like me, who would use her neck as the stem of my glass and feed her the alcohol directly from my mouth.

Nah, I'm not the solicitous or good one.

Deliberately relaxing my jaw, I shift my attention back to the chatty politician and slide my hands into the front pockets of my suit pants. Either that or slap my palm over his mouth, or worse—cuff both of these women up by the neck like the bitches they are and hand them over to Eli. See how fucking tickled they are after my head of security drags their asses down to the subterranean basement and I let him off the chain to . . . play. Their own fucking mama wouldn't recognize them by the time he washes and puts up the extensive collection of knives, hooks, saws, and other devices that make up his torture kit.

I murmur a generic answer to the congressman, ready to move on from this man and his dry begging. Yeah, I'm a self-admitted sociopath, but even his politics disgust me. He can get a visit in the middle of the night from me and my Glock for all the racist, xenophobic bullshit he backs and promotes, but he won't get a fucking dime from me or House of Cross. But it's fun letting him think he has a chance. Imagine him trying to get money from a Black man who he probably thinks is another DEI hire.

Bitch ass.

"Anyway, fuck her. Did you see Aryn Murray? I saw her as soon as I arrived," the nosy-ass brunette continues. An ache pulses along the line of my jaw. It would be interesting to see if she could run off at the mouth without a tongue. "Have you noticed that

Prince hasn't even glanced in her direction, much less talked to her. He's ignored her for the last two hours."

Malicious glee damn near drips from her words, and her girl chuckles.

"Of course I noticed. Do you think they're still together? Trouble in paradise?" The blond sighs. "I hope so. Let the rest of us bitches have a shot at all that man."

I wouldn't fuck either one of them with the congressman's dick. And as for Aryn, she has never been my woman. Yeah, we've been fucking for a little over a year, but she's free to do her own thing when not with me because I for damn sure do mine. Ours is an equally beneficial partnership. She uses me for exposure that has already elevated her supermodel career, and I get easy, convenient pussy.

Win fucking win.

". . . nasty rumors circling. Not that I believe—"

"Repeat that." I abruptly focus back on the congressman, and the murmur of conversation in the small circle surrounding us abruptly ceases. He flinches before he covers the telltale reaction with a strained, nervous smile.

He should be nervous.

"I said, I heard the rumors about Marcus's death, but I—"

"What rumors?" I softly ask, staring him down in his watery blue eyes. Moving forward the slightest inch and invading his personal space. The small party of aides and sycophants he approached me with slowly eases back, leaving him on his own. Abandoning him to my displeasure. "I'm not sure I know what you're talking about. What rumors?" I press, daring him to repeat it.

Yeah, the gossip surrounding Marcus's death wouldn't just die off right along with him. He was a powerful man, so talk of him being offed was more titillating than him having a heart attack or stroke. Even now, his body chilled in a cold, wet grave waiting for the worms to start playing "don't drop the soap" with his ass. And the asshole deserved every peek-a-boo. But murder?

This wasn't the fucking *Godfather*, and Marcus couldn't put a horse's head in nobody's bed. His bitch ass would've been too afraid about getting blood on his Italian loafers. Sometimes people just fucking died from bad diet, bad choices, and playin' in God's face.

If the congressman doesn't watch himself with spreading this kind of talk, he's going to find out what happens when he plays in my face. God is a little too busy, but I got time today.

As if he can read his obituary on my face, he blinks, swallows, and his prominent Adam's apple slides up and down his throat.

"No rumors. I misspoke," he whispers.

I scan the faces behind him and none of them are brave enough to meet my gaze.

Satisfied, I nod. "We all make mistakes. Now, Congressman, if you'll excuse me." I clap him on the shoulder. "There's something I need to handle."

"Oh yes, sure. We can talk later . . ." He rambles to my back because I don't hear shit else he says as I walk away.

I need to get away from his long-winded ass and those two hoes before I pull my Glock and shoot this bitch up. I clench, then stretch out my fingers, already feeling the grip of the gun in my hand like a lover I can't stay away from. When I find out who let that shit about Marcus possibly being murdered, I'm stripping them clean of their flesh, Buffalo Bill–style. Do I have my suspicions about the true nature of Marcus's death? Yeah. Strong suspicions. But until the truth is confirmed one way or the other, I'm shutting down all speculation. Ruthlessly.

Flipping my wrist over, I peep at the time on my gold-faced Patek Philippe. Nearly six o'clock. A little over three hours since we first arrived. More than enough time to start wrapping this up. If these people haven't stuffed their faces with free food and guzzled enough alcohol by now, that's their problem. I'm about ready to shut this shit down.

I maneuver my way to the full bar without stopping to acknowledge the various people who speak to me. The throngs of people crowded there part like I hold a staff and got ten plagues notched under my belt, allowing me a clear path. They scatter, leaving me by myself as I wave the bartender over. She immediately approaches, and I ignore the invitation for more than alcohol in her smile and eyes. The white shirt, black pants, and bow tie can't conceal that sexy-ass body with large titties, wide hips, and an ass I can see from the front. She's bad as fuck, and another time, I might've taken her up on her offer. But right now, all I want is a shot of that Henny she has behind the bar. No side of pussy.

"What can I get you?" she asks, showing me all thirty-two of her teeth.

"Double shot of Hennessy."

Her smile dims a little at my abrupt answer, and with a small nod, she fixes my drink.

"Here you go."

I accept the glass filled with the cognac and hand her a hundred-dollar bill for her tip. That grin returns, and I turn away, lifting the glass for a long sip. In the time I've been here, it's the first drink I've allowed myself. I don't trust none of the mu'fuckas in here. For Michelle and even Kareem, this is more of a social event, an opportunity to network. And yes, I've been socializing, but for me, it's more about showing every mu'fucka in here that House of Cross might've lost its leader, but we're far from weak. There's nothing vulnerable about us, and it's business as usual. That force of strength requires being aware and sober. Being impaired around these people would be stupid as fuck, and I may be a lot of things, but stupid isn't one of them.

Because forget God willing. By my hard work, all the lying, the swallowing of my hate and pride, I've earned every last ephemeral brick of this empire. I've spent years in servitude to a man who shoved the blade of disgust and betrayal deeper with every second spent in his company. I've bled literal and figurative blood for House of Cross, and no one and no thing will take it from me.

And I swear fo' God right now, if Marcus's bitch ass

double-crossed me, I will dig his corpse up with my bare hands and beat the shit out of him. It'll be a DIY cremation.

Just as I raise the glass for another sip, my cell vibrates in the inside pocket of my suit jacket. Except for essential personnel, the offices are closed today because of the occasion, but for me, it's business as usual. Funeral or not, my money doesn't take a backseat to anyone or anything. Shit, Marcus would probably appreciate that sentiment.

I remove the phone and glance down at it. A notification fills the top of the screen. Tapping the message box, I stare down at the text from Aryn.

Seeing you in that suit makes me want to drop down to my knees right now and suck your dick in front of all these people, Daddy.

A spark of annoyance flickers in me. Some men might like that daddy kink shit, but that ain't ever been me. Low-key, the shit gives Electra complex. Lifting my head, I scan the room, and, as if she was waiting for me to find her, my gaze connects with Aryn's.

A small, sultry smirk that has become her signature in the modeling world curves her lips. I've seen grown men and women blush and get weak at the knees over that smile. And luminescent golden-brown, blemish-free skin. And gorgeous face of wide, oval-shaped eyes, patrician angles, and lush curves. And tall, slim body with a handful of perfect breasts and a firm ass. None of that do shit for me. Aryn might opt to believe that what we have is more than it is, but that's on her. I've always been brutally honest with her. And keeping it one hundred, she better thank her mouth that I still keep her around. The pussy is subpar, but the head is fire.

I tuck the phone back in my jacket without replying to the text, then turn back to the bar to finish my drink. But not before catching the anger that tightens her beautiful features. Like I give a fuck. My dick doesn't run nothing over here.

"There you are." My mother glides up to me and slides an arm under mine, tipping her head back to peer up at me.

At fifty-two, my mother is stunning. With her flawless, dark brown skin, delicate facial features, and tall, slender form, she could give a woman fifteen years younger competition. She keeps the best plastic surgeon on retainer to ensure it.

"Lorenzo Rossi from Agosti wants a quick word with you," she says.

"Later."

"Prince." Her grip on me tightens, and when I glance down, her social mask with its not-too-big, not-too-small smile is very firmly in place, but her slightly narrowed dark eyes issue a warning to me. Like I give a fuck. The time when she was able to control me has long passed. My mother has the maternal instinct of a fucking piranha, so it shouldn't be a leap or surprise that she raised a predator for a son. "He wants to talk about a possible collaboration between us and his house. Imagine an exclusive line of House of Cross shoes paired with Agosti's newest collection. The prestige alone is priceless exposure, and we could assign any price point on the collection."

"Don't get it twisted, Michelle. He needs us more than we need him; I don't give a fuck how long his fashion house has been around. And he knows it, which is why he's been calling the office for four weeks now." I remove my arm from hers and meet her annoyed gaze. "Like I said, later."

Her deep red–painted lips flatten and anger flickers in her dark eyes, but she doesn't say anything further. Because although Michelle gave birth to me, she knows she can fuck around and find out, too, just like any random bitch on Melrose.

"Fine," she quietly snaps. "It's after six. We should say a few words before people begin to leave." When I nod, she squeezes my arm. "I'll get Kareem."

She walks off in search of my younger brother, and I head for the raised, gleaming wooden platform that's more of a stage toward the front of the ballroom. In the past, live bands would play from here. But today, only I climb the side steps, joined by Michelle and Kareem moments later. A wave of applause fills the room as an HoC staff member hurries over, microphones in hand, passing one to each of us. I decline with a small shake of my head, sliding my hands into my pants pockets. Michelle switches her microphone on and smiles, turning to the "mourners" watching us from the floor.

"Hello, everyone." In seconds, people quiet, and Michelle is in her element as all eyes fix on her. There has never been a spotlight Michelle didn't love or claw and backstab her way into. "Thank you so much for joining my family in celebrating the life and homegoing of my dear husband, Marcus Cross. He would've been so touched by your presence and the unflagging support you have given me and my sons."

Touched.

That's bullshit.

Marcus Cross would've considered their attendance and sycophant behavior his due. That entitled son of a bitch would've needed a heart to be touched. Not that I'm judging. Hell, that's probably why we got along. Two emotionally barren mu'fuckas. I still don't understand how he fathered someone like . . .

I survey the room, searching for her.

And like always, I find her. Standing in the back of the room, surrounded by her lab mice.

She might be all back of the bus 'n shit in this ballroom, but ain't shit cowering or submissive about her. With her shoulders drawn back, head slightly tilted up, face stoic, and wineglass clutched in her hand, she's a queen, surveying her subjects and judging us all lacking. And yet . . . even across the space of a cavernous ballroom, she can't conceal the fierce fire seething beneath all that luscious skin.

Maybe it's all that burning hate that damn near emanates from her that draws me. It reaches out to me, heats my skin, and I want to bathe in it. Let all that rage and animosity consume me in huge, greedy bites. Yeah, her pain has always been a balm to my soul.

If I had one.

My mother's voice drones on, nothing but an irritating buzz in my ears as my gaze clashes with *hers*.

The two women from earlier were jealous bitches. No way in fuck anyone with a working dick or pussy could take one look at Ember Cross and not see all woman. Did she smear pounds of makeup so that the color of her face didn't match her neck? Did she clothe herself in tight, short-ass dresses where, if she bent over, her whole pussy would be on display? Nah. But she didn't need all that shit.

Like today, a black pinstripe suit strokes every voluptuous curve. Perfect, almost more than full breasts shoving against a vest that strains like fuck to contain all that soft-looking flesh. It's holding up admirably. Wide-legged pants encase beautifully rounded hips that have my fingers itching to grip and bruise as I slam into that wet-ass pussy from the back, obsessing over the sexy arch of her back and the ripples of an ass that people get under the knife to get. Thick thighs that would be the perfect pair of all-year-round earmuffs. She's covered from wrist to feet, yet sex damn near seeps from her pores.

I allow my gaze to roam over her face—a face that has tortured me for more than a decade. Her long, dark blond hair is secured in a bun at the nape of her neck, providing an unfettered view of those haunting honey-colored eyes, wide nose, wider mouth with lush lips created for sucking skin off a dick, and that shallow dimple in the middle of her chin.

Yet, as beautiful as she is, none of it compares to that big-ass, lethal mind.

She's the deadliest combination walking. People like to whisper behind my back. Saying I'm dangerous and ruthless. They tend to overlook the real threat in their midst. Ember's like a deadly virus. Invisible to most. Sneaky. And deadly as fuck.

A threat doesn't always come in the form of thick muscle or heavy artillery. Sometimes, it's the mastermind in the background, the silent, patient killer behind it all that's the most lethal. That's Ember Cross. Unsuspecting. Underrated. Unassuming.

She's also my every punishment and penance wrapped in silken skin and bad attitude.

". . . so as we move forward without my beloved Marcus, we'll do so as a strong, united family leading House of Cross into the future. It's what Marcus would've wanted." As if on cue, a server appears with a tray holding three glasses of wine. I snort, and Michelle cuts her eyes at me. Leave it to her ass to make her final farewell to her husband a production starring her. She chooses a glass, as does Kareem. I give the server a look, and he ducks his head as he moves backward, disappearing from my sight. "If you have a glass, please raise it for one last toast." She pauses, and more than half the people lift their glasses in the air. "To Marcus. The world of fashion will never be the same without you. You will be missed. I love you."

"To Marcus." The room echoes with the toast.

I don't raise shit.

And as my gaze connects with Ember's again, neither does she.

"I thought we were doing this reading at the Castle?" Michelle snaps from the chair set in front of Marcus's desk, her foot swinging like a highly pissed-off pendulum. "It makes no sense for us to move everything here at the house when we had a perfectly good conference room where we were."

"I'm assuming Sam thought reading the will in Marcus's home would be more secure," Kareem murmurs.

"Bullshit," she mutters. "Sam just loves to inconvenience anyone when he possibly can. If he wasn't Marcus's best friend, I doubt he would even have a job with Cross. God knows I tried to tell him that very same thing too many times to count." Michelle huffs out an aggravated breath, drumming her fingers on the armchair. "Where the fuck is Ember?" she demands, switching subjects with the speed of light. Her foot swings harder. "The little bitch has always been so damn disrespectful. You'd think she could get her shit together on the day her father's laid to rest. So fucking selfish."

From the chair on the other side of our mother, Kareem looks at me, eyebrow raised.

Yeah. The audacity of that shit.

Marcus's study used to be his sanctuary where no one except me was permitted. No doubt he's cursing us all out for congregating on his holy ground. The room full of heavy, richly upholstered furniture, tall bay windows, dark, velvet drapery, stuffed bookshelves, and art that didn't move him as much as the price tag did is a far cry from a chapel. And yet, here we are, waiting to hear the benediction of his portfolio. I shift, leaning back against the wall nearest to Marcus's desk. It's the perfect vantage point of the entire room—and its inhabitants.

"Mom, it's all right. Sam isn't even here yet. Ember still has time to get here," Kareem placates her.

"God, Kareem." She flicks a hand in his direction without glancing at him, her body turned toward me. "Always so fucking chivalrous. Don't you get tired of being the hero?" She spits out "hero" like others would say "hot dogshit." "I swear," she snorts, "the way you pant after that girl is fucking pathetic and sad."

Like always when it comes to our mother, he remains quiet. My younger brother is more of the suffering-in-silence type, while I'm just the make-you-suffer kind. And Michelle takes full advantage of his disposition. Kareem owns a nasty desire and obsession with earning our mother's approval. He'd have a better chance of turning water to wine. Michelle dangles that illicit fruit in front of him, and he never fails to take a bite, only for her to snatch it away like the manipulative bitch she is. I wasn't born with Kareem's affliction.

"I'm sorry. I was unavoidably held up." Samuel Chavis strides into the study, his tall, lean frame clothed in a tailored suit that probably cost more than someone's monthly mortgage, a leather briefcase in hand.

The light from the chandelier strikes his immaculately styled black-and-gray hair and smooth, light brown skin. Sam Chavis, Marcus's and the House of Cross's longtime lawyer, is an imposing figure who exudes power, wealth, and menace. Only a privileged few know that the courtroom isn't the only place where Sam kills. Well, correction. Only a privileged few who are alive possess that knowledge. The others who're aware are too busy being dead to share that piece of intel.

"It's about time, Sam." Michelle huffs out a breath, crossing her arms. "Time is precious to some of us and shouldn't be wasted."

Sam rounds Marcus's desk and pins his flat, unblinking gaze on my mother. I've never been face-to-face with a snake—not the animal-kingdom kind, anyway—but I easily imagine his stare might be identical to that particular reptile's just as it's about to strike. And like any judicious prey, my mother falls silent and still. Michelle is a bitch, but she's a smart one.

"As I was saying, I apologize for my tardiness," he finally says, his low but powerful voice carrying easily as if he's in a courtroom instead of a nearly empty study. Settling his briefcase on the desktop, he spreads his fingers out across the gleaming leather surface. "I won't hold you long—wait." He frowns. "Where is Ember?"

Michelle snorts. "That's what we would like to know. Can we just move forward without her?"

"No, we cannot. Marcus's will stipulates that his family must be present. That includes his only daughter." A slight sneer curls Sam's lips, and condescension damn near drips from his voice. A good son would've checked him, demanding he show the proper respect for his mother.

That ain't me.

In order for me to be a good son, I would've needed a better mother.

"It's just ten after. Let's give Ember a few more minutes." Kareem tries to placate Michelle. "I'm sure it's been a trying and stressful day for her—"

"Like it hasn't been for all of us? For me?" Michelle snaps.

"Marcus was *my* husband. But I'm still here, showing the proper respect. No wonder Marcus couldn't stand the little bi—"

"Did I hear someone say my name?" Ember glides into the room, bringing a kinetic energy that electrifies my skin.

She still wears the suit from earlier, and I imagine it scattered on the study's floor, and her thick ass propped on the edge of her father's desk, legs spread and pussy glistening and soaked. Ready to be sucked and fucked. By me.

Is it incestuous to want to beat the lining out of my stepsister's pussy? Want to grip that slender throat and squeeze while lust and fear darken those honey eyes? Maybe. Now ask me if I give a fuck.

On a daily, I vacillate between needing to feel those undoubtedly tight and slick walls collapse around my dick and seeing that beautiful brain decorating the wall behind her.

I'm obsessed with fucking my stepsister and killing her.

Up until today, I haven't done either. But depending on what this will reveals, the latter will be another sin to stain my already dirty, questionable soul.

Will justify why I've remained this long with House of Cross.

Nah, not justify.

Reward. Finally, I will receive my reward for sowing all these long years as Marcus Cross's loyal second.

He owes me. And I'm about to collect in not just money but flesh.

His daughter's flesh.

"Now that we're all here, we can begin," Sam says as Ember sinks onto the couch across the room from the rest of us. Nothing in the casual cross of her legs or the relaxed slope of her shoulders belays the tension riding everyone else in this room. Her expression remains cool as glass, revealing nothing of her thoughts or feelings. But then again, this has been the dynamic of our "family" for the past thirteen years—ever since she was twelve and me, seventeen. Different. Distant. Separate.

"Finally," Michelle mutters.

Sam glances at her, and wisely, she shuts the fuck up. Then he glances at Ember, and that black gaze slightly softens. Though he's been in her life since Marcus nutted in his wife, a fierce, brutal urge to snap his neck punches me in the chest. She's not mine. And this damn near primal need to harm is not rational. But then again, neither am I.

"As I was saying"—Sam stares at Michelle—"since we're all here, I can begin." He opens his briefcase and removes a stack of papers. "I, Marcus Lamar Cross, a resident of Los Angeles, California, being of sound mind and body, do hereby make, publish, and declare this to be my Last Will and Testament."

Silence permeates the room, and a fine tension invades my body. It seems as if I've been waiting for this moment for half my life, and now that it's here, a foreign burst of nerves crowds my stomach. It takes every scrap of control to remain leaning against the wall and to school my expression.

"Let it be known that if any beneficiary under this will contests this document or any of its provisions, any share or interest given to the contesting beneficiary is revoked and will be disposed of as if he or she had not survived me." Sam pauses and his dark gaze meets each of us in the room. "To my wife, Michelle Denise Cross, I bequeath the Pacific Palisades home, the second home in Aspen, Colorado, ten billion dollars, and ten percent ownership of House of Cross. If she precedes me in death, her sons, Asad and Kareem Prince, will receive her inheritance."

Anyone else receiving a fortune in real estate, money, and stocks would be ecstatic. Fucking transcendent. Not my mother though. Her lips flatten until they damn near disappear, and her fingers ball into tight fists on her thighs. Knowing her like I do, she probably expected Marcus to leave her everything. The money, the property, the company. All because she let him fuck on her for the last thirteen years. I shake my head. That mu'fucka didn't even do shit for his own flesh 'n' blood. I don't get why Michelle thought she was so special just because she spread it low and wide.

"To my stepson, Kareem Malcolm Prince, I bequeath the Bel Air penthouse, eight billion dollars, and five percent ownership of House of Cross."

Unlike our mother, Kareem seems pleased. He nods and gives Sam a small smile, but I glimpse the gleam in his eyes. Greed. That's more money than he's ever seen, much less possessed. I can practically see his brain calculating how many bitches he's going to trick off on.

"To my daughter, Ember Belle Cross, I bequeath the trust left to her by my first wife and her mother, Kimberly Jacobs Cross, in the amount of twenty-three billion dollars. I also leave Ember an additional twenty billion, also to be held in trust until she reaches thirty years of age or enters into marriage, whichever comes first. I nominate my stepson, Asad Grayson Prince, to serve as trustee of the trust. If Asad is unable or unwilling to serve as trustee, I nominate my wife, Michelle Denise Cross, to serve in his place. Lastly, I bequeath Ember thirty-four percent ownership of House of Cross, with Asad Prince as proxy to the voting shares."

Her swift intake of breath pierces the silence like a razor-sharp scalpel. I switch my attention from Sam to her, and though her expression remains aloof and reserved, those light brown eyes tell another story. Scream that story. And it's one of rage, betrayal, and pain. Of hate. Seeing as how I've seen those emotions reflected in that gaze often over the last thirteen years—shit, I've been the cause of them more often than I can count—I easily recognize them.

But in the next moment, it's as if those eyes shutter, and there's . . . nothing.

Like everyone else in this family, she's mastered the art of pretending. But of us all, she's perfected it. She's had to, given the family she had the misfortune to be born into.

Marcus was as disloyal and dismissive of her in death as he was in life. When, in truth, House of Cross wouldn't exist without her.

That knowledge won't stop me from stealing her birthright though.

With a will that's been forged in the fires of rage, pain, and helplessness, I don't move a muscle. Not even an involuntary flinch. Nothing in my face or demeanor betrays the vicious and primal exhilaration sweeping through me like a destructive twister.

Three inheritances read and revealed. Only one more left. I can nearly taste the victory, fuckin' feast on it with bloody, grasping hands. *Mine.*

Michelle turns in her chair and looks at Ember, a malicious smile turning up the corners of her mouth. Even before the words escape her, I know they're aimed to maim, to eviscerate. To see Ember bleed. I won't allow it. Not here, not in this room with the ghost of her father not even fully formed yet. Nah, Michelle won't get the chance to draw that first blood. Even if it's me who has to make the initial slice.

"Anything to say, Ember?" I ask, embracing the ugly, slick slide of anticipation weaving its way through my veins like a bloated, filthy river.

That unblinking gaze of sunshine and syrup shifts to me, and my dick thumbs against my thigh, stretching and hardening at the heated punch of her eyes meeting mine. My whole body tightens with an eagerness that's usually reserved for dirty fights and dirtier fucking.

Will this be it? Will this be the time she unleashes all that banked and beautiful rage on me? I've waited for over ten years for it to happen.

But as she inhales, then slowly exhales, and her head slightly tilts to the side, apparently today won't be that day.

Fuck.

"No. Just sitting here being quietly thankful for all of my blessings," she evenly says.

Her reply leaves a distinct scent in the room. Smells like bullshit and broken dreams.

"If we can continue," Sam says, his voice possessing a warning that I ignore for a protracted moment where Ember and I engage in a visual *fuck you*.

I almost smile.

Almost.

I shift my attention back to the company attorney and find myself entrenched in another game of warfare. A muscle ticks along his strong, tight jaw, and his narrowed gaze is drenched in suspicion. The older man has never liked me, and the feeling is entirely mutual. Unlike her father, Sam has always sought to protect Ember, shelter her. For that, I resent the fuck out of him. Not because I want the role he's assumed.

No.

It's because he stands between me and my self-appointed victim.

"To my stepson, Asad Grayson Prince, I bequeath the rest and residue of my estate, including but not limited to real estate in Los Angeles, Miami, New York, London, England, and Paris, France, sixty billion in assets, forty-six percent ownership, and the position of CEO of House of Cross and all of the Cross Corporation entities. If he does not survive me, his brother and my stepson Kareem Malcolm Prince will receive his inheritance."

A roar invades my head, thundering and deafening me to everything but the bloodthirsty howl of *mine*.

Finally fucking all *mine*.

For all intents and purposes, I own eighty-five percent of HoC. Forty-six percent belongs to me outright, but with Marcus granting me voting proxy of Ember's thirty-nine, no one—not even my mother or brother—can defy me. Marcus didn't screw me. He screwed his daughter, but not me. A sensation too hot, too blinding, too primal to be labeled mere joy soars through me like a meteor crashing into earth. All the lies, the scheming, the years of submitting myself have proven worth it.

House of Cross is mine now. Mine to take in any direction I want. Mine to shape how I decide. Mine to shatter right down to the corrupt, bitter roots and erect in my reflection. No more Marcus Cross. Just Asad Prince.

I glance at Michelle, and her eyes glitter with pride and triumph. Even though I could give two shits about how my mother feels about me, the tightening of my chest makes a liar out of me. In my thirty years, I can easily count the number of times Michelle looked at me with delight etched into her features and brightening her gaze.

Every single one of them had been when I inflicted some kind of torture on Ember.

My mother raised a sadistic sociopath, and she's gotdamn tickled pink.

"I hereby nominate, constitute, and appoint House of Cross's legal counsel and my lifelong friend, Samuel Chavis, to act as the executor of this, my Last Will and Testament. In the event that Samuel Chavis declines to act or precedes me in death, I nominate and appoint my stepson Asad Prince to act in his place." Sam pauses, and I can't tell if he's having a moment of mourning for his friend . . . or silently calling him a bitch-ass muthafucka. Maybe both. "That's it. If any of you have any questions about the details of this will, you have my contact information. If you don't mind, I'd like to have the room and speak to Ember in private, please."

It's not a question or suggestion; it's an order. Though a sneer curls Michelle's lips, she stands from her chair. I don't need to possess telepathy to know she wants to tell Sam fuck him and she's not going anywhere. But as loose as she is with the mouth, Michelle doesn't have a death wish. And Sam would wrap his hand around her throat and wouldn't let go until she pissed on herself. And if she counted on me to save her, well, meeting her husband in the afterlife would dispel that belief.

Wisely, she remains quiet and stalks for the study door, Kareem on her heels. As they pass Ember, my brother's steps falter, and he pauses in front of our stepsister. His fingers flex near his thigh, straightening, then curling in a fist.

As if he longs to touch her but is afraid to. Instead of laying a hand on her, he leans over and whispers something in her ear that's too low for me to catch. Ember nods and grants him a small, strained smile.

That's more than she's ever offered me.

An equally unholy and dark possessiveness swims behind my rib cage, slamming against it like tsunami waves desperate to swallow and destroy everything in their path. My body locks, and I force myself to remain still and not charge across the room, throw my younger brother to the floor, and stomp a mud puddle in his ass. Thankfully for him, he straightens and follows our mother out the door.

"Prince," Sam says, voice hard, ice-cold.

"You just read that will, Sam." I drag my gaze from the direction my brother disappeared in and return it to the older man. "I own all this shit . . . including you. I'm not Michelle or that fuck ass Marcus. You tread lightly with me, and I won't pay a visit to your youngest up there at Stanford. Florence Moore Hall, right?"

Red rushes into his face, staining his patrician cheekbones. Deep lines etch his forehead and bracket his mouth. Shit, he better calm down. If his old ass strokes, I'm just going to roll his big ass under the desk and keep it moving. Fuck I look like.

Sam slaps both palms down on the desktop and leans forward, pinning me with a glittering, narrowed stare. "Muthafucka, did you just threaten my family?"

I chuckle, pushing off the wall.

"Nah, not me. Just a friendly reminder of who I am and what I'm capable of." I see my death in his dark eyes, and that shit don't move me. "I'll leave you to your meeting now."

Best he remember that and not lose sight. As soon as that will was read, all this became mine.

And everyone.

And by everyone, I mean Ember.

He might be her godfather, but she only had one daddy. That mu'fucka's sucking the devil's balls, and mine are about to be slapping against his daughter's pussy. Now Sam can either get out the way or get run the fuck over. His choice before I make it for him.

I stride across the room, letting my gaze sweep over Ember on the way out. In one swift glance, I take in the swell of her breasts over the vest, the slight pooch of her belly as she sits, perched on the couch's edge, and those thick thighs shoving against the material of her suit pants. When I lift my scrutiny to her face, I nearly stop, push her to the cushions, rip those pants down, and go deep-sea diving between her legs.

That face, man.

It's eerily composed, beautiful. But those eyes are flat, unemotional. The eyes of a killer. One thing I've never doubted about Ember Cross. The bitch is crazy. Not "sneak in your house while you're sleeping and drink your milk" crazy. Nah. She's "feed you dinner and continue eating as you die from the cyanide she added as seasoning" crazy.

That's how I know the pussy is good.

Pregnant and crazy pussy are always good.

I lick my lips, smothering a growl, as if I can taste her juices now. I bet that shit's so thick and creamy I wouldn't need any beard balm. That wet would keep it glistening and growing.

Clenching my jaw, I force my feet to head for the door and not make a detour for that couch. I'm high on the victory of winning her father's company, and she would be spoils of this war.

I exit and shut the door behind me and draw up short at the sight of two men wearing dark suits standing right outside the study doors.

Just as I'm about to demand to know who they are and how the hell they got inside this house, the shorter, bulkier one nods at me.

"We're with Mr. Chavez," he informs me, tapping the lapel pin I didn't notice on my first perusal. The small oval displays the logo belonging to Sam's firm.

"Fine." I return his nod, then stride down the hall toward the rear of the house. Marcus soundproofed the study long before me, Michelle, and Kareem came along. That's not gon' keep me from learning why Sam needs a private conversation with Ember. I've come too far, done too much, lost too much to allow her and her godfather to plot against me just when everything's falling into place.

House of Cross is mine. Ember is mine. And I plan on keeping all of them.

I don't stop to figure out where my mother and brother have gone—probably in the living room toasting their windfall. Turning in the opposite direction, I head for the library, enter, and lock the door behind me with a skeleton key I had made years ago. There isn't a room in this mausoleum that I can't enter—whether I'm invited or not.

The library is a slightly smaller replica of Marcus's sanctuary. Same masculine furniture, heavy drapery, expensive art. Instead of bay windows, floor-to-ceiling bookshelves line two of the three walls. I don't pay attention to none of this shit as I quickly move across the hardwood floor for the wide, ebony desk near the French doors and round it. Sinking into the black leather chair, I pull open the middle drawer and waste no time locating and pressing a hidden button on the wooden lip. A panel on the desktop noiselessly slides back, and a computer monitor slowly rises from the depths of the piece of furniture.

I press the power button on the thin side of the monitor, and after several seconds, about sixteen small squares fill the screen. One for each room in this house, except for the bathrooms, and for the immediate outside areas surrounding the property. Without hesitation, I tap the square that reflects the study, and in the next instant, the view takes up the entire screen. Sam emerges from behind the desk as Ember rises from the sofa. They meet each other in the middle of the room, and she walks into his outstretched arms.

Tapping the bottom-right corner, I turn the volume up and lean back in the chair, watching and listening to the scene unfolding in the room I just abandoned. Maybe I should feel shame about eavesdropping. But I don't.

I'll do anything to protect myself and what's mine.

And I'll kill anyone who even thinks about trying to take it away from me.

CHAPTER THREE

Ember

I stare at Asad's wide shoulders as he leaves the study. Even when the door closes behind him, I can't remove my gaze from it.

Can't stop myself from imagining freeing him of the gun he hides under his suit jacket and gifting him with a third eye right in the middle of his forehead.

Or driving a knife deep into his neck and severing his spinal cord, Predator-style. That's my favorite vision, even though I don't know how to handle either weapon. It's just the dagger is more . . . personal.

God, I want to get up close and personal with my stepbrother.

Especially when it ends with blood coating both of us.

"Ember."

I snatch my attention from the study door, shelve my mental musings of homicide, and look at my godfather. The softening of his sharp, handsome features nearly unleashes the tight harness I have on my emotions. I love Sam; he's the only person in whose presence I would dare to close my eyes or turn my back. But right now, with my father's words—his edicts—still ringing in my ears, I don't want softness. I don't want his pity. Because either might trigger something other than my rage.

And I need my rage.

If I'm going to survive, I need it.

"If you're going to give me some excuse for why Marcus is a misogynistic asshole, don't bother, Sam."

I rise from the couch, and for a second, I sway, my head swimming with so much of . . . everything. And none of it good. Rage—searing hot, roaring and racing like an out-of-control forest fire—swells within me, almost capsizing me in its powerful undertow. Bracing myself, I curl the fingers of my left hand into a tight fist, digging my nails into the flesh of my palm. I don't stop until the first bite of pain radiates through my hand. I press harder, making the pain flare hotter, brighter. After several moments, I inhale, hold my breath, and release it. Then, starting with my shoulders, I deliberately relax each muscle down to my toes.

The lie I tell myself: I'm unlovable.

The facts: My mother loved me, and if she'd had a choice, she wouldn't have left me. Sam loves me, even if it's just because I'm all that's left of the woman he secretly worshipped—Kimberly Cross, his best friend's wife and my mom.

The lie I tell myself: I don't belong here. I'm unwanted.

The facts: I'm not just the last living person with Cross DNA running through their veins, but neither this fashion house nor empire would survive without me. I'm more than wanted; I'm needed.

I knock down the automatic negative thoughts one by one using the cognitive behavioral therapy tools taught to me by my therapist, as well as the relaxation techniques. I've battled intermittent explosive disorder since I was eight years old. After being diagnosed and entered into therapy at nine, I've learned coping skills and have managed my condition over the years, and my outbursts have lessened as I matured. Shit, with my father and stepfamily, I've had plenty of opportunity and years to put those mechanisms into practice. But right now, with my skin prickling like tongues of fire are lapping at it, my limbs tingling with painful pinpricks, my rib cage constricting around a heart running a hundred-yard dash . . . Yeah, I'm afraid even the CBT method won't be enough to prevent the imminent explosion.

"Ember." His low yet soft voice ripples through me, somewhat soothing the savage beast crouching inside me. He crosses the room toward me. "Sweetheart."

It's that endearment, wrapped in a tenderness I so rarely hear, that accomplishes what my coping mechanisms couldn't. With a vicious fist squeezing my throat, I walk into his outstretched arms and lock my own around his tall, lean frame. The scent of Eau Sauvage by Dior greets me, and I lean into the comfort of his embrace and familiarity. Sam is my godfather. There isn't a time in life when he hasn't been there. And unlike my father, he's always been a safe space.

"He hated me," I rasp against his chest, my gaze fixed on the far wall mounted with awards from the fashion industry over the years. They cover the surface, more than a few from the era of Marcus Cross.

My era.

"No, sweetheart. He didn't hate you," Sam murmurs against the top of my head. "He could never hate you, his daughter. On the contrary, he loved you."

The caustic burst of laughter that escapes me razes my throat. "How can you say that? I know he was your best friend, and it's shitty to speak ill of the dead, but fuck that. It's just me and you, Sam. Marcus might've been a good friend to you, but he was a fucked-up father." I loose another laugh that's just as scalpel sharp, just as painful. "Not like I'm telling you something you don't know. He hid me away, for God's sake."

It's no surprise no one really knows of my existence, because Marcus orchestrated it that way. Homeschooled by tutors until I left for college, my only freedom was when Mom took me outside the state or country on vacations. She and Sam were my only friends, my constant companions. Their love aided in shielding me from the reality of Marcus's disappointment and shame in me and my gender—until it didn't. It wasn't until I was older and he found a profitable use for me that he peripherally allowed me into the Cross world. And even then, he still didn't acknowledge me as his daughter.

"Yes, Marcus was . . . complicated." When I snort, he leans back, cupping my shoulders and staring down at me. Sadness—at what? His friend's death, or his behavior?—darkens his eyes.

"Okay, Sam. There's nothing complicated about him thinking so fucking little of me he literally gave my inheritance away to a man who has no blood relation to him." My father sold me out because of his wife's so-called good pussy. There's absolutely nothing "complicated" about a man thinking with his dick. Hell, that story's as old as time.

"You still have thirty-four percent ownership of the company—"

"Which doesn't mean shit." I slash a hand through the air, cutting Sam off. "Not when Asad owns forty-one percent, and his mother and brother own fifteen. Even if he didn't have them to vote whatever way he decided, he is the fucking proxy for my thirty-four. I own mine on paper only. He might as well own seventy-five percent of my family's company." I laugh again. Longer and lower. "And you want to talk about Marcus loved me. That man couldn't give two shits about me. Not when I'm the only living Cross this side of the grave and he hands over my legacy to someone who got where he is because his ho-ass mama spread her legs for a bag. I know this fucking business better than any person here—know it better than my own soul. But I'm good enough to carry this goddamn house and family on my back, but not even to vote my own shares, make decisions regarding the company I've dedicated the last seven years? More, if we're keeping it one hundred."

Sam scrubs a hand down his face, suddenly appearing more haggard and tired.

"I get it, Em—"

"Do you? Do you really?"

"Marcus wasn't an emotive man; he never has been, and that's how I knew he loved your mother. He went against his father's wishes and married her. Marcus lived for Nicholas's approval until the day that old man died. Hell, until the day your father died. But Kim? He defied Nicholas to be with her, and the day you were born was the happiest day in his life other than when he married your mother."

"And he despised me for living when she gave him only me and no more sons."

I take a step back, letting his hands fall from my shoulders, taking the warmth and solid, grounding strength with him. I like it better that way. Pain and disappointment are the best teachers. They've educated me fully that the only stable foundation that can never be shaken or snatched away is one laid brick by brick by yourself. Anything else is fallible and fickle. Even one that appears the most stalwart and steadfast. Like Sam.

Like my mother.

"My birth might've been a good day for him, but as soon as he realized his wife birthed a daughter instead of a son, that joy started to dissipate. And then when he found out his perfect princess had flaws, and required even more precious time, well, then I became a fucking parasite as well as a burden. No, Sam. Don't try and rewrite history in some pitying attempt to make me feel better. I knew Marcus Cross better than most—even better than you since you only saw what he wanted you to, and I got to peer behind the curtain. So excuse me if I respectfully say fuck all that you're talking."

An array of emotion tramps across his features, but after several long moments, he bows his head, pinching the bridge of his nose. I stare at the thick black hair liberally sprinkled with strands of gray and for a second wonder what my life would've been like if he would've been my father. *Who* I would've been.

But in the next instant, I eject the pointless thought. Wishes are relegated to fairy tales and silly princesses who really believe a man can change their luck for the better instead of fuck their existence up the ass.

I've been called a lot of things in my twenty-five years—li'l bitch, ugly-ass bitch, ho—but never silly.

"Ember." Sam lifts his head, meeting my gaze, and the sadness there has deepened, and in those few seconds, as impossible as it is, it seems like he's aged by ten years. Grooves bracket his mouth, his olive skin pulls taut over his stark cheekbones, and the fine lines flaring from the corners of his eyes appear to etch deeper. "Sometimes I feel like I've failed Kim because I failed you," he whispers. But before I can address that or ask him what he means, he lightly shakes his head and continues on, his voice hardening, "We need to talk about your future with House of Cross. You—"

"Future?" I bark out a biting laugh. "You've got to be fucking joking. What future?"

I shake out my hands, stalking away from Sam, and head for the fully stocked, built-in bar across the room. The smoked-glass counter and shelves contain all the premium and top-shelf alcohol in thick crystal decanters. A bottom cabinet contains an assortment of glassware, and I grab a squat tumbler from the front, then place it on the bar top. I weaned myself off the meds for IED three years ago against my doctor's advice because I didn't like the idea of anything controlling me, not even prescriptions. Reckless? Yes, and a negative, foolish message for anyone living with mental health issues. But dealing with the nest of vipers I do, I'd rather increase my therapy sessions and chance the explosions than not be clearheaded.

Still, as I snatch the stopper from the decanter of whiskey, I can admit mixing alcohol with my simmering temper is probably as unwise as combining it with meds. Not that it's going to stop me.

Only after I fill the thick glass tumbler nearly to the top do I turn around to face Sam again. His brow wrinkles as he stares at the full glass of amber liquid, and the wrinkles deepen when I lift it to my mouth for a long sip. My eyes close as the smooth, smokey caramel flavor rolls over my tongue and down my throat before hitting my belly with a burst of heat.

"Whatever you're planning, Ember, don't," Sam sternly warns.

I open my eyes and slowly smirk at him. Not because there's anything faintly humorous about this situation but because if anyone can claim to know me, it's him. Though that's not exactly true either.

He groans. "Now isn't the time to act off emotion."

I snort. "Since when has that ever been me?" I gaze at him over the rim of the glass, taking another sip. "Contrary to what most of you probably assumed, I wasn't surprised at the terms of Marcus's will. Shit, I was actually stunned that the muthafucka left me anything. Was it a smack in the face that he left Asad CEO and stole my birthright from me, yes. A shock? No. I was angry at the disrespect, the humiliation. Marcus couldn't resist one last chance at taking my pride and shitting on it. So, no, I'm clear-fucking-headed about my next move, and it has nothing to do with what Marcus left or didn't leave me just now. I've been planning my next move for years, but misplaced loyalty and guilt kept me here longer than it should've. And that's my fault since my dear departed daddy has never given me anything but his ass to kiss. But now that he's in hell playing don't drop the soap with Satan's little minions, my conscience is clean."

"Goddamn, Ember," he snaps.

I shrug. "I'm just saying. There's absolutely no emotion involved in my decision to walk away from House of Cross."

"The fuck!"

"Exactly." I nod as if he asked a question. "Fuck this company. Fuck this so-called family. And fuck Marcus Cross. May he rest in piss. I mean, peace." I tap my lip and scrunch my face as if in deep thought. "Nah. I said what I said."

"No." He gives his head a hard, emphatic shake, holding his hands out in front of him. "You can't do this, Em. I *won't* let you do it. You're letting them run you off. Letting them bastards fucking *win*."

"No offense, Sam, but I'm a grown-ass woman, and you can't *let* me do anything. This is my decision and mine alone. And the only person winning is me. I'm exorcising hate, negativity, and the ugly out of my life. I've only stayed because of some misguided, warped sense of loyalty to a muthafucka that ain't never had any for me. Do you know one of the last things my mother said to me was to keep loving him, to not leave him? I kept one of those promises even when he made the other a near impossibility. I stayed. I kept my word to a name and legacy that's never recognized me publicly or privately. To a man who was a figment of my mother's imagination. To a woman who is just a memory, and if she was alive, I have to believe would tell me to get the fuck on. And let's be real. They need me way more than I need them."

"Technically, that's true, Em—"

"There's no 'technically.'" I interrupt him with a wave of my hand while setting the half-full tumbler down on the bar, irritated he would try to downplay my worth. "It's the fucking truth."

"Dammit, listen to me," he snaps. "That rumor about Marcus being murdered. It's more than just rumor. I found out just before coming here tonight. The medical examiner confirmed that your father died from a massive injection of heroin."

I suck in a breath that stings the back of my throat with freezing needle pricks.

"That's ridiculous. Marcus was a lot of things, but not a drug user. And the man would act like a damn manbaby when the doctors at HoC had to draw blood for insurance purposes. There's no way he would voluntarily stick a needle in his arm. Are you sure they said . . ."

Sam nods. "I'm certain. The ME even sent over a picture of the pinprick in his arm at my request." I didn't ask to see the image because . . . yeah. "He was killed, and we don't know by who or why."

I stare ahead, over Sam's shoulder, not really seeing the sturdy furniture, the books lining the walls, or the massive door.

He was killed, and we don't know by who or why.

My father was murdered. From an overdose.

Yes, there'd been speculation and innuendo since his death, but to have it confirmed as fact . . . Damn.

I reach down inside me, attempting to analyze how I feel, determine exactly what are the emotions swirling around inside me. Am I upset, despondent? Regretful that someone prematurely shortened his life? Enraged that this unknown person has taken the only father I've known from me?

Maybe.

Underneath a thick sheet of ice, a viscous, convoluted . . . mess twists and writhes, but I'm either too numb or too afraid to touch it right now. So I don't. I edge away from it as if one nudge will send cracks spider-webbing across the surface, allowing the emotions to seep, then spew forth. And no one wants that.

Especially me.

"Do you now understand why you just can't up and leave? We have no idea who killed Marcus. Or their motive. We have no idea if this hit originated within the company or outside of it. Your identity as Marcus's daughter isn't common knowledge, but if there's the slightest chance that the order is from within our circle, you could very well be their next target. Without complete knowledge of the motivation behind his murder, it could be anything from business related to wiping out the Cross line. Either way, you're safest at the Castle, here in this house, or at your place with security until we have the threat contained."

I blink, waiting for the punch line. Because there has to be one. But when he doesn't crack a smile or hit me with a "just joshin'," I let my own frown loose.

"Oh, you're serious." I huff out a breath and pour a healthy amount of disbelief into it. "This house? Safe? The place that has been my torture chamber until I moved out on my own? The same place now owned by the woman who beat the shit out of me too many times to count? Who I still wouldn't eat a dinner with or her pathological son unless I had a taste tester?" I squint at him. "And my home is the only place of peace I have. I already have a state-of-the-art security system installed there, and no one can pee in my direction without an alarm going off. Damn if I'm inviting strangers into my one and only safe space. Nope, I'm good. Besides, the only time I'm *safe* in the Castle is when I'm in my lab, locked behind a steel door requiring a retinal and fingerprint scan to enter. And I *still* make sure I'm carrying. So please, tell me again how safe I am with my so-called family close. No, Sam." I shake my head. "I'll take my chances on my own among all the strangers and serial killers California seems to spawn like starlets and weed."

Turning around, I pick up the glass and finish off the whiskey in two big gulps, not even flinching at the potency. Hissing a little at the tingle in my jaw and along my neck, I set the tumbler back down, debating whether I should make it a twofer.

"You would really not just watch your grandfather and father's company—your legacy—fall, but be the cause of it?"

I stare at him for several seconds, then slowly smile, showing all thirty-two.

"And roast corn nuts over the open flames."

We both know what he's referring to. Even now, with just the two of us alone in this room, he won't say the words aloud, but it's the dirty, illicit truth behind House of Cross and the Cross empire.

Most people recognize HoC as the premiere house for exquisite shoes, high-fashion shoes. But the underworld knows it as a front for the biggest international drug empire in the world. Some of the shoes are carefully constructed shipping mules for Glass Slipper, a highly addictive designer drug created by yours truly. I may have a rage problem, but I'm also a genius. Like, card-carrying Mensa genius. After graduating from USC with a bachelor's in biology and two master's in biochemistry and chemical engineering at twenty, I immediately went to work at the lab in the basement of the Castle creating the drugs that would earn the company and my family billions a year. More than the Cross empire earned in my grandfather's and father's generations. Good ol' Gramps might've initially gotten rich by transporting twice-stepped-on product from an overseas plug, and that was fine for his time. It got HoC started, and he built a name and empire to be feared and respected. But it's my mind, my creativity, my ideas and hard-ass work that fund this empire and the lifestyles of all the muthafuckas who despise every breath I take. And yet I'm still treated like shit scraped off the bottom of a sneaker.

Or maybe worse.

Invisible.

But I shouldn't hope for its downfall? Yeah, he could miss me with that. Once upon a time, I dreamed of HoC being my legacy, my future. Now it's just going to be my competition. Any figments of loyalty Marcus didn't manage to kill within me died when that machine lowered him into the ground.

A mixture of sadness and recrimination creeps across his stern features, and I can already tell he's on bullshit and I'm not going to appreciate what he's about to say. Matter of fact, it's probably going to make me flip my shit.

"Ember, I know you've been hurt, but this is beneath you. Your mother wouldn't have wanted this for you. She wouldn't have wanted you to become—"

"Don't finish that fucking sentence," I snarl, stalking closer to Sam and not stopping until mere inches separate us.

See, most people wisely fear my godfather, but not me. And not because he loves me and treats me like family. No, because while other people believe monsters are make-believe and just villains in stories to scare children to act right, I have firsthand experience that they're real. I've lived with them. Felt their fetid, hot breath in my ear, on my damp skin. Been scarred by them.

As a result, I don't fear shit.

"I love you, Sam, more than the man whose nut sack I came from and who barely raised me. But don't do that. Don't bring my mother into this. And you don't get to tell me how I should react to people who have done me dirty since the moment they laid eyes on me. Longer, if we're talking about Marcus. Since you don't have one scar, one nightmare, one . . ." I bite my lip to contain the scream building and swelling inside of me like an Oklahoma twister. "It's the stink of privilege to think you can dictate that for me when you weren't there to endure either the brunt or the pain. It's fuck them and House of Cross forever. And if you can't see that, it's fuck you, too. Respectfully."

His eyes narrow. "Watch your mouth, little girl."

"I said, respectfully."

A deafening silence thrumming with a menacing tension hovers over the room, vibrates between us. This isn't the first time we've butted heads, but this is the first time it's been this personal, this . . . antagonistic.

"If I'd known what was going on in this house—the extent of what Michelle inflicted on you and what Marcus allowed—I would've moved hell and earth to get you out of here. You know I would've."

The pain and disgust aimed at himself that echo in his voice soften my heart, and I dip my chin.

"I do know. That's why I didn't tell you. He was your best friend. And as confusing as it sounds—shit, it doesn't make sense to me—I didn't want him to be without you. Michelle is a selfish, self-serving bitch, completely out for herself. She didn't love him for real. And he didn't let me get close to him. After losing Mom, all he had was you. So, no, I couldn't tell you, but knowing you would've knocked all this shit over if I had was enough."

His heavy breaths punctuate the room like deep gouges. He lowers his head, his chest lifting and falling. The internal struggle is all over him. Because of the man he is, I know he's battling his own guilt, a sense of betrayal, and even maybe some disgust. This is my real father figure; he's the reason I understand affection and relationship.

"I don't blame you, Sam," I murmur.

"Maybe you should."

"Well, if you were going to make this about you, I would've kept this shit to myself."

His head snaps up, and when I smile at him, his flattened mouth and narrowed eyes soften. With a soft snort, he shakes his head. And though the shame lingers in his gaze, so does resignation. And acceptance.

For now, the storm has passed. But this is Sam. He isn't done with himself. Not by a long shot.

"You'll have security with you wherever you go. That's not up for discussion. I'm going to personally provide it so I can be sure they're trustworthy and capable," he says.

"Okay, I can work with that."

He sighs. "What are your plans? When do you plan on letting Asad know? Are you going to at least leave the formula for Glass Slipper behind?"

"I'm not even formally on the payroll, remember? Can't remind the masses that Marcus Cross has a daughter. This isn't some shit where I have to turn in my two-week notice to HR. He'll know when I tell him. But hell, he's smart. As soon as that will was read, he should've figured that shit out. And they can reverse engineer the drug. I don't owe these muthafuckas a thing. As far as my plans?" I grin. "They're my own." I shift forward and close the distance between us and kiss his lean cheek. "See you later, Sam."

"I have guards already waiting for you outside, Ember," he warns me. "Where are you headed? Home, I hope. It's been a long-ass day."

"I can't argue with you on that, but mine isn't over. I'm going in to work."

He frowns. "To the lab? What the fuck for? You attended your father's funeral today, for God's sake."

"I know." I shrug. "Threw my schedule all off. Talk to you soon."

Throwing a hand up in a wave, I set off for the doors. I have some business to handle that can't wait. And putting my father in the ground isn't reason enough to put it off.

Forty minutes later, I step off the elevator into the bowels of the Castle and enter the stark white antechamber outside the lab. Within seconds, I press my thumb to the fingerprint scanner next to the lab door, and a green button at the top corner of the small black box beeps. Next, I lean forward to the retina scanner and wait for the low-level infrared light to beam through the eyepiece. Seconds later, the green button beeps again, and the stainless steel, pneumatic-seal APR doors silently slide open.

As soon as I step into the sterile lab with its stark white walls and spotless workstations, the heaviness and stress of the long day evaporates from my chest and shoulders like a poisonous gas. Taking a moment, I scan the room, visiting the workstations, sinks, array of beakers, test tubes, microscopes, incubators, and exhaust hoods as if they were old friends instead of standard lab equipment. The silence is a cocoon of ambient noise that soothes my soul from the past fifteen hours. The faint whiff of chemicals and cleansing solution smells better than the most expensive perfume.

I inhale my first weightless breath of the day that doesn't contain death, rage, or avarice. Simply put, in this place of lab equipment, tools, and deadly compounds, I feel . . . home.

Crossing the large open space, I stop at the far wall and press my hand to a panel, and a section of the wall swings backward, revealing a spacious locker room. And that's a bit of an understatement. Yes, there are four cubbies, but they are huge, a beautiful oak. A long, matching table, cabinets, and full kitchen complete the room. And tucked in the corner is a bathroom with a full shower.

I quickly open my locker, pull out my lab coat, and shrug into it. Sure, it's just an article of clothing, but in a way, it's like putting on a new skin. The right skin.

When I emerge from the locker room, Perla, Jarrod "Gus" Gusner, and Jaq Merritt enter the lab. Together. That's them. Always together. They even showed up for their interviews for the positions as my lab assistants as a trio. Three people couldn't be more different in appearance and personality, but according to Perla, they've been best friends and inseparable since middle school. Most of the time I love that for them since this world is known for being cruel to anyone born or who dares to be different.

And other times I'm envious that they had each other during those confusing, sometimes toxic years, and I had no one.

"Oh good, you're here," Perla says in her sweet, slightly squeaky voice. "We weren't sure if you were still coming in tonight, given . . . you know, your—"

"Your father being dead 'n' all," Jaq states in their usual blunt manner. When Gus and Perla hiss their name, they blink at them. "What? She knows he's dead; she buried him today. And it's not as if she's broken up over it. Other people might be off, but this is just a regular workday for all of us, so I don't know why you're over there stuttering and shit."

We all stare after their tall, slim frame and the long, fishtail braid riding their spine as they head toward the locker room. I smirk while Gus glares and Perla just looks mortified and apologetic. I don't know why. Jaq's right. Now if anyone else but one of these three had fixed their mouths to speak to me like that, I can't promise they wouldn't find something odorless and colorless seeping out of the car vents next time they turned the engine on.

But Perla, Gus, and Jaq aren't just my lab assistants. They're the only friends I have. Aside from Sam, they're the only people I trust.

"We'll be right back," Gus mutters, then he and Perla follow behind Jaq.

Though he walks ahead of her, as soon as they reach the door, Gus holds it open for his much smaller friend to enter first. With his nearly seven-foot frame, the wide, powerful body to match, thick, auburn beard, sharp-as-an-axe cheekbones, and deep-set blue eyes, he could be Paul Bunyan's Gen X, liberal cousin. He's also a gentle giant with manners that would have him in high demand at a *Bridgerton* dinner.

Fuck y'all judgmental hoes. *Bridgerton* is the shit.

Moments later, they reenter the room, their white lab coats and game faces on. The regular day-to-day HoC business might've been postponed for the day, but *my* business? It begins when everyone else's workday ends. What we're working on right now?

My liberation.

"Ready? We got a long night ahead of us. I want to run several tests on the various subjects we have. I think we're closer than we've ever been before to perfecting this new drug." I head toward the back of the lab, passing by the contamination shower and stopping at the rear wall that to the naked, unknowing eye appears just like that—a wall and not another door inside the lab.

"I'm curious to see what effects increasing the MDMA will cause," Perla says, excitement causing her voice to rise even higher.

Other people her age would be hyped at just using ecstasy. She's excited at examining the chemical effects of it.

Yeah, we're nerds.

I lean forward, and an infrared light beams out of the undetectable retinal scanner embedded in the white wall. The activation of the door also triggers the cameras in the lab to loop so if anyone does go snooping, they will only see an empty room. In the next second, a panel slides open on a sibilant hiss, and I enter, Jaq, Perla, and Gus close behind me. I don't need to glance behind me to see Gus press his hand to the black device just inside the door to seal us in. It's routine by now.

Only the four of us know of this secret laboratory.

It's a replica of the one beyond the door, except it's much more spacious. It needs to be for the cages.

My father may own—Goddamn. This is going to take some getting used to. *Asad* may own this building and everything in it, but this lab within the lab? It's mine. I had it clandestinely constructed. One of the perks—maybe the only perk—of having a father who doesn't give a fuck what you do as long as you're providing his drugs is he's not all up in your business. Used to seeing the four of us at HoC after hours, security doesn't pay attention to the three-man team I've granted access through the rear of the building. And with the lab already being soundproof? That's how one gets a secret lab up and running under a drug kingpin's nose.

Now, did I have the construction team murdered so they couldn't betray my secrets? Yes, but that's just self-preservation. My money supplied every piece of equipment, every chemical, every experiment. And the results from here would only belong to me, not House of Cross or the Cross empire.

My exit plan from HoC has been over a year in the making. Twenty-two months to be exact. About as long as this lab has been in existence. Marcus's death just shoved the timeline ahead. This new drug? It's going to fund my way out of here and my new empire.

Yeah, I'll probably be a little sentimental when I shut this space down. I'm going to miss it.

"Damn, I'm going to miss this place," Jaq says, damn near reading my mind as they turn their head to scan the area.

"Same." Gus thrusts his large hands into the pockets of his coat. "We've had some good times and have done some of our best work in here."

"But we'll still have more of those good times in the new lab," Perla adds, always the ray of sunshine of the group. She sweeps her purple bangs out her eyes, tilting her head. "This might be our last night here, but it's not our last night together."

"Aw, shit. If she breaks out on some Sister Sledge 'We Are Family' bullshit, I'm knocking her the fuck out and shipping her back to whatever fucking fairy tale she escaped from. Ain't nobody got time for that," Jaq warns with a jab of their finger toward Perla.

Gus snorts, and Perla does a combination of fancy tap footwork while holding both of her middle fingers up. She once told me her mother made her take dance when she was little, hoping it'd make her more social. It didn't work—one of the little girls in the class ended up mysteriously dying, so it was shut down early—but Perla does remember some of the steps. The girl has talent.

"What Perla said." I pause. Then snort. "Without all the sentiment. Grab your tablets. Let's get to it. We got a drug to perfect and still have to officially close this lab down tomorrow night, so we need to get as much work done as possible before then."

Because starting two days from now, we'll be in our new lab, located in the basement of my apartment building. Since no one knows of this space, and the door can only be opened by the four of us, I'm not worried about dismantling it.

"Roger that." Gus moves toward the cabinet next to the occupied floor-to-ceiling cages and pulls four tablets free.

He hands one to me and the others, keeping one for himself. We pull up our previous notes from a couple of nights ago. Though the information is branded into my brain, I still study the calculations and formulas from both my control and test groups. Nodding, I slip the tablet into my coat pocket and stride over to the first pen. I pluck the binder hanging from the front and flip through it, perusing Jaq's meticulous notes from last night's observation. As soon as we step into this lab, a recorder, both visual and audio, automatically clicks on. But I still require the three of them to log in their data. Technology can fail, and it would be negligent to not have a backup.

"Day eleven. Subject one. Control group. No change in appearance or symptoms," I narrate, narrowing my gaze on the specimen crouched in the corner of the cage, shivering like a dog left out in the elements too long. Its low, continuous whimpers echo off the lab's walls. They're irritating as fuck and distracting. Besides, when he was busy breaking into the homes of elderly women, robbing and beating them to hell and back, I'm sure they whimpered, too. We match energy in here. "The subject shows signs of increased swelling in the hands, ankles, and feet. Possible hypervolemia. Previous notes record a marked lethargic response and loss of appetite." I remove a thin flashlight from my pocket and aim it into the cage, right into the subject's eyes. It gives a slow blink, belatedly frowns, and sluggishly raises its arm to shield its eyes. "Slow response. Perspiration on the forehead, chest, and arms. Skin is flushed. Appears to be febrile response to a possible infection. We'll need to check its temperature and take a culture sample. Also, note the phlebitis at the injection site."

Normally, in most clinical trials, a sugar pill or saline solution is given to the control group. The subjects in my control group are special though. So they've been administered a sodium chloride solution. In other words, salt.

Makes for a slow, painful death.

Perla hums. "We should have another week with it. Possibly a couple of days more before we have to dispose of it," she says.

"We'll keep it until it's served its purpose, just like all the others."

I move to the next pen, but I hear the dismissal in Jaq's voice and silently agree with them.

"Then the real fun begins," Gus says, a smile curving his mouth. Red paints his cheekbones, and when he looks at me, excitement gleams there. The same thread of glee prances through me like an auntie fucking up the Electric Slide at the cookout.

Yes, my lab assistants are brilliant, dedicated, and loyal, and to many, unassuming and meek—even Gus with his big ass. Which is why they've been dubbed the "lab mice" by the employees in the Castle.

While I appreciate and admire those qualities about them, they aren't the most useful to me.

It's their sociopathy.

All three of them are sociopaths.

Like me.

Don't get me wrong. I grew up in a house brimming with a Disneyland of personality disorders and antisocial behaviors. But even there, I didn't *belong*. I for damn sure wasn't ever safe. But here, with my lab mice? I've found my people. They're mine, and I'm theirs.

For the next hour, we go through, running the same physical examinations, studying and recording our observations for the rest of the subjects of the control group. Once we finish, we move on to the next set of cages lined against the opposite wall.

As soon as I stop in front of the first one, the subject inside whimpers and scrambles away, pressing its spine against the back bars. Its head swings from side to side, a wild glaze in its eyes as if it's desperately searching for an exit, a way out of the kennel.

A smile stretches across my face, and as its gaze lands on me, it visibly flinches, body jerking. Oooh. I think my clit just swelled.

The first thing I love about my job. Designing new drugs and constantly besting myself.

The second thing. Torturing murderers, pedophiles, rapists, and other muthafuckas who the justice system allowed to get away with their crimes.

Slightly hypocritical? Sure. Am I losing sleep over it? No.

Am I feeling like a fucking Avenger? Hell yes.

"Jaq," I say, my attention still fixed on the thing in the cage.

"Day two. Subject one. Test group. Seems to have recovered from the last trial. The seizure and convulsions didn't cause permanent, adverse damage. The CAT scan and MRI returned normal. Although, the subject hasn't spoken since the trial, but this could be due more to psychological trauma than physical." They remove a light from their lab coat pocket and shine it between the bars directly in the subject's eyes. Animalistic sounds claw at the back of its throat as it scratches its arms. "Dilated pupils. Clenched jaw. Common signs of methylenedioxymethamphetamine usage."

"They couldn't just say *molly* like everyone else, huh?" Perla mutters.

Jaq side eyes her. "Just because you're the size of a mustard seed doesn't mean you need to be bitchy with me, sweet pea."

"That's faith the size of a mustard seed, Bishop T. D. Fake," Gus corrects them.

Jaq shifts his side eye to Gus. "I said what I said."

I snort, because these three can go at it all night if I don't intervene.

"Continue, Jaq."

With a superior sniff, they turn back to the cage. "As I was saying, along with the dilated pupils and teeth grinding, there's been excessive perspiring and he hasn't been asleep in two days. Some of these symptoms can occur over habitual drug use, but these have appeared almost immediately."

"That could be a positive result, because the onset of usual MDMA effects takes about an hour and hits its peak at seventy-five minutes, give or take. But from the recorded notes, the subject exhibited the effects much sooner. Within ten minutes. And while the customary reported euphoria lasts about three and a half hours, the subject's lasted eight. That's remarkable. But the adverse effects also presented much sooner—within an hour."

"Damn," I murmur. "No vomiting though. Or hallucinations or signs of paranoia."

"None." Perla shakes her head. "And we took a urine sample, too. Did you see that? We saved that as a little gift." She grins, and her eyes sparkle behind her blue-and-gold frames. Bending her head over her tablet, she taps the screen, then tips her chin. "Check your email."

Arching my eyebrows, I go to my inbox and tap on the attachment inside the waiting message from her. Moments later, I lift my head and smile wide.

"You're shitting me."

"Nope." Perla laughs.

"And good news. It won't show up in that either," Jaq adds.

"Ew."

"Really? We're having a moment here."

Perla and Gus throw at their friend, who just shrugs.

I chuckle and once again glance down at the lab results Perla sent me. According to the PDF, subject one's urine and blood samples came back completely clean of any drug substances.

Satisfaction and triumph burn hot inside me like the fucking Olympic torch. Not even Glass Slipper was undetectable. But *my* new drug—Fairy Dust—the one I'm creating in my secret lab, the one that will fund *my* new empire, is untraceable. Imagine, a designer drug that people could take in the club on Sunday night and pass a urine test at their jobs on Monday. One that would send them as high as the goddamn U.S. Bank Tower and keep them there longer than any other drug out there, without the crash. One with more power than even Glass Slipper, the best synthetic substance in the streets right now.

Addicts would be flooding clubs, bumrushing pushers, hounding suppliers for this product.

And they would only be able to get it from one source. Me.

The billions Fairy Dust would generate didn't motivate me as much as knowing it would topple the House of Cross throne and the usurper and his bitch-ass mama who sat on it.

The usurper.

Asad Prince.

My fingers involuntarily clench around the edges of my tablet. The memory of him pausing in front of me just before he left the study earlier this evening floods my mind, and I inhale a low, deep breath, battling back the rush of rage that wants to drown me in a crimson wave. He'd peered down at me with his usual inscrutable gray stare—like a pathologist examining me right before he gets to work dissecting and collecting. In my sophomore year of college, I visited Surgeon's Hall Museum in Edinburgh, and I can just see him storing pieces of me in those jars and under slides to analyze, then throw away when they start to bore him. Because I learned that early about *Prince*, as everyone else calls him, except me. Send useless prayers up that you didn't catch Asad's attention. And if you did, hope he lost interest sooner rather than later. Because the only person who had fun when Asad toyed with his things was him. He left all his playthings broken. Which was why I couldn't understand why so many women and men flocked to him, begging for that gunmetal gaze to just trip over them. They offered him everything, from every hole in their body to their stock options.

Bitch, you a lie. You know good and damn well why they throwing the coochie and dick at him.

I growl at myself, disgusted that my mind would even go there. Even Asad's haters—mainly me—couldn't deny the man's face card. After years of being in my stepbrother's presence, you'd think I'd grown some kind of resistance to it. But like a virus that mutates into a stronger, deadlier variant that renders immunity useless, his beauty only matures, deepens . . . darkens. He reminds me of the orchid mantis that uses its beauty as a disguise to lure in its prey before it attacks them. Since I'm a biological animal, my body's primal response to Asad's appearance can be excused. The heating of blood in my veins, the hardening and ache in my nipples, the tug and tightening low in my belly, the swelling and quiver in my pussy, the moisture that spills from it, dampening my underwear . . . They're all instinctive responses to that lovely mask. Nothing more than an animal jerk.

The difference between me and the many people who fall victim to that lure is I know what monster exists behind that brutally pretty face with its silver eyes, fierce angles, and fuckable mouth. I've witnessed and been on the receiving end of those claws and teeth and forked tongue.

Giving my head a small, abrupt shake, I purge my Asad-stained thoughts and return my focus to the tablet and the most recent results regarding Fairy Dust.

"This is amazing. And huge." I look up, smiling at my assistants. "Great work."

A whimper from subject one's cage draws my attention back to him, and a ripple of excitement undulates through me.

"Get him out and ready," I order Gus.

I don't miss the gleam in his eyes. This is his favorite part. It is for all of us. And not just because of the scientific work we're doing here.

No.

It's for the pain we're about to inflict.

Subject one's whimpers elevate into ear-piercing howls as Gus opens the cage door and enters. It begins to flail and try to fight, but its skinny stature and weakened state are no match for Gus's much larger, heavier frame. My lab assistant doesn't even seem to flex a muscle as he picks up the subject with ease and carries it over to a black surgical chair with chest and thigh straps, as well as wrist and ankle cuffs. Jaq assists Gus in securing subject one in, then they fix the halo brace over the subject's head, attaching the bottom to the chest strap. Next, they insert a "bite block" into his mouth to hold it open.

"Perla, do you have the new sample prepared?" I ask. With this altered sample, we hope for a reduction in the adverse effects.

"It's ready."

She approaches subject one with a pair of tweezers, and it attempts to buck and strain against the bindings with no success. Gurgles roll out of its throat, and it tries to rear and thrash, but all of it is useless, and that shit doesn't move any of us.

Perla lifts a small, square film from a white, round dish, lays the drug on his tongue. With the piece in its mouth, the subject can't spit it out. But even if it could, the construction of the film is intentionally thin, intended to quickly dissolve.

We step back, our tablets out, and study the subject like a specimen. Well, that's what *it* is. Because the moment this piece-of-shit excuse for a man decided to rape the seven-year-old daughter of his girlfriend, he ceased being a human and became a *thing* that deserves to suffer, to die. What the laughable justice system refuses to hold it accountable for, I will. The laws of society claim no person can be judge, jury, and executioner.

I say, you got me fucked-up.

And every cage in this lab contains a rapist, a molester, an abuser, a murderer—those who prey on the weakest and most vulnerable of our society.

God forgives.

But before they leave this earth and discover if He will indeed meet them with open arms, they'll fuck around and find out with me.

Ten minutes pass with no change in its demeanor other than the panicked roll of its eyes, the soft but rapid pants and heaving of its chest. But at eleven minutes and thirty-two seconds, its body slumps into the chair. Subject one's facial features go lax, and its eyes glaze over. A throaty, almost hedonistic groan fills the room, and a smile curves its mouth, softening its features. It appears euphoric. Hard to believe that just minutes earlier it'd looked like a cornered, terrified rat.

For the next eleven hours, we rotate shifts. I study it, recording notes, and Perla remains alongside me, taking vitals and keeping it hydrated. Gus and Jaq head back to the main lab and attend to our regular workload. Aside from my secret work, I'm still the lead scientist for House of Cross . . . for now. If anyone wanted to investigate, they would appear like employees engaging in overtime that I signed off on. We do have a couple of irons in the fire though, so it's a good thing our schedule isn't exactly nine to five.

Right now, I'm perfecting a new drug called HEA for them. It was almost there and ready to roll out. The first batch had tested well with local fiends. But I wasn't satisfied. The high hit like cocaine, with none of the crashing-out side effects. Plus, it was intended to be an aphrodisiac. A dopamine agonist increased sexual arousal, making it the perfect party drug for its intended target customer—the wealthy, young party crowd.

Right now, Asad has enough Glass Slipper supply for the next month. And besides that initial test batch, none of HEA. But I'm not unreasonable. I'm willing to sell the formulas for both to him.

For a price.

"Ember."

I lift my head from the microscope and slide I was hunched over, and Perla waves me over to where she's standing next to subject one. Immediately, I turn and head toward them. Moments later, the lab door hisses open and Perla and Gus enter.

"Subject one. Test group. After eleven hours and"—I glance down at the timer on my tablet I started after the dispensing of the drug—"thirteen minutes, the subject is heavily perspiring. There's rigidity of the muscles in his extremities. Teeth are clenched. Acceleration of breathing." Another ten minutes pass. "Subject one is seizing, foaming at the mouth. Blood is leaking from the corners of his eyes and his ears. Subject is choking on his tongue."

None of us move to perform any lifesaving measures.

Cries and screams of horrors fill the lab from the other subjects in the cages as they witness this one die an agonizing, bloody death. Probably because they're scared this will soon be their immediate future.

That's fair.

"Time of death 8:22 a.m." I call it, jotting the information down in my tablet. "It's been a long night. You three go home and get some sleep. I'll see you here tomorrow."

Perla stretches, yawns. "I'm not going to argue with you. See you guys later."

She returns her tablet to the cabinet and exits the lab, Jaq behind her.

Gus starts to release the brace and straps from the body.

"I'll take care of the body, Ember. You don't have to wait on me," he says.

"You sure?"

He nods, walking over to another cabinet and grabbing a long black bag. Dropping it on the floor in front of the chair, he tosses me a smile.

"Of course I am. I got this. See you tomorrow."

"Be careful."

"Always."

I leave him to the disposal. Hell, he enjoys it, and who am I to deprive him of his little thrills. Besides, he's damn good at it. Not one trace has been found of the bodies yet.

Heading back to the door, I tap in the code to stop the audio and visual recording, then exit the lab. Instead of taking the elevator up several floors to the main lobby, I hop on it and ride it one floor down to the lower-level floor opening right next to the parking lot. Minutes later, I exit HoC property and ease into the early LA streets. With the traffic clotting the streets this time of morning, it takes me nearly an hour to pull my Aston Martin DB11 up to the gate of the former private compound converted into a four-unit luxury apartment building instead of the usual thirty minutes.

Four acres of lush, beautiful gardens surround the property, granting privacy and the illusion of a quiet, peaceful oasis on the west side of Los Angeles. I should be exhausted given I've been up a little over twenty-four hours. But I'm wired, a kinetic energy racing through me. It's hard to believe that this time yesterday, I was preparing to put my father in the ground. Almost like it happened to someone else, not me. Because if it happened to me, I should feel more than indifference and a hard knot of anger lodged between my ribs.

Yeah, let me get off thoughts of Marcus before I end up ramming this car into the garage bay wall.

Minutes later, I key in the code to the gorgeous atrium-style foyer with its high ceiling and marble flooring and climb the stairs to the second level. Though I occupy one of the two apartments on that floor, I own the entire complex. The other three units are empty of tenants because I value my space and I only like about four people. And I don't like anyone enough to have them living with or near me.

An hour later, I emerge from my bedroom, freshly showered, dressed in a black sports bra and leggings, with a yoga mat under my arm. When I stopped taking my medication to cope with IED, I integrated yoga and meditation into my daily schedule. And blunts. My therapist recommended it as a relaxation technique to release endorphins and lower stress. I created my own special blend of marijuana that relaxed me even more. Believe me, I'm surprised as much as anyone that it works, *and* that I actually enjoy it. The yoga, not the weed—

My mat drops to the living room floor as my body stiffens.

"What *the fuck* are you doing in my house?"

CHAPTER FOUR

Asad

That disrespectful mouth is going to be the death of her.

Literally.

Fuck the fact that I am sitting in a large leather armchair stationed in front of the floor-to-ceiling French doors in her living room. Or that I've been here, waiting on her to arrive home, for the past five hours. She left the study and the house nearly fourteen hours ago.

Also fuck that I broke in here to offer a proposition that I've spent literal hours analyzing and working all angles of how to deliver to her. And with each minute that's passed, my patience has retreated, while my anger at not knowing where her current location is has advanced.

Anger. Irritation. Jealousy.

I'm here for a specific purpose, but that's taking a backseat to my needs to know where she's been and with who.

Knowing her workaholic habits as well as her usual schedule, I'm assuming she returned to the lab after leaving the house. But damn. This was long even for her.

Ember is usually self-aware and sharp. But this morning, she came in this apartment and walked through the room without noticing my ass sitting here.

The possible answers march through my head like well-trained soldiers. And my blood grows colder and colder with each one. Her ass better have been at the lab, because the alternative—that she might've been out up under someone and full of dick—has me battling the urge to put a hole in someone's forehead. Yeah, as soon as I leave her, I'm going to be putting a call in to the Castle to pull tapes.

If I'm not fucking her, no one else will be either. And I put that on everybody's life.

I've been waiting here all these hours because she and I need to talk about the terms of Marcus's will. What those terms mean for her immediate future. And yet . . . I shake my head.

Yet, I'm sitting here, slowly drumming my fingers on the arm of this chair, needing that deliberate motion to calm and divert me from going with my initial and instinctive urge.

Snatching her up, gripping that slender and delicate neck, and demanding the name of the person whose death would be on her conscience.

Shit.

Who am I kidding?

Ember Cross doesn't have a conscience.

"I *said*, what the fuck are you—"

Before she can finish the question, I abruptly shove out the chair and cross the space separating us in three long strides. And I don't stop until my personal space is all up in the guts of hers. Until that sharp and sweet citrus and fresh, crisp air scent invades me like a stealth bomber, exploding in my chest, my belly . . . my dick.

"That's your problem now. Focusing on the wrong shit."

Knowing my stepsister as well as I do, she would slit her own throat before admitting to the discomfort that flickers in her eyes. But I see it. And knowing it's because of me? Because I'm so close I can taste the mint toothpaste on her breath? Because the memories of our past and the pain I inflicted are probably playing in her head like a twisted reel?

Nah.

That attitude, the hostility and cutting sarcasm can't completely disguise the uneasiness my presence stirs.

The knowledge that I can inspire that kind of vulnerability—any kind—in *this woman* is a narcotic more powerful than the one we pump out into the global community. And we have some good shit.

"Okay, I'll bite." She crosses her arms and edges back a step. I don't misinterpret that move. A retreat. Smart on her part but still a mistake. Never let the enemy know they have an advantage, an edge. Ember just did, losing a little bit of ground in this war between us—make no mistake; we are most definitely the fuck at war. "What should I be focusing on other than you committing a little B and E first thing in the morning? Or do you start off most of your days with felonies?" She huffs out a small, dry chuckle. "Look who I'm talking to. Of course you do."

"Go put some clothes on, ma," I say, staring into her honey-brown eyes.

Her head jerks back, thick eyebrows arrowing down and damn near meeting over the bridge of her nose.

She's a breathing distraction in these clothes. Nah, she's not to blame for my body's reaction to her perfect tits, juicy ass, and thick thighs. Still, I'm not hearing shit she says until I can no longer see her nipples outlined underneath that top. Or feel the phantom rub of them over my tongue.

"The fuck?" She laughs again, and it is just as humorless as the one from moments earlier. "You broke into my house. I never issued an invitation. And last time I checked, this"—she sweeps a hand down her body—"is the appropriate clothing for working out. In case you don't remember, let me refresh your memory. We buried my daddy yesterday, and unless he's pulled a Jesus 2.0 between then and now, I don't have one. And I haven't voted you into the role."

Men and women have lost their fucking lives talking less shit to me. One thing I don't play about is my muthafuckin' respect, and her being my stepsister isn't going to save her. Shit, I'll kill Kareem if he ever loses his mind and lets his mouth get loose.

Neither he nor Michelle is that fucking insane. And Michelle is gotdamn certifiable. So, nah, it's not a familial relationship that has her lungs still residing on the other side of her ribs.

It's because she's Ember.

She's a cancer that no amount of radiation or chemo can eradicate.

She's the secret enemy set on my destruction.

She's my weakness.

I've lost count of how many times over the years I've stood beside her bed like some angel of death, watching her sleep even as the barrel of my Glock hovered only an inch above her forehead. Even after I moved out of Marcus's house and she remained there, I still returned and snuck into her room, convinced that this time—*this time* I would take her life and get rid of this *sickness*.

This vulnerability.

Obviously, since she's standing before me, dark blond hair pulled up into one of those buns that should've looked sloppy but instead makes her look freshly fucked, light brown eyes narrowed and that fuckable mouth curled into a sneer, I failed to pull the trigger.

A part of me can't handle that. I've never failed at anything I've set my sights on. And Ember Cross is my ultimate failure.

So if I can't kill her, I'll consume her.

"Let's get one thing straight, little sister. If I wanted you to call me 'daddy,' you would, right after begging me to let you be my good girl."

Funny how just yesterday, the thought of Aryn calling me that shit annoyed the fuck outta me. But imagining Ember's sultry, edged-in-barbed-wire voice wrapped around *daddy* as I punished that pussy? That has my dick so hard, it's a physical ache, and it's taking every scrap of control not to bend her over the arm of that chair.

I step forward, eliminating the space she's placed between us. Confusion and that delicious anger she used to unleash like a raging wildfire flash in her eyes, and they're both irresistible.

I trail my fingertips along the stubborn yet delicate line of her jaw, the flexing of the muscles underneath sending a bolt of heat straight to my dick. She's done a commendable job of learning how to cope and manage her IED; I'll give her that.

But I've never been afraid of her fury, her explosions. Quite the opposite. I've wanted her to use me and let go. Slap the shit outta me. Scratch me. Punch me. Bruise me.

Mark me.

She's always seen me as her tormentor.

Good. I want her fear. I *need* her fear. Because if she ever suspected even a sliver of the truth . . .

I slowly drag my caress down her neck and feel the soft catch in her breath before I hear it. Satisfaction sears me seconds before I strike, gripping her slender throat . . . squeezing it. Her eyes flare but not with fear. Nah. I should've known her hardheaded ass wouldn't give me what I want. Those honeyed eyes stare back at me with hatred and a delectable defiance that has a beast rising up inside me, roaring and snapping to crush, to tame.

"Get your fucking hands off me," she calmly says, the ice in her voice licking over my skin and leaving a coat behind. "Is this your game? I guess you've forgotten that I'm familiar with all of them. *Intimately* familiar." She inches closer, and on pure reflex, my hand presses tighter against her windpipe. Not that she seems to notice—nah, that's a lie. That flash of darkness in her golden eyes telegraphs full awareness of her actions and mine. It's a dare. A gauntlet thrown down. "Hide-and-seek, where you locked me in a closet, not fucking *seeking* me for six hours. Or musical chairs, where you tied me to a chair and blasted music so loud for so long, my eardrum ruptured. Or what about blind man's bluff, when you forced me into your car, drove me to Topanga State Park, and dropped me off, making me walk home. In the dark. And that's just naming a few. So this . . ." She taps the back of my hand with a nail. "You're going to need to come harder, *Prince*." She sneers the name that everyone calls me.

Everyone but her.

I shift my grip upward, and instead of letting her go like she demanded, I cradle her chin in a hard, bruising grip. Even when I lower my head until my nose bumps hers and her breath is heated, minty blasts on my lips, I don't release her, don't allow her to look away from me.

Was her reminder supposed to stir guilt inside me? Remorse?

If so, she should know better. Should know by now that she got the wrong muthafucka for that.

"You don't think I've learned some new games in the last few years?" I murmur. "Promise, ma, you don't know everything I'm capable of. But if you don't watch that mouth, I can help you find out."

"You can—"

My cell vibrates against my chest, and because every call is a potential business opportunity and I never miss out on money for anyone or anything, I release Ember and slide a hand into the inner pocket of my suit jacket. Irritation flickers inside me when a swift glance down at the screen reveals Aryn's name.

The fuck does she want? After leaving Marcus and Michelle's house—well, now only Michelle's—I went and took Aryn up on the offer she made at the reception. I even beat up the pussy along with that bottomless throat and left her in the damn fetal position with a pillow between her legs. I got a nut and she got several of them, so ain't shit for us to talk about.

Silencing the phone, I slip it back into my suit pocket.

A snort drags my gaze back to Ember's face and the twisted smirk riding her mouth that's about to get her good and fucked.

"As I was saying, you can go now. Play with your bitch, don't play with me." She adds a little wave of her fingers, apparently trying to dismiss me.

She got me fucked-up and confused with one of her little lab rats. I got something to fix that shit though. Sometimes muthafuckas just gotta be reminded of who the fuck you are. Lucky for Ember, I don't mind writing recaps.

Before she can lower her hand, I snatch it, curling my fingers around hers and tugging her forward. Her free arm rises, breaking her fall against my chest, but that shit doesn't work, because I step into her so it's trapped between our bodies. The tendons running along her neck stand out in sharp relief, and her deceptively soft, thick body quivers with the rage radiating off her. I absorb each tremble and savor it like a well-earned trophy.

"Nah, I just had my dick drained, so I'm good on that. But don't worry, ma." With the hand not gripping hers, I gently tug on a shorter strand of hair that's escaped her top bun and slide it behind her ear, nudging the diamond-encrusted hoop piercing the upper and outer cartilage. A small shudder passes through her, and this close, I don't miss it. Grim, fierce satisfaction snarls inside me, and gotdamn, I want to drop to my knees, press my open mouth to that beautiful peanut-brown skin, and let every one of those shivers vibrate over my tongue. "In all these years, I've never found anyone capable of replacing you. No one's able to take pain like you so beautifully can. Nah, Ember. You'll never need to worry. You, ma, will always be my favorite playmate."

I loose her hand and shift my hold to her sports bra. Thrusting three of my fingers down the front of the top, I fist the tight spandex-and-cotton material. A soft cry escapes her, and her palms slap against my chest, breaking her forward fall. That light pop vibrates through me, but not as much as the rapid flutter of her heartbeat against my fingers. Or all that silken flesh encasing my fingers in that damp heat . . . I clench my teeth, and a throbbing ache pulses along my jaw. In this moment, it's the closest I've come to imagining what it would feel like being plunged into the damp, fleshy warmth of her pussy.

And that quick, I'm addicted.

Fuck that. I've been addicted. For years.

Now I'm obsessed. Consumed. Gotdamn fucking *feral*.

"Now, do what the fuck I said and go change your clothes." My grip tightens on her sports bra . . . But instead of tugging her closer and sucking on her until a violent dark blue and purple bruise rises on her skin, I shove her away from me. Ember stumbles back several steps but quickly regains her balance, glaring at me. "Either that or I have a conversation with the print of that fat-ass pussy instead of you."

She stares at me, her chest heaving up and down on the loud blasts of breath punctuating the deafening quiet of the living room. Her fingers flex and straighten next to her thick-ass thighs, those golden eyes reflect the need, the hunger to inflict damage. To be the harbinger of pain.

I smile.

And though it feels foreign as fuck and strained on my face, it's still genuine.

Her "fuck you" isn't spoken. Then again, what's understood doesn't need to be explained.

After several more seconds where she continues to silently consign me to hell and back, she whips around and stalks out of the room toward the marble staircase leading up to the second level of the apartment. I couldn't tear my starving gaze from her slender back and plump ass, rippling with every angry step, if I wanted to. And fuck if I want to.

As soon as she disappears, I exit the living room, walking past the elegant dining room with its wall of glass-block windows and long, gleaming ebony table with matching chairs. The area, with its brick fireplace, formal serving buffet, and bar, was designed for family and friends—a particular group, aside from her lab rats and Sam, Ember had neither.

I made sure of that.

If I couldn't have her—couldn't get close to her, be inside her, fucking have her—then no one else would either.

Call me an asshole, a bully. I really don't give a fuck.

I've been called worse and deserve every one of the names. I own them. Don't give a fuck about them either.

My footsteps echo on the hardwood floors as I make my way into the kitchen toward the refrigerator. I open it, grab a cold bottle of water, and close the door. I'd be a liar if I claimed to be surprised at the beautifully appointed room. Top-of-the-line appliances. Freestanding indoor grill and separate island. A bar, large double oven that wouldn't have been out of place in a restaurant, range and hood, warming drawer, gorgeous stone counters. Huge breakfast nook with a cedar table, chairs, and sitting area looking over the covered patio, fire pit, and pool. It's a kitchen for someone who enjoys being here. Someone who loves cooking, creating.

"You really have no boundaries. Marcus leaves you the kingdom, and you walk up in my shit—illegally, I might add—and act like you own it, too. This is what happens when muthafuckas never hear the word *no*. Spare the rod, spoil the child, and all that shit."

I turn around, eyebrow raised, careful not to exhibit any expression other than that as Ember strolls into the kitchen. It's a struggle though. Because she's trying me. I swear to fuck, no one pushes me like my stepsister. Yeah, I'm a violent man, and I embrace it. Fuck, I love that shit. Everyone else goes out of their way to avoid inciting that side of me. But Ember? She does it like the government is handing out mu'fucking stimulus checks for the shit.

This woman. I twist the cap off and lift the bottle to my lips, swallowing water along with a harsh, sarcastic chuckle.

The dark blue, ankle-length, sleeveless dress should be modest, boring even. And on someone else, it probably would be. But this isn't "someone else." It's Ember. And there's not shit boring about her.

She's gon' make me order her to take her hardheaded ass back up those fucking stairs and change—again.

Gorgeous, thick thighs and those sexy-as-fuck, round hips press against the thin material, stretching it to the max. Even though she's facing me, I can still see the spread of her ass, and my fingertips tingle, desperate to dent all that juicy flesh as I grab all on it while delivering death strokes from the back. My stomach knots, my dick lengthening, hardening behind my suit pants with just the thought. With the hunger to have my hips slapping against her as that undoubtedly tight, gushy pussy drowns me.

Fuck.

The dress clings to the small pooch of her stomach and to the thrust of her full breasts. She's not a small woman; the thin straps are damn near fighting for their lives holding up the weight of those titties. Still, they're sitting up pretty, stirring a deeper, gnawing ache in the pit of my gut. Imagine me sitting in a doctor's office trying to explain an ulcer from hungering to be face-deep in titty and balls-deep in pussy.

Wait.

I narrow my eyes on her chest . . .

Nah.

Can't fucking be. My dick jerks, and shit if I'm not seconds away from cummin' in my gotdamn pants.

"What the fuck did you do?" I growl even though it's quite fucking obvious what she did. Yeah, I sound like a rabid animal. Fuck, I feel like one.

I pride myself on being aware of Ember's movements, of keeping tabs on her. So this . . .

Ember mimics my gesture from moments ago, arching an eyebrow. "What're you talking about?"

Instead of replying, I slam the bottle on the island, not caring about the water erupting out of the top and splashing across the spotless surface. I stalk across the kitchen, not stopping until she's caged between my body and the grill. She leans away from me, and a sibilant voice warns me to back off, give her space. But the hungrier, much louder part of me ignores all whispers of caution. It just needs to feed, and I surrender to it. My hands curl around the edge, and I grasp it like it's the only thing saving me from falling ass-first into a pitch-black pit.

"Is this what we're doing?" I chuckle, and though she recovers quickly, it's not fast enough to conceal her slight flinch. I don't blame her. Wasn't shit humorous about the sound. And ain't shit jokey-jokey about the lust tearing at my insides in great, greedy, bleeding handfuls. I shake my head, loosing another low, mean laugh. "You out here sounding like a broken record with all the shit I supposedly put you through—"

She snorts, mugging me. "Supposedly. Muthafu—"

I crush a finger to her lips, pressing so hard, the ridge of her teeth lightly scrapes my skin.

"Unh-unh. Watch yourself, little sister. I let you slide, but disrespect me again, and I will choke you up in here and hang you on that fucking wall right next to those pots and pans like a gotdamn coatrack. Try me if you want to."

She snatches her head to the side and drags her hand across her mouth as if wiping away the taste of me. Anger wraps around my rib cage in red-hot barbed wire, and maybe her father is down on his knees sucking Satan's dick as a favor for his little girl right now to keep me from going upside her fucking head.

"I'm not your sister," she snaps, voice dripping with derision.

"Ma, you don't need to remind me." I lean back, staring into those narrowed honey-colored eyes that glare back at me with so much contempt. Yeah, if she understood how all that hatred is like fucking photosynthesis to me, she'd at least attempt to hide it better. "If you were my sister, I wouldn't do this."

Without tearing my gaze away from hers, I lift my hand and flick the very visible nipple piercing outlined under the dress's thin material.

"The *fuck*?" She gasps, her entire body jerking as if experiencing a seizure. Her hands fly to her breasts, covering them.

But I'm faster.

Cuffing her wrists, I snatch her arms down, transferring both to one hand in front of her. A snarl curls her full, fuckable lips and she twists and bucks against my hold. I shift forward, crowding her, corralling her with my bigger body. Ruthlessly and shamelessly using my strength to subdue her struggles.

And gotdamn.

It's a mistake.

I'm not Jesus; I've made a few errors since sitting under Marcus and learning the reins of running HoC and the Cross empire he left in my hands. And I've learned from every one of them, never repeated them. But a mistake I've never committed was touching Ember in a sexual manner. Have I aggressively handled her? Snatched her up? Bullied her in all the ways she listed? Yeah, and in more ways she left unsaid. But get so close my thighs cradled hers? That my chest and shoulders curved over her, providing a safe space for her to ply her teeth and nails? That my dick finally feels the soft give of that sweetly rounded stomach? Nah. I've never been that close to her. And there's a reason.

I was protecting her.

Protecting myself.

Because now that I have the most minimal glimpse into hearing what kind of raspy sound she might make as I finally grind and thrust into that pretty, wet pussy . . . have a nebulous idea of how all those sick-ass curves would bear my weight . . . possess the barest sense of how that badass body could fuck me back . . . Now that it's all branded in my mind, imprinted on every cell in my body, I'm wide open. There's no forgetting.

There's no turning back.

I fucked up.

So we're both fucked.

"Look at me, Ember." I grab her chin, pinching it between my thumb and forefinger, giving her head a small but firm shake when her gaze rests north of my nose and not on my eyes. "There you are," I softly praise when she obeys. The lush curves of her mouth are flattened into a firm line, as if she's biting back a vitriolic tirade aimed directly at me. If only the frantic flutter of her pulse at the base of her throat didn't telegraph something altogether different than anger, then I might take my hands off her. Might. "You've been keeping secrets, ma. When did you get this done?" I ask, dipping my chin toward the hoops with the little balls pressing against the dark blue dress.

"Fuck you," she hisses.

I cock my head, studying her for a long moment. "If you want. Is that your dying wish, ma? Because I can tear that little pussy up before I slowly watch the life drain out of you." I shift my hand from her chin, lowering it to her throat and squeezing. Hard. "You keep poppin' off like I'm one of those mark-ass mu'fuckas you used to dealing with, and I'll make it happen. Last time I'm warning you about disrespecting me. You got me fucked-up, ma."

I give her neck another squeeze, and just as my grip loosens, something . . . dark flashes in her eyes. Not rage. I'm very familiar with the sting of her fury. But that glint—I know it. Have seen it before. Just not on Ember.

Never on Ember.

It's lust. Need. Confusion and resentment swirl there as well, but . . .

My stomach clenches so tight, pain mauls me like a rampaging beast, and my hold on her wrists almost slips. For a moment, I'm so caught off guard, the same bewilderment in her gaze trickles through me. What the fuck did I just see? It couldn't . . .

Desperate to see more of that emotion—desperate to convince myself I didn't imagine its presence—I flip my hand and trail the back of my fingers down the front of her neck and over her bare shoulder . . .

Got. *Damn.*

I release her as if her skin suddenly resembles a biblical plague, and my flesh is in danger of bubbling up and peeling away. For the first time since my father died, leaving me and Kareem victim to Michelle's tender mercies, fear skulks through me like a starving rat. I believed grief, hate, hypocrisy, and resentment had cauterized that part of me capable of feeling that particular emotion.

But here I stand, in this gourmet chef's dream of a kitchen . . . retreating. Physically frozen but on the run.

If I followed the first rule taught to me by Marcus, I'd reach over to that butcher block of expensive-looking, sharp-ass knives, pull the biggest, longest one free, and slice the blade across her throat. Eliminate all threats. Expeditiously. As the new head of a crime family, that rule isn't a suggestion, it's a mandate. It's the difference between power and insurrection.

And Ember . . . She's a weakness. A fucking phobia.

That makes her the biggest gotdamn threat of all.

"Answer me," I say, not letting the subject of the piercings go. This isn't why I sat in her apartment for hours waiting for her to arrive. Still . . . As it is, I want to hunt down the body piercer, take the same needle he or she used on Ember's nipples, and drive it through their eyes and then crucify their hands for seeing and touching her. "When did this happen?"

Her teeth sink into her full bottom lip, and I almost introduce her flesh to the edge and bite of my own teeth. We can nibble together, because this is the only situation in which I'm willing to share what's mine.

Her shoulders draw back and she tilts her chin up, her breath a soft pant, but nothing other than steel runs through her. "A year ago."

I nod. Pause. I should let this line of conversation go right here. Leave it alone . . .

Yeah, fuck that.

"Who did you get it done for?" I growl.

She barks an abrupt crack of laughter. "I'm sorry, what?"

"You heard me. Who, Ember? What bitch ass got you so fucking gone that you out here poking holes in your muthafuckin' body?" I step backward, tilt my head, and aim my stare toward her thighs. "They turn that pussy out, too?"

If she says yes, I'm flipping all this over.

Am I stupid enough to believe no one has been inside her? No. Am I unhinged enough to want to kill anyone who has?

You damn fucking right.

And anyone—man, woman, them—who's even sniffed the pussy had best be prepared. Because there's gonna be some slow singing and flower bringing when I find out who they are. And don't get it fucked-up—I will.

"There's this little thing called *autonomy*. I don't know, maybe you've heard of it? What I do with and to my body is all for my benefit and pleasure—no one else's. I don't need another person's permission or validation, nor do I give a fuck about anyone's opinion of it." She pauses, tips her chin up. "That goes double for who's bussin' this pussy wide open."

"Names." I snap out the demand, fury, red-hot and howling, boiling inside me. My veins are a conduit for the rage until I'm breathing it, organs pumping it. Shit, I *am* it.

Am I being irrational, unreasonable, and hypocritical? Fuck yeah. All of that and more. But it is what it is. When it comes to Ember, I've never been sane, sensible, or fair. I've played dirty from the moment I walked through the doors of her childhood home, the seeds of plans to steal it all away from her already germinating in my mind. Ain't nothing changed this way. Demanding a list of her sexual partners though? That might be a new low for me. It's degrading, objectifying, and shaming.

Fuck if I'm gon' take it back. I said what I said.

I want names. Every one of them.

I need to know exactly who I need to kill between my two and four o'clock meetings.

Ember blinks. Then the disgust for me that seems to be a permanent fixture on her face makes its reappearance.

"You first," she fires back, lip curled. "Hold up though. I got a papyrus scroll stashed next to the silverware drawer. You'll need it if you're going to get down every bitch you've fucked."

Amusement tickles my rib cage before I can smother it as ruthlessly as I suspect Michelle killed my father. And thin skeins of hate and . . . fear creep under my skin, spread their deadly spores into my bloodstream.

Michelle once called Ember an abomination.

And in this moment, staring down into those amber eyes that somehow possess the mystical power of appearing warm and so fucking frigid at the same time, I almost agree with my mother. Because only something, or someone, with some kind of corrupt, dark power could make me *feel* as much as her. Like I'm one six-foot-plus raw nerve ending.

Only she could make me . . . scared.

I'm the first to look away, to lose our visual square up. And for the second time in just minutes, I retreat. And not just emotionally. Physically.

Shifting backward a couple of steps, I place distance between us. A much-needed distance where my head isn't crowded with the delicious heat emanating from her soft body. Or the delicate and precarious thump of her pulse at the base of her throat. Or the no-nonsense citrus and sharp, fresh scent that's like fresh fruit in the crisp, early-morning air.

I take another step back.

"Meet me in the study. We have something important to discuss." I don't wait for her agreement—shit, this is Ember, don't wait for her argument.

Pivoting, I exit the kitchen without the water I'd initially gone in there to retrieve. Fuck, no man-made liquid could quench the thirst yawning wide inside of me.

Seconds later, I enter the study that's as far from her father's as the east is from the west. The only similarities are the walls of books and hardwood floors. Otherwise, the one I'm standing in isn't a showpiece carefully curated to display the owner's wealth, status, and power. Nah, this study is lived-in, used . . . loved.

The same block windows from the dining room claim a wall, while overstuffed bookcases occupy the others. A group of chairs and low table congregate in front of another massive fireplace. Instead of a bar, there's a state-of-the-art entertainment center with a TV monitor and music system, including a record player and albums. Small glass containers fill the other section, and I don't need to inspect the contents to figure out what they contain. Ember is a fucking pothead. She loves the shit, and if it were possible, she'd probably fuck it. Yeah, she got down with the Mary Jane like that.

Giving my head a small shake, I take in the rest of the room, landing on the large, cedar desk. Unlike Marcus's, whose desktop always remained ruthlessly clean, Ember's looks like the stereotypical scientist works there. It's the only thing clichéd about her, the avalanche of papers and notebooks, memo notes stuck to the back of the monitor, a collection of random pens jammed into containers. Behind the desk stands a huge whiteboard crowded with equations, numbers, and notes that make my head hurt just looking at them.

My stepsister is a gotdamn genius.

And that's another reason I trust the bitch as much as I trust anyone, other than an auntie named Reetha Mae, to cook the macaroni and cheese on a Jesus holiday.

People say there's a thin line between genius and insanity for a reason . . . And that reason is Ember Cross. She's crossed back and forth over that line so many fucking times, she needs a visa by now.

"What is it that we have to discuss, Asad?" she asks from behind me. "You've already disrupted my yoga session, and I'm working on no sleep. Can we make this fast so I can take care of one of those two things?"

Where the fuck you been for all these hours?

Once more, the question blinks in my head like a twenty-four-hour diner sign, but I've been distracted enough. And if she's been somewhere other than the lab, it isn't like she's going to tell me. Ember is more secretive than fucking KFC with that original recipe.

But I'll find out.

I always do.

Until then, I need to get to why I'm here.

"Sit down." I dip my chin toward one of the chairs in front of the dormant fireplace.

Her full lips roll inward, and her nostrils flare, but after a long moment, she heads toward the sitting area and sinks down onto one of the seats.

I follow her, the sweet and sharp scent leading me like I'm a doomed mouse caught up in the Pied Piper's haunting and lovely snare.

Deliberately, I choose a chair with my back toward the windows, with her and the study doors in my view. Anyone looking in on us might mistake us for acquaintances, or even friends, being cordial and catching up with one another. They wouldn't glimpse the proverbial line drawn in the sand visible to only the combatants sitting on either side of it.

During the long hours waiting on Ember to arrive, I went over how to approach her with my proposal. Ember was stubborn, could be petty, and if she didn't fuck with you, would screw you over even if it meant going against her best interests. I fell into that last category. If we were trapped in a burning car, and freeing herself meant saving my life, we'd both just be two burnt muthafuckas.

So I need to tread lightly in how to approach her . . .

Fuck it.

"You're going to marry me in a month."

CHAPTER FIVE

Ember

I blink.

Stare at Asad.

Blink again.

No, his stoic, flat expression doesn't change. No bare hint of a smile. No glimmer of amusement in those gray eyes. Nothing.

Still, I laugh. And laugh. And laugh some more. I can't stop. Every time it's almost under control, *You're going to marry me in a month* echoes in my head, and I'm gone all over again. Tears sting my eyes, and wheezing out a breath, I press my fingers underneath them, wiping away the moisture.

"Whew. I needed that," I rasp. "Who knew you had a sense of humor?"

"Are you finished?" he asks, voice even, void of emotion.

"Are you?" I curl my legs under me and yawn. "Thanks for the laugh, but your idea of a joke is weird as fuck, and I don't get the punch line. Then again, I threw out any fucks I had left to give last night along with the leftover shrimp egg foo young. Should've broken in here yesterday."

My unbothered tone is a charade and a shield. As Asad's steady gaze roams over my face, moves lower to my breasts, stomach, and thighs, I force myself not to fidget or cross my arms in a fruitless effort to conceal the effect that stare has on my body. Because, fuck, it's having an effect. My skin prickles with this awareness that's damn near painful, like tiny needles. And I'm so disgusted with my hot-in-the-ass pussy, who can't differentiate between the enemy and a less psychopathic potential lover who wouldn't consider fucking foreplay to be murder.

"First thing I'm going to do after we're married is tame that mouth. And make no mistake, I'm going to enjoy it."

Slowly, I straighten, my spine pushing against the back of the chair. Panic flares inside me, hot and bright like an SOS to my brain that Asad isn't fucking around. This whole marriage thing just might not be some sick joke. The last vestiges of humor evaporate under the heat of the dread and fear eddying in my belly, and I stare at him, at the coldness of his gaze, the aloof expression, as if threatening me with unholy matrimony bores him.

"Asad." I carefully say his name. "What the fuck is going on? No more cryptic-ass messages."

"Cryptic?" He tilts his head. "Tell me what I've said that confuses you."

"That would be the *marry* and *me* parts," I say, with a sarcastic chuckle.

Shaking my head, I drag a hand over my hair, my fingers bumping against my bun. It takes everything in me not to rip the band out of my hair and scratch the hell out of my scalp like a woman who's lost her shit.

I deliberately inhale a breath and stretch my arms high above my head, aiming to appear calm. Trying to seem as if my heart isn't playing kickball with my rib cage. Especially when his attention dips to my breasts, and his inquisition about my piercings replays verbatim in my head. My nipples seem to have perfect recall as well, because they tighten to the point of pain, sending a throbbing ache straight to my clit.

The *fuck*?

What the *actual* fuck?

That, that . . . abomination of heat that briefly flared in my belly and had my pussy quivering in the kitchen was an aberration. A delusional—and forgivable—blip from being up for nearly twenty-four hours. But this . . . This spasmodic clenching of my walls around an aching emptiness is inexcusable.

This is *Asad*.

My fucking nemesis.

Talking about marriage. Why *marriage*? No engagement? Just skip that—wait. What am I thinking, and where am I going with *that*? Marriage, engagement. It's all bad, and all a big-ass *no*.

"Okay." I hold up a hand, palm out. Anything to distract him from the beaded tips of my breasts that have no goddamn shame. "I'll play. Why are you under the impression that we will be husband and wife in a month?"

"Because it's in your best interest to do so."

I scoff, waving him off. "It's also in my best interest to get a caffeine enema, but you don't see me bending over and shoving Folger's breakfast blend up my ass, sooo . . ."

That frigid, gray stare settles on me for several long seconds. Then he smiles. It's a slow, gradual curving of those almost too-lush lips. It's stunning. It's breathtaking.

It's unnerving.

"My dick," he murmurs.

"Excuse me?" I jerk my chin toward my neck, scowling.

"My dick," he repeats, still wearing that unsettling, beautiful smile. "That's what I'm going to use first to break that mouth in."

The explosive puffs of air escaping my lungs competes with the deafening silence in the room.

"The fuck?" I rasp.

He didn't just say that to me. He couldn't have . . . Asad doesn't . . . We're not . . .

Oh shit. Now I can't even complete whole thoughts. I'm a fucking double-master's-degree-holding scientist, for God's sake, and he's reduced my mental to, to rubble. Instead of words, vivid, revolting, and—shit—hot-as-fuck images crowd into my head. Images of me, down on my knees, head tilted back, mouth wide open as Asad feeds me his big, long, veiny dick until I'm choking on it . . .

Fuck.

Fuck.

"Muthafucka, I don't even *want* the dick."

That smile widens and it's still beautiful. Still disturbing.

"Okay, ma." He chuckles. "You're seeing it."

It's not a question. He's stating fact in that smug tone, and I hate it and him even more because of the accuracy.

Bitch.

"All I'm seeing are the hours of sleep passing me by because you won't get to the point of this little visit." I cross my arms over my chest. Fuck pride. I can't die on that hill when my nipples are saluting like good little well-trained soldiers. "Now, please. Explain how my idea of entering hell on earth would be in my best interest."

"Because I assume you enjoy living."

I blink. This muthafucka just threatened me. That in itself shouldn't be shocking. I know what Asad is—a liar, thief, psychopath, murderer. But that he's in *my* fucking house, sitting in *my* study, threatening my life to *my* face? It's the audacity for me.

"Married to you or breathing." I wrinkle my nose, pretending to weigh the pros and cons. "I'll take Breathing Is Overrated for two hundered, Alex. Now." I uncurl my legs and arms and prepare to stand, ending this pointless, inane conversation. "If that's all—"

"Ember, if you move your little ass out of that chair, I'll tie you to that mu'fucka and make what you endured as a kid seem like recess. Try me." He doesn't raise his voice, but that doesn't prevent a shiver from trampling down my spine.

I believe him.

Just the mention of what I'd suffered at his hands is enough to ossify my muscles. I remind myself every day that I'm over the abuse of my childhood, that I'm no longer a prisoner to it. But the primal part of me stills like prey catching scent of a stalking predator on the wind.

Asad Prince is my walking, living nightmare. Him and Michelle.

But while I've outgrown—desperately fought my way free of—my fear of Michelle, it's not so with her son. Maybe because

I sometimes find myself foolishly captivated by all that pretty, nut-brown skin, brutally sharp angles, beautifully dirty mouth, and startling silver eyes. Maybe because at times my pussy forgets he's the enemy and weeps like a Kardashian after she's been cheated on . . . again. This makes him far, far more dangerous than any drug, any weapon. No . . .

This *makes* him the drug, the weapon.

And my guaranteed destruction.

So it's fuck him forever.

If only my gotdamn ignorant-ass coochie would get on one accord with me.

With his quiet warning echoing in my ears, I ease back into the chair, body rigid, fingers like claws gripping the arms, pulse like rapid gunshots in my ears. Still, I force my muscles to unlock, to deliberately relax so I at least appear to not be on red alert. The worst thing one could ever do is show weakness in the face of a hunter, a predator.

Asad taught me that. In spades.

"There are several reasons you're going to marry me," he says as if he's reading the details of a new distribution contract instead of dictating the terms of my immediate future. "One. Marrying me grants you access to your trust five years ahead of schedule. And as an incentive, I'll relinquish my role as trustee—"

I snort in disgust. "And have your bitch of a mother take your place? No thanks. I can't believe these words are actually coming out of my mouth, but I'd rather have you than Michelle. Letting that ho near anything associated with my mother . . ."

Fuck. I bite the inside of my cheek. *Shut. Up.* God knows I didn't intend to let that much slip out. I should know better than to give Asad anything personal that he can later weaponize.

"No trustee at all, Ember. Marcus relied on your intelligence and knowledge to fund his entire operation. It makes sense you can also manage your funds without a babysitter," he says, his full lips twisted into a sardonic half . . . shit, I'd say *smile* on anyone else, but this is Asad.

"You're right." I nod. "That is an incentive. But not enough of one to sell my soul. You, Marcus, Michelle, Kareem—the whole fucking lot of you would do and probably have done anything and anybody just to acquire money and power. Hell, I don't have to look too far behind you to see all the bodies littering the streets like piles of steaming dog shit. If I have to wait five more years to access that trust, or even never access it at all, I'm good on you. On all of you."

If he really believed I was as smart as he claimed, then Asad had to know I'd never fully depend on Marcus, him, or anyone to take care of me. Yes, I pull a hefty salary down from HoC, but I've also invested in stocks, real estate, saved. I've known about Mom's trust ever since I was thirteen and Sam sat me down and explained how she'd set a fund aside for me apart from the Cross fortune because she wanted me to have my own. Never wanted me to be out here fighting for financial independence because a man shackled the purse strings with tradition, misogyny, and "love." *That* fucking four-letter word that had tripped up many a woman onto her back and out of her power. Kimberly Jacobs Cross hadn't wanted that for me.

She should've wanted that for herself when she married Marcus.

I did learn the lesson she desired, just not in the manner she intended. As the creator of the drugs that funded his empire, I've been paid millions and, except for my home, lived a nine-to-fiver on a budget. I knew this day would arrive. Knew the time would come when I could taste the precursor to my freedom like a refreshing remise en bouche—the palate cleanser erasing the bitterness of the past before I gorged on the liberation of my future.

In other words, not Marcus, Michelle, or fucking Asad gon' catch me slipping.

I got my own.

I don't need his fucking money.

And though my mother's trust rightfully belongs to me, I think she would agree with me from wherever she is saying, fuck that money and her baby daddy.

"You good on breathing?"

Said breath catches in my throat. Not out of fear—okay, I can lie to others, and do so on a regular basis, but I don't make a habit of doing it to myself. So yes, a frisson of fear does skitter down my spine at his explicit threat. Those gray eyes don't blink, don't waver from mine, and he's not shittin' me. He will squeeze the breath from my throat, staring down at me as my soul flails, clawing and biting to hold on. Then he would drop my cooling carcass to the floor and step over it without a shred of remorse or guilt. That's how that muthafucka's built.

Which makes the quicksilver strand of, of . . . reckless excitement trembling underneath my skin, racing along the highway of my veins, an indictment. A gotdamn aberration.

And yet my pussy flutters like a fucking swooning Victorian virgin.

Shit.

Ignoring the caving and knotting of my stomach, the uncomfortable dotting of perspiration under my arms, I scrape tooth and nail for normalcy.

"I see we've reached the threatening portion of our program," I say.

"No threat necessary, ma."

He stands, and I lock down my muscles to prevent myself from jackknifing to my feet along with him. That big body towering over me? Nah. We don't do shows of intimidation over this way. But to follow through with that plan would also betray to what extent his display of dominance affects me. Either way, I'm fucked. And either way, I'm gotdamn *affected.*

"That's not—*what the fuck are you doing?*"

Shock damn near catapults me from the armchair. But it's the same shock that chains me to the seat easier than lengths of hundred-pound iron chains. I can't move. Can't speak. Am afraid to even think past this moment that has no precedent to guide me so I don't stumble into territory so full of land mines and disasters that there is no walking back.

In one moment, Asad stood in front of his chair, and in the next, he kneels before mine.

Asad.

Kneeling.

Before me.

My heart repeatedly slams against my chest in an attempt at a jailbreak. But I've lost all control over simple motor skills, so I can't lift my hand to rub my knuckles over the spot to calm the panicked pounding.

Even in that position, his tall, wide frame seems to block out the study like the moon eclipsing the sun. I can't see around him, above him. No, all I glimpse is *him*. The range of his chest and shoulders, the corded neck with incongruously delicate pulse at the base. The thick, dark beard surrounding that wide, ridiculously lewd mouth that has no business on a man as hard as him. The startling silver eyes under black, dense eyebrows. The long, curly hair still pulled up in its bun, exposing every beautiful, brutal line of his face.

It's too much.

It's too much.

Fucking overload.

My breath slams back into me after being unable to draw a thin draft of air into my lungs, and it slices into me like a razor-edged scalpel. I'm halfway surprised I'm not drowning in my own blood.

"Back up. Get away from me."

My low rasp of a voice trembles, and I don't care. Survival has wrenched control of the wheel and pride has climbed in the backseat of this ride. Horror at his nearness, at the memories of the past, at the tightening and pinch of my nipples and the sharp, tugging ache high in my pussy . . . I'm angry, afraid, confused. And a deafening *tick, tick* fills my head like the ominous countdown on a detonator.

If he doesn't move, if he doesn't grant me space that isn't permeated with Creed cologne, cedarwood, and skin-warmed musk,

I'll blow up, leaving him splattered in my rage, my deceit, my hatred . . . my shameful, dirty need.

My fingers ball into fists, my nails digging into my palms. Fire licks at my skin. Sweat dots the valley between my breasts, my upper lip, and under my arms. A thin, pink-tinged film colors my blurred vision.

"Breathe, Ember." Asad's deep rumble sounds as if it's traveled a long, hard night through a crowded tunnel. Yet, I clearly hear him. And feel the warm, mint-scented brush of his breath over my chin as he leans forward, his big palms clapping the sides of my face. He shoves his directly in mine, and my entire world becomes those beautiful and deadly gray eyes glaring down into mine. "You better breathe, because if you black out and swing on me, we gon' be like Ike and Tina in that mu'fuckin' limo up in here. In and out, ma. In and out. That's it. With me," he coaches. And as if my body is a sycophant to that terrible, irresistible voice, it follows his instructions.

"Focus, ma. Five things. Tell me five things you see."

I frown. But when he gives my head a little but firm shake, I do as he says and focus.

"The desk. My grinder. Record player. Fireplace. *Sticks and Stones*." I list the painting by Ernie Barnes that hangs above the mantel last.

"Good. Next. Four things you hear."

I close my eyes, inhale a deep breath, and close everything out except for my sense of hearing.

"The central air clicking on. Your even breathing. The Pandora station I left on in my room. The chirping of birds . . ."

We continue the exercise with him guiding me, and by the time I get to one, the howling in my head quiets to a whispering wind. My heartbeat slows from a furious stampede to a gentle cadence. And the air in my lungs . . . It calms and follows his measured rhythm.

The rage grudgingly loosens its greedy grip on me, and I'm not peering at Asad through a watered-down crimson tint any longer. As impossible as it should be, that unblinking, uncompromising stare grounds me in my own body, in the here and now. He's both my trigger and my coping mechanism.

"I thought you had that IED shit under control. Are you still taking your medication?" he asks, hands still clamped around my cheeks. Muscled, solid stomach still pressed to my knees. Big body still knelt in front of me.

"I did. I do," I say, not bothering to answer the question about my meds. Shit, he doesn't see me asking how he knows about the 5-4-3-2-1 grounding technique. And believe me, I really want to know. But curiosity and Asad are a bad mix. Like cyanide and living.

Instead, I lift my hands and circle his thick, tattooed wrists. I tug at them, trying to remove his palms away from my face, trying to insert much-needed space between us. But I might as well be pulling at a two-ton concrete block—immovable and pointless.

I suck my teeth. "It's not like I take a pill and I'm cured. It's not a disease. I live with it; I treat it. I manage it. Now, can you get your hands off of me and back up? Please?"

Maybe it's the "please" that finally makes him decide to concede. He removes his touch, and relief rolls through me on a seismic tidal wave. My skin tingles, and I silently threaten my fingers with amputation if they dare caress the area that feels branded by his palms. My plea was enough of a sign of weakness; I'll be damned if I give him another one. And Asad Prince has always been one of those give-an-inch-take-a-whole-fucking-country-mile muthafuckas.

No boundaries, that one.

Like right now. My relief shuts off like a celestial hand twisted a faucet as he drags an ottoman over and sits on it directly in front of me. With massive thighs spread wide, he pulls my chair even closer, and once more, I'm battling against the claustrophobic sense of panic scrabbling at my throat.

A loud, ominous silence pulls taut between us. His gaze runs over me from the top of my messy bun, over my bare shoulders, lingering on the thrust of my breasts and pierced nipples, and down to my dress-covered knees curled beneath me. Everything in between sizzles and hums under that all-seeing, all-knowing inspection.

I will not fidget. I will not fidget.

I will not admit that in one glance the seat of my panties is destroyed.

It's wrong. It's all so fucking wrong and a betrayal to the girl who was his victim for years. Disgust and lust twist and wrestle, and there's no clear winner. That only makes me hate myself more.

"I had you hemmed up in the kitchen and you didn't almost crash out on me. Why now?" he probes.

"You weren't talking about binding me to you in matrimonial hell then," I lie. "Which brings me back to the subject. Still a hard pass."

He leans forward, propping his elbows on his thick thighs, his tatted hands dangling between his spread legs. I force myself to focus on those piercing eyes and not dip to the cruel yet beautiful curve of his mouth, the long, dark beard surrounding it, or the strong brown neck liberally painted with ink.

No, those ice-cold, pitiless eyes are much safer.

"Yesterday, you sat in the same will reading as I did where I inherited the Cross—"

"Stole."

"—empire," he continues, ignoring my interruption. "I already have muthafuckas gunning for me, ready to test me as the new head of this shit. You got me all the way fucked up if you think I'm going to just let you walk, taking away my main income source. And nah, I'm not reverse engineering shit when I have the scientist right here. And she's not going anywhere."

A sliver of ice slides down my spine, and my belly twists into trembling knots. How the hell . . . ? Sam would've never shared our private conversation with Asad. Never. So how is he sitting here repeating almost verbatim what I told Sam about leaving and taking the formula for Glass Slipper with me?

I narrow my eyes on him, but keep my expression schooled in the aloof mask that I've perfected over the years around his family. Or at least, I attempt to. It's difficult when my insides feel scraped raw and bloody.

"Sitting there wondering how I know about your plans to try and leave me?" He arches an eyebrow. "When're you going to learn ain't shit around this mu'fucka that I don't know? One being you're not going anywhere except down the aisle. To me."

He's still on this bullshit, and I laugh, despite the alarm banging in my pulse, ricocheting off my skull.

Leaning forward, I shake my head. "You done lost your gotdamn mind. Even if I was going to marry—which Jesus Christ Himself would have to come down and do a burning bush, water-into-wine kind of miracle in order for me to even consider it—I would never make that mistake with a sample muthafucka like you. Respectfully."

His thick beard can't hide the tightening of his jaw, nor could he completely hide the flash of anger in his eyes like dry lightning.

I mean, I did say "respectfully."

"A sample muthafucka?"

"Yes. 'Cause everybody gets to try it." I dip my gaze down his large form and drag it back up. "If I was into that, I'd just hang out at Costco." My bread and butter is death, but until this moment, I didn't know I wanted to embrace it with open arms and a tongue fuck. And apparently, I'm not done. "And since we're on the subject of husband material, what kind of sad bitch would I be to marry my childhood bully? A BookTok-made-for-Netflix-movie sad bitch, and she ain't me."

For several long moments, he stares at me, and the heat from those eyes . . . It slips around the front of my neck and tightens its hot, thick fingers. I try to drag a breath in, but that's next to impossible.

"Ember, I promise you. The only thing I'ma bully is that pussy."

Holy. Shit.

I blink. He . . . he's never spoken to me like that. *No* man has ever spoken to me like that. But Asad . . . Asad hates me as much as I detest him. So what in the *fuck* was that?

Confusion, shock, and an indescribable, dark ache pulse within me like a thick, sluggish pulse. Since he's arrived . . . his innuendoes, crowding into my personal space, guiding me back from the ledge of an episode . . . It's almost as if blinders I've refused to rip all the way off are torn away by the shuddering, wild wind of lust, and I can no longer ignore that this man has said my name and "pussy" in the same sentence. Can't pretend that this hungry, annoying heat isn't one-sided.

My pussy throws up jazz hands, volunteering as fucking tribute.

I swear, if the ho could detach herself from me and throw herself at him, she would be a fucking fastball right now.

As if the bitch knows what she's begging for anyway.

But my head, my stutter-stepping heart? They're not on board with my kitty-kat. They're still holding ticket stubs to the "What the hell are we doing?" train, and I don't know if I'm willing to jump off.

This man, he could break me in more ways than one. Definitely my body. I have zero doubts he would shatter me with a pleasure that would have me looking for his ass in the daytime with a flashlight.

But Asad has also *broken* me in the past. I've been there, done that, and have the therapy bills to show for it. There is no way I could risk being vulnerable with him. Stripping nude with him, beyond my bare flesh, is a no. It's a hell no.

"I'm still going to have to pass on behalf of me and my pussy.

She's anti-bullying as much as I am." I stack my hands, crossing them in an X.

If it'd been anyone else except Asad, I would call the glimmer in his silver eyes *amusement*, but this *is* Asad. So no, it was more likely a warning or excitement at the thought of possibly murdering me.

"A shame. I thought we could negotiate this like two adults, but unfortunately, we're one short for that conversation." He straightens, and I frown at his insult. My comeback leaps up my throat and roasts my tongue, but he holds up a hand.

It isn't that age-old "stop" gesture that prevents me from speaking though. It's the ice-cold mask hardening his features and the freezing of those eyes, turning them to dirty sleet. A shiver tracks down my spine, and I'm no longer staring into the face of my childhood tormentor, my stepbrother, or the merciless bane of my existence.

No, I'm peering into the visage of the monster I've heard whispered about. The Asad Prince that trades his custom suits for blood-covered skin. Montblanc pens for fillet knives. Boardrooms for torture chambers stained with fluids and screams.

The only thing keeping me from shrinking back into the chair is the curse of my pride. Outside, I angle my head while my lips curl into a condescending sneer. But inside . . . inside, I'm shaking. I'm a killer, but the . . . male staring at me out of Asad's eyes is something altogether different. And more terrifying.

"I've tried reasoning with you, Ember. Given you more concessions than most. Let anyone else talk to me like you have, and their mamas would receive their tongues along with a gift certificate for a funeral home. Say 'thank you' for my patience."

When I don't immediately reply—because shit, how this muthafucka want my gratitude for not snatching the tongue out my mouth?—Asad leans forward and wraps his hand around the front of my throat. In reflex, my fingers wrap around his wrist, but that implacable grip only tightens, shutting off my air. Panic flares, and I drop my hand. There's no mercy in his steady, unblinking gaze. I could be a random bitch off the street, not his stepsister, and he could easily strangle me or snap my neck without any remorse.

I'm not ready to die.

I want to live.

And I'm ready to beg for it.

Bile churns in my belly and races for my chest as I tap his upper arm. Asad gradually loosens his grip, his stare never leaving mine. If I expected to see satisfaction and triumph in his eyes—and I did—I'm wrong. There's nothing there. Nothing. Just like his soul. And his conscience.

"What do you have for me?" he asks.

Hatred spills over and through me. I've had years, more than a decade, to detest this man. But those instances seem like petty grievances compared to this moment. Him and his mother have repeatedly tried to break me, and now he's attempting to take my pride. And I can't lie—he's ripped a strip away.

"Thank you," I grind out.

"There." He slowly eases the pressure on my neck even more, then finally lowers his arm. "That wasn't so hard, was it?" Right there. He's gloating. My hatred doubles down. He doesn't wait for an answer but taps the hand I hadn't even realized I'd curled into a fist. "Unless you're gon' do something with that, li'l baby, let it go." He does pause until I straighten my fingers, stretching them along the arm of the chair. "Wise choice. Now, you're going to marry me. Four weeks from now."

Just seconds earlier, I was silently screaming I wanted to live, that I was ready to beg for it. Beg him for it.

Well, the fury coursing through me has altered my options. I want to live. But I'm willing to tap out of here if I can take him with me.

"It's a woman's prerogative to change her mind, and muthafucka, you gon' have to kill me." And I mean that.

After what he just showed me of himself? Nah, I'll end up shooting him up with the foulest drug I have or he'll flay my skin from my bones. Either way, it would be shorter than a Britney Spears marriage.

He shakes his head, leaning forward and, once again, propping his elbows on his thighs. "Nah. Just call us Bobby and Whitney, 'cause I changed my mind, too. Killing you would be too easy, and it'd defeat the purpose. Nah. It wouldn't hurt you, wouldn't cost you. But those lab rats of yours." A sinister smile curves his mouth. "Me putting a hot one through each of their heads in front of you—now that would be a heavy price for you to pay."

His words are a solid haymaker to the chest, caving in my rib cage.

Did I say I hated him minutes ago? No, I *abhor* him now.

And for the flash of a second, I hate Perla, Gus, and Jaq for being my weaknesses that give him this leverage over me. A person who is alone, who has no attachments, has nothing to lose.

You'd think my crash course in Marcus Cross would've pile drove that home. Blind love and loyalty kept me bound to him through the abuse of his new wife and family. By the time I realized what a piece-of-shit father he was, and that he didn't deserve either my love or loyalty, it was too late. I'd been tangled up in the Cross empire, and those strings bound me tighter than chains, twisting and strangling me the harder I fought.

So yeah, you'd think I would've learned about the fallacy that is relationships and love.

But obviously, I truly am my mother's daughter. Right down to allowing love to be my downfall.

"Fuck you," I whisper.

"We'll get to that," he says, making my stomach drop to my ass. "But first things first. Do you understand what I'm telling you? I will take each of those lab assistants of yours, kill them one at a time, and let you watch them die. But not before letting them know that you could've saved their lives but chose yours over theirs. Let you witness all that admiration they have for you turn to disappointment, betrayal, and finally hate before there's nothing because their brains will decorate the wall."

I close my eyes, trying to block out the sensual, deep voice discussing the murder of the only people I care about as if he's ordering a porterhouse at Chi Spacca.

"Move." I lower my legs, my shins brushing his knees. Ignoring the electrified pulse that crackles through me, I scoot to the end of the seat, not caring that I'm crowded into his space. "Move, Asad."

For a moment, he doesn't, but then he stands, pushing the ottoman back and allowing me the most minimal of space to edge past him. Striding over to the entertainment center, I'm practically buzzing with the need for a blunt. Rage kindles under my skin, deep in my bones, and underneath, anxiety crouches in the recesses and nooks, waiting for its big break to make its appearance. I quicken my strides, and seconds later, I open the glass door and pick up my bag of pre-rolled blunts. Snatching one out and grabbing my lighter, I almost run out of the study for the balcony off the second library.

I don't glance around the room, with wall-to-wall books and plush chairs and couches specifically purchased for comfort. My sole attention is focused on the floor-to-ceiling French doors at the back of the library. Flinging one open, I step out on the balcony and drop down onto one of the basket chairs hanging from the overhang like a pendulum. My ass barely hits the cushion before I'm firing up.

My lips close around the end of the blunt, and I puff, drawing the acrid but sweet-flavored smoke into my lungs. I hold it several seconds, then blow it out. This blend is one of my own strains. Strawberry with a hint of cream and lemon. I hit it again, closing my eyes and tilting my head back to blow the smoke to the sky. My body has already started to loosen, the tension fading. My mind stops screaming, calmed by the drugs entering my system. I'm not floating yet, but I don't want that feeling. Not while Asad is here. He's too dangerous to completely lower my guard and be vulnerable around.

Part of me is surprised he didn't follow me out here. He isn't known for space or allowances. Then again, maybe he realized that if he didn't back the fuck up off me, one or both of us were in very real peril of going over this railing.

I take a couple more pulls, then ash the blunt out on the balcony's pebbled flooring. The soft breeze brushes over my skin as I take several more minutes to myself before I have to return and face the devil.

Shit, Satan is probably down in hell asking why I gotta bring him into this.

I sigh, bowing my head and pinching the bridge of my nose.

I'm trapped. I have no choice, and he knows it just like I do. He played the one card that I would never say fuck it and risk it all on. Huffing a dry chuckle, I stand and head back inside, shutting the French door behind me. Maybe that's another reason why Marcus left everything to Asad. Maybe he knew as small as it might be, I still had a conscience and Asad didn't possess one whatsoever. Just like him.

When I reenter the study, Asad stands where I'd left him. He leans against the mantel above the fireplace, arms crossed, his gaze catching mine as soon as I walk through the door.

"Why marriage?" I ask the question that's been bugging me since he brought up this blasphemous proposal. "Why can't I just sign a contract or something promising to stay employed with House of Cross?"

"Because I say so." *Gotdamn, I can't stand him*. "Now that you look more"—he raises an eyebrow—"relaxed, what's your answer?"

A wild something cries inside me, the piercing howl echoing in my head. And it only takes me seconds to recognize it.

That's my once chance at freedom screaming goodbye.

"You already know what my answer is," I snap.

"I want to hear you say it," he growls back, his arms lowering to his sides. The evidence of anger in his voice rolls over my exposed skin like tongues of dark fire. "Fucking say it, Ember."

I swallow every curse and name crowding into my throat. Smother my dreams of being free of everything Cross.

"I'll marry you."

CHAPTER SIX

Asad

Triumph glows in my veins as I descend the steps outside of Ember's apartment and reach the lobby. If I was one of those goofy-ass, smiling mu'fuckas, a grin would stretch across my face from one ear to the other. Sitting in her place all those hours and going back and forth with Ember had ultimately been worth it.

She's marrying me.

She's mine.

Did it require threats to the lives of people she loved? Yeah. Did she probably hate me more than ever? Most likely. Did I give a shit?

Fuck no.

I'm of the end-justifies-the-means school of thought.

I wasn't walking out of there without what I wanted. Unfortunately for Ember, she's just that. Years I've waited—waited for the right circumstances, the perfect opportunity. The stipulations in Marcus's will provided that chance, and fuck I look like, not taking advantage?

Shit, will or not, Marcus dead or not—Ember was going to end up mine. Too many times over the course of the years, I stayed, tethered to Marcus, playing second to him. Biding my time. Because sooner or later, she would've been ready for me. And nothing would've stopped me from claiming her as my own. Not her father. Not my mother. Not even her. I refused to walk away from this without Cross or her.

Yeah, I hadn't been completely honest with Ember when she'd

asked why this had to be marriage instead of a contract binding her to HoC. Before Marcus died, he'd called me into his office and spoken to me about what was required of me if I intended to inherit his empire. He and Michelle had their ideas of what that would look like.

And I had mine.

Stepping out of the building and onto the circular driveway, I glance over my shoulder toward the windows that belong to her space. The glare of the sun prevents me from seeing into her apartment, but I don't need to in order to picture Ember standing at that glass. That thick, sexy-ass body on display. Her gold-and-brown hair pulled up and away from that stunning, strong face.

Mine.

In only days, all those curves will be laid out on my bed, naked, damp with sweat and cum, that hair a messy halo around her head, that face twisted in pleasure I'm doling out.

Fuck.

'Cause that's what I intend to do. Fuck. Hard, and so often she'll feel me in her chest. And shit, as long as I've been waiting on her, baby girl will probably spend the first few weeks full of dick. I hope Ember doesn't harbor any crazy-ass idea of this marriage being in name only. If she does, her pussy cumming all over my dick will let her know different.

I turn around as the blacked-out Range Rover pulls up and stops in front of me. Just in time to prevent me from charging back inside and demanding she gives me a taste of what's been driving me crazy for years. Ember might claim to hate me, but the way those thighs were clenching beneath her dress says at least her pussy might have feelings for me.

The rear door opens, and Eli Rodney's huge frame eases out. I'm not a small man at six feet, five inches. But the head of my security is damn near seven feet and is a gotdamn wall of pure muscle. When people see him coming behind me, only the bravest of souls—or those flirting with death—will try him.

"We're headed to the Castle," I tell him, sliding into the backseat.

Instead of answering, he scans the immediate area and then follows me into the vehicle. As soon as the door closes, Tre, my driver for the day, pulls off.

"Everything good, Prince?" Eli asks.

I nod. "Yeah. Anything come up while I was gone?"

"No, it's been quiet."

"Good." I pull my phone free of my suit pocket and check my messages and emails. After about ten minutes of replying to the ones my executive assistant marked urgent, I look at Eli. "Did Ro get back to you about any CCTV or traffic-cam footage around Marcus's condo?"

As soon as I overheard Sam inform Ember that Marcus had been murdered, I put the members of my small, private circle made up of soldiers I implicitly trust without question to investigate. Yes, I had my suspicions, but once I had full confirmation—first by Sam and then later with the ME herself—I immediately moved. Not for myself.

I'ma keep it one hundred. I really don't give a shit. Marcus has wronged so many people in life, it's play silly games, win silly prizes. It's the nature of the beast when living in the world we do. But now I can't let it go for two reasons.

One, the heads of the other crime families who do business with Cross ain't trying to hear that.

And two, Ember deserves the truth. Even if from the sound of her conversation with Sam, she give less of a fuck than I do. One day though, she might. I want to have those answers for her.

So yeah, I put my people on this. And they've been with me for years as I secretly built my own power base outside of Marcus and the Cross empire. They're not loyal to HoC—they're loyal to me. Eli is one of those people, and so is Ro, short for Rochelle, Mills. She might not say much, but she's proven herself many times over and is a fucking genius when it comes to all things tech. If she can't find it or hack it, then the shit just can't be done.

I'm lucky to have her on my side and not the law's.

Unlike Marcus's misogynistic bullshit, I don't believe just because you don't possess a dick you have no place in this organization. Now that I'm head of this, all that shit gon' change. And whoever ain't with it can get the fuck on. And by that, I mean leave with a bullet in the back of their heads. I'on trust not one muthafucka to come at me on some get back shit. Fuck, I would. Nah, this ain't that. Blood in, blood out.

Ember should've remembered that.

"Nah, she hasn't found anything yet. She managed to get the security and Ring camera footage from the neighbors and surrounding businesses this morning, so she's got that to go through, too." Pause. "You really think you're going to find something? I don't know, but I think whoever was smart enough to make it look like Marcus overdosed would also have enough intelligence not to get their faces caught on video. Especially since that couldn't have been their first time visiting him. Think about it. No sign of forced entry. He had to let them in. And that was his fuck pad. Only a limited number of people had access to it. Which means he had to grant it."

I shrug, pocketing my phone. "All true," I concede. "But on the other hand, that same person didn't have enough information about Marcus to know of his fear of needles. So their attempt to make his death look like a heroin overdose is unbelievable. Not to mention he had no track marks—shit, no marks at all except the one that took him out of here. And for a lot of addicts, heroin isn't the gateway drug that gets them hooked. Weed, coke, even opioids. Then they move to the harder shit. Marcus fucking ran a drug empire—a drug empire with the best designer drugs available, here and abroad—and the one he goes out on is heroin? Nah, I'm not buying it. Not then and not now. My stepfather was a whole host of things—a kingpin, a whore, a thief and murderer. But an addict, or even recreational user, wasn't one of them. And whoever killed him should've known that, too. The fact they didn't means they damn well could've slipped up somewhere because they're not careful enough."

"I'll give you that." Eli stares ahead, his eyes squinted. For the years I've known him, that's his tell for him being in deep thought. "Why kill him? What's the motive?"

Damn if I know. If I had to gather a list of criminal heads to murk—and let's be clear, I have—Marcus only made my top five because I want his spot. I can't see him charting anyone else's though. Was Marcus a ruthless asshole? Yeah. But shit, what CEO isn't at least a little sociopathic? That doesn't mean all them out here getting Luigi'd.

"Power. Money. Revenge. And if that's the case, you got mad people to choose from. Shit, start with everyone named in his will, including me."

"Facts. You know once the news of his murder goes public, most people are going to be looking at you, 'cause to them, you gained the most from his death. Then your people," Eli says.

Ask me if I give a fuck.

Maybe Eli reads the answer in my silence because he laughs, shaking his head. He knows what type of time I'm on.

"You still plan on having that dinner at your place tomorrow night?" he asks.

"Yes, Mars got everything in place," I say, referring to my executive assistant. "Only thing left to do is let Michelle and Kareem know about it."

And Ember. I'll need to shoot her a text about her required presence.

"Prince, man." Eli blows out a breath. "This shit is a logistical nightmare, you realize that, right? Listen, I'ma give you credit that you're not holding this at your main residence. Ain't no way that many people should know where you lay your head. Especially ones we don't trust, for real. Still"—he shakes his head—"you got the heads of the Bratva, Yakuza, and Italian Mob, as well as all our street bosses all in one place." He lists the names of the other crime organizations operating in LA, California, and this side of the country. "The odds of all this going left? Man, there are better odds in Vegas of the fucking Browns winning . . . anything."

"You sound like a bitch with all that whining." I tilt my head, arching an eyebrow. Eli smirks in return because he knows just like I do that ain't no man ever put fear in my heart. And just because they happen to be the leaders of the deadliest criminal families on this side of the country don't mean shit to me. They bleed red just like I do. "I have to meet all of them anyway, so it's better to get it over with at one time. And having them all together at my table is a show of power and authority they won't be able to ignore. Introduce them to the kind of man who's now in charge of Cross. And how that man ain't no fucking Marcus Cross."

The thought of all I have planned has a warm slide of anticipation skimming through me.

"Just make sure you have security in place. Hire out if you need to. I'm sure they're going to be bringing their own men to this dinner, and I won't be outnumbered in my own house." Eli nods and takes out his cell. "And make sure you have someone to temporarily replace you for the evening. I need you at the table, too."

Eli silently studies me for a moment. "You sure that's where you want to announce this change?"

"What change?" I frown. "The will was just read last night. If muthafuckas assume shit, I can't be responsible for their assumptions. Like I said, I'm not Marcus. I get to decide who my underboss and street bosses are. Hurt feelings ain't got shit to do with me."

"Even if those hurt feelings belong to your brother?"

"They family, but this is business." I arch an eyebrow. "You saying you don't want the position?"

Eli's head jerks back. "The fuck? Be for re—*shit*!"

A blast ricochets like a nuclear boom outside of the vehicle, rocking it seconds before a hailstorm of bullets pings against the windows and side panels. The screams of metal against metal penetrate the nearly deafening and constant banging of guns.

With a curse, Tre swerves, and my shoulder crashes into the door, the shuddering impact singing up my arm, across my shoulder blade, and up the back of my neck. The side of my head slams into the window. Shoving off the interior panel, I brace a hand against the back of the passenger seat and another on the headrest behind me.

"You better keep this muthafucka on the road!" I bark.

If not for the Range Rover being completely bulletproof, we would've been fucked.

Tre nods, but I peep the throbbing at his temple and the bead of sweat rolling down the side of his face. Shit. If his bitch ass gets us caught up, he's not gonna have to worry about catching some fucking bullets. I'ma kill him myself.

A swift but thorough glance out the window reveals a hot-ass mess. The blast of horns and panicked screams fill the air, barely muffled by the glass separating us from the outside. Cars attempt to swerve out of the way, but the thick choke of traffic and the other flustered and terrified drivers make that an impossibility. Just feet from me, a Rogue slams into the rear of a Benz. Shifting my attention away from the accident, I instead focus on the motorcycle edging up close to the Rover's rear tire. A dark blue Hellcat with heavily tinted windows attempts to box us in from the front.

Bet.

Turning to the door, I locate the button disguised to blend into the side panel. I press my thumb to it, wait for the scanner to read my print, and then pull the panel down, revealing a store of weapons. I grab my CZ Scorpion Evo 3 and SIG P365, tucking the smaller gun at my back. A glance over shows me Eli has the other hidden compartment open, and he's fastening an extended magazine to a Koch MP5.

"What you got?" I demand, shoving two more guns in my shoulder holsters.

"Bike and Altima right on our ass."

Whoever sent these hittas after us wasn't playing. Good thing I'm not either.

Rage and a hedonistic, fierce delight sing through my veins. My mouth curls into a smile. Yeah, Marcus had been grooming me for years to one day replace him as head of his criminal empire. But this shit? I lower the window and aim the CZ Scorpion at the rider with the black-and-red helmet who's roaring up next to my side on a Kawasaki Ninja. I was born for this shit.

With one shot to the neck and another to the front tire, the biker crashes out. A car in back of him jerks to the right with a squeal of tires to avoid hitting him. But the car ends up running right over his body and the bike anyway.

Yeah, ain't no coming back from that.

"One down," I inform Eli just before jerking back as another volley of bullets sprays the side of the Rover. Thank God for the bulletproof exterior or shit would be looking real different. The Hellcat pulls up alongside us, and another hitta wearing a ski mask leans out the back window, firing a SIG MPX. More bullets dance over the outside of the Range Rover.

"How many more?" I ask Eli, shoulders pressed between the backseat and the window.

"Just took out the muthafucka firing on us in the Altima. Still got the other motorcycle on our ass."

"Got it." Out of the corner of my eye, I see the Hellcat pull even with us and the gunman lean farther out, gun raised again. "Tre, brake." When he doesn't react, only glances at me in the rearview mirror with wide eyes, I shout, "Brake, gotdammit!"

His head bobs, and a second later, he complies. The Range Rover skids to a stop, and the Hellcat shoots pass us, but it can only go so far in the LA traffic. It brakes, wheels spinning, the acrid scent of burning rubber corrupting the air. A cacophony of horns, screams, and the screech of metal and tires peppers the air, but I block it out, lowering my window farther down. The

Hellcat doesn't get far, unable to turn left or right, blocked in by vehicles with frantic drivers.

Lifting my CZ Scorpion, I pop the gunman hanging out the window in the head, then take out the two tires on the driver's side. The car careens wildly as the driver tries to control it, but it's too late for that. He crashes into the other vehicles, and within seconds, a second motorcycle plows into the driver's door, the rider flipping over the hood.

Everything in me demands I jump out of this car, head over to that Hellcat, and make sure there are no survivors. My hand fists the door handle, but I stop and inhale a deep breath. Too many witnesses. Nah, correction. Too many witnesses with cell phones and cameras.

"Aye, get us out of here," I order Tre, raising my window.

Next to me, Eli breaks down his gun, and I return the CZ Scorpion and the SIG P365 back into the hidden compartment, replacing the panel. As soon as we get back to the office, I'll have Eli get rid of all the weapons.

"The road is blocked in front of us—" Tre stammers.

"Bruh, if you don't back this bitch up and get us the fuck up outta here," Eli snaps. "I don't care if you run into every gotdamn car in our way, do what he said. The fuck?"

Tre wastes no time throwing the gear in reverse and whipping the Rover in a sharp K-turn. The big-body vehicle jolts as it smashes into cars behind it, triggering another round of screams and profanity from outside the car. Then he spins the car around and barges his way across the street into the opposite flow of traffic. Sirens blare in the near distance, but Tre hooks a right off the main road, taking us farther away from the site of the drive-by.

"Shit," I hiss. Hiking my hips, I snatch my phone out of my front pocket and dial a familiar number. As soon as it connects, I start talking. "This is Asad Prince. You have officers on their way to a shots fired, drive-by call right now involving a black Range Rover, two motorcycles, and two more vehicles. PCH and Sunset Boulevard. Fix it."

I hang up on the chief of police without waiting for his reply.

Fuck. I pinch the bridge of my nose. What the *fuck*? I'd be lying if I said this was the first attempt on my life. Shit, you can't be in the line of business I'm in and not have people make it their business to snatch your soul. But this? This shit was messy, too public. Chief Miles can handle burying the police report and halting the investigation, but he can't make the witnesses disappear. Ro can scrub the internet of the videos posted, but erasing people's minds? Impossible. So again . . . what the *fuck*?

Only one gotdamn day as boss and already a hit.

And right on the heels of Marcus being taken out?

Nah. This feels personal. But at the same time . . . it doesn't.

Scrubbing a hand down my face, I blindly stare out the window. The bloodlust slowly ebbs, but the rage remains, roiling and clawing in my gut. For some reason, a face of bold, slashing angles with a mouth composed of lush, damn near indecent curves and a sick-as-fuck slim-thick body flickers in front of my eyes like images flashed across a phantom movie screen.

Could it be her?

Could Ember be behind the attempt on my life?

A quiet voice warns me not to underestimate her just because she's a woman. That's some Marcus-type thinking. Shit, some of the most brilliant bosses and deadliest killers I know are women. It's not about what she has between her legs. That low whisper cautions me not to disregard the loathing I glimpsed in her gaze either. Her hatred for me didn't start with me forcing her to accept my "marriage proposal." Hers is old, aged. Like wine. The older it gets, the more potent and intoxicating. Maybe now is just when she's decided to finally pop the cork on it, let it breathe. It could be the timing of today's drive-by was just a coincidence with my appearance at her house.

Love. Hate. Lust. Greed.

They're the greatest motivators for any crime. Especially murder. And the irony would be that I'm finally claiming Ember only to have her gunning for me.

My fingers curl into a fist on my thigh. If Ember is behind this shit, not her gender, her beauty, or my inexplicable obsession with her existence will save her.

Nothing will.

She'll die screaming and begging like any of my enemies.

But another, cooler part of me scoffs at the idea. Dismisses it. Hell, I just left her house. For one, she didn't know I planned on turning up at her house today, so her having time to plan this level of ambush is insane. And she for damn sure wouldn't have been this messy.

And this just isn't . . . Ember. It's not her style. Silent. Unseen. Smart. That's her. Her failures wouldn't be caught on iPhones or Facebook live.

Ember Cross just wouldn't be caught.

Still, neither argument is enough to cross her off the list.

A list that unfurls to include about fifty people who just became *my* soldiers, the members of *my* organization. Include the very people who are about to show up on my doorstep for dinner tomorrow night. Shit, include my own mother and brother. No one's exempt.

The car slows, dragging me from my thoughts. Tre pulls up to the black iron double gates with elaborate scrollwork, and they slowly open before he can come to a complete stop. The untrained or unaware eye would only see the security guard in the booth who nods at Tre. They wouldn't notice the sensor implanted in the ground that scans the undercarriage for bombs. Or the high-security weapons detection system installed into the posts of the gate that examines vehicles for weaponry, similar to the technology at airports. Or the strategically placed guards along the perimeters of the property and on the roof of the house.

Fort Knox don't have shit on my estate.

Tre rolls down his window and leans out, extending his arm to tap in a code that will cut off the silent alarm our hidden weaponry is triggering. The gate swings open, and returning inside of the car, Tre pulls through.

As soon as the Rover circles the marble fountain with the clear water bubbling from snarling open mouths of a pride of lions, the front door of the sprawling villa-style mansion opens, and Makeda Hannah, one of my street bosses, exits. She descends the steps, her petite, slim body taut with anger and a frown darkening her pretty face. She's one of my hand-chosen inner circle, having been with me for the last couple of years. Only now, with Marcus gone and me in his place, I can officially bring her on, those archaic, patriarchal mandates a thing of the past.

When the car rolls to a stop, I shove my door open and step out, rounding the rear of the vehicle.

"What the fuck happened?" Makeda demands, approaching the Rover. Lips pursed, she bends down, running her fingertips over the dented doors. "Ro called and said there was a shootout with a Rover coming from the direction of Brentwood. She accessed the traffic cams from that area and deleted it but not before seeing your license plate number on the vehicle. What the hell's going on, Prince?"

"Some muthafuckas pulled up on us on the way here and tried to take us out."

"Shit." Turning to face me, Makeda sweeps a hand over the top of her waist-length box braids. "Who? And how did they know where you would be?"

"That's what I plan on finding out. Bet on that."

Makeda rocks back on the heels of her black platform boots, shoving her hands in the back pockets of her dark gray jeans. "I tell you what." She huffs out a sharp chuckle. "Whoever did this is bold as fuck. I saw the footage before Ro scrubbed it. Those shooters didn't care who saw them or who else could've been hit while trying to get at you. Bitches who give zero fucks like that ain't done. You got to know whoever sent them gon' be gunning for you again. This is only the beginning."

For a moment, the melodic gurgle of the fountain behind us provides the only soundtrack to our individual thoughts. I rub a hand across my jaw, my beard scratching against my palm as I acknowledge what she said.

Makeda isn't wrong, and she hasn't said anything that I haven't already considered. And now that they not only failed to kill me but tipped their hand about coming for me, most likely they would be coming harder, hit faster. Hell, it's what I would do. There's no bitch in my blood; I'm on the verge of having everything I've worked, schemed, and killed for. Everything owed to me. I'll be damned if I allow anyone to take that from me.

These streets'll run red first.

Even if it's my new fiancée's blood staining them.

"You right," I say to Makeda and hike up my chin, shoving off the front passenger door. "Hold that thought."

Turning, I reach beneath my suit jacket, grab the SIG from its shoulder holster, and shoot Tre point-blank in the forehead. His big body sags against the driver's door, then drops to the ground, face forever frozen in a mask of surprise.

Eli grunts behind me, and it's a sound of satisfaction while Makeda flinches.

"Goddamn, Prince," she shouts. "Why . . . What—" She shakes her head. "Tre's been with us for years."

I shrug, reholstering the gun. "That don't mean shit to me. Either he was in with them bitches who came after me or he's a punk ass when under pressure. In both scenarios, he's a liability and had to go." I glance at Eli. "Get someone out here to clean this up."

"On it," he says, already pulling his cell out.

"You know his father and uncle are both street bosses," Makeda reminds me. "They're not going to take his death well. There could be retaliation or worse. And with people already coming for your head, we probably don't need dissension within our own ranks."

"Mack, I hear what you're saying, but I could give a fuck. They're bosses, but they're soldiers first. They know how this go. Demarcus will get the death payment for his son. And he's only receiving that because, at the moment, I don't have concrete proof that Tre sold me out. But best believe I'm getting Ro on that shit, and if she gives me that evidence, he's gonna hand over every last cent of that payment back. And then both D and Gray better hope that I don't turn nothing up on their asses. Now, if they got issue with that or me, we can handle it another way. But that other way gon' end up with fish fries and their faces on T-shirts."

We fall silent as several men roll up in a black van from the side of the house and park next to the Rover. Three of them shove open the rear doors and jump out the back. They nod to me, and within seconds, they stretch a dark gray tarp out next to Tre's body, hike his deadweight onto it, and then roll Tre up like a pig in a blanket. While two of them lift his corpse and tote it back to the van, the last man gets busy spraying the blood on the asphalt down with a bottled solution.

The three of us turn around and climb the curved front steps to my house, leaving the cleanup crew to do their work.

"Did you manage to get a good look at the shooters?" Makeda asks me and Eli, entering the house first and waiting until I close the door behind us all. Her thick-soled heels fall against the black-and-white-checked marble floor, the sound echoing under the cathedral ceilings. She doesn't pay any attention to the fireplace against the far wall and golden mantelpiece, continuing past the formal living and dining room and smaller parlor toward the rear of the house. "Ro couldn't really tell anything from the video except that they were either Black or Latino. That doesn't mean they couldn't have been hired by damn near anyone."

"They were brothas." Shrugging out of my jacket, I stride to the ruthlessly clean, state-of-the art kitchen. After sitting there waiting on Ember for hours and that shitshow on the PCH, I'm starving. Nothing stirs an appetite like murder. "And true, they could've been hired out, but the Bratva and the Yakuza aren't fucking with us like that. While I don't put it past the Italians to hire a few of us as hittas to do their dirty work, I just don't think this is them. We don't currently have beef with the mob. Nah." I frown, tossing the jacket onto a chair in the breakfast nook. "This was someone else."

"Not the gangs either. We have an alliance with them, and they don't want to go to war with us," Eli adds, jerking a chair from under the table and sinking down into it.

He's not wrong. The Cross organization and the street gangs of LA have enjoyed an understanding that was forged by me five years ago. Marcus didn't see a need in it, same with his father and his father before him. All of 'em were shortsighted. Yeah, we were a strong-ass family. But we were still surrounded by the Russians, Italians, and Japanese crime families. Having the Black gangs who have ruled the streets of LA for decades as allies just makes sense in numbers and dollars. That's the problem with us as a community now. Other races gon' have each other's backs. They gon' share information, ensure capacity building within their own communities, network, and partnership to safeguard their power and financial success.

Fuck if I'm making that mistake on my watch. Marcus, in his arrogance, fought me on it. Didn't see past his own house. But shit, I wasn't asking for his permission; I was informing him. If the largest Black underworld on the West Coast was eating, the table was big enough to feed *all* of us.

That bred fidelity, faithfulness.

Which means I have zero doubts those hittas coming after us weren't from the outside. They didn't have anything to gain. No, some intuition, sixth sense, insists this originated from within.

Someone from within my own family wants me dead.

Maybe I should start listing the names alphabetically.

"Like I said, this dinner is gon' be some shit," Eli murmurs, then sliding me a look, laughs. "You wild as fuck, Prince."

"No doubt." Makeda circles the large island in the middle of the kitchen and opens one of the cabinet doors lining it. She's been in my house so much, she doesn't bother asking permission as she removes the box of Cinnamon Toast Crunch and sets it on top of the island. "Ain't no way I'm missing it."

"You over here sounding like you hope some shit jump off." I swing open the cabinet door above the stove and withdraw two bowls, and then grab the milk from the refrigerator.

"I'm not *not* hoping." Makeda tugs open the silverware drawer and removes two spoons as I set one bowl down in front of her and the other before me.

Neither one of us bothers offering Eli any cereal. He refuses to eat sugar, carbs, or pussy. No wonder he's a fucking workaholic. His life holds no joy.

Before I can reply, my cell buzzes in my pants pocket. Sliding it free, I glance down at the screen and immediately answer it.

"Ro," I greet Rochelle Miller, my tech analyst. "You get any name recognition hits off that video?"

"So far nothing, but I'm still working on it," she says, the clicking of tapping on a keyboard sounding off in the background. This woman works more than Eli does. "I got something else though I think you should look at. I just sent an encrypted file to your email."

"Aight. I'll check it out and hit you back."

"Bet."

When I end the call and set the phone on top of the island, Eli is already rising from his seat and making his way across the room. Makeda drops her spoon in her bowl and studies me, her body turned toward me, going still, as if bracing for action.

"Do me a favor and grab my tablet off my study desk?" I ask Eli.

With a nod, he disappears from the kitchen, and not a minute later, he's striding back into the room, coming to stand next to me and Makeda.

"'Preciate it," I murmur, powering the device on.

As soon the screen blinks to life, displaying a lovely but boring screen saver of ice-capped mountains, I maneuver to the email app. On either side of me, Makeda and Eli shift closer. They didn't overhear my conversation with Ro, but it's as if they sense some shit is about to go down.

They wouldn't be wrong.

The encrypted file sits right at the top of my inbox, and I waste no time right-clicking on it. The tablet's screen fills with a black-and-white video of what appears to be a lobby. Maybe at a hotel or office or . . .

"Oh shit. This is Marcus's apartment building."

I've only visited my stepfather's Brentwood condo a handful of times, but it's hard to forget the pretentious-ass stained glass that sits high on the wall above the revolving entrance door. Other than that one identifying factor, it's just any other lobby in another building. Security desk lining one wall, nondescript couches, chairs, and tables creating a fair-sized sitting area, and a bank of elevators just out of shot.

"Look at the date." Makeda taps the top corner of the screen with a jet-black painted nail.

"Yeah," I say.

"The night Marcus was killed," Eli murmurs, flattening a palm on the marble surface and leaning forward, his focus fixed on the device.

For at least five minutes, the lobby remains clear. Not even a guard stands on post behind the desk. Impatience scratches at me. Impatience and a . . . knowing. Something is coming. I can feel it sitting on my chest. I deliberately slow my breathing so it doesn't echo in my head, but there ain't shit I can do about the jumping of my pulse or the acrid aftertaste of trepidation coating my tongue.

Just when I'm about to jab at the fast forward button, the revolving door begins to slowly spin. A figure steps into the enclosure and, seconds later, walks into the foyer. A hood covers their head, but the tallish figure strikes me as familiar. A woman. Neither the material concealing her face or the long raincoat covering her frame can hide those feminine curves. She steps farther into the camera's view.

And pulls the hood back.

Ember.

Shock rips through me. I stare at her beautiful face, so clear even in the slightly grainy quality of the video. Gaze still pinned to the video, I shuffle backward a step, away from it. A rush of emotion floods into my chest, threatening to crack my sternum open like the gotdamn Jaws of Life.

Shock, yes. But also disbelief, confusion, anger.

Pride.

Ember had been at her father's place that night. The night he was murdered. And she never said anything to me. Never so much as mentioned that she'd seen her father hours before his death. There was only one explanation why.

I can't tear my eyes away from the tablet, watching her disappear from the camera's view. After continuing to watch the video for another twenty minutes, she still doesn't reappear. That's when I pause it.

Silence permeates the room. None of us move or utter a word.

"What're you going to do?" Eli asks after several tension-thick moments.

There's no need to discuss if Ember killed her father. We all watched the same incriminating footage. And Ember's own omission is a testimony to her guilt. Now it's about action.

Consequences.

I pivot, stalking over to the sink and slamming a hand down on the counter next to it.

Fuck.

Gotdammit. Fuck. *Fuuuuck.*

Wrapping my stinging palms around the cool, stainless steel edge of the sink, I stare out the window into the trees and mountains in the distance. As much as I planned and committed damn near every unthinkable act to be right here as the head of HoC, sometimes I just want . . . My fingers curl tighter around the sink edge.

Sometimes I just want to run. Run and disappear into those

trees or those mountains. Shrug off the weight of decisions, responsibilities, lives and walk the fuck away, never to be seen again. How freeing that shit would be. To walk without the ever-present concern of who might be running up to my back to pump a bullet in it. To not always be thinking three steps ahead. To not map out a room as soon as I enter it to be aware of the fastest exit should something pop off. It's fucking exhausting, and gotdamn, I'm tired.

Of the lies.

The betrayal.

The greed and envy.

The people.

I could never admit this to Ember, but I get it. I get her desire for freedom, to abandon it all. Besides being unwilling to allow her to leave this organization, leave me, maybe that's the other reason for my refusal. Jealousy. I don't want her to experience what I at times so desperately crave.

Yeah, that makes me a selfish li'l bitch.

"Prince?" Makeda softly calls my name and, inhaling a deep breath, I briefly close my eyes. When I open them, gone is the would-be wanderer, and the head of House of Cross returns.

I can't afford to be anyone, anything else.

Spinning around, I face my street bosses again.

"Nothing," I announce.

Makeda and Eli glance at each other, then back at me. Both wear identical frowns.

"What?" Eli asks, with "the fuck you mean?" all up in that one word.

"That's what we're going to do. Nothing." I shove off the sink and retrace my steps to the counter, picking up the tablet and powering it off. Setting it back down on the island, I meet their confused, angry gazes. "I'll get with Ro, but we're the only four who know this exists, and that knowledge stays here."

"Why?" Makeda demands, flicking a hand toward the device.

"Ember murdered Marcus, the head of Cross, *her father*. We can't just ignore what we saw or the implications of it. If she can take her own father out, then what else is she capable of? What else has she already done? She can't be trusted."

"I'm aware of their relationship. It's because of that connection I'm deading this shit," I bark, pacing away from Makeda, over to the stove, then retracing my steps. Over and over. "That"—I jab a finger in the direction of the tablet—"was personal. If she'd sent someone else to kill him, I might agree with your argument. But Ember didn't; she handled that herself, and it was between father and daughter. Whatever happened in that apartment didn't have shit to do with Cross or me. Don't get me wrong. Ember Cross is very capable of more, and I'd turn my back on a starved pit bull while wearing a meat suit before her. But what happened to Marcus don't have shit to do with us. So. Forget. It."

I halt mid-step, pin an unblinking stare on Makeda. To her credit, she meets it without flinching.

"But get one thing straight and never fuck it up again—I'm the head of Cross. Offer me your opinion, I welcome it. But don't ever fix your mouth to tell me what I can and can't do. Understood?"

After a moment, Makeda, arms crossed tightly in front of her chest, nods. "Understood."

"Good."

Neither of them was privy to the dirty, raw details of the history between Marcus and Ember. So they couldn't fully grasp why I didn't give a fuck that she shot her father full of smack and left him like some dope fiend in a condemned crack house. Given the father he'd been to her—the mu'fucking man he'd been to her—it was better than he deserved. And shit, fuck I look like trying to swoop in and avenge him? Fuck Marcus.

My anger stems from her not confiding the truth with me. Not letting me fucking protect her. Not letting me protect what's mine. Trust between us an ideological concept, but . . . No but.

I *want it* from her. Call me unreasonable and irrational considering I'd just threatened and blackmailed her into marriage, but I *needed* it.

Sighing, I drag a hand over my hair, then roughly scrub it down my face.

"So you don't think she's behind the drive-by today?" Eli asks, walking back to the table and reclaiming his seat. Leaning forward, he props his elbows on his thighs.

I shake my head. "I didn't say that. I don't know if she's involved in that or not. Ember has her own reasons for wanting me dead so we continue to look into her and everyone else. Marcus and today's attempt are two different instances. We treat it like that." I look over at Makeda. "We good?"

Frowning, she lowers her arms and reaches for the milk. "Yeah, of course. Listen, I'm into that toxic shit. If you ain't threatening my life, you don't love me."

I snort and head to the refrigerator. Pulling the door open, I grab a beer, no longer in the mood for Cinnamon Toast Crunch.

"Now . . ." I twist the cap off and lift the bottle for a long, deep pull. "Let's go over this dinner. Everybody's about to find out the difference between me and Marcus."

CHAPTER SEVEN

Ember

So this is what Daniel felt like?

Except he was a whole punk in those biblical streets.

First, he got to kick it in a lions' den. Try hanging out in a drawing room with exquisite, prettily upholstered furniture that invites no one to sit their asses on, art that is pricier than good, and a large, looming fireplace that feels more like a threat than an offer of warmth. Do that, then come talk to me about discomfort.

Second, those lions' mouths were sealed shut while he was in that den. Standing here in the middle of this elegant and luxuriously appointed drawing room, the mouths of these predators are wide the fuck open, flashing razor-sharp teeth that are just ready and waiting to tear into vulnerable flesh.

Am I being a little dramatic?

Given we're congregating in Marcus's—no, now Asad's—Malibu property instead of Asad's home because he wouldn't dare invite anyone to where he lays his head?

No. I'm not being dramatic in the least.

Still . . . I dislike most people under ordinary circumstances. They're annoying, ignorant, rude, and talk too much. As a person who values quiet, I can't put up with all that noise for too long. Which is why I'm ducked off in a corner of the room, alone except for my drink.

Add my natural aversion to a room filled with the heads of powerful crime families—families who share a tenuous history—several of the Cross organization's soldiers, my stepfamily, and of course, Asad, and my tolerance level is nearing flash point. And then there's Aryn Murray.

Her light, slightly husky, and sensual laugh floats above the conversation in the room. It's not garish or rude. And judging by the expressions on most of the men's faces, they find it alluring, delightful.

I'm not a man.

Asad is.

Though his usual stoic expression gives nothing away, including how much he appreciates his lover's laughter, he doesn't try to avoid her slim hand on his chest. He doesn't ignore all the smiles she directs up at him. No, my "fiancé" allows another woman to loop her arm through his and press her body against his. Sure, we're an exclusive party of two that knows about this "engagement," but the disrespect of inviting the soon-to-be side chick to the same party as your almost wife?

The fucking audacity.

My hand tightens around the cut crystal whiskey glass. The sharp edges press into my fingers and palm, and I relish the small bite of pain. It blunts the fringe of anger simmering in my chest, combating and keeping it under control.

I've been trying not to glance in the direction of the supermodel, but shit, it's a damn difficult thing to do. Kind of like attempting not to stare at a giraffe in a room: It's tall as hell, with long legs, and if you move in any direction, you can see its pussy.

The ends of her long, dark brown hair nearly reach her ass, making the silken length only several inches shorter than the black lace cocktail dress. On another woman, I would assume she had some business to attend to down on Figueroa Street. But Aryn, with her astonishing beauty, glowing brown skin, and innate sense of sophistication, pulled it off with grace and style. You had to admire her for that.

And yet, I'm over here still calculating the amount of rocuronium I would need to inject in order to lay her out like a fucking mummified mannequin. At least then I wouldn't have to hear her gotdamn voice speak *his* name.

Is it crazy that I'm battling the urge to snatch up my "fiancé's" ho for peering up at him with the knowledge of a woman who knows exactly how he looks when he cums? Hell yes. Especially when I would rather be anywhere but in this bitch with all these strangers. Especially when I don't want a gotdamn thing to do with said "fiancé." When I don't want a fiancé *at all*. Particularly *that one*.

Yes, it is crazy as fuck.

But Aryn reminds me of the women I went to college with—beautiful, carefree, laughing, *unspoiled*. I've always held a . . . disdain for them. They've never known neglect, rejection, uncertainty, instability. Being so young when entering university, I didn't participate in or enjoy the usual collegiate experience. I didn't party, drink to excess, or fuck. And not only because of my age and social immaturity. Let's be honest, that's never stopped a lot of teens. But I had—have—a healthy mistrust in people, particularly men. Given the ones in my life—my grandfather, father, Asad—is there any wonder? I couldn't trust a man with any part of me—my mind, emotions, heart, body—for fear of manipulation, deception, cruelty, and abuse of control.

So, yes, knowing all of this about myself makes it ludicrous that I give a damn about Aryn touching or smiling at Asad . . .

Am I willing to analyze why I still want to inject homegirl with a paralytic so I can eviscerate her and splay the flaps of her torso wide like a dissected frog?

I'd rather stay here for another hour and engage in small talk.

In other words, hell no.

Lifting the glass to my lips, I take a sip of the seventy-two-year-old Macallan whiskey and savor the delicate sweet oak, citrus, vanilla, and smokey flavor. I already received several raised eyebrows and disapproving looks when I requested the same whiskey as the men, instead of the wine most of the women were indulging in. Fuck that. When they broke out a bottle of alcohol carrying a $121,000 price tag, there's no way in hell I'm partaking of some weak-ass Jesus juice. Asad must be really trying to impress his guests given there are less than six hundred of these available in the world.

Who am I kidding?

This has Michelle scrawled all over it. Asad couldn't give a shit about impressing anyone. But his mother, my stepmother? One of her favorite pastimes is shoving her wealth in others' faces. And now that her golden child is the ruler of the entire kingdom? Oh yes. She's in her element and wants everyone to know it.

In particular, me.

As if I summoned the bitch with the full moon and nut of a hellhound, Michelle glances at me from across the room. She says something to the circle of jeweled, plucked, and surgically enhanced women gathered around her like ladies-in-waiting playing court with a queen and heads in my direction.

Fuck.

Who got time for the bullshit she's undoubtedly on? I purposefully found a corner to duck off in to be by myself since that's whose company I prefer above any person in this place—mine. Here I am, minding my business, and this ho gotta make her way over here and make an already painful evening more agonizing with her stench of gloating and Black Opium.

I hastily down the rest of the whiskey just in case I need the glass to crack her upside her head for coming at me wrong. Tonight ain't the night for shenanigans.

"Over here alone, I see," Michelle says, coming to stand in front of me with her signature smirk. "Some things never change. You always were too awkward and inept for social occasions. That's why your father never insisted you attend them with us and your brothers. You were always an embarrassment."

If she expected me to cry at her corrosive words like I used to when I was younger, she's going to be sorely disappointed. Not because they don't burn and eat away at my soul. I don't think there's been a Teflon coat invented that can protect against the cruelest words meant to strip emotional skin. But Michelle fucked up and let those wounds she inflicted over and over again grow into inches-thick keloids. I hide behind them like masks, concealing my rage, my pain, my humiliation.

This bitch had enough of all three over the years from me. Damned if I give her a peep show for free now.

"Believe me, Michelle, I had other plans tonight rather than be here with you and your venerated guests."

I held up my glass, signaling to the roaming server to bring me another drink. I would need about five more of these things to make it through this evening without stabbing myself in the carotid with a salad fork or starting a gang war by telling Don Amato that his wife eye-fucking Dimitri Petrov, the pakhan of the Russian mob, was bad form.

Michelle scoffs, raising her wineglass for a sip, eying me over the rim. "You have no man, no life, and soon, no position within this family once I speak with Prince. What could you possibly have on your busy social calendar this evening that would trump being here with people who you'd never have the pleasure or chance in hell of being in the same room with?"

I barely smother a bark of laughter at her poor but very ironic choice of words. No man? No position in this family? Shit, if my presence at this little affair is headed where I think it is, she might want to buckle up.

And who is this "Prince" she speaks of that she can bend to her will or influence to do what she wants? Have we met? Shit, have *they* met? Because she can't be talking about the Asad Prince I know or she pushed out her tired-ass snatch.

The server approaches me with another cut crystal glass, and I exchange my empty one for a full one. Or I almost do. Instead of letting the staff leave with the empty glass, I discreetly place it on the table behind me. You know. Just in case I need a quick weapon. Preparation is key 'n' all that.

I take a sip, humming in appreciation before giving my attention back to the ho who seems to so desperately want it.

"Reruns of *Bill Nye the Science Guy*. PBS has a marathon going on. Oh, and figuring out how many licks it takes to get to the center of a Tootsie Pop."

For a moment, she stares at me, as if not fully comprehending my answer. But when it hits, I hold back another chuckle as her face screws up in an ugly scowl, her eyes darkening to damn near black.

What? She cares about fake shit like this. I don't. I'm here under duress. As a matter of fact . . .

"For real, Michelle," I say, leaning a shoulder against the wall, "if you have an issue with my presence here, take it up with your son. He demanded I attend. Why, I have no clue. Ask him," I add, throwing Asad under the bus.

I wish Asad would come get his mother. My patience level with her runs somewhere between none and sewing lips shut to keep her from talking to me. But I get why she's asking me. Asad would quickly tell her to mind her business. Still . . .

When is this engagement announcement going to happen so I can get the fuck up out of here? The delicious aroma of whatever food is being prepared tickles the air, but I'll stop and get an Animal Style cheeseburger from In-N-Out if it means escaping this hell sooner.

"Kareem invited you?" She frowns, voice dripping with disbelief. "He would never."

"And didn't." I sip more Macallan. "You have another son."

Her mouth slackens, lips parted. Then fury tightens her features, and I swear, if she pops off, she got the right one. I was with all the bullshit and have no one to impress up in this bitch.

"You a fucking lie."

I slowly smile.

"Not the Leimert Park coming out."

"Bitch—"

"Michelle." Asad appears behind her, his low, midnight voice rumbling with a silken menace that even his mother isn't safe from. She stiffens, her mouth snapping shut around whatever else abusive shit she'd been about to spit at me. "The caterer needs to speak with you about what time to start serving dinner. She's in the hall outside the kitchen."

His tone, threaded with I-will-show-the-fuck-out, has her giving an abrupt nod and turning to leave us . . . but not before pinning me with another hate-filled glare. As if that shit bothers me.

"If you came over here to reprimand me about getting into it with your mother, save it. She came for me," I say, preempting him.

His gray eyes narrow on me, probably not appreciating me speaking out of turn like a bad little handmaid.

"Don't assume you know what I'm thinking or about to do. Fuck that making-an-ass-out-of-you-and-me shit—it's just you. Now, let's try this again before you opened that big-ass mouth and pissed me off. What did Michelle come over here for?"

Well, damn.

He read me down, and my dumb ass kind of likes it. At least my pussy does from the way she's pulsing and wetting up.

Jesus.

I feel like I need to give her a sermon on being careful what you wish for, but she'd probably just turn around and do some bald-headed ho shit like pray for Asad to lay hands.

Clearing my throat, I straighten from the wall and imperceptibly squeeze my thighs together, to try and extinguish the heat between them. But I forgot this is Asad I'm standing in front of—he misses nothing.

His silver gaze fixes on my face, gliding over my cheekbones and mouth in a damn near physical caress before moving to my dark blond hair that I wore in its natural curls in a thick halo around my face and brushing my shoulders. I'm frozen under that hypnotic . . . molten stare as it drags down over another one of my signature pantsuits, lingering on the deep, French-lace-adorned V-neck of the black blazer, searing the bare flesh between my breasts. That scrutiny continues down over the asymmetric bottom of the jacket and loiters on my thighs and the pussy cradled between them. There's no way he can see through the material of my high-waisted, flared pants to notice the moisture soaking my panties but, God, the way he's staring . . . I don't know. And—*fuck*. Did my body not receive the message from my brain not to fidget?

The gleam of satisfaction, of damn victory in his eyes after they travel back up my oversensitive body and land on my face again, has my fingers clenching tighter around my glass.

"What I tell you about that, ma?" he murmurs in a voice low enough for only us to hear. "Ball that hand up, you better be prepared to throw it. That's my last warning. Next time we'll be moving furniture in here, but know that it's gon' end up with you bent over it. So tread careful, li'l baby."

Ma. Li'l baby.

Endearments that should be exclusive for intimate partners, for lovers.

His voice wrapped around them, especially as he threatens me with fighting *and* fucking, shouldn't have my breath coming in shallow pants. Shouldn't have my skin heating like a Bunsen burner is lit underneath it. Or have electrical currents crackling from the nape of my neck to the soles of my feet.

No, none of this should be happening since the woman he's currently fucking is no less than five feet away from us, chatting within a circle of male and female admirers but still casting not-so-subtle pointed looks in our direction.

The reminder dries me right on up.

The anger that had been simmering flares into flickering flames, evaporating the lust that had just seconds ago invaded my veins. Disgust and rage replaces it now.

Bastard.

Why invite me to this business dinner when you fully intended to parade your lover in the same space as your so-called fiancée? It didn't matter that the only two people who knew of the "engagement" were him and me; it was fucking humiliating.

And in this moment, I had a crystal clear vision of how any marriage to him would be. From the time he left my apartment yesterday, I've actively avoided thinking about my imminent future. But I can't avoid it anymore.

Side chicks out the ass while I would be expected to sit there like a good little Mafia wife and suck it up 'cause men would be men.

Fuck. That. Shit.

That had been my mother's life. Michelle's life. But fuck what Asad thought, it would never be mine.

"Answer me," he demands. "What did Michelle want?"

"Same ol', same ol'." I wave off his question. Like he doesn't know his mother. Shit, they cut from the same cloth. "I ain't shit. I'm a lonely bitch. I'm not worthy of breathing the same rarefied air as everyone here. Blah blah blah."

Raising my glass, I peer at him over the rim, and sipping my whiskey, I frown at the bolt of . . . something in his eyes. Couldn't be anger; hell, he cosigned her bullshit from the time Marcus introduced him, his brother, and his mother to me.

"Funny thing though." I pause, mimicking him and tilting my head. "She wasn't aware I was here at your invitation. Not that I can blame her, considering you have your girlfriend and fiancée"—I damn near choke on that blasphemous word—"at the same dinner together. Still, I thought you two were besties. Don't tell me you didn't let your mother know of our intended nuptials." I hike an eyebrow. "Let me find out you're ashamed of me already."

That *something* moves in his eyes again, and I stiffen, coils of disquiet and an unsettling . . . eagerness twisting low in my belly.

He chuckles, and the sound is raspy, and utterly absent of humor.

"We just had a conversation about assumptions and here you go. You claim you know me, and yet, it's like you trying me on purpose, fully aware how I get down. Are you that desperate to see how much of a beating that pussy can take, ma?"

I mug him even though my heart beats between my legs. "You got me fu—"

"Hey, everything okay over here?" Kareem asks, standing next to me, his arm brushing my shoulder.

Asad and I had been so focused on each other, we hadn't noticed his brother approaching us. And while I was thankful for Kareem's timely interruption, from the flattening of his full lips and flaring of his nostrils, Asad looks like he seconds from forgetting Kareem is his little brother. His narrowed scrutiny lowers, momentarily fixing on where we touch before lifting to meet Kareem's gaze.

"Does it look like it isn't?" he asks, his voice calm. Too calm. Like the eye before a destructive, deadly storm.

Kareem's either gloriously oblivious to the quiet warning his brother is issuing, or he's just decided to ignore it. I can't decide if that's brave or foolish.

"It just seemed a little . . . intense. And some of our guests were beginning to notice." Unlike the other men at the dinner party, Kareem opted for a beer, and he raises the dark brown bottle to his lips for a sip. I admire that about him. He doesn't give a fuck to be different, though he often gets the backside of his mother's tongue for it.

Asad keeps his focus trained on his brother, but I surreptitiously glance around the room. A couple of women brave enough to perch on those ornate, too-fragile-looking chairs. Aryn and Michelle hovering in the doorway between the drawing and dining rooms. And sure enough, several pairs of eyes are focused on us—Naoki Sato, the Yakuza oyabun; Don Amato and his wife, Chelsea; Demarcus and Carter Williams; Michelle and Aryn.

The weight of their attention crawls across my skin like a battalion of ants in search of a picnic to ruin. The fragrant scents I'd found so delicious just minutes earlier congeal in my stomach like a ball of old, greasy lard. I barely keep the hand not clutching my glass restrained to my side and not rubbing over my arms. Exposed. I feel exposed.

Fuck.

I hate being the center of *any* attention.

Another reason to resent Asad.

Why couldn't he leave me alone and bother his fuck buddy? She appears to love his attention. And dick. Can't forget his dick.

"Like I give a fuck who's noticing what. I didn't invite them here to mind my business," Asad coldly says.

"Oh." Kareem glances between the two of us. "So you and Em have business?"

Shit. I rear back just a little. Questioning Asad? Is Kareem drunk?

I'm not God. I'm not protecting babies or drunks. If his brother goes for his throat, I'm not jumping in the way of a gotdamn thing. Kareem might be the lesser, kinder evil of his family but nothing I'm willing to sacrifice my body over.

"Hold that thought, bruh." Kareem holds up his beer bottle like a church finger and shoots a pointed look over Asad's shoulder. "Incoming."

Again, Asad doesn't bother glancing behind him, but I do. And inside, I cringe and smother a huge sigh. Michelle and Aryn are walking our way.

God, this evening is like fucking *Groundhog Day*.

Endless.

"Prince, your mother said dinner is ready. We should be heading in." She loops an arm through his and offers me a polite if bland smile. "I'm sorry. I don't think we've met before."

I don't return the ingenuine gesture. I'm too busy staring at first, that hand on his body, and then Asad. Too busy waiting to see if he's going to push this bitch away or let her lay claim to him in front of me. When he does nothing—doesn't admonish her, step away from her—I loose a low, dry chuckle. And shift backward, my shoulder brushing Kareem's chest.

"She's no one of importance," Michelle butts in with a flicker of her hand. She shifts in front of Asad and Aryn, giving me and Kareem her back, dismissing me. "Asad, as the host, you should lead the guests into the dining area. You and Aryn shouldn't keep everyone waiting. I'm sure our guests are ready to finally eat."

The shit Michelle just pulled is childish and expected, and yet . . . it stings. It shouldn't, but it does.

Maybe because, although Asad's gaze is still fixed on me, he doesn't disagree with her.

Doesn't defend me.

Doesn't protect me.

I disgust myself for the hurt trickling through me. What did I expect? This is him; this is his MO. Who he is. Who he has shown me he is since we were young. Why should I expect anything different now?

No man has ever shielded me. Not my grandfather. Not my father. And for damn sure not Asad, my childhood bully and would-be husband.

The only person I've ever been able to count on is Ember Cross.

The sooner I remember that—the quicker I stop believing that maybe, just maybe people can change and exhibit just a little humanity—the less disappointed I'll be.

"Kareem." Michelle turns to her youngest son. "I have you escorting Demarcus's daughter—"

"I'm sure D will be fine taking his own daughter to the table. I'll go in with Em." Kareem shuts his mother down with a finality in his voice that brooks no argument.

I blink, stiffening, and Michelle gawks at him, lips parted. I don't know who's more shocked—me or her.

The Kareem I'm used to usually bows to his mother's every order with little resistance. For him to buck a demand now? And for my sake? What number beer is he on?

Michelle's smile freezes in place, the corners strained, but it doesn't reach her eyes. No, they flash with promises of retribution, and for a second, I almost feel sorry for Kareem. Almost. This isn't *Who Wants to Be a Millionaire?*, and I didn't ask for a lifeline or phone a friend. And if I did, it certainly wouldn't be from him or anyone in his family.

"Fine," she grits out between clenched teeth, that phony smile still in place. After several seconds, she spins around and faces Asad and his girlfriend again. "Asad, baby, you—"

"Michelle."

Just that one word. In that voice. And she shuts right the fuck up. Even Aryn looks uneasy, slightly fidgeting beside him. They can sense in the air what we all can—the impatience of the predator in our midst. Even Michelle knows she can push her son only so far. That unblinking stare moves from his mother to me, and I meet it without flinching.

I want him to glimpse the loathing in my eyes. Hope he chokes on it.

But who am I kidding? Not only does he dine on my hate, he gorges on it with relish.

'Cause that's what monsters do.

I should know.

Just before our visual battle becomes awkward for those around us, he pivots and stalks away, leaving Aryn, who still clings to his arm, to keep up with him. Michelle follows them.

Clapping her hands once, she stops in the middle of the drawing room. "If you'll follow my son, dinner is ready and waiting to be served. Thank you," she announces, face wreathed in a wide smile.

Some of the men and women set their glasses down on the smaller tables littering the room, and they break into couples, filing behind Michelle to the adjacent room, appearing like a macabre bridal party.

"Something you want to tell the class, Ember?" Kareem asks, arching an eyebrow at me.

"Nope."

He chuckles and offers his arm out to me. I glance down at it, then back up at him, my face balled up. Again, he laughs and lowers his arm to his side. Like I thought.

"Understood." He waves his hand in front of him. "After you." I move forward, and he falls in step beside me. "If you don't mind, I'll accompany you to dinner and sit beside you at the table."

I stop mid-step and turn to face him, frowning.

"Why? What's with the sudden concern?"

He holds up his hands, palms out, shaking his head.

"No ulterior motive, honest. You might not believe this—or you may, I don't know—but I'm just as much of an outsider here as you are." When I arch my eyebrow at that, he gives a low laugh. "Okay, maybe not *as much*. But I'm a runner-up." He smiles. When I don't return it, he sighs and rubs a hand over his neat, short, tapered beard. "There's no need for me to stand here and lie to you. We both know who's the favored son. Who's the respected one. When we walk in there"—he jerks his head in the direction of the dining room—"it will be like a king holding court, and his subjects paying tribute. And I'm one of those subjects. Not a brother. Not family. Not in that room."

He falls silent, and he slides his hands in the front pockets of his suit pants. There's no anger in his voice, nor in his eyes. Just a faraway look of . . . acceptance, resignation. And maybe a hint of loneliness.

That, I can relate to. A little too well.

In this moment, memories of times in the past when Michelle was preoccupied with running after Marcus, plotting how to position Asad, or shopping, and when Asad was busy being mentored by my father, waver in my head. That left me and Kareem alone in my childhood home. And in those times, we got along. We actually had . . . fun. Watching reruns of *Supernatural* together. Him trying to teach me how to play his video games. Me teaching him how to make explosive stink bombs with my chemistry sets. Yeah . . . I forgot about that. They were few and far between, especially as we grew older. But Kareem had been my rare ports of warm kindness in a protracted, bleak, and cruel storm.

Funny how I didn't remember that until just now.

"Sometimes being invisible is better than being seen. Less of a target on your back that way," I say. "Also, in a room full of people who love to hear themselves talk, silence can't be repeated or misquoted."

That distant glaze dissipates, and his full lips curl into a slight smile. Without the blinding intensity of Asad's magnetism and innate, burning sexuality casting its long, deep shadow, Kareem's handsomeness is in full bloom. The lovely, dark eyes he inherited from his mother, the strong facial features, and wide, sensual mouth combine to form an attractiveness that undoubtedly draw him his fair share of attention. Even though just a few inches shorter than Asad and with the leaner build of a swimmer, he still exudes a quiet strength, albeit less intense . . . overwhelming.

It's . . . pleasant.

"I don't think I've ever thought of it that way. Can't say I've ever considered being ignored a benefit."

"I don't have a problem with being invisible to people. I could give a fuck about that. The issue is when I begin to feel unseen. There's a big difference."

He nods. Then smiles, and it reaches his eyes, the dark brown gleaming. "I love my mother and brother, but sometimes them muthafuckas gotta be the most obtuse muthafuckas breathing."

I frown, a little taken aback. "What do you mean by that?"

"Just what I said," he says, still wearing that smile before walking forward again. "You're the best of us and neither one of them see or value that."

"And you do?" I snort.

"I do." He cups my elbow and guides me into the room where almost all the guests sit on either side of the long, beautifully laid table. Kareem pulls a chair out for me nearest the door and waits for me to sit before leaning down and murmuring close to my ear, "And I'm learning to more and more."

Not a little puzzled and surprised, I follow his tall, wiry form as he rounds the end of the table and sinks into the chair across from me. A server offers him another beer, and okay, it suddenly makes sense.

Hell, I might join him on whatever bullshit he's on since I'm about to be on my third drink. When I hold up my nearly empty tumbler, another waiter appears as if out of thin air with a refilled whiskey.

I set the glass on the table and shift my gaze—and find myself ensnared in Asad's. That unblinking, hard stare reflects nothing, his expression as blank as the sheet of glass in the window behind him. And yet, his rage reaches me from the length of the table, seeking me out from among the other guests, skimming my cheek with blunt, ghostly fingernails. It's in the almost indolent manner he holds his tumbler of whiskey. To the untrained eye, the grasp is relaxed, casual. But the tight skin across his knuckles, the tendon running along his wrist betrays the emotion no one but me most likely sees. Feels.

Asad sits at the far head of the table, with Aryn one side of him and Michelle on the other—places of honor for his woman and his mother. My chest tightens, a titanium band of pressure squeezing tight around my chest. Prickles of heat sting my scalp and race down the nape of my neck to streak along my spine. It's ridiculous. I don't want to sit at his side, don't want to be claimed by him. To be acknowledged by him. Yet . . .

Yet, I can easily imagine my salad fork buried in his neck for playing with me.

This shit right here is why I've stayed single and preferred my hand and toys over dealing with a man. Men like Asad—like my grandfather, like Marcus—they're good for nothing but games and felonies.

Tearing my attention from him, I focus on the first course of velouté, with a choice of seafood or vegetables. Lively banter flows around me as I consume the savory, creamy soup. Amir Brookson, a Cross street boss, who sits on my left and Akira Sato, on my right, attempt to draw me into conversation. But I politely but firmly shut that down when I realize they're just attempting to figure out who I am and my purpose in being there.

Is it pathetic that my own father's soldiers aren't aware of my identity? That they don't know I'm the reason they eat? Yeah, it's sad and misogynistic as fuck. So is the fact that the women gathered at this table are only here for decoration for the men. But hell, if Marcus, and now Asad, refuses to enlighten them about who I am and what I mean to this organization, then I won't either.

But this display of sexism is why I've kept my activities separate from Cross secret. One day, I'll be the plug, and all of the men sitting here will need me. Will come begging me.

I smile.

"Hmm. That random-ass smile is both pretty and scary as fuck."

Looking up from my plate of glazed salmon and asparagus with gorgonzola butter, I meet Kareem's amused smile. I shrug, then slide the fork loaded with fish between my lips. He smirks and then turns to a Cross soldier beside him.

"Ember, is it?" Don Amato's smooth voice that bears a light hint of a New York accent carries over the several different conversations at the table, the clatter of cutlery meeting plates, and the soft melody of classical music.

I set my fork down next to my half-filled dish and shift my attention toward the middle of the table where the head of the Accardi crime family, one of the United States Costa Nostra's four families, sits. His piercing brown scrutiny rests on me, and I steadily meet it, not looking away even as a server appears next to me, refilling my glass. The distinguished, elegant man, who appears to be in his midforties and wears power as easily as his obviously custom-made and gorgeous black suit, probably intimidates many people.

I'm not one of them.

"Yes."

He pauses, as if waiting for me to say more, but "yes" is a whole sentence, last time I checked.

"We weren't formally introduced earlier. I'm Julian Amato, and this is my wife, Chelsea." He nods toward the beautiful, thickly curved brunette seated next to him—the one eye fucking the Russian pakhan earlier.

"A pleasure." I nod.

He picks up his whiskey glass and sips, and though his gaze is heavy on me, it doesn't feel sexual or inappropriate. More . . . speculative. More as if he's trying to figure out how I fit into the present company.

"I apologize for my forwardness, but you seem familiar to me. Are you certain we haven't met before? Maybe I've had previous business with your husband?"

"No."

Across from me, Kareem lets out a low groan, and I blink. What? The man asked me a question and I answered. Just like "yes," "no" is also a complete sentence. And it's better than asking why he assumes I have a husband or a man simply because I'm a woman. Now that would've been as rude as his assumption.

Julian chuckles, and though it's dark and a little menacing, it also contains humor, as does the glint in his eyes.

"I think I like you, Ember . . ." He trails off, inviting me to supply my last name.

Even I, with my disdain for social situations and people, know it would be a direct insult to ignore him, and stuck, I glance down the length of the table toward Asad.

He lowers his knife and fork to the plate in front of him, his stare shifting from me to Julian, then back to me. My belly trembles, bottoming out, and I mimic his actions. Because I can read in the slight narrowing of his eyes, the minute firming of his lips, that he's about to—

"A toast." Michelle's chair shoots backward, sounding like nails scratching down a chalkboard as she damn near leaps to her feet, wineglass in hand. A broad smile stretches across her face, but the corners of her mouth are pulled taut, making her resemble Pennywise the Clown rather than a gracious hostess. Her gaze flickers over me, and the malice there warms my heart. Even as fire flickers in my chest at her interruption. At her aversion to any of these guests discovering my true identity. Discovering I'm a Cross. "First, please let me thank you all for joining my sons and I here tonight. This has been a season of loss with the passing of the great Marcus Cross. He was a strong leader, a wonderful husband, and a loving father to Prince and Kareem. He is and always will be greatly missed."

She takes a dramatic pause, and allows beat of silence to draw out where, once again, her eyes briefly connect with mine. Silently letting me know her omission of me in her little speech wasn't a mistake; it was deliberate. An intentional reminder that my father belonged to them, not me.

She wins this round.

I force myself not to look away from her, refuse to allow her see she scored a direct hit, and my heart, my pride, sullenly bleed from the wound.

I despise her and myself for that scarring. That victory, too.

Clearing her throat, she waves a hand. "I apologize," she continues as fraud-ass grief thickens her voice. Michelle very well might miss Marcus, but those billions he left her are a hell of a comforter. "Tonight, we not only remember a great man but celebrate the passing of his bright torch to his heir, our son, Asad Prince."

She dips her head and peers down at Asad, and I do, too. Surprise whispers through me, and I battle back the frown wanting to take residence on my face. He's never been an emotive man—colder than a witch's tit would be more of an apt description. But this is something different. Maybe his mother, his girlfriend, or his guests don't notice the tension pulling him so tight a nudge would make this man snap. See the storm darkening his eyes to soot. Or the tic of a muscle not fully concealed by his thick beard.

His mother is in full nauseating praise mode. What did she say . . . ?

"Marcus placed full trust and confidence in Prince to carry the House of Cross and the Cross family into the future. And with you, our allies, friends, and family, I am excited for that future under his rule and direction. Please, lift your glasses and join me in toasting a new, prosperous, and even stronger era in the Cross organization."

Everyone rises to their feet, and I do as well, though slower, more reluctant. And when they hold their glasses up in the air, I sip from mine. My tolerance for hypocrisy will only stretch so far tonight.

When I set my whiskey glass on the table, my gaze collides with Asad's. The residue of that anger shadows his eyes, tautens his mouth and body, but the barest hint of a smirk twists his mouth, and he dips his chin to me before lifting his own glass and drinking deeply.

My skin tingles with awareness, and I look next to him and find Aryn's contemplative scrutiny on me as well. She glances back and forth between me and her man, eyes narrowing before landing back on me again. Shrugging a shoulder, I sink back down in my chair and resume eating. If she needs answers, she needs to take that up with her boyfriend. He's the one who owes her loyalty, not me.

"So, Prince, now that you've stepped into position as head of the Cross organization, how close are you to fulfilling the terms of the other conditions set by Marcus?" Dimitri Petrov asks, leaning back in his chair, allowing the pretty server to pick up his dinner plate.

He smiles warmly at her, causing the young woman to blush even as she steps back and hurries out of the room. His wife, a petite, icy blond with beautiful green eyes, sitting on the other side of him, pretends not to notice his blatant flirting. And *this* is what I have to look forward to as a Mafia wife? Yeah, no thank you. Dimitri would be foaming at the mouth and shitting himself by now fucking around with me.

"Other conditions?" Kareem echoes, frowning. "What are you referring to, Petrov?"

The pakhan arches a black eyebrow. "I'm sorry." He reaches inside his suit jacket and removes a small silver case, opening it and sliding a thin, brown cigarette free. He can't hide the gleam in his bright blue eyes as he looks from Kareem to a quiet Asad. The Russian is obviously a shit stirrer. "I had no idea you weren't aware of the marriage contract Marcus had in place for whoever assumed head of House of Cross and all its . . . entities."

Marriage contract?

I glance around the table. Most of the women either continue eating or sipping from the wineglasses while the heads of the families lean back in their chairs, studying Asad. Waiting, like the rest of us, for his answer. But from their obvious *lack* of reaction, they're aware of this contract.

"Marriage contract?" Kareem demands, voice sharp. "Why is this the first time I'm hearing about this?"

He's not the only one.

A dull roar fills my head as I stare down the length of the table at Asad. Heat builds under my skin, pouring into my face, licking at the palms of my hands and under my arms.

"Why marriage? Why can't I just sign a contract or something promising to stay employed with House of Cross?"

"Because I say so."

He lied to me. The bastard fucking lied to me about why I had to marry him instead of another alternative. If I'm picking up even a little bit of what Dimitri Petrov is implying, then here's the true reason why Asad needs to marry me. Not just the voting shares and ironclad ownership of HoC. It's to keep it.

Son of a bitch.

I loose a low chuckle, and though there's no way Asad could've possibly caught it, his gaze seems to sharpen on me. Not that I give a damn.

Not when these muthafuckas stay using me.

"Not now, Kareem," Michelle hisses at her youngest son, and though his lean frame seems to damn near vibrate with the anger tightening his face, he sits back in his chair, shutting up.

Oh, so none of this comes as a shock to Michelle either. Poor

Kareem. It must hurt having the fact that you're an outsider in your own family rubbed in your face.

"I apologize. Did I speak out of turn?" Dimitri asks, the wide smile on his face contradicting the remorse in his deep, rumbling voice. "I assumed that was the reason behind this impromptu dinner—to introduce us to your betrothed."

Betrothed? I silently snort. What are we, in medieval England?

But then again, our world has more in common with that patriarchal society than a modern, progressive existence where women are recognized and valued as equals.

"It is one of the reasons," Asad finally speaks, indolently reclining in his chair, eying the Russian crime boss.

Though I suspected the truth, hearing him confirm it shoves me back against my chair. Fucking bastard. Playing me like I'm some toy. No, worse. A pawn. Just a thing he can maneuver around on this chessboard only he and a select few know the rules to. But me? The person whose life will be directly affected, whose future hangs and turns on every one of *his decisions*, doesn't matter. Not my voice, my dreams, my needs. They don't matter.

I drop my hands to my lap, curling my nails into my thighs, embracing the flare of pain.

"Dimitri, I have respect for you as a businessman and an ally, but I don't tolerate disrespect from anyone. Especially in my own house. We can start this relationship off with the same cordiality you shared with Marcus, or we can go another route. It don't make one difference to me which one we do because I'm with the shits either way."

Across the room, two members of Dimitri's security detail move forward, scowls darkening their faces, but the Russian mob boss holds up his hand, even though his back is to them. They halt, but they don't retreat to the wall or lose their frowns.

I might be the only one not holding my breath at the terrible tension arcing between Asad and Dimitri. The rest of the crime family heads remain seated, their bodies taut, gazes alert, watchful. Julian leans slightly forward, shifting his frame so it's a barrier between the other guests and his wife. Michelle's frozen, perched on the edge of her seat, and Kareem, although fury had just darkened his handsome features, unobtrusively lowers his hand, and reaches inside his jacket.

Eli, sitting next to Michelle, slides his hand behind him, as do the other members of the Cross family, no doubt reaching for their weapons in case someone in here jumps bad. The select members of the other mob bosses' security teams allowed in the dining room step forward from their posts against the wall. They don't reach for the guns that are probably on their persons, but one wrong move made, one wrong word spoken, and no doubt they will pull those weapons.

No wonder unease and anxiety fill this room like heavy storm clouds ready to burst and wreak havoc at any second.

Only Asad and I appear unaffected. Him, because, hell, he issued the threat, or choice, however you prefer to look at it. And me, because I sincerely hope all these muthafuckas off each other and save me the trouble. When or if the bullets start flying, I'm ducking beneath the table, pride be damned. Self-preservation will first and always be my concern. They can all go to hell, starting with my *betrothed*'s ass.

Finally, after a handful of nerve-screaming moments, Dimitri nods.

"No disrespect meant. I apologize if it came across as such."

This time, I can't hold back my snort at that half-ass apology. All eyes swing my way, and though I hate being the center of attention, I meet each and every pair. Don't nobody in here intimidate me. True, I bleed like everyone else, and a bullet has no respect of persons. But men aren't the only ones not afraid of dying. Do I want to? No, but none of them put fear in my heart.

Besides, they don't know me. If they come for me, they better not miss. I can have their brains oozing out of their dicks or pussies if they try me.

Like Hallmark, I have a drug for every occasion.

"Excuse me. Who are you again?" Dimitri's wife—Elena, Helena?—asks, plump lips curled into a sneer.

"No one," Michelle hurriedly interjects, mugging me. "She's no one at all."

"Then why is 'no one' at this table?" Elena/Helena demands. "She needs to learn her place."

My place? Oh, this bitch loose . . .

"Because it's *my* table," Asad says, a vein of pure steel threading through his voice. "And as she is my fiancée, I'm the only one who determines where 'her place' is—and that's right here. With me."

Well, fuck. This is happening.

I slowly inhale, hold that breath, then exhale.

The room erupts with gasps, murmurings, and "what the fucks" from Michelle, Kareem, and Aryn. Horror spreads across Elena/Helena's face, and she pales as if one of the Four Horsemen just rode through the dining room door and took a shit on top of her glazed salmon. Hell, it's not *that* far off. She's staring Death in the eyes, and he's wearing Asad's face.

Dimitri cuffs the back of his wife's neck and from the wince she doesn't manage to fully cover, I can only imagine what awaits her at home. She unknowingly just insulted the fiancée of the newly appointed head of the Cross organization, and by doing that, the boss. Yeah, her ass is going to pay. And Dimitri doesn't appear to be the gentle sort.

"Prince, is this some kind of prank?" Michelle snaps, slapping her hand on the table. The crystal glasses tremble. Soft, feminine gasps follow her outburst, and Chelsea, Don Amato's wife, throws a disgusted look Michelle's way. Dimitri's lip curls up in distaste, and the rest of the men stare at her, their expressions stoic. "This is in extremely poor taste. You have Aryn sitting right next to you, and you want to joke about marrying that, that . . . thing." She jabs a finger in my direction.

"That's Mrs. Thing to you," I say, lifting my crystal tumbler in a mocking toast, the petty retort concealing the thick, deafening thudding of my heart and the damn near primal urge to grab my steak knife, fly across this table, and send fine china scattering to bury the blade in her throat. This ho has made it her life's work to disrespect me, and a bitch can only be expected to take so much. None of these men would ever accept it, but because she's Marcus's wife, I'm supposed to?

Miss me with that. Especially now.

"Ember," Asad growls, and I shrug, sipping my drink. Tightening my grip on it so I don't commit the venial sin of throwing the fucker at his head.

"Could you please answer your mother, Prince?" Aryn asks, voice trembling and reed thin. She sounds on the verge of crying, but a closer glance at her face, and there's no evidence of moisture gleaming in her eyes. Just a fury hot enough to burn this whole damn house down to its foundation. "Are you seriously marrying someone else?"

The "and not me" isn't spoken, but it's definitely implied.

"Ember?" I look across the table at Kareem and meet his inexplicably hurt dark gaze. "Is this true? Are you and my brother engaged?"

Before I can reply, abruptly Asad rises from his chair, the screech of wood scraping wood jarring.

"Quiet." He doesn't raise his voice, but the low, sensual, authoritative timbre silences every sound in the room. "Ember. Come here."

My mind screams *fuck you!* but my body is already on the move. It instinctively heeds him as if he's Geppetto pulling my invisible strings and I'm his helpless puppet. In this moment, I'm a slave to my flesh, and as I near him, the shouts to keep walking until I hit the front door and freedom ring in my head. But they're overruled and drowned out by the primal governing of the physical.

What is this fucking power he has over me? He displayed it

at the cemetery, in my kitchen, in my study . . . I shake my head even as I near him, and he encircles my wrist, those long, elegant, and lethal fingers branding my skin.

More importantly, how do I break free of it?

"As I just mentioned, the reasons of this dinner are twofold. The first is to reforge the alliances between the Cross family and the organizations represented here. The second is to announce my engagement. Let me formally introduce everyone to my fiancée, Ember." He pauses. "Ember Cross. Marcus's only daughter."

A silence so loud blasts in the room, I restrain myself from lifting my hands to my ears and covering them like muffs. The expressions range from astonishment to confusion to rage at the bomb he just dropped.

Then, in the next heartbeat, a cacophony of voices rise, shouting questions or exclaiming disbelief. Aryn and Michelle, both on their feet, shout, but their complaints are lost in the rest of the noise.

But none of them are louder than the pulse thundering in my veins, ricocheting against my skull.

Ember Cross. Marcus's only daughter.

It echoes in my head, louder and louder, stronger like the wind of a hurricane, screaming, drowning everything else out but its destruction. Because that's what his outing of me is. A destruction of who I was before this moment. For the first time, my whole name, my paternity, my *existence*, is being declared aloud. And I'm shaken. I'm humbled. I'm vulnerable. I'm lost. I'm . . . liberated.

And this man, my tormentor and enemy, set me free from the chains of secrecy.

"Quiet." Once again, Asad doesn't yell, but that even, almost soft tone shuts everyone up. And quickly. He looks at his mother and girlfriend. "Sit down. Now."

They instantly obey him, and even with how annoyed and *done* I am, amusement trickles through me.

"I apologize for our rudeness at your table, Prince," Naoki

Sato says. "Your . . . announcement has taken most of us by surprise. I wasn't aware Marcus had biological children. In the years we've been associates, he never mentioned a daughter. I only knew of you and Kareem."

"Which brings us to the next question that everyone in this bitch is too scared to ask," Carter Williams spits, his face balled into a disgusted mug. "What in the hillbilly incest is going on here? How're you marrying your sister?"

If it wasn't for the street boss's disrespectful tone or the coldness that seems to seep from Asad's pores as Carter speaks, I would've laughed. I mean, he's not wrong. At first glance, this does seem like some *Deliverance*-banjo bullshit.

Since Asad is standing, I sink into his chair. Taking myself out the line of fire.

"This is the one and only time I'ma explain this because I don't owe a muthafucka a gotdamn thing." He pauses, his frigid gray gaze sweeping the table. "Ember is Marcus's daughter from his first wife, who died when she was twelve. He married Michelle shortly after, making him my and Kareem's stepfather, not biological parent. Why Marcus chose to not expose Ember's identity is his business and, with him in the ground, something he can't explain. Doesn't that satisfy your questions?"

Not by any stretch of the imagination is he asking an inquiry; Asad is telling them it *better* satisfy their curiosity and to drop the shit.

Though I loathe my stepbrother, I'm very fluent in Asad Prince–speak.

"It's a pleasure to officially meet you, Ms. Cross," Naoki says with a slight bow of his head.

"You as well," I say, nodding.

"Now I know why you seemed familiar." Don Amato smiles, a gleam I can't fully decipher in his dark gaze. "You must favor your mother, but I can see the resemblance to Marcus." He chuckles, shaking his head. "Didn't see this coming. That would make you the last Cross, wouldn't it?"

"With all due respect, Don Amato, but no. She is not the last Cross. My sons are Crosses. Marcus wouldn't have left his empire to my oldest son if he didn't consider them family, his sons," Michelle interjects, her tone heated, affronted.

I've heard this shit over the last decade of my life. But for her to continue with this now? After everything that has been stated? I slowly reach for the fork next to Asad's plate, but a hard, implacable hand covers mine, squeezes it. Prevents me from picking up that utensil and driving it into her lying-ass tongue.

Glancing down, Asad narrows his gaze on me. Shakes his head. Then releases my hand. Exhaling, I pull free of his grip and meet the dark, knowing stare of Noaki, who obviously caught the exchange.

In front of me, and everyone else at the table, Don Amato's congenial demeanor shifts, and a hard cruelty creeps across his expression, turning his face into a harsh, frigid landscape.

"As your son said earlier, Mrs. Cross, I, too, insist on respect. And being the widow of the former boss and mother of the current one doesn't make you exempt. I understand very well how familial dynamics work," he says, voice dripping with sarcasm and a simmering disdain. "But marriage does not trump biology or DNA. Marcus would've left his position to Asad because, like most of our organizations, a woman cannot rule. Yet that doesn't negate the scientific fact that Asad's fiancée is the only relation left with Cross *blood* running in her veins. No matter how much you may wish to the contrary."

Gotdamn.

I slide a glance at Asad to catch his reaction to the Italian mob boss reading his mother down. But he doesn't have one. His expression doesn't change from the aloof, impassive one that hides his every thought and emotion.

"I can't believe Marcus kept this a secret from all of us though," Demarcus murmurs, his hazel gaze fixed on me, a frown wrinkling his forehead. Unlike his brother, he doesn't appear upset, just confused and maybe a little . . . hurt.

Though most of the Cross soldiers weren't aware of my identity, I'm fully aware of who they are, and Demarcus was one of my father's longtime and most loyal soldiers. I get why he'd be disillusioned and offended by Marcus's lie of omission. Shit, he was out here like a deadbeat baby daddy, denying an offspring that most people didn't know existed.

"He's not here to explain himself, and this isn't about him," Asad reiterates, essentially deading the subject. Demarcus nods, but his expression remains troubled. Maybe he's realizing how much of a bitch his friend and boss was. "Since Marcus had you, Naoki, Dimitri, and Julian sign as witnesses to the addendum to his will regarding my requirement of a bride within sixty days of assuming leadership of Cross, I thought it only fair you be here for this announcement and invite you to the wedding that will take place in a month's time."

"I can't believe this shit!" Aryn shoots up from her chair and storms from the dining room.

I feel you, baby girl.

"Asad, how can you humiliate Aryn like that?" Michelle snaps. "She's been around much longer than her. She's more loyal and worthy to bear your name and stand by your side. She doesn't deserve this treatment from you."

I sigh, loud and wholly aggravated. My stepmother's glare shifts to me, and I smile, daring her to take her best shot. The ho better not miss. When she leans toward me, I start to rise from my chair, but once again Asad stops me. His fingers clamp down on my shoulder.

"You invited her here, Michelle, I didn't," he coldly says to his mother. "So any humiliation she's experiencing is on you, not me."

Relief and a fierce satisfaction sings through me hearing that Asad didn't invite his girlfriend to the dinner party. On the heels of it though is self-directed disgust. I shouldn't care; it shouldn't faze me. But fuck if it doesn't.

"I have one more"—Asad pauses, and a slow smile slides

across his face. It's not pretty, not warm. It's fucking terrifying—"surprise for the evening. What's a party without entertainment?"

As if they were waiting for that cue, the servers enter the room once more. Instead of dessert and coffee, they carry a huge plastic roll and a chair. Within seconds, the plastic is spread across the floor like a tarp, and the large, heavy armchair is set right in the middle of it.

He sheds his suit jacket and loosens his tie. "Eli, guide Carter over to the place of honor, will you?"

"The fuck? Prince, what's going on, man?" Carter shouts, twisting in his seat, alarm raising his voice.

Demarcus jacks to his feet, moving in front of his younger brother's chair, blocking him from Eli, who advances on them.

"Wait." The street boss holds up his hands, palms out, traces of panic edging his even tone. "Prince. The hell is happening here?" Demarcus scans the long table, but no one jumps to his side. None of the Mafia heads, and none of the other Cross street bosses seated there. "Ain't no way . . ."

Asad jerks his tie over his head and casually rolls up his shirt sleeves, as if relaxing after a long day at the office. I scoot closer to the edge of my chair, riveted. Out of my peripheral vision, I catch a flash of movement. Kareem rises out of his seat and stands at the end of the table, his face void of emotion.

"I'll explain in just a minute what your brother has been up to, D. But first . . ." His face and voice harden to the consistency of flint, and even though his cold fury isn't directed at me, a tremble still trips down my spine. "Eli, get his overgrown bitch ass up like I said."

Shoving Demarcus out of the way, Eli snatches Carter up out of his seat and drags him over to the armchair. Carter's not a small guy, but even struggling and yelling, he's no competition for Eli's size and weight. His forearms and ankles are swiftly bound to the chair by zip ties. Demarcus yells, charging forward to help his brother, but a wall of Cross armed soldiers circle around him, caging him.

A soft but firm tap on my shoulder momentarily distracts my attention from the scene in front of me, and Asad dips his chin. I nod, correctly interpreting his order to remain sitting. The last thing I want is to be in any proximity to Michelle, who reclaimed her own seat to my right, but I'm also wise enough to pick my battles. And challenging him here, in front of Mafia bosses—Cross allies—and their wives, is the very definition of *un*wise.

I'm not afraid of anyone in this room, but I'm also not itching to be the next person occupying the chair on the tarp.

"Carter." Asad strolls over to the street boss, sliding his hands in his suit pockets. The Glock cradled against his lower back gleams and appears bigger and more threatening against his stark white shirt. "Yesterday, someone took shots at me while I was headed toward downtown. Well, a few someones, to be specific, in cars and on motorcycles. I'm guessing they didn't expect my car to be bulletproof or for Eli and me to bust back. Or whoever paid them didn't warn them about who they were coming after. Either way, they're some dead muthafuckas, and I'm left wondering who sent their roadkill asses after me." He stops in front of Carter and bends down, cocking his head. "Or, I *was* wondering."

"Prince, man—"

"Shut the fuck up," Asad quietly says to Demarcus without looking away from his brother. Demarcus stacks his hands on top of his head, his feet doing a little shuffle, going side to side. But he does shut up. Carter mugs Asad, but his fear seeps into the air, saturating it like a cloying perfume. "Carter, do you know why I'm no longer wondering who sent them after me?"

"Nah, man, I don't," he grinds out.

"No?"

"No," Carter snaps. "D, bruh, this is bullshit." He looks in his brother's direction.

The crack of Asad's open hand across Carter's face is loud and hard enough to swing the other man's head back the other way.

No one makes a sound. We are all spectators in this dark show. Even the soldiers lined against the wall don't move, glued to the play Asad orchestrates.

"I'm talking to you, muthafucka. Didn't yo mama ever teach you it's rude to not look at someone when they're talking to your bitch ass?" Asad asks, his calm voice contradicting the violence of his assault. "Now, I'ma give you one more chance to nut up and tell me the truth. What do you know about those hittas coming after me?"

A quick glance around the room reveals varying reactions to the display unraveling before us—excitement and satisfaction from the dons, unease and distaste from their wives, anger, apprehension, and fierce pride on the faces of the Cross family members. I don't peek over my shoulder at Michelle, but I can practically feel the bloodlust and pride emanating from her. This ruthless, intimidating, heartless monster . . . This is who she created, who she raised.

Disgust should swim in my chest. Horror should churn in my stomach. The itching, clawing need to be far, far away from this chilling tableau should be crawling through me, have me inching toward the door to escape.

Instead . . .

Instead, a twisted, perverted anticipation—no, eagerness snakes through my veins, lighting up nerve endings and carving out a craving in my belly that can only be filled by pain, screams, blood.

I briefly close my eyes. But only for a second, lest I miss anything.

And there's my secret, the one I've buried so far deep that I have a hard time wiping off the grime and admitting it to myself.

I survived the monsters of my childhood by becoming one.

"I don't know nothin'," Carter spits. "And even if I did, I'm no snitch."

"Okay, okay. I get it. I can almost even admire that kind of loyalty," Asad says, straightening to his full height. "Almost, if you hadn't taken an oath of fidelity and allegiance to me rather than the people you're protecting. That's some shit."

"I gave that to Marcus, not you," he shoots back, and that boomerangs around the room like a ricocheting bullet.

From my position, I can only see Asad's profile, but with his long, dark hair weaved into beautiful and intricate stitch braids, nothing hinders my view of the arch of a thick eyebrow and slow curl of his lips.

"Is that so? Good to know." He turns to Demarcus, who's still barricaded by Cross soldiers. "What about you, D? Is your loyalty to me, or are you still sucking Marcus's cold, dead-ass dick along with your brother?"

"Both, Prince," Demarcus says, a heavy resignation and, if I'm not mistaken, sadness weighing his voice as he stares at his brother. "My allegiance was with Marcus and now it's with you."

Carter's chest heaves up and down, his breathing audible in the room, but he doesn't glance at his brother. His cheek must still be hot from that slap.

"Good answer."

Turning, Asad strides across the room to a small sideboard that I hadn't noticed. A linen-covered tray sits on top of it, but when Asad whips the covering off, pastries don't cover the silver surface.

Knives. A machete. Scalpels. Ball peen hammers. Pliers.

A varied and beautiful array of torture tools.

Murmurs sweep through the room from where the Cross soldiers stand, and excitement quivers within them. I can practically taste the anticipation and lust for blood that saturates the air like droplets.

"Gotdamn, Prince. Please, man. That's my brother," Demarcus pleads. "He said he don't know about a drive-by. Off the strength of your father—"

"Marcus ain't got shit to do with this, D. Your brother helped some muthafuckas to try and come for my head. There's no fucking exile in this bitch. You been in this life long enough to know there's only one punishment for that kind of betrayal. Letting your boy go? Nah, I ain't even built like that."

He turns around, rolls the sideboard in front of him until it's next to Carter.

Demarcus looses a low, pained groan, but I have to give Carter his flowers—he keeps silent, doesn't even flinch when Asad picks up a big stainless steel pair of shears. His eyes though . . .

They damn near glisten with fear.

I lean forward, my breath catching in my throat, my skin tingling.

I've never seen Asad at work, and I'm thirsty to witness it. Witness him unleash the demon that lurks behind four-thousand-dollar suits, a fortune in watches, and civilized manners. The powerful yet sexual play of muscles under his shirt, the almost graceful glide of his big body, the loose and familiar clasp of long, elegant fingers around the weapon . . . They're all hints at that monster, and I'm eager for his appearance like a child on the watch for St. Nick.

Or Krampus.

"Now, because I don't want your brother out here thinking I'm an unreasonable muthafucka, he should know why you about to go to hell a few inches shorter." Asad pulls a cell phone out of his pocket and passes it to Eli. "Give that to D, Eli. The password is 365432," he tells Demarcus.

Several seconds later, Demarcus frowns down at the cell.

"This is Tre's phone."

"Trust me, he don't need it anymore." Asad circles Carter, stands behind him. "Go to messages and find the thread between him and Carter." Taps the blunt edge of the blade against Carter's shoulder.

I, like everyone else who's a captive audience to this theater, wait in complete silence as Demarcus navigates to the app and texts. His frown deepens until his eyebrows practically meet. Finally, he lifts his head and stares at Asad.

"What the fuck is this?" he barks.

Looping his arms around Carter's shoulders, Asad clasps the machete in front of him, the blade braced up against his throat.

"Read it, Demarcus."

Demarcus hesitates, but with Asad's flat, frigid gaze settled on him, he lowers his head over the phone again.

"Tre texted 'Unc' at 10:28 a.m. yesterday morning, 'We're leaving now.' Unc at 10:29, 'Bet. Take the 10 Freeway. They'll follow you from there.' Tre replies back. 'Bet.'" Demarcus briefly closes his eyes, but a second later, keeps reading. "Unc texts again ten minutes later. 'Keep head on swivel. Two Ninjas. Hellcat. Challenger.' Then an hour later, another text from Unc. 'You good? Hit me up. Let me know what P sayin.'"

"What was that about he don't know shit?" Asad asks Demarcus, the first hints of anger seeping into his voice. "I don't know what I'm more pissed at. That he was in on setting my ass up or that he did it through text messages on an unsecured phone."

"Prince . . ." Demarcus whispers.

"Don't beg him for shit," Carter snaps. "He gon' do what he gon' do anyway. Fuck him."

"Fuck me?" Asad chuckles and a delicious shiver dances down the middle of my torso, between my breasts, past my navel, and two steps over my clit. I shift in my seat. "Y'know what I say? Fuck those fingers. Grimy muthafuckas who text like bitches don't need 'em."

He steps to the side, opens the shears, and closes them so fast that I don't realize four of Carter's fingers are severed until his high-pitched screams pierce the air. Blood spurts, spraying Demarcus and the soldiers standing beside him.

Just a couple of days ago, I made a man bleed out of his ears and eyes, but that was in the name of science. This . . . I stare at the appendages on the floor next to Carter's feet. This is pure grisly art. And Asad is a macabre Picasso.

In this moment, he has never been more fascinating to me. More savage.

More beautiful.

"Jesus, Prince! Jesus Christ," Demarcus shouts, surging forward, but he's held back. "Please, not my brother."

"Now, Carter, you can tell me who you working with, and I can end this now and your brother can make sure Ms. Rachel has most of you to bury. Or you can keep quiet like the disloyal bitch you are and go back to them in jigsaw-puzzle pieces. Makes no difference to me. Your choice, bruh," Asad says to a whimpering Carter, ignoring his brother's cries.

When Carter only continues to groan, Asad nods, and the chandelier's light glints off the shears once more as Asad takes Carter's thumb.

Screams assault my ears, and I close my eyes, hold my breath. Block out everything but that sound. In this dining room, surrounded by some of the underworld's worst, the man I consider my biggest, worst enemy is unlocking something inside of me. Introducing me to a side of myself that I'd hidden behind the cold, detached wall of science and sterility. But this . . . this is personal. Personal, intimate, and messy.

And I'm utterly captivated.

"Cauterize it." The words leap out of me before I realize they even formed on my tongue.

I feel the weight of gazes on me, but mine is fixed on the reaper that stands behind the bound and bleeding Cross soldier.

Asad studies me, the silver depths impenetrable.

"If you don't want him to bleed out too soon, cauterize his wounds," I say again.

"I'm not new to this, ma." He peers at me for several more seconds, then nods his head toward the sideboard. "But come here and get that blowtorch."

I don't mistake the order for anything other than what it is—a taunt, a challenge.

Standing from the chair, I barely pause before striding over to the tray of his tools and picking up the handheld torch. Asad doesn't say a word, but his silver eyes gleam, daring me.

Excitement sparking through me, I move closer, not caring about the blood smearing the toes and bottoms of my House of Cross pink-and-black stilettoes. I bend down and twist the gas cylinder before clicking the igniter. Blue fire flashes out, as does the hiss of gas, and without hesitation, I apply the flame to the open wounds where Carter's fingers and thumb used to be.

He writhes in the heavy armchair, his feet scrambling against the tarp-covered floor as if trying to get away from the pain. His screams bounce off the walls, echoing in the dining room in an agonized crescendo.

"Bellissima," Julian murmurs. I'm not sure if he's referring to the piercing screams or my technique.

Dimitri chuckles, and straightening, I glance in the direction of the table and catch the Russian Mafia head's wide smile, as well as Naoki's subtle nod. I don't miss the disgust painting their wives' faces or the hatred twisting Demarcus's.

"That's disappointing." Asad tsks. "He's passed out. Guess he couldn't take the heat. Literally. Wake him up, ma."

I shouldn't feel like we're on our Bonnie and Clyde shit . . . That hint of pride in his voice shouldn't send a tingle down my spine like a warm, big hand sliding a caress straight to the small of my back. Neither of those should have my feet instantly moving toward the table before my brain gets the message.

But they are. And I am.

I bypass the goblets of water sitting toward the center. Instead, I nab two half-filled tumblers of whiskey and retrace my steps. Reaching Carter, I stare at his face, slack in his faint, but it's the wounds that get doused in the alcohol.

His eyes fly open, black with pain, his mouth stretched wide on a silent scream. His back arches, looking like a tautly pulled bow until his body shudders and slams back into the chair.

"Oh good. You're back with us." Asad roughly pats Carter on the shoulder. "I was worried you were crashing out on me for a minute there. Where were we?" He rounds the chair and lays the shears on the tray, then crosses his arms over his chest. "Who gave you the order to come after me? Who you working with?"

Carter's labored breathing punctuates the air, and he shakes as if great blasts of wind buffet his body, but he remains silent.

Asad chuckles, and it's mean, ugly.

My nipples harden, the rings going through them pinching my flesh.

"A'ight, muthafucka. Play it your way." He looks over Carter's head and says, "Bring them in."

One of the Cross soldiers moves and opens one of the double doors at the back of the room. Seconds later, a couple of men in black suits usher in an older, beautiful Black woman and a man who resembles her, appearing to be in his mid-twenties. They wear stoic expressions until they catch sight of Carter and his fingers littering the floor.

"What the fuck?" the younger man yells. "Dad! The fuck! Uncle D, what's going on?" He turns to Demarcus, his hands cupping the back of his head.

"Baby." The older woman tries to approach Carter, but one of the soldiers who led her in prevents her by a firm grip on her upper arm. "Baby," she says again, voice cracking. "What have they done to you? Why?" She looks at Asad, confusion wrinkling her face. "Why are you doing this?"

My heart twists for her, because no mother should have to see the person they birthed hurt and in pain. But on the other hand, revulsion and anger flicker in my chest as I glance at Carter. A man who cared about his family—especially a man in this world—wouldn't put those he loved in this position. If he was going to do some foul shit like betray the head of his organization, then he at least could've made sure his immediate family were moved out of harm's way. He's been in this shit long enough to know those closest to him would be the first casualties in this war he initiated.

Hit people where they're weakest. It's what I would do.

"Ask your son," Asad replies, his tone flat. He beckons her closer, and once her guard releases her, Carter's mother rushes forward, but Asad stops her before she can touch her son. "Carter, explain to your mother why she and your son are here."

"Ma," he rasps.

"Prince, this is too much. They have nothing to do with this. Let them go, man," Demarcus demands, straining against the soldiers holding him back.

But Asad ignores him, his attention fixed on Carter.

"Speak up, Carter. Tell your mother why she and her grandson gotta see you like this. Explain what their bitch-ass son and father has been up to."

"Ay, that's my fuck—"

From one instant to the next, Asad's gun is out and pointed in Carter's son's face. The younger man stumbles back a step, his hands flipping up. "I wasn't talking to you, young buck. Don't act like you don't know who I am. Let disrespectful shit fly outta your mouth and you'll be meeting your cousin in the upper room. So shut the fuck up and listen while grown folks are talking."

"What? What do you mean, his cousin?" Demarcus whispers. "Tre? Are you talking about Tre? My son?"

I'm not sure how he didn't put that together before now. Especially with the texts. But maybe the, uh, excitement of the situation didn't allow him to piece two and two together.

"Yeah. I was going to hit you up about that. But I got distracted by finding out who was trying to take me out. Well, besides your son." Asad switches his focus from Carter to his brother. "I killed Tre, D. But take that shit up with your brother, not me. You read the text messages; he involved your son in what he had going on. He got him killed. Carter and whoever he was in with might as well as have pulled the fucking trigger."

A hoarse sob rips from Demarcus, and only someone with a heart made of stone wouldn't be moved by the grief-stricken and tortured sound. In this moment, I want to march over to that tray, grab that machete, and chop off Carter's hand instead of his remaining fingers. His thoughtlessness or greed or selfishness or . . . whatever cost this man his son. And might cost him their mother. And yet, he still sits there, silent. What a whole bitch.

I take a step toward him . . .

"Nah, I got it." Asad's big hand palms my belly, holding me back.

How he knew I was about to follow through on my thoughts, I don't know, and I don't analyze. Not right now when a red haze is misting my vision and static crackles in my ears. Gently shoving me back, he grabs Carter's mother and tugs her forward so she's standing in front of him and her son. The Glock lodges right up against her temple.

"You ready to tell me what I want to know now? Or are you willing to let your mother get popped over it? 'Cause make no mistake, Carter. I will blow her fucking brains out right here in front of you and then follow up with your son. And that'll just be for starters. Every person you love can get it until there's a fucking pile of bodies right at your feet. Then I'll go back to cutting you up until even your dead-ass mama won't recognize her baby boy. Is your loyalty to whoever you're protecting worth the lives of family?" He presses the barrel of the Glock harder against his mother's head. Screaming, she recoils from the barrel, twisting as if she can get away. "Start talking or I start busting. You got five seconds."

"Gotdammit, Carter! That's our mama," Demarcus yells. "Fuck them people! You done already had my son killed, bruh!"

Carter's son is quiet, but I glimpse the war in his brown eyes—stand by his father but the love and fear for his grandmother.

I'm a little surprised no one has jumped forward to intervene on behalf of Demarcus. His son is a treacherous piece of shit, but he didn't seem to know anything about it. But no soldiers step forth in his defense. Several of them move forward, including Kareem, but to form a line behind Demarcus, as if preventing any chance of him running if he decides to take that course of action. Most of the guests stand from the table, silent but enraptured.

"Three seconds," Asad says.

"I—" Carter hesitates.

"I'll fucking kill you myself!" Demarcus screams.

"One second," Asad warns, and his fingers tighten around the trigger . . .

Their mother closes her eyes, her lips moving . . .

"Okay, okay!" Carter hoarsely yells. Resignation and pain weaken his voice, but he meets Asad's gaze. "Let her go and I'll tell you what you want to know."

Asad mugs him, and I silently ball my face up, too. He's in no bargaining position. The fuck?

"Talk, muthafucka," Asad quietly orders without lowering his gun.

After a long moment, Carter sighs and bows his head. "Xavier. And Deacon."

Shock reverberates through me in seismic waves, damn near rocking me on my feet. Marcus didn't include me in the management of Cross business, but I still made it a priority to know everything about the empire that bore my last name and was part of my blood. So I understood the importance of those names. Xavier Holloway and Deacon Martins are two powerful street bosses who have been with Marcus for years. Their fathers served under my grandfather, and even their sons were members of the organization. No one could've ever convinced me they weren't loyal to HoC.

They were supposed to be here tonight but had business in New York. Sounded plausible at the time. Now it's suspect as fuck.

But here Carter sat, saying they were the instigators of this plot to kill the new boss.

The fuck is going on? Did they . . . Shit, could they have anything to do with Marcus's death, too?

I look at Asad, and his expression is a blank slate. It reveals nothing of his thoughts or emotions. But standing beside him, I note the tendons in his neck popping out in stark relief against his toasted-brown skin. Catch the stiff set of his shoulders. The pounding of his pulse at his temple.

Finally, he nods at Carter. "Thank you," he calmly says.

Then, in rapid-fire succession, he puts bullets through Carter's mother's, son's, and brother's heads.

A horrific cry tears out of Carter, and it's worse than when Asad severed his fingers or when I cauterized the wounds. This is soul-deep and raw.

Low murmurs underscore the weeping. And a glance at the Cross soldiers reveal some of them nodding or wearing fierce expressions of satisfaction and pride.

I feel nothing hearing it. Their blood is on his hands.

Besides, he had to know his actions would cost them their lives. Asad couldn't afford to let them live; I already saw in Carter's son's eyes Asad was creating an enemy. And once Demarcus recovered from his immediate grief over Tre's death, that sadness would likely turn into rage and a hunger for revenge. Nah, all this could be laid at the feet of Carter. Right next to his fingers.

"Get him out of here," he orders.

Eli moves forward, along with two more men, and they free a sobbing Carter, dragging him from the room, his blood streaking the floor.

"Well, when I agreed to dinner, I didn't know it would be dinner and a show," Dimitri says with another of his signature chuckles. He begins to slow clap, but the glint in his eyes is cold, speculative. "Браво."

"Traitors are owed no mercy," Naoki says in his quiet but powerful voice. "Neither are their bloodlines. That was a pleasure to witness. And allow me to congratulate you again on your choice in wife. She's your equal in strength."

"I second that. I'd like to offer another toast." Julian stands and waves a hand to the servers. They move quickly, and within moments, everyone's glasses are refilled. Everyone at the table remains standing, a little disturbingly unmoved by the events that just passed. These men underestimate women, but their wives must be as strong and cold as they are; none of their faces betray any disgust or fear at the violence that occurred.

A wave of heat rushes over and through me as I walk back to the table, Asad next to me, his palm a hot brand low on my spine. A part of me screams out an objection; the nearly feral excitement that consumed me during Carter's torture fades, and I'm right back in reality, where Asad is my nemesis and I'm being forced into a life I want no part of.

The other part fills—overflows with it. Because that same part thrills at being called his equal. Fucking preens at it. That approval isn't just of me as Asad's future wife. It's of my last name, showing as a Cross. It's sick, twisted. I don't need their praise, their recognition. I for damn sure don't need Asad's. But that kernel of warmth, that . . . *thing* that lifts its head toward the heat and light of his approval, contradicts my claim.

It's obvious I have daddy issues.

Because the alternative . . . it's untenable.

"Michelle." Asad's deep rumble of a voice vibrates against my back, snatching my attention from my internal existential crisis, and landing it on his mother. If anything lightens my mood, it's the repulsed expression riding her face as she glares at me standing there with her son. Oh hell yes. That does wonders for me. "You're not joining in the toast?"

The question isn't one at all—it's a warning. And Michelle knows better than to disrespect not just her son but the head of the Cross organization.

With a smile, Michelle raises her wineglass. "Of course I am, Prince," she says, giving him a tight smile.

The waiters bring Asad and me our drinks, and surprise ripples through me when he selects a whiskey for me instead of wine. Murmuring a thank-you, I accept it.

"To the future of House of Cross," Julian says, his beautiful, rich voice booming in the room. "Asad, as we've witnessed here tonight, you are a wise choice to usher in this new age. Someone once said, 'This is a ruthless world, and one must be ruthless to cope with it.' I'd like to add that one must be ruthless to rule it. You're that man and that ruler, Prince. And from what we've seen, you've chosen a queen who shares your unflinching willingness to do what it takes to govern it. Congratulations to you both."

A chorus of congratulations peppers the air, and as I lift my glass to my lips, my gaze meets Kareem's. Like his mother's, there's no acceptance or joy there. Anger tightens his smooth brown skin and hardens his jaw.

Noticing my stare, he forces his mouth into a smile that doesn't alleviate the flatness of his eyes. He nods his head and lifts his glass, taking a sip.

I don't return the acknowledgment or the gesture. I'm too busy spiraling. Because this is suddenly too much.

Chatter and laughter follow the toast, and like all the air was suddenly vacuumed out of the room, I'm struggling to breathe. It isn't the torture or murder; it's the blinding, hot exposure. The nearly overwhelming sense of being seen . . . and accepted with admiration by this lethal circle when my own "family" had rejected and reviled me for most of my life. I'm like a mountain climber who's gone from one altitude to another. Disoriented. Sick. I need space that doesn't include Asad or these people. I've overstayed my welcome here, and more than anything, I crave the safety and familiarity of my home.

"Excuse me," I murmur to no one in particular as none of them are really paying attention to me. I head toward the doors, but hard, long fingers cuff my wrist.

"Where are you going?" Asad bends his head over mine, and his lips are a sensual threat as they almost brush the top of my ear.

"To the bathroom." *And then out of here.*

He studies me, and my heartbeat pounds in my ears because

for an illogical moment I think he's able to read my mind. But then he nods and releases me. Silently loosing a sigh of relief, I wind through the servers entering with pots of coffee and plates of dessert, making my way out of the dining room. Leaving the rest of them to toast, dine, and laugh and . . . do whatever party-goers do.

For several minutes, I weave and stumble through this maze of a house. This might've been my father's at one time, but it's still foreign to me. Bypassing closed doors and furnished but empty living rooms, parlors, and a den, I eventually locate the bathroom, and I spend about twenty minutes in the luxurious, tastefully decorated space. I wash my hands and using one of the towels, clean up the few flecks of blood that splattered on my chest and neck. There's nothing I can do about the fluid on my shoes and hem of my pants. I'm not tossing them though. Tired, and hoping it's possible to avoid seeing any more people before I skip out, I exit the bathroom and heave an audible sigh this time when the hallway appears free of people.

"Ember."

Fuck.

"Kareem." I turn around and don't bother pasting on a smile. My polite life expectancy expired for the evening. "I didn't see you there."

"I'm sorry. I saw you leave and followed to make sure you're okay." He chuckles, sliding his hands into his pockets. "*A lot* went down in there."

"It did." I nod. "Thank you, but there was no need to check on me. I'm good." Irritation and an urgency to get the hell up out of here war with each other, and I glance over his shoulder. "Look, I don't want to—"

"You sure you're okay? I don't mean to pry, but when Prince announced your engagement, you didn't exactly look like a blushing bride." He gives a dry, short laugh, shaking his head. "Ember, if anyone knows my brother, it's me. And I love him, but he can be . . . focused. And when he has his mind set on something, he doesn't allow much to deter him. Not even the word *no*. I'm going to be honest with you, Ember. I can't imagine in what world you would willingly go into this marriage . . ."

"And if that is the case, what could you do to help me?" I tilt my head, studying him, curious about his answer.

Because like he said, he possibly knows his brother better than anyone. So he also understands that there isn't shit he could do to save me. Shit, he can't even save himself from the hell of this family. I've never once witnessed him stand up to his mother, much less Asad. So how in the *fuck* could he do anything for me?

He huffs out another laugh, and it's just as bitter as its predecessor.

"I already know what you're thinking. You don't think I can do a damn thing. But you're wrong." He edges closer to me, and not willing to appear weak, I stop myself from retreating, but an unease begins to creep through my veins. "You let me know—give me the word to get you out of this bullshit, and I'll do everything in my considerable power to help you. You see, Ember, plenty of people underestimate me, and I don't mind that. I can show you better than I can tell you. Are you going to give me that word, Em?" He inches even closer.

The unease blooms into a chasm of discomfort low in my stomach. Though I want nothing more than to be extricated from the miserable trap that marriage to Asad would be, I'll use the shears still coated with Carter's blood on my own hand before offering it to Kareem for help.

"I got it under control," I say.

Fuck it. I don't care how he perceives it. I retreat a step, inserting more space between us.

He arches an eyebrow and moves forward, reclaiming that space. Reaching up, he wraps a finger around one of my curls and tugs on it.

"Em, I shouldn't have to remind you who or what Prince is—you grew up with him. He showed you more than any of us. Now imagine being married to him. When he can legally claim you as his property and you'll no longer have any control over your life. Do you really think he's going to change and give a fuck about you? Do you honestly believe he's going to be faithful? Prince is going to fuck everything that moves just like he does now and expect you to sit at home like good little silent, obedient wifey, wasting away. Is that how you see yourself? Is that the life you want?"

The life I want? I almost laugh in his face but manage to swallow it back. This hasn't been the life I've *wanted* for thirteen years. But at twelve, others made those decisions for me, and at twenty-five, Asad was still trying to steal my choice, manipulate and sculpt my future into a nightmarish something that I didn't recognize.

But why does Kareem suddenly give a fuck? He never did all these years. At least not enough to step in and defend me against his mother's and Asad's "tender mercies" before. So why now?

No. I don't trust it. I don't trust him. At the end of the day, he's his mother's son.

I guess he takes my silence as me considering his little speech because he smiles at me, rubbing my hair between his fingers.

"Look at tonight, for example. Mom may have invited Aryn here this evening, but Asad damn sure didn't tell her to leave. And then he had her sit beside him at dinner instead of you. They've been together for a while now, and it's been no secret. It's also no secret, at least to me, why he's forcing you to marry him, and it has nothing to do with actually wanting you. The Cross DNA. Keeping you chained to this organization so you can't take your talents elsewhere. You're the moneymaker, Em, and Asad and Mom will never let that go."

He's not informing me of anything I'm not already aware of or hasn't occurred to me. That shrewd, too-sharp gaze studies my face like hard calculus, but I'm proficient in concealing my thoughts and emotions. He and his family instilled that in me long ago. So though his well-aimed darts struck their target, he'll never know it.

But I'll never be my mother, though I love her with all my heart. I will never be a man's trophy—golden, silent, and decorative—while he disrespects me, fucking anything that moves and expecting me to shut up and take it. I'll walk away. And if that's not an option, I'll kill all of us first. And I mean that shit with everything in me.

"Kareem, you know what they say about touching a Black woman's hair." I wrap my hand around his and squeeze, digging my nails into the sensitive flesh between his fingers until his mouth flattens and he releases me. "Don't."

"Ember . . ."

I cease listening to whatever else he's saying. His words are drowned out by the deafening pounding of my pulse in my head. My heart lodges in the base of my throat, the rapid beat nearly strangling me, while a shower of heat pours over me.

The door to a room a little farther down the hall opens, and Aryn walks out with Asad behind her. This shouldn't have fury and humiliation pumping through me. Slivers of betrayal for damn sure shouldn't be sliding between my ribs like splinters under fingers. A terrible . . . ache shouldn't be yawning wide inside me like an empty, dark abyss.

And yet . . .

Yet, as I stand in this hallway with Kareem as a witness to my goddamn *fiancé* exiting a room with his lover after probably fucking her in apology, all of that shit is coursing through and over me.

"I told you," Kareem murmurs, not bothering to hide the pity in his eyes as they head in our direction. "I warned you. He didn't wait until you were out of the house to go back to her. I'm sorry, Em."

Shut the fuck up, my mind screams at him. But the words stick in my throat, crazy-glued by the hurt I have no business experiencing.

Asad and Aryn notice us and stop mid-step. Surprise flickers across both of their faces, but then a smirk curves Aryn's wide, full mouth. A mouth with smeared lipstick. Even as I yell at myself to not give a flying fuck, I can't stop my gaze from traveling over Asad's aloof, impassive mask, down his shirt, and lower, to his pants . . . to the red stain dirtying them right over his dick print. It's almost indecipherable on his black pants, but I see it; I know what it is.

And when I drag my gaze back up and meet his narrowed, molten eyes, he knows what I've seen. Knows that I've guessed exactly what went on in that room between him and that bitch.

I don't care.

He's forcing me into this charade, bullshit marriage.

It doesn't mean—

"Fuck you."

CHAPTER EIGHT

Asad

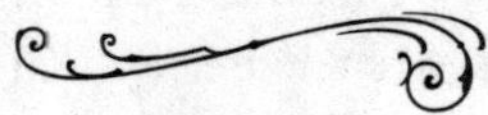

Xavier. Deacon.

Gotdamn.

I grip the sides of the bathroom sink and bow my head, forehead almost pressed against the cool glass of the mirror.

I'm not even gon' lie. This one fucks me up.

I've known those two since Michelle first brought me and Kareem into Marcus's house. When Marcus started introducing me to the House of Cross business and then the underworld side when I turned eighteen, they became like honorary uncles to me. They'd taught me the rules and ropes of this game as much, if not more, than Marcus. My stepfather was savvy and knowledgeable in the boardroom, but in the streets? Xavier and Deacon dirtied the hands Marcus insisted on keeping clean and callus-free. I respected them for that. Admired them for that. When I imagined stepping into my rule over this organization, that vision included them by my side along with Eli and Kareem.

Now what? How deep did this go? Were they working on their own, or did they have an army behind them? Did they object to just me, or was this plan in process against Marcus, too? Were they responsible for Marcus's murder and now making sure all obstacles were out the way?

Shit. Just . . . shit.

Running a hand over my braids, I shake my head.

I never saw this betrayal coming.

Keeping it a hundred, I would've foreseen my mother coming for my neck before they did.

I exhale, the long, hard breath fogging the glass.

It hadn't even been four whole days that I'd been in control of this shit and already I had a fucking conspiracy and uprising. I chuckle. Good thing I didn't give a fuck about burning this shit all the way to the ground and starting all over if that's what needed to be done. Yeah, I did everything in my power to end up here, at the top, but none of this shit owns me. I'd salt the gotdamn ground to make sure nothing grew and move the fuck on to grow what I wanted before letting any muthafuckas play on my top.

That's what my little demonstration was about tonight. A message to not just my allies but to my own street bosses and soldiers. I was loyal to those who were loyal to me. But cross me? Cross me and the T-shirt business will be extra busy for you and your loved ones. I'll wipe out your whole bloodline, fucking around with me.

As Carter found out tonight.

The corner of my mouth curls into a faint half smile.

Carter damn sure fucked around and found out tonight.

As did I and everyone else in that room.

I don't need to close my eyes for an image of Ember holding that blowtorch to materialize in vivid HD. That had been . . . unexpected.

And hot as fuck.

Not just her using that torch on Carter without flinching or without hesitation.

Nah.

The sexiest thing had been that sheen of excitement, of lust, in her eyes.

I've known Ember was dangerous. Known what she was capable of. But *fuck*.

Seeing her hard nipples and those muthafuckin' rings press against that jacket at the sound of Carter's screams had my dick bricking up. And I wanted to shove her down to the floor on her hands and knees in his blood, cuff the front of her neck, and beat her pussy up until it molded to my dick. Have her cry out my name as I spelled it out in that tight-as-fuck hole. Have her pussy shiver and weep until we were both coated in cum and the blood I spilled.

Something tells me, Ember wouldn't have minded a little blood either.

It's me she would object to.

My jaw clenches as I twist the faucet and let the water run. Even as I strip out of my dress shirt that has flecks of blood splattered on it, I try to douse the anger simmering inside me. That anger that has been set on you-about-to-see-the-other-side-of-me for most of the evening. For years, Michelle has taunted Kareem for having a soft spot for Ember, but tonight he seemed to be pushing up on her extra hard. And I love my brother, but every time he stepped too close to her, smiled at her, touched her, I was visually measuring his suit for a burial plot.

I loose a soft chuckle, but ain't shit funny. Kareem didn't know Ember and I were engaged, but shit, she did. And I can't even count how many times I wanted to snatch her little ass up for giving him what she refused me. Conversation. A smile. Softness. Only our guests kept me from nutting up.

Grabbing a washcloth, I run it under the water with soap and quickly clean up. This isn't my main residence, but I keep some clothes here. Before coming into the study, I'd stopped by the master bedroom and grabbed a replacement shirt. Once I finish washing off, I slip into the garment. Dressed again, I turn off the light and exit, prepared to return to the dinner party and my guests. And to hunt down Ember. It's been about twenty minutes since she left the room. Now that I've announced who she is to me and our engagement, I'm not letting her far from my sight for long.

Mine.

As I reach for the knob, it twists, and the door opens. I step back in time to avoid being hit, and Aryn enters. She closes the door behind her and irritation pricks at me. From the first time I saw her tonight, I'd had to stop myself from grabbing her by the back of her neck like the little bitch she is, dragging her from my house, and putting her outside. She's fucking lucky some of my guests had already arrived and I cared more about not causing a spectacle and managing Michelle in front of them. I didn't want to gift wrap the heads of the families and their wives something to talk about other than what I planned for the evening. Otherwise, her humiliation would've been on her since *I* didn't invite her here tonight. Play stupid games, win stupid prizes.

"What do you want, Aryn?" I ask, not hiding my impatience. "I have guests to return to."

"How could you treat me like this, Prince?" she snaps, planting fists on her hips. Her beautiful face twists as if any moment tears are about to spill and screams will tumble out of her mouth. Her long hair falls about her face, over her shoulders, strands clinging to her cheek. "How could you humiliate me by announcing an engagement when I was sitting there right next to you?"

"Check it." I angle my head, sliding my hands in the front pockets of my slacks. "Did I ask you to be here tonight?"

Her mouth twists and she flicks her fingers, rolling her eyes. "Your mother reached out and invited me."

"Yeah, keep rolling those eyes at me and watch me snatch them bitches out your head. But I repeat, did *I* ask you to be here tonight?"

She's quiet for several seconds and looks everywhere but at me. "No," she quietly says.

"Nah, baby girl. Say that shit with the same energy you walked in here with."

"No," she repeats louder, glaring at me.

"Exactly. I didn't invite you to shit. My mother doesn't and never will speak for me. And I'm not even sure why you're here, Aryn. We don't even rock like that. We fuck. You suck me off. I don't even put my mouth on you. Occasionally, I'll escort you to an event, and rarely, I'll take you to one of mine. But I can count on one hand the number of times I've been to your place since we meet at hotels to bust a nut. You've never been to where I lay my head. What does that tell you?"

"Whatever, Prince. I've never seen you out with any other woman. My name is the only one that's connected to yours. And yours has been the only connected to mine. That means something, and you can't play me now by telling me it doesn't."

I shrug. "Yeah, it does mean something." She starts to smile. "It means you're good at keeping your other fucks on the down low, just like I am." That smile freezes before disappearing. "C'mon, Aryn. You know what it was between us. Don't try and make it out to be more than it was."

"Was?" She stalks closer, and her sultry, earthy perfume reaches me first. Most men find it alluring. I always make her shower the shit off before we fuck because it messes with my allergies. If she were my woman, I'm certain she'd notice that quirk. "What it *was*, Prince? Are you really ending what we have for that, that fat bitch in there?" she damn near screams.

I laugh, and my palm is itching with the urge to choke the shit out of her.

"Why the first thing you insecure bitches always go for is the appearances of other women you feel threatened by?"

Aryn's chin jerks back, and she blinks as if appalled. "Insecure? She is not me, and I've never been threatened by another woman in my life, especially not that one." She jabs a finger toward the door.

"Yeah, you are." I smile, and she flinches. "A woman confident in her own appeal and worth wouldn't have to tear down another sista to make herself appear more valuable in the eyes of another person. A secure woman understands that her value isn't tied to her tits, ass, or pussy but the inestimable shit that can't be bought—ambition, drive, courage, perseverance. A secure woman would tell a man like me to get the fuck on and flipped that whole muthafuckin table on her way out if I passed her up for someone else. Because she'd understand she was the muthafuckin prize, not me. And Aryn"—I pinch her chin hard enough for her to wince—"you say that fat shit like it's an insult. Shiiiit, Ember got grown-woman curves. She thick as fuck, and best believe every man in that room tonight wanted her ass. Literally. But that's mine."

She jerks her head away from me and stumbles back a couple of steps. But not before I catch the flash of anger and hurt in her eyes. I can't help that shit. She pissed me off, and we been dealing with each other for over a year. She know my mouth by now. Ain't nothing nice about it.

"I don't care what you say, Prince. If you didn't want me, didn't want this"—she cups her breast with one hand and slides the other under the short hem of her dress and palms her pussy—"you wouldn't have kept coming back all this time."

Before I can stop her, she drops to her knees and fists me through my pants. Pressing her lips to my dick, she mouths it, letting me feel that overly talented tongue and graze of her teeth. For a moment, I let her do her thing because, *fuck*, it feels good as hell, and Aryn has always been a throat goat.

I palm her head, pressing her hard against my shit, and she releases a throaty moan. But that sound turns into a yelp when I fist her hair and yank her to her feet. Aryn scowls at me, her fingers circling my wrist, attempting to tug my hand away from her.

"Listen to me, Aryn. Are you listening?" I give her a little shake until she nods. "Treat this dick like last season's whatever the fuck. You don't want to look at it, have nothing to do with it. If you ever see my dick on the street, cross it. If you and my dick are ever in the same room, exit that muthafucka. You get where I'm coming from? Nod if you get where I'm coming from, Aryn."

She frantically nods. "Yes, Prince, damn. Let me go."

I abruptly release her, and she stumbles again, but this time, she maintains her distance.

"Aryn?"

"Yes?" She sniffs, smoothing down her hair, her full mouth pursed in a pout.

I tilt my head. "You and my dick are in the same room."

Sucking her teeth, she spins on her heel and stomps to the door. She wrenches it open and walks out with me right behind her. I've wasted enough time with this bullshit . . .

The fuck?

The rage that had been absent while dealing with Aryn's annoying ass rushes back like a tidal wave, breaking against me and splintering into my skin.

Kareem hovers over Ember, standing so close he's damn near sharing her gotdamn breath. Her gaze shifts over his shoulder and my brother turns around, moving next to her, as if guarding her. From me?

Smart.

Because what I'm about to do to them is going to make what I did to Carter look like a fucking Care Bear Stare. Kareem leans down and whispers something in Ember's ear, and a growl rolls up from deep inside me. I stalk closer, and Aryn keeps pace with me with her messy ass.

An emotion spasms across Ember's face, and it jolts me to halt. I can't decipher it at first, but then her gaze sweeps over Aryn, then moves to me, dragging down my body, lingering on my dick. Specifically on the spot Aryn had her mouth.

Fuck. Gotdammit.

Suddenly, that emotion I couldn't make out becomes crystal clear. Disappointment. Hurt. Betrayal.

Hate.

"Fuck. You," she enunciates, sending fury surging hotter and brighter through me.

"Oop," Aryn instigates with a petty laugh from next to me. "You think she guessed what went on in that room, baby?"

"Bitch, I will kill you," I say to her, and that grin slowly falls away as her slim fingers lift for the base of her throat. "Get the fuck on."

"Sure." She gives me a tight smile. "I'll just follow your fiancée out."

I glance from her to see that Ember is no longer in the hallway. Shit. Leaving her and Kareem standing there, I take off in the only direction she could have disappeared, but he grasps my arm, stopping me.

I chuckle, staring down at my younger brother. I love him, but he's playing with his life right now.

"You should leave her alone, Prince. You and Mom have done enough damage tonight."

Gripping his fingers, I slowly peel them off me, making sure to squeeze them. Hard.

"This isn't your business, bruh. Sit this one out." I pat him on the back and continue down the corridor. "Tell Michelle to give everyone my regrets but I got called away, and send them home. Thanks," I call over my shoulder.

It's only been three minutes at the most, so even if Ember made it out the house, she couldn't have gotten far. Possessing knowledge of the house's layout is an advantage. I bypass the dining room and the closed doors of the salon where Michelle would've corralled my guests. That would've been the last place Ember went. I glance on the other side of the house, and the second living room and parlor are empty. And she wouldn't have gone deeper into the house toward the kitchen. Dammit, that leaves outside.

I grab the knob, but just before I twist it, instinct whispers to head to the library. There hasn't been one time my instinct has failed me, so I release the doorknob and retrace my steps down the hallway. I make a left at the stairs and head to the wide, closed double doors of the library.

It makes sense. Even as a child, the library had been one of Ember's favorite hiding places from my mother.

From me.

Clenching my jaw, I open one of the doors and step inside the shadowed room. It doesn't take me long to locate her lush, thick body perched on one of the huge armchairs in front of the desk. Her head is bent over an open book, and as I cross the room, she doesn't lift it or acknowledge my presence in any way.

"I didn't take you for a runner, ma."

"I didn't take you for a bitch-made asshole." She flips a page. "No, wait. That's exactly what I've always taken you for."

"Look at me, Ember." When she doesn't, I move to the side of her chair. "I'm not gon' say it again."

Sighing, she closes the book, and the cover reveals the title: *Titus Andronicus*. Shit. I'm not surprised she's reading a tragedy where a man cooks his enemies' sons into a pie and serves it to their mother. She'd appreciate that kind of creative get-back. Hell, I do, too.

She turns in the chair, tilts her head back, and silently meets my gaze.

"I've warned you about that mouth. It's reckless as fuck and gon' write a check that fat, juicy ass can't cash. If anyone else talked to me the way you have tonight, they wouldn't have a tongue."

"So I can't be disrespectful, but you can."

"How have I disrespected you, Ember?"

She barks out a sharp crack of laughter. "Calculated obtuseness isn't a good look, Asad. Do better." Standing, she circles me to the shelves and returns the book. Dragging a disgusted look up and down my frame, she huffs out a rough chuckle and heads toward the doors. "Let me get out of here before I commit bodily harm."

"Nah." I move and step in front of her, blocking her from leaving the library. "You had your chance to leave. Answer the question."

"Nah," she mocks me, curling her lip in a derisive smirk. "Everybody in this house, this *family*"—she sneers the word as if it tastes like deep-fried shit on her tongue—"in this fucking organization bows to you. You get what you want, whether it's by misguided loyalty, that li'l dick that's for everybody, or threats.

Who the fuck tells you no? Well, you know what, muthafucka? No. Dig deep in that problematic brain and figure out the answer to your own question because I'm fresh outta explanations. Ninety-two percent, muthafucka. I'm resting."

Those golden eyes glow with her hatred, and that slick-ass mouth has the same antipathy burning in my chest.

Gotdamn.

I want to choke slam the shit out of her.

I want to fuck the lining out of that pussy.

My fingers curl. Straighten.

Curl.

Straighten.

I can almost feel the flutter of her pulse under my palm. Feel that same tremble around my dick as she stretches to accept me. Molds to me.

Now it's me who takes a step in retreat.

Either that or we're both going to have an epic case of rug burn.

"First, li'l baby," I say, lifting a hand and trailing my thumb over the shallow dent in her chin and down to her throat. It's a mistake to touch her, but one thing she said about me is correct. I get what I want, and I don't deny myself shit. I press the tip of my thumb into the cradle of her collarbone, savoring the evidence of life that flows through her veins. "Ain't nothing little about this dick, and you just talking shit with that one. Second, I stand on me not disrespecting you. When did I do it, Ember? Was it when I introduced you as my fiancée? Was it when I invited you to come up there with me so you could show everyone in that room you're not to be fucked with? Was it when I didn't jack your li'l ass up for saying fuck me in front of Kareem and—"

"Don't say her name to me," she snaps, slashing a hand between us. "Maybe it's when you let her hang all over you like a thrift-store suit or let her sit at your side in a place of honor at your table. Or maybe it's when you crept off to get your dick sucked after a sideshow of murder and torture."

Several moments of silence throb between us like a primitive drumbeat.

Gotdamn. None of that other shit meant a thing to me, but I can see how it would look to her. And possibly others. Yeah, I get it. But . . .

"Didn't shit happen in the study." She scoffs and attempts to move around me, but I shift, blocking her once more. Lowering my head, I shove my face close to hers until I can taste the smokey and citrusy flavor of her whiskey-scented breath. "Didn't shit. Happen. In that. Study."

I stare into her honeyed eyes, not looking away. Letting her see the truth there.

"She tried it. And for a moment, I considered letting her, but only for a moment. Nothing happened, ma," I reiterate.

She releases a shuddering puff of air, and it teases me. I slick my tongue over my lips, catching that whiskey-and-sex taste. Her eyes flare wide, her pupils dilating. I stiffen, for a moment, believing she's going to force-feed me that sweet smoke and fruit air. *Do it, li'l baby. Give it to me.* The rough growl in my head reeks of desperation and demand. Hunger and hope.

And when she withdraws from me, backpedaling until she reaches the desk, rage and revulsion screwing up her face, that growl transforms into a howl that holds nothing but anger and frustration.

And loss.

"I don't really care," Ember lies. The room stinks with that lie. I saw her face in that hallway. It's branded on my brain. "All of it—your bitch, the wives at dinner, and some of the conversation—drove home the hell that awaits me, and you can threaten me and my people, but it's a no for me."

Everything inside me stills, goes dangerously quiet.

"What's a 'no' for you?" I murmur, warning her with my carefully even tone that she better tread real fucking lightly.

"Tonight, I had a preview of what my life would be like

chained to you. Having a courtside seat to Marcus and Michelle's happy union all these years clued me in, but I never saw the side chick up close. At least as far as I saw, Marcus kept the hoes away from his wife. But no, I had to sit at a table with yours." She shakes her head, those beautiful, thick curls brushing her cheeks and shoulders. A sneer rides her mouth, and she lifts her hand, palm out. "That's what I mean by 'no.' Marcus shackled me to this life with guilt, duty, and the foolishly stubborn bits and pieces of love. And you want to do the same thing—chain me to a family, an organization that bears my name but has never bore no love for me. I almost left after leaving that dining room." She waves a hand toward the library door and the rooms beyond it. "But then I decided to stay so I could tell you that you're no better than Marcus, but this time, I'm not handing over my life, my future, my *fucking everything* to you."

I've never experienced panic before.

Not when Michelle sat me and Kareem down and informed us that Dad was in the hospital and it didn't look good.

Not when she beat Ember so badly that she couldn't move for a week.

Not when the security at Marcus's ho pad called and said they'd called several times and couldn't reach him.

So no, panic isn't an emotion I'm familiar with, which may explain why I don't immediately recognize it. But I'm fast becoming intimate with that burning, pressurized tightening of my chest, relieved only by the sensation of razor-sharp claws sinking into my skin.

Only years of battle-won self-control keep me from revealing the chaos roiling inside my body, my head.

But that same control smothers the panic—no, not smothers. It morphs it into something cold, hard like steel. A sword to cut whatever bullshit argument she's about to give me into so many pieces, she won't be able to reassemble them.

She doesn't have to hand a fucking thing over to me.

I'm taking it. Stealing it by any means necessary. Just like I did her inheritance. Don't shit about me say I play fucking fair. Not when it comes to her.

She should really start paying attention.

"You're right." I cross my arms and lean a shoulder against the bookshelf behind me. "I'm not better than Marcus. I'm worse. He gave you some concessions because you were his daughter. I don't possess even an iota of those sentimentalities."

She snorts. "What house did you live in? He didn't give me shit."

"He didn't kill you. I don't have those constrictions."

"Marcus had the paternal instinct of a quokka," she says, rounding the desk, and despite the lingering dregs of anger and disquiet at her threat, I almost laugh. She ain't lying. That muthafucka would launch his own flesh and blood in the path of a gotdamn herd of roaming hyenas if it meant him getting away without a scratch. "I've had time to think about our"—she scoffs—"negotiation yesterday. Tonight only solidified my decisions. You bullied me when I was a girl, but you won't be doing that to the grown woman." She opens and closes several of the drawers until she finds a sheet of paper and a pen and slaps both on top of the desktop. "I would get Sam here to be my legal advisor, but since you know very well he'd kill your ass if he had any clue what you're up to, I'll be my own counsel."

I arch an eyebrow, thoroughly amused. "You think I'm scared of Sam?"

"You should be. It'd be a mistake to underestimate him."

"I don't underestimate him or anyone; only fools are arrogant enough to do that. But, ma, Sam don't put no fear in me. No one does." I dip my chin toward the paper and the pen in her hand. "And I don't negotiate with terrorists."

She sinks into the leather chair, and unbidden, the impression of a beautiful Black queen sitting on her throne invades my mind. Regal. Indomitable. Powerful. And that's how she stares at me with that almost haughty expression and tilted chin—like I'm a peasant beneath her feet.

"You need me more than I need you. House of Cross needs me. Fact. And there's no getting around it," she states. I don't argue with her because we both know it's the truth. "I'm not staying with you."

I tilt my head, maintaining my composure, but in reality, I'm seconds away from jumping over that desk. "The fuck you're not."

"Go ahead, Asad. Go ahead and threaten Perla, Gus, and Jaq. That's not going to work this time."

"No?" I push off the bookshelf and stalk across the room until I reach the desk, flatten my palms on the top, and lean forward. "Since when you know me to bullshit, Ember?"

"Never. I have zero doubts that you would blow away the closest things I can call family right in front of me. But that's not enough to make me indenture myself to you and this fucking organization for the rest of my life just to be used up and eventually discarded. No, been there, done that. Have the dead mother and impulse control disorder to show for it."

She removes the cap from the pen and starts writing.

"Here's what I'm proposing—No marriage. We'll remain engaged for a year. At the end of that time, I'm free to leave House of Cross with my mother's trust and my share of the inheritance my father left me in his will—you keep my voting shares and all stocks in HoC. I want nothing to do with the fashion house or the organization. You can also keep the formula to Glass Slipper, but I continue to receive a thirty percent share of all profit from it. I will retain the formula to HEA for a year after I leave. If, once that period concludes, you honor your end of the contract, I will release the HEA formula to you, with me receiving the same percentage of profit as Glass Slipper. Do you accept these terms?"

"Fuck no." Straightening, I hold my hand out for the pen, which she hands over, mugging me. I cross a line through the first condition. "No to the yearlong engagement and no marriage. We're marrying, and there's no negotiating on that. Your father made it clear that the head of Cross had to marry, and he had the heads of our allies there to sign a document attesting to his wishes."

"Yes, the document you failed to mention yesterday when I asked you why there had to be a marriage. The document I discovered existed along with your brother tonight at the dinner table," she sneers.

"Yeah, that one," I say, unrepentant. If she expects remorse from me, she's in for a long-ass wait. If I'd told Ember about it, that would've been leverage. I'm not in the business of handing my adversaries the advantage. And make no mistake, she's my adversary. "And the month is also nonnegotiable. I announced that tonight and to change it now would weaken my new position with Cross allies, and I refuse to do that so early in my leadership. It's happening, Ember. Wrap your mind around it."

She stares at the paper several moments, then finally lifts her head, pinning me with a honeyed glare.

"Fine, but for a time limit. I'm serious about not spending my life in a loveless, hostile prison. Did the document say anything about not being able to divorce?"

I want to lie to her. It's on the tip of my tongue to do just that—

"No."

Relief washes over her face, and she nods. "Okay, then. We marry, but after three years, I'm able to receive a divorce, and you don't contest it."

Shit, I'm already contesting it. I'm already refusing to let her go, imagining locking her away, holding her hostage until she capitulates and realizes she can't go. She doesn't *want* to go.

I inhale a deep breath, then deliberately exhale, looking away from her. Only when the dull roar and thoughts of marital kidnapping swirling in my head are under control do I return my attention to her.

"Yeah, I agree." I focus on the next item on her list. "I already offered you the trust and the portion of the estate Marcus left to you. The thirty-four percent is also yo—"

She shakes her head so hard, her curls whip around her face. "No, I said what I said. I don't want any parts of HoC. They're yours. Hell, they weren't really mine anyway since Marcus made sure I didn't have voting control," she says, bitterness coating her tone.

Though Marcus's decision granted me more power, I can still admit it was a mark-ass move. Especially for a so-called father to his daughter.

"If that's what you want, I can't do anything but respect it. As far as Glass Slipper, fifteen percent of the profits."

Her head jerks back, and she barks out a laugh. "The fuck? That's all me. You lucky I'm not asking for fifty since you wouldn't have shit to sell or have a delivery system if it weren't for me. Thirty."

"Twenty."

"Thirty."

"Twenty-five."

"Thirty."

A reluctant smile tugs at the corner of my mind. I was willing to give that thirty percent to her all along; I was just curious to see how hard she'd fight for it. This is Ember though. I should've known.

"As far as HEA, that's still in the works for HoC," I continue, circling the last item on her list. "As far as I know, it's still not perfected. How close are you to having it distribution-ready? Because that affects our discussion on it."

"I'm close. It tested well with our focus group, but there are some things I want to fine-tune. I'm saying another two weeks. Three at the most."

"Okay." The woman was a fucking beast at what she did. "Here's my counter with HEA. You retain the formula for three months after you leave." She frowns, parting her lips to argue, but I shake my head, stopping her. "Let me finish. In those three months, we would be dependent on you to still supervise the cooking of the drug, which means you'd continue to have a foot in the company even after you've officially walked away from it. I can't have that. We'll be divorced. You'll no longer work here. But you'll still have access to Cross facilities? Personnel? To sensitive information? Nah, that's not good business, and it puts you in a dangerous position as well. So, three months, and in exchange, you receive thirty-five percent of the profits from HEA."

She contemplates my suggestion, and after a long pause, she dips her chin.

"You have a deal." Turning the paper around, she slides it across the desk. "Put those changes down, then sign the bottom."

I blink.

"Fucking seriously, ma?"

"Completely fucking seriously. If Lionel Messi's first contract was written on a napkin and was binding, ours should hold up, too." She taps the top of the paper. "I'll wait."

"Nah." I fold my arms across my chest, still holding the pen. "There are a few more things we have to discuss since we're putting everything down in a . . . contract." She sighs, and I'ma let that slide. For now. "I don't know what you have planned in your head, but this will be a real marriage. No separate residences. You'll be living with me as husband and wife."

"Oh hell no," she balks, backing away from the desk as if creating distance between my words. "I'm not giving up my home for this shit that's not even real. That's my property. My . . . *mine*. I'm not abandoning the only peace I have."

"I'm not demanding you have to sell it. Keep it. Rent it out. Hold on to it. I really don't give a fuck. But in four weeks, you will be moving into my home and living with me for the next three years."

She laughs, but it's caustic, resentful. And her gaze gleams with those same emotions.

As well as fear.

My stomach hollows, as if a huge spoon scraped it out. The fuck? I doubt she's even aware of what that stare holds. If she did, I know for a fact, Ember wouldn't allow me to see it. She's been fly at the mouth with me, stood up to me in ways no one else would dare if they valued breathing.

So what . . . ?

"What're you afraid of?" I bluntly ask.

"What?" she snaps. "I'm not afraid of shit."

"Yeah, you are. You're mad as fuck. And right now you want to go for my throat. But you're also afraid. Don't bullshit me. What is it?"

She starts to shake her head, but then stops and turns away from me, tunneling her fingers through her hair. In a moment so quick that if I wasn't obsessively watching her, I would've missed it, her shoulders sink, as if a huge weight bears down on her. On instinct, I move forward, about to round the desk and get to her, but before that step is completed, she straightens, those same shoulders drawing back, her back arrow straight. And when she pivots to face me again, she's expressionless except for the small smile touching her mouth.

"Don't bullshit you." The smile deepens but it's heavy with disdain instead of humor. "Okay. Let me ask you a question instead. Can you think of any reason why I would object to living with you again? Especially given how truly fucked-up the last time we cohabited went? You really believe I would willingly consign myself to that hell again?" she asks, her voice rising with each question.

Fury pours through me, burning like a corrosive acid. I'm flush with it, fucking sweating. I backpedal several steps because if I don't . . . if I don't, I just might take my anger out on that pussy or throw her through that window—it's a toss-up.

All these years and she still doesn't fucking *see*.

And short of stapling her fucking eyelids to her forehead, I can't force her to.

"Willingly or not, it is what it is. And come four weeks from now, your li'l ass is going to be in my house as my lawfully wedded wife. Being happy isn't a requirement of this arrangement. Fake that muthafucka."

"I'm not faking shit," she shouts, slapping her hand down on the desk. "If you wanted a phony bitch like your mother, you should've had that ho who was just sucking your dick marry you. Fuck I look like pretending to be ignorant of or delighted with my *husband* slinging dick all over the fucking West Coast while I bury myself in a lab earning his ass money. You got me fucked-up. Michelle might've been okay with looking like a fool for Marcus as long as he threw a black card and jewelry her way. But I'm not her. Never will be."

"You seem real preoccupied with my dick, Ember."

Pure, unadulterated joy and brutal lust punch through me, so strong my veins sizzle with the power. My body sways a bit before I go still.

Even across the distance that separates us, I catch the stiffening of her voluptuous frame. I wish I would stop myself from tracing the heavy, full curves of her breasts, the deep valley between them bared by that jacket that I both want to worship and incinerate. Her catch of breath is as loud as a bullet's report as I don't conceal my open scrutiny of the lushness of her hips and that fat, perfect ass that I can see even though she's facing me. The high-waisted pants only emphasize those thick-ass thighs, and shit, I want to switch out the diamond studs in my ears and wear those instead. Li'l baby got a sick-as-fuck body. I have to suppress an almost animalistic urge to make her list every man who had the pleasure of exploring it so I can take their lives before our wedding. It'll be her gift to me.

"And you seem real enamored with it," she sneers, although there's still a little tremor threading through her voice. "My point remains. If you're expecting me to be one of these silent, turn-a-blind-eye Mafia wives, then you're going to be disappointed. I match energy and body count."

That has me charging across the room and in her face, backing her up against the curtained window. Slapping my palms on either side of her head, I cage her in between the glass and my body. I lower my head, then my hand, and slowly wrap it around the front of her throat. Given the nature of our . . . history, I don't tighten my grip—I don't hurt her—but it's firm enough to let her know I can. At any time, I can.

"Say it again. I dare you. Tell me again how you're going to give away my pussy."

She glares up at me, fisting my shirt at my waist. Unease shimmers in her golden eyes, but it's nearly drowned out by the anger. Anger and more. It's the *more* that has my hand remaining around her neck.

"Ain't nothing over this way yours," she says. And I would've believed she meant that shit if not for the shivering in her voice.

"Nothing?"

"No."

"You sure about that?" I murmur, pressing my fingertips into the sides of her throat, savoring the throbbing of her pulse against my palm.

Her grip on my shirt tightens, and it pulls taut across my stomach. I inch closer, answering that unconscious plea for me to invade her personal space. The tremble that was in her voice transfers to her body, and I absorb it, take a dark, vicious delight in it.

"Yes," she whispers, her gaze lowering to my chin.

"Nah, look at me," I order her, and when she obeys, those honeyed eyes snapping up to meet mine, pleasure and surprise wing through me. I lower my other hand from the wall and, with my gaze still on hers, cuff that fat flesh between her thighs. A high, shocked whine escapes her and she shoots to her toes, but I follow her. I open my mouth on her jaw, sucking it, drawing hard on the flesh in a wet kiss that gifts me with another of those cries. With a low hum, I drag my tongue up her cheek until I get to her ear. "If this pussy"—I squeeze her flesh harder and grind the heel of my palm against her clit—"ain't mine, then why is it so fucking hot and wet, I can feel it through these pants? Huh? Tell me something, ma."

Head tipped back and teeth sunk into her ripe bottom lip, Ember doesn't speak to me. But her face does. It's saturated, fucking drenched with pleasure, with hot, grimy need. Her chest heaves, and those big, rounded hips move like she's working somebody's fucking pole, riding my hand. Seeking what I'm holding just out of reach for her.

Taking a chance, I tighten my grip on her throat just as I press hard on her clit.

She gasps, her eyes flaring so wide I can read every emotion in their light brown depths. Shock. Lust. Uncertainty. Her body stiffens, and then a shudder rips through her like a seizure. I frown even as her lashes lower and soft whimpers break on her parted lips. Her hips continue to buck, but the rhythm is jerky, uncoordinated. My frown deepens.

The fuck?

"Muthafucka, did you just nut?" She doesn't reply, but the small aftershocks shaking her body like a leaf supply my answer. Shit. Lust and the hot lick of possession roar inside of me, searing me from the inside out. *This* is what I wanted. All these years of watching, waiting, this right here is what I wanted, hungered for. Not just her coating those panties in that juice I need on my tongue. But her desiring me. Her needing me. Her pussy hot to fuck me. *That's* what I wanted. And now that I have it, literally in my hand, I'm damn near feral and ain't no turning back. I chuckle and, dipping my head, clamp my teeth around the tendon running down the side of her throat. "You know you done fucked up, right?"

Snatching my hands from between her legs and from her neck, I grab her hand and haul her the few feet from the window to the desk. Trapping her between my body and the furniture, I press my chest to her back, almost bending her over as I pick up the pen, slide our "contract" closer to us, and hurriedly scribble the item regarding our living arrangements to the bottom, along with—

"We're fucking," she reads the last condition. "Seriously?"

I sign the bottom of the paper and slap the pen down on top. "Sign it."

When she's slow to move, I pinch her chin and turn her head to the side so she can look at me. My thumb skims over the sexy little dent in her chin before migrating north to her plump bottom lip, rubbing over it. Her dark red lipstick stains my skin as I make a mess of hers. I'm not gon' lie. This might be the prettiest, the sexiest, I've ever seen her.

Freshly fucked.

I like this look on her.

Nah, I fucking love it.

"You brought this contract to me, making demands. I did my part," I remind her. "Now it's time to do yours and see it through. You knew who you were coming to with this. You even knew I wouldn't go for that engagement bullshit. If I didn't know better, I'd suspect you wanted me to press you into the marriage. Why? So you can convince yourself later that you didn't have a choice? I mean, you don't, but this way you can make yourself believe you tried and I'm the big bad in your story. Again, you're not wrong. Since you went to all this trouble, let me not disappoint." I pick up the pen off the desk, press it into her palm, and fist her fingers around it. With my free hand, I cuff the back of her neck, applying slight pressure. She initially resists me, body slightly stiffening. But then her back bows, muscles loosening. When she leans forward, I do as well and deliver a sloppy, nasty kiss to her nape, tonguing the flesh as I would that dick tease of a mouth. "Sign it, Ember," I growl in her ear.

She hesitates, but when I push my large frame harder against her, grinding my dick against her ass, she bows her head . . . and signs the paper.

Like an atomic bomb detonates inside me, I explode into

motion, sweeping the contract, pen, lamp, and other shit off the desktop. Spinning Ember around, I cup her small waist and hike her up in the air, then set her down on top of the furniture.

I wrap a hand around the front of her neck and don't miss the shiver that races through her. This is what I'm talking about. She just came from me just cupping that pussy and already she's aroused again. So fucking responsive. I dreamed of this, fantasized about how she would quiver at my touch, come apart under it. If that beautiful brown skin would redden from me just dragging my tongue down her cheek. Now I know.

And now that I do? No one and no thing is safe.

Especially this pussy.

I'm wrecking it with my mouth, fingers, dick. By the time I'm finished, these walls will crumble at just the sound of my gotdamn voice because they recognize their owner.

"There's no tapping out, Ember." I lick a path up her throat, just above my palm, and drag it over to her ear because I need for her to hear every word. "This is your one and only chance to tell me no, because after that, I'm punishing you for making me wait all this time, all these years. So tell me now if you want to walk out of here."

Three seconds. That's all I give her, but they're the longest fucking three seconds of my life.

And in that short span of time, she shakes her head.

"No," she whispers.

"No what, ma?" I nip her earlobe, suck it hard. "No what?"

"No, I'm not walking out of here."

A damn near feral growl rolls out of me, and I crash my mouth to hers. Her fresh, tangy flavor explodes in my mouth and I lap it up. Suck it off her tongue, lick it off the roof of her mouth. I'm loose, wild, and though a voice in the back of my head whispers to slow down, I can't. Fuck that. I won't. She better keep up.

"This ain't gon' be slow, baby girl," I warn her, dropping my hands to the top of her pants. Within seconds, I have them unbuttoned and, hooking my fingers in the open flaps and the band of her panties, I roughly drag them down over her wide, sexy hips and down those thick, round, dimpled thighs.

Her gasp and soft "wait" force me to step back even though I just told her I wasn't stopping. But I do. I pause for her. Grant her the opportunity I need—to get a hold of myself before I say fuck it and drive myself deep in those slick, tight walls.

Ember sits there on top of the desk, half-naked, blinking up at me as if a little lost. A hand lifts to her hair, then drops back to the top of her thigh as if she's unsure what to do with herself. The same hand flutters between her legs, attempting to hide my shit from me. I didn't think I could get any harder at that small, probably unintentional show of innocence. But shit, here we are.

"You good?" I rasp at her, my gaze dropping to that brown and pink bald pussy that glistens in the library's weak light. "Move your hands."

She hesitates, but then shifts them away, dropping them to either side of her legs. Swollen folds of the loveliest pussy I've ever seen are on display. Making my mouth water.

Gotdamn, I need a taste.

"What do you think you're doing, carrying around that fat, pretty mu'fucka, Ember?" Shrugging out of my jacket, I let it fall and go for the buttons on my shirt. Impatient, I jerk at the sides and don't even flinch at the sound of them hitting the floor. My skin is hot, my body is burning, and I need air and all that thick juice decorating her bottom lips to rub over me.

"Fuck, baby girl." I shake my head like a ravenous dog. "How can you be so beautiful? Don't make no gotdamn sense," I murmur to myself.

Approaching her, I grip the back of her neck, hold her still as I stroke my free hand up her thigh and cup that pussy, grind the heel of my palm against her clit. She gasps again, arching tight and strong into me, pressing those gorgeous breasts into my chest. I need eyes and hands on those, too. I'm going a little crazy, desperate. Suddenly wishing I had more mouths and hands on deck so I could multitask. But just one dick. I don't need more than one because I don't like to share. I'm a jealous mu'fucka.

Her sticky heat coats my hand, flooding it. Unable to help myself, I lift it to my mouth and lick all that fresh, sweet essence clean. The unparalleled flavor bursts on my tongue, and in one hit, I'm hooked. I'm addicted.

"You gon' let me eat this pussy?"

She gives me a fervent nod of her head, and that's all I need.

Releasing her neck, I fall to my knees in front of her, and glancing up her trembling thighs, rounded belly, and still-clothed chest, I meet the nerves in those pretty eyes. Still, she props herself up on her palms, and I don't even have to say "get those eyes on me." They're already there.

Trailing a burning path up her leg from her knee to the crease where her torso and thighs meet, I bow my head and dive into heaven. Into hell. Into mine.

Her sharp cry echoes in the room as I swirl my tongue around her clit, then place an almost chaste kiss on it. That juicy button of flesh flinches, swells, and a rumble rolls in my chest.

"That's what the fuck I'm talking about. She knows me, ma."

"Asad," Ember whines, and I reward that pretty sound with a hard, long lick up her slit.

Ember screams, her ass clenching, lifting off the desk, and I hum my pleasure into her sex. Her body jerks, and I wrap my hands around her hips, holding her still.

"God, Asad, no. What? I don't . . ." Words tumble from her in a frantic, frenzied free fall, and my dick jumps in my pants, demanding it have what my mouth enjoys. I'm fucking hurting, in pain from wanting to slide inside of her, to ease this ache that's clawing at me, roaring at me.

Fuck her. Fuck her. Claim her. Mark her.

I've gone animalistic, and it ain't shit I can do about it. But eat. And eat some more. Fire. With a groan that vibrates against her flesh, I taste, suck, and tongue her, leaving no inch of her unexplored. She writhes and twists, my puppet, my plaything.

My fucking everything.

Feverish cries punctuate the air, and I gently bite a fold, then suck on it hard. Fractured pleas caress my ears, and I rim her entrance with a fingertip. Then plunge a finger deep.

Her sex sucks at me, and damn, I knew she'd be tight, but this is almost ridiculous. I manage to wedge in one, working her, loosening her. Ember stiffens, her body going taut and not out of pleasure. I know the difference. When I glance up, her eyes are squeezed shut, her eyebrows drawn tight in a pained frown.

"Relax, ma," I urge. "Relax and let me in."

It's either been a long time or whoever she called herself being with wasn't hitting it right. Gradually, her muscles loosen, and I push her legs wider apart. I withdraw my finger, then dip back inside her, trailing a caress along the sensitive skin connecting her sex and ass. She moans, going still again, and I shush her. After some coaxing, I get inside her, and with a groan at the extra-small, extra-tight fit, I latch on to her clit, tonguing it, French-kissing it.

"Oh God, please," she begs.

"That's it," I praise, continuing to thrust in and out of her, getting her good and wet and messy. "You tight as fuck, baby girl. Somebody ain't been hitting it right. But that's aight. I'm about to take care of that."

Her thighs shake around my ears, and I hook my finger, rubbing the tip against that spot high within her. And she explodes, splinters.

Not giving her any time to recover, I grab at my pants, jerking and shoving until they pool at my feet. Kicking them away, I move forward between her legs and cup them, hiking them high to ride my waist. My breath heaves in my chest, my heart a primal drum against my sternum as I notch my dick at her entrance.

"Asad, wait." Ember splays her fingers wide against my bare chest, and I push them away, focused on burying myself inside this pussy, this woman who has tormented me for years. But she cups my face, forcing my head up to meet her eyes. "Asad, I need to tell you the truth. I . . ." She swallows, and both impatience and tenderness well within me. "I haven't done this before. I'm a virgin."

Shock pummels me with meaty fists, and I rock back, almost losing my grip on her. Shaking my head, I stare down at her, wanting to tell her to stop lying, but the truth shines in her eyes. The nerves, the traces of fear that can't be hidden by the glaze of lust.

"The fuck, Ember," I breathe. Shook.

"I know, I should've told you sooner—"

I smother her words with my mouth as a fierce, primitive joy surges in my chest, my soul. I've called her mine, but gotdamn. She is. All. Mine. No one has touched her, has been inside her. As hypocritical and misogynistic as that sounds, I don't give a fuck. I'm happy. She only knows me. She only belongs to me.

"Let me in, Ember." I slowly push forward, penetrating her. Her tight flesh resists me, but I don't stop. Just the tip stretches her, and she whimpers, cries out, the clasp of her stealing my breath. "I want in, baby. If it takes all night, you're going to let me in this pussy. It's mine, and you're going to give it to me."

I withdraw, then thrust. Withdraw, then thrust. With every slide forward, I claim more of her until I'm completely seated inside and she's pried open, bare, full of me.

"I can't," she pleads, tipping her head back.

"You're doing so good, Ember," I praise, kissing her cheeks, her mouth, her chin. "You took all of me like I knew you could. Just like a good girl." I stop, feeling her flesh flutter and quiver around my dick, attempting to let her acclimate to the power and size of me.

Soon, she starts shifting, moving underneath me, and I loose a low chuckle.

"That's it, ma." I reach between us, sweeping a caress over her clit. She cries out, flinches, but I keep up the featherlight caress. "That's it, Ember. Get your dick, baby girl."

Finally free to move, I withdraw until only the tip remains in a chokehold by that tight-ass pussy and then plunge back inside, pressing my balls to the bottom curves of her ass. She screams, the sound muffled against my shoulder, but still echoing in the room.

"Look at me." I wait as she obeys me, tilting her head back, staring at me with lust-glazed eyes. With a low growl, I wrap my fingers around her throat, squeezing hard enough for her eyes to widen then flare brighter. Hotter. In reaction, my hand tightens, and her throaty moan is like the wettest, dirtiest hand job. "You know you done fucked up, right?" With my grip still around her neck, I thrust harder, riding her deep, and she writhes, undulating into each drive of my dick. "You let me in this pussy. She knows me. Knows who she belongs to. Sucking me deep like a hot mouth. Fucking gripping me tight." Another hard, heavy stroke. Another firm squeeze of her throat. "Mine, gotdamnit. Mine. Give my shit away, and a mu'fucka's death gon' be on you."

She whimpers, and I cover those luscious lips in a nasty kiss. For the next several minutes, whimpers, groans, and grunts punch the air along with slaps of sweat-drenched skin against skin. The suction of her flesh releasing and welcoming me inside her. It's lewd, carnal, raw. Beautiful.

"Asad. Fuck, Asad," she cries, and I go harder, a grimace twisting my face, passion and pain contorting hers. "I'm about to . . . I have to . . . Help me, please."

Placing an open-mouthed, hot kiss along the side of her neck and the crook where neck and shoulder meet, I deliver a sharp, firm pat to her clit and another stroke.

Her legs quiver, her head flies back and the scream she releases will live in my memory until I draw my last breath. Her pussy clamps down on my dick, and I fall over the edge with her. Hammering at her, I empty everything I got inside her.

And one word fills my head as I shudder, losing every ounce of control and sanity.

Mine.

CHAPTER NINE

Ember

"Sooo . . . Something you need to tell us? I don't know." Jaq shrugs, sliding their hands in the front pockets of their purple plaid suspender pants. "Anything you'd like to get off your chest? Maybe—just a wild guess here, but—an engagement?"

Shit.

I pinch the bridge of my nose, squeezing it. The headache behind my right eye throbs a little harder. Not only did I not get a lot of sleep last night—my mind instinctually skirts away from *why* I didn't—but I had to be at the lab early to meet Perla, Gus, and Jaq to update them on the change in plans. And I needed to do that in the secret lab at HoC where we would be safe from any eyes and ears before the workday started. A pain unfurls in my chest, and I rub the small ping. I can't help but think how we should have been in the lab at my house by now, but because of recent events, this will continue to be our home for at least the next three years. I have to remind myself a dream deferred is not a dream denied.

"Please tell me how you're aware of that, given the announcement was made just last night to a select amount of people at a private dinner," I say, dropping my arm and fixing a steady, unblinking stare on them.

But this is Jaq, so they are completely unbothered by the threat implicit in my voice. They prop their arm on the shelf holding the tablets and shrug.

"I have my sources." When I tilt my head and narrow my eyes, they smile. "Perla. Perla is my sources."

I silently groan and shift my attention to my lead lab assistant.

"The fuck, Perla."

"Justus came over last night," she says with a chagrined smile. Adjusting her glasses, she holds up her hands, palms out. "We fucked and then had a little pillow talk afterward."

"In other words, she put the power of the pussy on him, and he confessed his Social Security number, where Jimmy Hoffa was buried, and every detail of what went down at that dinner last night." Jaq snorts. "Hard to believe the unassuming li'l pixie got the Jaws of Life between her legs."

Perla grins, skimming her purple bangs out of her eyes and picking up one of the cups of coffee that I brought in for the four of us this morning since I called them in so early.

"Are you attached to Justus?"

She's no fool; she knows what I'm asking. This Justus could be a loyal Cross soldier—if he was allowed to be in attendance last night, then chances are he is—but obviously his mouth runs like a geriatric bladder. If a good nut can make him gossip about an engagement, then how easily would he tell other shit under the right, or wrong, circumstances? Nah, Justus gotta go. Like I said, Perla understands my reasons for asking about her affection for this man. Yet, her smile doesn't slip as she shakes her head.

"Not particularly."

I nod and pull out my cell phone. Reluctantly, I text the burner phone of the one person I intended to avoid for at least the next month, letting him know he has a leak in the house that needs to be tightened up. I follow it up with an emoji of a set of scales. Before I can tuck the phone away, it pings with a reply. An "Okay." That's it, that's all. I don't know why I expected a little more. Something a little more . . . personal. I mean, just because I gave Asad my virginity and he reshaped my pussy so it now looks like a mold of his dick, that's no reason for him to text me anything more than "Okay." Just because he sucked the lining and the soul out of my pussy doesn't mean he should've asked if I was "Okay."

Dammit.

I stuff the cell back in the pocket of my lab coat and violently shut down that line of thought, in turn sending another bolt of pain to my temples.

Focus on immediate business and not how my guts were rearranged.

"Since you already know about my"—my mouth twists, and I clench my jaw before grinding out—"engagement, this changes things up for us. Plans to move this lab to my property? They will have to be postponed."

"For how long?" Gus asks with a frown, straightening up from his sprawl in the chair where we do our experimenting on the test subjects.

"Three years."

"The fuck?" he snaps, crossing his arms over his barrel chest.

"What he said," Jaq cosigns. "What's going on?"

I sigh, running a hand over my hair. "The abridged version is this marriage with Asad isn't by choice, but I had to make the best out of a fucked-up situation." I deliberately leave out the part about the threat to their lives. "I have to stay married and an employee of Cross for three more years before I'm completely free, no ties except for a percentage of the profits from Glass Slipper and HEA."

"What about Fairy Dust?" Perla frowns. "We're closer than ever to perfecting it. Are you going to put that on hold for three years, too?"

I'm already shaking my head. "Hell no. We're going forth with that as planned. I already have a distributor lined up. His territory is in the South—from Atlanta to Miami. So there's no conflict with Cross. For now." Relief passes over their faces. "And to be clear, we're partners in this. I might have designed the drug, but you three have been invaluable in bringing it to fruition.

Same with Glass Slipper and HEA. When the time comes, we'll take numbers so you'll receive a percentage of those profits as well. You've more than earned it."

"Ember, you don't have to—"

"Speak for yourself," Jaq cuts Gus off. "Don't be blocking my blessing."

Perla giggles, while Gus mugs Jaq. And I find my first smile of the day.

"I know three years sounds like a long time; I get it," I say, holding my hands up, palms out in the age-old gesture of *hold on*. "But it's just a setback. In the meantime, we could use that time to design another drug after we see how Fairy Dust does in the streets. The time will fly by, and then we'll all be free of this place and this organization."

I try to inject optimism into my voice, but if the raised eyebrows and scrunched noses are anything to go by, I failed. Epically.

"Shit, fine." I sigh. "These next three years are going to be long as a muthafucka and probably just as hard, but we can use them to our advantage so we come out of it set for life."

"That has to be the most depressing pep talk ever," Gus says after a long, silent moment.

Jaq nods. "Big facts."

"Ember." Perla studies me from behind her blue-and-gold frames. "Are you good? I feel like there's more to this than you're sharing with us."

That's the trouble when your employees become friends—they come to see beneath the facade. But as badly as I need to share this burden with someone, I can't. Not only am I still their boss, but keeping the whole truth from them is for their protection. They may work for the Cross organization, but they're still not privy to the inner workings and information that could have them end up like Carter.

And I love them enough to continue to shield them from that possible ending.

"I'm fine." I don't force a smile because they would see right through it. "Did I foresee this happening? No. But it is what it is, and this is just another pool of bullshit I have to wade through." I retrieve my cell from my pocket again. "It's seven. Let's head out to the main lab."

Seeming to get that I'd like to drop the subject, they walk ahead of me to the door. Within moments, we exit and step into the sterile room to begin our day. Jaq, Perla, and Gus move to their stations, and it doesn't take long before they're immersed in their work.

As I head to the temperature-controlled cabinet to grab a sample of HEA, my phone chimes with a notification. I remove my cell from my lab coat pocket once again and glance down at the screen. A text box from Asad fills the bottom of the screen. I tap on it and scan the message and frown.

"The hell?" I mutter, reading the words on the screen for a second time, and then a third.

But no, they remain the same. Asad is demanding my presence in the conference room on the second floor. A burst of emotions scatter through me—confusion, disquiet, nervousness.

In all my years of working at HoC, I've never been called to the second floor, the secure space where Cross business is discussed. I've had no reason to—as a woman, I had no place there. So to be summoned to the inner sanctum of the organization now . . .

"Hey, I'll be back. I have a meeting. Not sure how long this will take, but I'll text if it's going to be longer than a couple of hours," I inform Perla, Gus, and Jaq.

Rightfully, the three of them glance up, wearing matching expression of bewilderment. They, too, recognize I've never been asked to attend a meeting. It's not just unusual, it's an aberration.

"Okay," Perla says, drawing the word out. She looks over her shoulder at the other two before returning her gaze to me. "Just hit us with a thumbs-up text in the group chat or something to let us know you're good."

"Or alive," Jaq adds. They're not joking.

Shit, me neither.

I nod, then turn and head for the lab door and slip out of my white coat. Minutes later, I step out of the elevator onto the second floor, and my footsteps are swallowed by the oatmeal-colored carpet.

Nerves jump in my stomach like a live wire. I'm not sure what I'm walking into, or why I'm walking into it at all. And there's no noise leaking from the closed doors on either side of the corridor to give me any hint since this whole floor is soundproof. The hallway is no different from any other in this building: carpet, generic photographs of famous LA hotspots and landscapes on the wall, just . . . plain and nondescript.

This space is the perfect setup. To the curious eye, all they see are business-casual-dressed employees entering the Castle, showing up for work, but they're not the everyday personnel of a fashion house. Unlike the designers, artists, publicists, and other HoC staff, the people entering the lobby are drug dealers, smugglers, thieves, killers. My grandfather and Marcus were the kings of "hide in plain sight." It's the reason why the Feds and law enforcement have never built a case around or even suspected House of Cross of fronting one of the largest drug empires on the West Coast. Well, that, and Marcus, just like my grandfather did, had most of the LAPD and high-ranking officials in the FBI in his back pocket, loyal to him by money and secrets.

Following the directions of the text Asad sent me, once I reach the door of the conference room, I notice the black box beside the jamb. I press my hand to it, and a blue light flashes, scanning my print. Seconds later, the lock clicks, and I pull the handle and enter the room.

Like the corridor outside, the conference room resembles any other that graces the floors of the Castle. A long, rectangular glass table bisects the room, bodies parked in the leather rolling chairs on either side of it. More of those chairs line the walls. A large monitor hangs suspended from the ceiling at the front of the room, ready for someone to hook up their laptop and display a presentation across its screen.

The main difference between this room and the one on the executive level is that about thirty lethal members of a crime family occupy these chairs instead of CEOs and marketing staff.

As if on cue, every head turns in my direction. Except for Asad. Standing at the front of the long glass table, his gaze is already on me. And of everyone, it's his gaze that's the heaviest. His that's the most . . . intimate. His that sends a rush of heat rushing through me like Noah's flood and has my poor abused pussy clenching around an emptiness that now is shaped like his dick.

I recognize several people in the room, including Sam and my stepfamily. And Deacon and Xavier. Surprise whispers through me at their attendance. I flick a glance at Asad. What game is he playing, allowing traitors and his would-be killers in the room?

To my further shock, not only is Michelle seated at the table, but so are several other women. Though beautiful, they all bear that sharp-edged, hardened demeanor of those who've seen a lot of things and done more.

He beckons me forward with a curl of his fingers.

The nerves that beset me in the hall dial up a notch, but damned if I'll let him or anyone in this cavernous room peep it. As much as I hate the bastard, Marcus's neglect and rejection are the gifts that keep on giving—they've empowered me with the talent to exude I-don't-give-a-fuck-ness like the loud-ass special-edition perfume HoC rolls out at Christmas.

So as I stride toward the only available seat next to Asad, with each step my sore thighs and vagina reminding me exactly what I had been up to last night. I lift my head up and my shoulders are back and straight. I meet every stare with a calm that is challenged by the whirlwind of questions in my head and twisting in my belly.

I approach Asad, and he doesn't bother to hide his molten perusal of my body in the black pinstripe suit with the matching corset top underneath the jacket. His nostrils slightly flare, and my nipples tighten in response. For a moment, I can feel his mouth at my breasts, feel his teeth grazing the tips before tugging on the piercings. Feel his tongue soothing the small sting with slow, thorough sucks and licks.

Shit.

Thank God this suit is black. Otherwise this whole damn room would have a front-row seat to the wet spot between my legs. Unable to hold his hot, silver stare, I glance away and crash right into Michelle's. The gleaming hatred there does the job of cooling the unwanted and resented lust for her son. I can always count on my stepmother to reality-slap me, to remind me that I don't stand among friends or colleagues. I'm among strangers and potential enemies—because unknowns are enemies until they're not.

I smile my thanks at Michelle.

Movement next to her draws my attention, and I notice Kareem. Unlike last night, his expression is closed off, distant. The flattened mouth and narrowed eyes don't give off disdain and animosity like his mother's, but this is not the man that joked with me either.

"Ember, have a seat right here." Asad motions to an empty chair at the head of the table and to the left of his. Reluctantly, I sink into the seat with a suspicion of what's about to come. "Thank you all for coming to this meeting on such short notice. I'll try not to keep you too long, but there are some things we need to discuss that can't be put off. The sooner we address them, the sooner and stronger we can move into this next phase of the Cross organization."

He takes a step back, and that steady gray gaze moves over the room, landing on each person. The protracted silence skates on, uncomfortable, but Asad seems unbothered by it. Power emanates from him, and it rolls through the air like crackling surges that skip over skin, lifting hair.

Goddamn.

It's not fair that one man has a soul so black, but is this

damn fine. The intricate stitch braids from last night still look neat and beautiful, as does his thick, glistening beard that frames his full lips. The navy-blue, three-piece suit fits him like it's obsessed with his ass, fawning over those wide shoulders and chest, clinging to that washboard stomach and strong, powerful thighs. When God was creating him, He said, *Nah, been here, done that*, and just passed him off to Satan to finish the job.

"You've no doubt already picked up on some of the changes, but still, look around you. Note the people in this room." I did as Asad directed even though I'd already done so when I first entered the conference room. One person I didn't see? Justus. "This is the new leadership of the Cross organization."

Murmurs and a low grumbling ripple through the space.

"Quiet," Asad orders in a low, even voice, and the noise instantly silences. "I understand the long tradition of this family, and I respect it. But traditions are guides, not gatekeepers. They shouldn't hold us back from progress and change."

"Not all change is good change," an older man with a thick salt-and-pepper beard sitting near the other end of the table says. Several people shift in their chairs, their discomfort obvious. While others nod, agreeing with this sentiment.

"Doesn't mean it's not needed either. Without the infusion of something new, innovative, and fresh, the old will grow stagnant and fade away into obscurity or death. No one here wants that, and it's not going to happen on my watch. And don't interrupt me again." The threat in Asad's voice holds the promise of blood and a thousand screams. Yes, I might be a little dramatic, but then again, not in this instance. The older soldier dips his chin and leans back in his chair. "As I was saying, there will be changes going forward. The first and most obvious being the inclusion of women in our leadership and organization. All respect to Marcus and the Cross men before him, but it's foolish to discount the strength, talents, and intelligence women have to offer this organization simply because they don't have dicks. Nah, we're Black men, and no one knows more than us that we're our strongest and most complete when our queens are beside us. And if that includes busting guns, if that's what they choose, then we in this shit together."

Well, damn.

My breath whistles between my ears, my pulse just as loud.

My pussy is ten times wetter.

"If anyone has an issue with that, now is your chance to leave—your one and only chance. If you remain seated in your chair, I'm assuming you're good with this change." He pauses. And under his scrutiny, no one utters a word. "Good. This next one shouldn't come as much of a surprise to anyone. Marcus had his advisors, and so will I. So thank you, Xavier, Deacon, and Malcolm, for your service, leadership, and loyalty. I know Marcus valued your friendship and wisdom."

Oh shit.

Shots fired.

He's sitting Xavier, Deacon, and Malcolm down. It's a move that's shocking. But . . . isn't. Asad would be a fool to keep them as his officers when their loyalty is questionable. And you can say many things about Asad Prince—trust and believe, I do—but being a fool isn't one of them. But demoting them is one thing. Killing them for attempting to take you out is something different, and I still don't understand why Asad's toying with them.

Unable to help myself, I peek across the table where Marcus's second and counselor sit. Xavier, a distinguished older man with wavy salt-and-pepper hair in a large frame draped in a tailored Italian suit, wears a congenial smile, but it doesn't reach his hazel eyes, and if his hands clasp any tighter, he might crack his own bones. Deacon, smaller in build than Xavier, with a gleaming bald head and dark brown eyes, stares at Asad with no hint of emotion. It's unsettling, but it's also more honest than the polite smile curving Xavier's mouth.

"Xavier, Deacon, Malcolm, we can speak specifics afterward about the change in your organizational roles going forward. But rest assured, there's always a place for you here."

He shifts his attention away from them after delivering the verbal version of a pink slip, and I don't know whether to be impressed by his lack of fucks or horrified by his cavalier pop-lock with death. Because I don't need to be a mentalist or body language specialist to peep that both Xavier and Deacon crave it. Even if I weren't aware of their betrayals, the coldness in their gazes as they watch Asad would put me up on game.

"All of you probably know my people, but let me reintroduce you. Eli Rodney, my new second. Samuel Chavis, my advisor."

Another current of murmurings undulates on the air, and I can't blame them. Shock catapults through me, and I jerk my head in Sam's direction. Traditionally, the leadership were members of the organization. Though being Marcus's best friend made him privy to all the workings of the Cross empire, Sam belongs to the corporate side. As if he's been lying in wait, he meets my gaze with a steady one of his own. The other night in the library, he never mentioned being one of Asad's newly appointed officers. Hell, I didn't even think the two liked each other. Oh, Sam has some explaining to do.

"And Makeda Hannah as my enforcer."

If discovering Sam's new appointment caused a stir, the announcement of a woman being in a key high-ranking position incites a tsunami that rushes through the room with shrieking winds.

"This is going too far," the same man from earlier snaps, rising to his feet. "It's one thing trying to force us to accept women in our ranks. But to place one in power above us? Having us report to a female? You're going too far now. What the fuck was Marcus think—"

The rest of his sentence is cut off by a bullet to the forehead.

Blood sprays, splattering a couple of people nearest the body before it drops to the floor with a thud, knocking his chair back and sending it rolling several feet away from the table. I blink. So that's why the floor in here is concrete. Easier to hose down the blood and brain matter.

Asad slides his Glock back into the shoulder holster under his suit jacket and continues as if he didn't just blow the back of a man's head out.

"His first mistake was interrupting me again. His second one was not taking the out I gave him and everybody in this room. I said if you couldn't deal with the changes, you could walk out that door. But since he decided to keep his ass in that seat, he chose the other way of leaving. Mistake three." He leans forward, planting his palms on the table. His rich, heady scent taunts me, and all that dominant power teases my pussy. "Challenging me. This is my first and last time saying this. Marcus is dead. His era as head of Cross is over, and now I'm running it. And this ain't a democracy; we don't vote on shit. Yes, I'll take your opinions and suggestions under advisement, but I have the final say. You have the right to not like it, but, muthafuckas, you better watch your delivery. I don't do disrespect well." He scans everyone seated at the table and against the walls. Including me. "Good, now that we're clear, on to the next thing."

He straightens and slips his hands in his pants pockets, his manner calm as if he didn't just threaten everyone in the room.

"Glass Slipper is still moving, and we've been contacted by the Morrel organization in Seattle. They've sampled Glass Slipper, and they're looking for a plug to distribute it up there. I'm taking the meeting next week, and if that goes well, we're going to expand. That leaves us with HEA. Ember?"

What? Me? I look at him, momentarily stunned. After arriving, I expected to be a spectator, not a participant. Him asking me to stand in front of a room full of Cross officers and *speak* is another break from a decades-long, patriarchal tradition. Not to mention, this will not only be outing *who* I am but *what* I am to this company. Outing a secret Marcus took such pains to keep concealed . . .

Asad tilts his head, and inhaling a low, deep breath, I slowly rise from my chair. Anxiety twists and knots in my stomach. I've operated in the shadows for so long that a part of me has found comfort there. Like I told Kareem, invisibility provides a defense, a natural shield. And moving to stand next to Asad—no, in front of him, as he takes a step back and lets me have the head of the table—I'm suddenly *too* visible. Too exposed. Too vulnerable.

But on the other hand . . .

On the other hand, satisfaction surges through me, hot and fierce.

I belong here.

Marcus did everything in his power to prevent me from being in this place, from seeing this moment. From anyone within this organization that bore my name knowing *my name*. Yet, here I am. And not from a position of weakness but strength. My own strength.

With the help of him.

Yes. As much as I hate to admit it, with Asad's help.

The *why* still lingers in my mind like a cardboard piece attempting to fit in the wrong jigsaw puzzle.

But trying to figure anything out about Asad lately seems the very definition of futility.

"As I discussed with Asad yesterday, HEA is nearly ready to be distributed. It's tested well with control groups. HEA resembles cocaine, and it's highly addictive, but without the hallucinations, paranoia, and aggression, just to name a few side effects," I inform them, fully in my element, talking about my area of knowledge and expertise. Despite the grumbling that could be a reaction to the information I shared or my presence itself, I continue. "The main difference between Glass Slipper and HEA is the latter's meant to be more of an aphrodisiac. It increases sexual arousal, heightens the senses, as it's also a stimulant. HEA is the perfect party drug for the affluent demographic between the ages of eighteen and thirty-five."

The silence damn near screams, it's so loud. Several people glance at one another, confused frowns wrinkling their eyebrows or turning down their mouths.

"When will HEA be ready for us to give to our crews?" a beautiful woman with long, dark brown locs asks.

Obviously, she's new to this HoC leadership. It's almost comically easy to distinguish between the old guard and the new. Most of the former wear dark frowns and are sunken lower in their chairs. Well, if she feels the disapproving glares from some of the men in the room for speaking, she doesn't acknowledge them. Or maybe she just doesn't give a fuck.

"Two weeks. Three at the most. And because it's created to be a more accessible drug at a less expensive price point, the shoe designed for it to be shipped in will also be sold at a less expensive price point." I glance at Asad, and he nods, granting me permission to disclose this new information. "House of Cross has always been known for couture, but as of the new season, we will roll out a new affordable line that will be stocked in department stores as well as outlet malls. We've already constructed how the shoes will be mules for HEA before they're distributed."

And by "we," I meant me. The new line consists of two designs—a beautiful knockoff of one of our best-selling open-toe stiletto sandals with ankle-strap rivet studs, and our version of a platform-heel saddle shoe in various colors. The rhinestones, studs, and laces of the shoes will be coated with HEA and covered in a formula specially designed by me that renders the drugs undetectable by canine units, X-ray scanners, and chemical field testing if the shipments are detained. And that's a big *if*. Who would suspect *the* House of Cross of smuggling drugs? No one has yet. At least if they had, they hadn't lived to share their suspicions.

The woman with the locs nods at my answer, and a younger man with long box braids, sitting against the rear wall, gives a low chuckle.

"Okay, I'ma ask what everyone else is thinking but don't have the balls to because they don't wanna end up like Jay." He nudges his chin toward the dead man on the floor. "No disrespect meant, but who are you?"

Michelle snorts. The first pinpricks of anger race over my scalp, down the back of my neck, and sprint down my spine. It wouldn't take much effort or time to reach over and snap her thin neck. I can just hear the crack of her cervical vertebrae. Can feel the hot spill of grim exultation in my veins lighting me up brighter than the Wilshire Grand.

Giving myself a mental shake, I refocus on the question and the man who issued it and away from my fantasy. Unlike some of the other men, I believe him when he says, "no disrespect." There's no aggression or disdain in his voice or face.

"I'm Ember Cross, the head scientist for Cross and the one responsible for designing Glass Slipper and HEA."

Another street boss pushes off the wall, shifting forward a step. "Cross?" he asks.

I nod. "Yes. Marcus was my father."

The room erupts with shouts that range from "The fuck?" to "You's a lie." A couple of them twist in their seats as if looking for a "punked" camera, while others turn to each other in confusion. The only people who don't appear shocked besides my stepfamily, Sam, and those who were at dinner last night are Xavier and Deacon.

I don't know why I'm surprised, as both men were extremely close to my father. And yet . . . I still am.

For years, I assumed I was Marcus's shameful secret he literally kept hidden away in the basement. The secret he did his best not to acknowledge to anyone outside of immediate family and Sam. Knowing of their betrayal, it has to make me wonder if they'd actually been privy to the information—from what Sam told me, once my mom had me, I was basically hidden away.

So it doesn't . . . fit that Marcus would've confided in his lieutenants about me. And if that's true, then it stands to reason that they discovered the truth about me some other way. But how?

Or who?

"Quiet." Asad's low command booms from behind me and reverberates through the room. The resulting silence is almost painful in its abruptness. "Ember is Marcus's daughter and only child," he says, his tone practically daring anyone to contradict him.

The same young soldier speaks again, his palms out. "No offense meant, Prince. Or to you, Ms. Cross. It's just, most of us here didn't know Marcus had kids. I mean, blood kids. And we for damn sure didn't know his daughter was the one responsible for creating our food."

Michelle softly scoffs, but it's loud enough to reach my ears, and my fingers curl into a fist on the table, a physical manifestation of the simmering rage that never fully extinguishes when I'm in her presence. Standing in front of this roomful of ruthless, streetwise soldiers with their calculating and way-too-perceptive eyes on me, I can't afford to let her trigger me. Don't have the time or privacy to perform one of my coping or grounding techniques. But this bitch is trying me. And the more she pokes, the hotter my anger burns. The more my control slips . . .

Fingers trail down my back, using my spine as a road map, and my skin pebbles. All of my senses laser focus on that touch and the man exerting it. It—he—grounds me in a way one of my coping mechanisms would have. I force myself not to lean into it. Not to close my eyes and indulge in it. That would be one of the worst mistakes I could make.

Because his touch isn't just offering me a firm foundation on which to resettle myself. It also extends a perverse sense of safety—perverse since Asad is the one I usually need protection from.

"Now you do," Asad says. "Like I said, I'll meet with each of you individually, but there shouldn't be an interruption in distribution or shipments. If changes are implemented, it will be to make the machine run smoother, not make what we have more difficult for you." He pauses. "One more announcement before I let you go. Some of you found out last night, but for the others, I'm getting married in a month. You just met my fiancée." He curves a hand around my hip, and lust wars with confusion and self-directed disgust. This man has been my nemesis since he entered my life thirteen years ago. And yet, here I stand, nipples beading, pussy creaming, skin heating as my body remembers how he'd mastered it, possessed it, fucked it. Who the fuck am I becoming? "You're all invited to our wedding in a month's time."

Various versions of "congratulations" filter through the air, the leadership nodding at me and some even smiling, but Michelle and Kareem remain on mute. The disgust and fury tightening Michelle's face is expected. But the same anger darkening Kareem's? Surprise sweeps through me like a drafty, whistling wind. From his words to me last night, I understand he disapproves, but this . . . rage? It doesn't fit. Especially considering we barely have a relationship. In my eyes, he's just slightly better than his mother and brother. And that's only because he's always been the weakest link among the three of them, the least threatening.

I narrow my eyes on him, and as if he feels my scrutiny on him, his gaze shifts, meeting mine. In the next instant, his expression clears, his mouth softening, jaw relaxing, eyes losing some of their intensity.

Unease tracks across the nape of my neck like the spindly legs of a daddy longlegs.

The swift change from infuriated to congenial is disturbing as fuck.

"If there aren't any questions, you're free to go." When no one speaks up, Asad nods, and everyone shoves their chairs back and stands, talking among themselves as they head for the door. Me included. I take a step in the same direction, but Asad's hand, still clamped around my hip, tightens.

"Stay," he murmurs before dipping his chin at two people, a man and woman, who approach him. "Everything good?" he cryptically asks. They nod, and he turns to me. "Ember, I want to formally introduce you to Eli and Makeda."

"Hi, it's a pleasure to meet you," I say.

"You, too," Makeda replies, her intense gaze staring into mine almost to the point of discomfort.

"Same." Eli smiles.

The three of them start engaging in a low conversation, and I tune them out.

My heart makes a jailbreak for my throat, and my mind howls an objection. I'm not ready to be alone with him. Not after last night. I haven't even had time to fully process how I feel about giving my biggest enemy something no one has ever had—my body, my virginity. I don't trust him. Damn sure don't like him. He and his mother made my childhood a living hell while I was still suffering through the most traumatizing experience of my life—my mother's death. He *is* my trauma.

And yet . . .

I shake my head, try to take another step, but again, his hold on me tightens. Harder.

Yet, I allowed him inside me. Was more exposed with him than I have been with anyone else. No, I don't trust Asad with my well-being, my safety, hell, my life, but I did my body . . . my pleasure. I trusted him not to hurt me. Not to take advantage of me in my vulnerability.

No, I don't want to "stay."

I want to get as far from him as possible.

Except for Michelle and Kareem, almost all of the street bosses pour out of the room, but Sam heads in our direction, his dark, penetrating stare fixed on me. I brace myself, already knowing what he's about to hit me with.

I sigh. "Sam—"

"Congratulations are in order," he interrupts, the resonant, deep voice that intimidates in the courtroom directed at me. I'm immune to that fear tactic, but not to the disappointment in his eyes. Regret swims in my stomach. "Let me speak to you. Privately."

Asad breaks off his conversation with Eli, his new enforcer he called Makeda, and a petite woman with lovely ebony skin and beautiful lemonade braids, and turns to us, his silver gaze skimming over me and focusing on Sam.

"This isn't your business, Sam," he warns.

My godfather frowns, not cowering in the face of Asad's threatening tone.

"Anything having to do with Ember is my business, Prince. That's not going to change, whether she's your fiancée or not."

The two men stare at each other, and the tension crackles on the air.

"Hello, still standing here." I wave between them, fighting not to roll my eyes. "I'm not some bone to be fought over. I can make my own decisions about who I can and cannot speak to. I don't need his"—I jab a finger in Asad's direction—"permission, Sam." Asad fucked this pussy; he didn't shoot my mother's up. So he doesn't get to dictate my actions like he's my parent.

Makeda snorts, but Asad bows his head over mine.

"Don't get fucked-up in here. You know I don't care about audiences," he threatens.

And I hate the ripple of heat that courses down my spine.

Ignoring the warning, I curl my hand around Sam's arm. "We can talk over here." *Here* being across the room and in the far corner. "Be right back," I say to Asad with an arch of my eyebrow.

Maybe he sees the "I will cut the fuck up" in my face, because after a moment, he nods and turns back to his people. Michelle and Makeda join him as we depart.

As soon as Sam and I are a safe distance where ears can't pick up on our conversation, he lights into me.

"What the hell is going on here, Ember? Why am I just finding out that you're engaged? And to Asad Prince of all people? Last we talked, you hated him and planned on leaving House of Cross, and now you're *marrying him*? Is he forcing you? Is that it?" he cross-examines me. "Because if that's what's going on here, I'm putting a stop to it right fucking now."

"Damn, Sam. Can I get an answer in?"

"Watch your mouth, little girl."

I sigh. "Sorry. But I can explain if you'll let me," I lie. Because I'm obviously not explaining *everything*. Guilt already eats at him for not protecting me after Mom died. If I confess the whole truth to him, he'll confront Asad and lose his life. I can't have that. "Yes, you're right. And honestly, not much has changed except that I'm not leaving Cross as soon as I planned. Asad approached me"—*broke into my house*—"and offered a proposition." *Threatened me.*

I break down the terms we negotiated last night, forgoing mentioning the threats and coercion that came before that. By the time I finish, the lines etched in Sam's face ease, and though he doesn't look pleased, he also doesn't appear to be in a murderous rage either.

He studies me for several long, uncomfortable moments, then finally, he nods.

"Okay. I can't lie, Ember. I'm not thrilled about this . . . arrangement. I wish there was another way other than you shackling yourself to Prince, even if it's for three years. Still, as mean of a son of a bitch as Prince is, he can provide the best protection for you right now. Your father's killer is still out there, and we're no closer to knowing who they are—"

"I can take care of myself, Sam," I grind out. "I've been doing it for the last decade."

"You shouldn't have had to."

"Doesn't change the past though."

He pinches the bridge of his nose, bowing his head. When he lifts it, regret drenches his dark eyes. "Believe me, I will never forget that I can't change the past. But I will do everything in my power to make sure your here and now is different. This transition in Cross isn't going to be a smooth one; I think you can tell that for yourself from what we witnessed here today. And all I want is your safety. And your happiness. You deserve it more than any of us. If that means being Prince's wife for a little while so you can walk away with your freedom and a piece of the empire you helped build, then I'll support you. Although I wish you would've come to me first—trusted me to talk this over first—before accepting Prince's proposal, I respect your decision."

I reach for his hand, wrapping my fingers around his and squeezing.

"This isn't about trust, Sam. Hell, you're one of the very few in this world I can say have that from me. It's about making the best decision for me and my future. I'm used to looking out for myself without anyone's input, so as difficult as it is for you to hear, I didn't think about consulting you. I did what needed to be done to survive." And to save the lives of the people closest to me.

"Shit, Ember." He glances away from me. "You're killing me. I promised your mother . . ." When he looks at me again, for the first time, he wears all of his fifty-plus years on his face.

"Sam, I didn't say that to punish you or make you feel guilty. You've been the one constant in my life. You've been more of a father than the shitty one I got. All the moments a child is supposed to have with their father, I experienced those with you. No, you couldn't protect me in my own house, but that wasn't your role; it was Marcus's. But when I think of my college graduation, you were there. Don't think I don't know it was you who convinced Marcus to hire me at Cross in the first place." I squeeze his arm, then drop my hand. "It is what it is. I just need you to support my decision, because at some point in these next three years, I'm sure you're probably going to need to talk me down from murdering that muthafucka."

"You mean your husband?"

I shrug. "That's what I said." He chuckles even though I'm dead ass. Tilting my head, I ask, "Your turn. How the hell you end up as Asad's advisor?"

"He asked. I agreed," he simply says. "I was your father's legal counsel but also his friend. That made me privy to all the inner workings of this organization, and he often came to me for advice. Stepping up to this role for Asad won't be much different. And it allows me to at least try and guide Cross into an even more prosperous future. Will let me preserve your legacy."

"My legacy." I scoff, ignoring the muted sting behind my rib cage. "You drafted and read the will. I don't have a legacy. Not anymore. Marcus and your new employer made sure of that."

I try to stem the bitterness trickling through me and to keep it out of my voice, but I fail at both.

"House of Cross will always be yours; I don't give a fuck whose name is under CEO. Nothing can change the blood running in your veins." Anger vibrates through his big frame, a scowl darkening his face.

"It's a nice thought, Sam, but I'm too old for sentimental shit." I give him a small smile. "Enjoy your new position. You deserve it, and Asad needs someone around him who won't kiss his ass. Me? I'm just going to ride out these next three years until I'm free of all this."

He studies me for several quiet moments before slowly nodding.

"Ember, I—"

"Asad, this is bullshit." Michelle's shrill, raised voice snatches my attention and interrupts Sam. He whips around to face the source of the disruption. Michelle stands in front of her son, her petite and slim body damn near vibrating with anger. Red tinges her light brown skin, and her full lips twist to the side while her shoulders hunch so high they almost touch the bottom of her short chandelier earrings. One hand is curled into a fist by her side, while she points a finger in Asad's face with the other. Oh yeah, stepmama big mad. "You know these people for what, a couple of years? And yet you promote them, have them occupying the most coveted positions closest to you. But what about your brother? You just cut him out. He's been here, been loyal from the beginning, and what do you reward him with? Street boss like all these other flunkies! It's unfair, and he deserves so much better than that, Prince," she shouts at him.

Thank God we are the only ones left in the room. One thing I know for certain about Asad is he doesn't play about his respect. And mother or not, she won't be exempt from his punishment.

"Give us the room, please," Asad calmly says. But that calm

doesn't extend to the grim set of his mouth or hard line of his jaw. His eyes glitter with malice, and a shiver races and trips down my spine. Most people shout when they're enraged. Not Asad. The more enraged he is, the quieter and calmer he becomes. And right now, staring down at Michelle, he must be pissed the fuck off.

Usually, I'd pay for a first-row seat to the carnage that's about to happen, but my desperation to be away from Asad outweighs my delight in witnessing Michelle get verbally molly whopped. I turn to leave with everyone else.

"Not you, Ember," that deep, midnight voice demands, stopping me before I've made a few steps across the room.

Fuuuuck.

My face contorts into a grimace as I watch Sam, my safety net, walk out the conference room. Swallowing a sigh, I smooth my face out before turning and retracing my steps back to the table. But I halt short of standing next to Asad. Bad enough that even from this distance his woodsy musk teases, no, taunts me. I need his body heat to stop doing the same. I don't like the man, but apparently my coochie is Team Pussy-Hound Stepbrother. Shit, she's on her Oliver Twist shit. *"Please, sir. Can I have some more?"*

Faithless heffa.

Michelle scoffs, waving a bejeweled hand toward me. "See what I mean? Why is *she* here? This is a discussion between *family*. Which brings me to my second issue, Prince. Since when did we all agree to bring her in on the family business? Marcus didn't want her here. He hid her in the basement—hid her fucking existence—for a damn good reason. And yet, here you go, introducing her as his daughter and your fiancée? Which, I might add, marrying her will happen over my cold, dead body," she snarls. "Then you had her up there, speaking as if she's a part of this organization. This is a betrayal, Prince. Of your father, me, your brother, and the empire Marcus left in your hands."

God, she's a scratched, broken-to-hell record. And so is the rage, the need to end her, to strangle her until that thin neck snaps.

"Are you finished?" he asks with no inflection in his voice. I brace myself for what's about to come next, and I'm not even on the receiving end of it.

"No," Michelle snaps, and I smother a sigh. I hope she's using a heavy-duty shovel because it's going to be needed if she's intent on digging an even deeper hole. "You had me here for this meeting as well, but you neglected to introduce me or my position just as you did Kareem. If it wasn't for me, Asad, none of this would be yours. None of it. Don't you ever forget that. *Now* I'm finished."

A sneer curls her mouth as she crosses her arms under her breasts, and I'm fascinated. I'm used to this rage and that attitude being directed toward me. But never Asad. He's the golden child, the one who can do no wrong. So the scene playing out in front of me right now is just . . . wrong.

And captivating.

"Michelle." He pauses and sweeps a hand down over his beard. "Michelle, you're my mother, and that's the only thing keeping my foot out your ass and my gun out your mouth."

"Asad." Kareem takes a step forward, holding out an arm as if to shield his mother from his brother's wrath.

But Asad pushes that arm aside and moves ahead, encroaching on Michelle's personal space and looming over her. Michelle tips her head back to maintain eye contact with her son, but even from my distance, I can see her throat move up and down as she swallows. Swear I can taste the metallic and grimy scent of fear on the room's recycled air.

Kareem doesn't fall back though, standing close beside his mother. "Asad, hold on. She's our mother." Kareem's low reminder barely garners him a flick of Asad's silver gaze.

"I don't want to hear that shit, Kareem. And I'm not talking to you," he says without removing his gaze from Michelle. "Let's get one mu'fucking thing straight, Michelle. Just because you popped that pussy for Marcus doesn't mean I didn't earn this seat at the head of the table. You married Marcus for yourself—for his money and to elevate your status so you could be stuntin' on those hoes who looked down on you. It wasn't about me or Kareem but always about you. So don't ever fix your mouth to tell me I owe you. This is the only pass you'll get with me. I'm the head of Cross first and your son second. For your health and safety, don't confuse the two, and don't ever question my decisions. You understand me?" When she doesn't immediately reply, he tilts his head, and I have to stop myself from running over there and jacking her head up and down. Anything to alleviate the murder stamped on his features. His shoulders seem to broaden, chest seems to deepen—shit, he just seems to *grow* with his anger. "Are. We. Clear?" he repeats, slower, quieter.

"Yes," Michelle finally grinds out between clenched teeth.

Asad stares down at her then, and after a weighty, intimidating pause, steps back.

"Good. I'm glad we're on the same page. Now, as for your concern. Kareem"—he turns away from Michelle and directly addresses his brother—"yeah, you're my brother and I acknowledge and appreciate your loyalty. That's not, nor has ever been, in question. It's your experience that's lacking. Marcus had you working for HoC, not the underworld side. Eli has his hand in both. And Makeda has been under me for the past three years. Maybe not officially because of the gender restrictions, but she's been there. Still, I want you to be with me, and not just with House of Cross. That's why I made you a street boss. You'll continue as Senior VP of marketing, but you'll also work directly under Eli and gain the experience needed in the drug operations. You have leadership skills, which is why you're not starting as a lower-level soldier, but I can't make you my second either. It's your choice though, Kareem. You can remain as VP and have nothing to do with this side of Cross, and I'll respect it. What do you want?"

"I want in," Kareem says without hesitation.

"Good." He nods, then switches his attention back to his mother, whatever warmth that had seeped back into his face and voice from talking to his brother leached clean now. "I had you here because you're Marcus's widow and my mother and you have ownership in this company. That alone affords you respect. But it doesn't automatically give you a position in either the company or the organization. When have you worked, Michelle? When have you *wanted* to work? I'm not in the practice of dropping titles on people like a fucking fairy godmother. Everyone here works, they earn their shit. And you pushing me out your shit gets you a thank-you but not a corner office. You want to know why Ember is here? Because she deserves to be. True, Marcus was a bitch-made muthafucka who hid her existence and her contribution, but none of that changes the fact that she's the reason this family isn't trying to compete in an oversaturated market. Cross is one of one, and that's owed entirely to Ember."

It takes everything in me not to sink into the chair behind me. My trembling legs fight the good fight and manage to keep me standing upright. But inside? Inside, every organ, muscle, and bone—the very breath in my lungs—quivers. My ears and soul ache with the echo of the rattling.

This is the very first time in my life that anyone other than my mother and Sam has defended me. Especially from the person most responsible for my pain and abuse. And for that person to be Asad, the other person who tormented my dreams with his treatment . . .

Confusion and an emotion that's too murky, too . . . uncomfortable to mentally touch or attempt to decipher swirl in my chest, my head.

Why? Out of all the volatile words we've lobbed at each other like dirty bombs . . . Out of all the painful and terrifying acts he's committed that's left behind keloid scars on my mind and psyche . . . Out of all the enmity and disgust that exists between us like a third in a sick-ass ménage . . . Why would he champion me with Michelle of all people, the person who was his favorite partner in crime?

"You're standing here defending this bitch?" Michelle's head jerks back as if his palm went across her cheek. Her voice trembles, but not with tears or hurt. No, pain doesn't suffuse her face; rage does. She glances at me, and there's death in that dark, narrowed gaze. I'd like to say I'm unfamiliar with that look, but it's as recognizable to me as the reflection that stares back at me from a mirror. Her hate brings me joy. "I don't give a fuck about this not owing me bullshit. I'm your *mother*. Your *blood*. You owe me your loyalty, your allegiance. Not Marcus. Not Cross. And for damn sure not this whore—"

"I've been a bitch and a whore. I'm not going to be too many more of either." I calmly interrupt her tirade. A whole grown-ass woman up here having a tantrum. Make it make sense.

"And what're you going to do about it? *Whore.*" Michelle sneers.

Heat flares beneath my skin like someone twisted the knob on a gas range and the flames leap high, licking at me. My heart crashes against my chest, the beat pounding out a primal rhythm in my ears. In one instant, I'm leaning against the conference table and in the next, I'm climbing on top and launching myself at my stepmother.

"Shit," Kareem hisses.

But he's too slow. Too late. I'm on his mother. Taking her to the floor. Punching her in her slick-ass mouth. Wrapping my hands around her neck, digging my fingernails into soft skin and squeezing—squeezing so hard something fragile yet vital snaps under my fingers . . .

I blink.

I still stand on this side of the table, Michelle unharmed, her neck intact.

Just a vision. A wish. A deep-seated need.

Inhaling a low, measured breath, I slowly release it.

And smile.

"The fuck are you smiling about?" Michelle snaps.

"Just thinking about your question." I tilt my head. "By the way, do you have any idea the number of poisons that are tasteless and odorless? Just imagine it. You're eating dinner or lunch . . .

or maybe having that must-have after-dinner old-fashioned, and suddenly your chest tightens to the point of excruciating pain. Then your eyes start to tear because they're on fire while your lungs collapse, and you drown in your own fluid. And all that is before your bladder gives up the ghost and you wet yourself like a geriatric with incontinence. Just asking though." I smile again. "But hey, be careful out there."

Michelle's lips part, and I can *see* her need to snap back at me. It's in the fierce frown darkening her expression. The hike of her shoulders. The digging of her nails into her thighs. But I also spy the flicker of fear in her gaze. And the power that rushes through me . . . It's fucking euphoric. It's a high that hits harder, is more addictive than anything that we could possibly peddle on the streets.

"We're done here," Asad says into the tension-filled silence. "Kareem, I'll get up with you later. Michelle, I'll call you." He bends down and brushes a kiss over the crown of her head, but the thread of steel in his voice leaves no room for argument.

Kareem slaps hands with Asad, and then they pull one another in for a half hug. For the first time since I entered the room, he gives me a small smile, then turns to his mother and cups her elbow. "C'mon, Mom. I'll walk you out."

"I don't need to be handled, Kareem." Michelle snatches her arm out of her youngest son's grasp. "Asad, we'll talk later." She doesn't bother glancing my way before marching from the room with Kareem trailing behind her.

The door shuts, leaving me alone with Asad. At one time, this would've been my biggest nightmare.

It still is. But for far more complex reasons now.

I turn to him, and we face off.

"Is there something else you needed to say to me? 'Cause if not, I need to get back to my lab. And somebody needs to come get the dead person on aisle one," I say into the stifling, taut quiet, tipping my head back.

He doesn't immediately reply to me, but that stormy gaze

runs over me, and I force myself not to flinch from the nearly physical touch of that too-intimate survey. My muscles quiver with the effort. But I already ceded a battle to Asad when I submitted to the greedy, bloody lust he elicited in me last night, transforming me into an insatiable creature I didn't recognize—one I cringe just thinking about in the cool, too-clear, and accusatory light of day. Letting him know just his eyes upon me affects me as much as his hands on my skin is another skirmish I can't afford to lose. Not when I intend to win this long-standing war between us.

"What did you see today?"

My head slightly jerks back, and I frown. "Huh?"

Yes. A Mensa member, holder of several degrees, and a leader in my professional field, and all I can come up with is "Huh?"

Asad arches a dark eyebrow. "If you can 'huh,' you can hear. Answer my question."

Muthafucka. "I . . ." Still frowning, I pause and gather my whirling thoughts and parse them. Inhaling a breath, I shake my head. "Shock at the changes, of course. But a quicker acceptance among the younger street bosses than the older ones, but that's to be expected, I would think. They're accustomed to the traditions of Cross being patriarchal, and the addition of women is going to take longer for them to accept. You will probably have to handle a few more how you did ol' boy though. And not to just make an example out of them, but because they won't be able to take orders from your enforcers and resent women being street bosses and having the same level of authority as them. They'll end up being a problem. And problems either become snitches or competition. Both need to be eliminated."

"Go on." Asad nods, sliding his hands in his pockets, exposing his powerful chest and abs. My clit thumps, and my pussy, even though sore and still a little swollen, clenches around phantom dick. Like a fucking ho.

"For the most part, everyone in the room seems receptive of your leadership. Which isn't very surprising since they're familiar with you. Doesn't hurt that you also promised them more money with a new product and a new distributor," I point out.

"And you said 'for the most part.' So that means not everyone."

I perch on the edge of the conference room table and study him, scrutinize each strong, masculine piece that congregates to form a beautifully brutal picture. What does he want from me?

"I think you already know, but okay, I'll play along. Xavier and Deacon. Malcolm didn't seem to be bothered at all. If anything, he appeared . . . relieved. I almost believe he's ready to sit it down. He's about Marcus's age and might be ready to get out of the game. But not Xavier and Deacon. They hate you. And want you dead. It's just my opinion, but of the two, I believe Xavier is more dangerous. He's the type to stab you in the back while asking how the fam's doing to your face. A Judas. Matter of fact, I'm surprised his ass didn't kiss your cheek on the way up out of here."

Asad snorts. "I never did trust him like that. But Marcus did, and neither him nor Deacon gave me a reason to think they were moving foul."

"Until now."

"Until now."

"Just out of curiosity, why are they still alive? I can't lie." I hike a shoulder up. "I was shocked as hell to see them sitting at this table when I walked in here. Not telling you how to do your new job or anything, but I would've thought they would've been more dead with a lot less limbs by now."

A gleam enters his gray eyes, and it reminds me of the glint that brightened his gaze as he stared down between my legs last night while his dick slowly muscled its way into my pussy.

Pleasure.

"'Cause it's fun." When I just stare at him, he smiles, and though it's twisted and mean as fuck, my breath catches in my throat and my pulse echoes in my clit. "You asked why're they alive. Because it's fun," he explains. "After some more time with

Carter"—from the quiver of his lips, I can just imagine what that quality time entailed—"I got all the info I needed to confirm that yeah, Xavier and Deacon are behind that hit. Now I'm not naïve enough to believe it hasn't gotten back to them that Carter's named them. Until I clean house, I don't know who's loyal and who isn't, so I assume everyone, except my own handpicked people, can't be trusted. So they sat here today knowing I'm aware they tried to have my ass taken out."

"And they're also left wondering when you're going to retaliate."

Psychological warfare. I don't know why I'm surprised. Asad has never been impulsive. He's not the snake, quick to strike; he's the spider, waiting, stalking, playing with their food before slowly sucking it dry for maximum pain.

"Do you think they're behind Marcus's death?" I quietly ask.

He studies me for several seconds. "Do you care?"

The question isn't confrontational or accusatory. And because of that, I take my time and consider my answer.

"Yes, as in I'd like to know. Not only would not having the mystery solved annoy the hell out of me but it would be bad for business. Rumors about the manner of Marcus's death are already circulating. To think we can squash them is unrealistic and impossible. And once the fact that he was murdered is confirmed, if people discover Cross hasn't identified and handled the person responsible, it makes the organization—and the head of the organization—appear weak. And that affects business and the bottom line. For *that* reason, I care."

He stares at me for a very long moment, and I almost think he isn't going to reply. And something about the glint in his eyes . . . I begin to regret saying anything. Those intense, piercing eyes—it's like being visually stalked and hunted down.

"That sounds cold as fuck, ma."

I pause, glance to the side, and catch my reflection in the heavily tinted, one-way window where I can view the heavy traffic of downtown LA. Instead of seeing myself, I glimpse the image of the woman I believe my mother must've looked like at my age. A little over average height, same body type, the same facial structure. Sam often tells me that I'm her twin, and since I've dyed my hair honey blond, the similarities are uncanny.

"My mother's been gone longer in my life than the time I actually had her," I murmur, still staring out the window. Even as the words are spilling out of me, there's a voice in my head screaming to shut up, to not give Asad ammo to use against me at a later date. But it's as if some circuit breaker flipped between my brain and mouth, because they're not connecting. And I can't stop talking. "Yet there are times I miss her as if she died last week, instead of thirteen years ago. That's why I changed my hair color." I lift my fingers to touch the long coils. "To feel closer to the mother that I can only see, talk to, smell, and hold in my dreams." I pause, then softly snort. "At least, that's one of the reasons. The one I'll readily admit."

I finally turn away from the window, and as if he were just waiting on me to look his way, Asad's gray eyes capture mine, and for a panicky moment, my throat squeezes closed, and I struggle against the sensation of drowning. My fingers flutter to the base of my neck, and his gaze drops to the movement. I drop my arm, forcing it to hang by my side. I'm already revealing too much with my word vomit, but this . . . this gesture suddenly and inexplicably feels too . . . vulnerable.

"Don't stop now, Ember." Asad takes a step toward me, his hands still tucked into his pockets, an urgency in his words, in the tight lift of his shoulders. "Get that shit out. What's the other reason?"

My lips part, but no sound comes out. Self-preservation shows her ass, and since that's my girl, I should listen. *Should*. But I don't know if it's some kind of magical dick left over from last night fogging my God-given good sense . . . or if these thoughts have been locked up deep inside me for so long that all it took was a question about my father and a thought about my mother to unlock that rusty door to free them.

I swallow, wetting my throat and tongue, attempting to wipe away the dusty layers of the past.

"I was about fourteen when I noticed Marcus never looked me directly in the eye; he'd look over my head or shoulder but not in my face. It didn't take therapy or an accelerated degree to eventually figure out it was because of my resemblance to my mother and his late wife. So a few years ago, I decided to make it even harder for him to ignore me by changing my appearance to look even more like the woman he so easily replaced in my mother's house and bed with an evil, crazy-ass bitch." If he expects me to apologize for calling Michelle out her name, well, people are disappointed every day. Shit, I could've called her a raging, STD-ridden cunt, so he needs to be grateful. "Marcus made neglecting me an Olympic sport, and that muthafucka won gold year after year. You explain to me how I miss a parent who's been gone for over a decade more than one who hasn't even been dead for a couple of weeks."

"So your other reason was to punish Marcus."

"Over and over," I admit without shame and with a perverse, delicious glee that I probably do a shit job of hiding. "What you call cold as fuck, I call my truth. I care about finding out who killed Marcus as much as Sherlock deducing who was behind the hound of the Baskervilles. Leaving mysteries unsolved is irritating."

Silence settles between us as we both fall into our own thoughts. I don't know what his are, but mine switch from my gone-on-to-glory father to another track that crowds into my head like the Beyhive at a Beyoncé concert. And while reason demands I let it go, I can't. The not knowing would eat at me until it would slowly drive me insane. More so than who dispatched Marcus.

"Why do you care about my impression?" I ask. *No one ever has before. Especially you.* "Why aren't you asking your second and Sam? That's why they're there. Since when did my opinion become important?"

He stares at me for so long that my questions seem to ricochet off the walls, growing louder and louder. Or maybe that's just how the regret and embarrassment churning in my gut make it appear. I should've kept my mouth shut. Never should've given him a glimpse into how his answer . . . matters. But it does. The not knowing will eat me alive. I need to pinpoint, to examine to death the moment I became important to Asad Prince.

Shit.

"I'm not Marcus, ma."

"I know that."

"Do you?"

I scoff. "Yes."

"Then act like it."

See? This is why we can't have nice things. Talking to Asad without feeling homicidal is like Yogi Bear waltzing through Jellystone Park and not committing a little larceny of picnic baskets. The shit's just not happening.

I hop off the table and head for the door. But before I can take a third step, a big hand cuffs the back of my neck, halting me dead in my tracks like a misbehaving puppy. The comparison sends anger spiking inside me, and I whip around—or I attempt to whip around. That grip tightens, and I'm jerked backward, almost off my feet, slamming into Asad's hard, wide chest.

Holy shit. Did this muthafucka just *365 Days* me?

"I'm beginning to think you like this toxic shit, 'cause you stay trying me, ma." That low, dark growl rumbles in my ear, his lips grazing the top curve.

I just manage to imprison the humiliating gasp scrambling up my throat. But there's not shit I can do about the bottoming out of my stomach or the liquid, molten heat filling it. Or the moisture already wetting up my lower lips and panties. This man doesn't mean my sanity or pussy any good.

"I don't like fuck all about you," I say, grasping ahold of my dignity with bloody fingernails.

He chuckles, and goddammit, a shiver crashes through me.

There's no way he missed it. The press of his chest to my back, the grinding of that big, long dick against my ass, clue me in that he caught every ripple that coursed through my body.

"Lie to yourself, but don't bother doing that shit with me, baby girl." He looses another of those rumbling, barely there laughs. "We both know there's at least one part of you that likes me."

He wraps an arm around my waist and dips his hand between my legs, cupping my pussy. If she wasn't already leaking, she would be now. I sink my teeth into my bottom lip and clutch his thick wrist. To tug his hand away . . . to hold it tighter against me . . . I'm as indecisive as my sex.

Scratch that.

My pussy is decisive as hell.

"She loves the fuck outta me." He squeezes my flesh, grinding the heel of his palm against my clit and setting off a chain reaction of electrical currents. They crackle up to my stomach, and it goes concave, before they double back and sizzle a path down my suddenly trembling legs to the soles of my feet. He just broke me in last night, and already my body responds to his touch like a trained circus animal. With immediate obedience and expecting a reward. "I can feel how hot she already is for me, and if I dragged down these dick-tease pants, I bet this pussy would wet me up. She knows who she belongs to."

I . . . *Oh fuck*. I can't.

This isn't a shadowed library where I can convince myself my choices were limited. That sex was inevitable and that he was going to take it one way or another and the act of surrendering was a way of retaining some of my power. That pleasure from fucking him was biological, with no emotional attachment.

That I still hated him.

No, this is a cold, brightly lit conference room where none of those . . . arguments will stand. Not when reason isn't clouded by greedy lust and desperate need.

Gripping his wrist tighter, I wrench it away from between my legs and tear from his hold. My neck and pussy burn as if branded, but I ignore them and turn to face him, inserting a safe space between us.

His gray eyes gleam, and for a second, I have the inane impulse to tilt my head back and bare my throat to him. Make myself vulnerable and submit to him.

Oh shit. This man is way more dangerous than I ever imagined.

He's a threat to my very existence.

My hard-fought independence.

"Answer my question," I say, the calm, even tone not reflecting the chaos wrecking shop inside me. "Why do you care about my opinion?"

"Do you or do you not hold a bachelor's degree in biology and two master's in biochemistry and chemical engineering?" He doesn't give me an opportunity to respond but continues. "Were you the only one in the room with an IQ of 158?" I frown, unaware he knew that information. "Were you the only person attending that meeting with the exclusive knowledge of our product? Are you or are you not the last living member of the Cross family?"

I wave a hand, dismissive, even though the frantic, wild knocking of my heart more accurately relays the mixture of panic, anger and—*God, I hate it*—yearning written inside of me.

"None of that mattered to Marcus."

He frowns at me as if genuinely confused, tipping his head to the side. "Maybe I was too quick in mentioning that high IQ 'cause I could've sworn I just said I'm. Not. Marcus."

"No, you're worse," I murmur. "At least with him, I could trust in his disinterest, his neglect. This"—I sweep the same hand to the right, encompassing the room—"I can't. Your outing me to the organization, introducing me as your fiancée, defending me to Michelle, and asking for my observations like they have weight . . ." I shake my head. "No. I *won't* trust it. Sex and playing like some fucking prince storming in to slay the dragon won't erase years of pain and torture. So you're absolutely right. You're not Marcus. I could never make that mistake. It isn't my father who invades my nightmares."

Storm clouds gather in his eyes, transforming them into a gray so dark they nearly appear black. A shiver backpedals down my spine, but I force my feet to remain in place. As much as I like to believe I'm not afraid of Asad, there's no denying he's bigger, heavier, stronger.

God . . . If only it was his strength that presented the biggest threat. I wish I could claim that.

But when I bled on his dick, it usurped the crown.

Even now, shame crawls through me on its dirty hands and knees, head bowed, because while fear treads through me at the menace brewing in Asad's narrowed gaze, so does lust. So does excitement as electric and stunning as lightning.

Head for the door. You don't want none of what's in those eyes.

My self-preservation is working time and a half today.

"You seem bothered by what I said."

Fuuuuck.

"You're one privileged muthafucka." He shakes his head, releasing a low, rumbling chuckle. But if "ain't shit funny" was a sound, that would be it. "A blind one, too."

I frown. It's the second time he's said something along those lines to me.

"Privileged?" The "blind" comment didn't offend me as much as that one. No, *insult* me. Because Asad had me *fucked up*. "Your big ass really standing here accusing me of being privileged? The same muthafucka who only had to walk through the front door of my home to be labeled the golden child by a man who couldn't even tell you my favorite color if I held a Glock to his forehead. Whose every wish and need were granted before he even opened his mouth to voice it? Who inherited a kingdom simply by owning a dick and a pair of balls?" I screw my face up. "And you wonder why I can't trust none of this bullshit—why I can't trust you. Because of the shit you just allowed to come out of your mouth. Standing there like the injured party when the reason for the hell I endured, the reason you have the keys to a stolen empire, was just sitting at the right-hand side of your table. You know what's fucking privilege? Being so goddamn arrogant to think I would ever believe you meant anything good for me as long as you remain aligned with that bitch of a moth—"

"Shut the fuck up."

He moves so fast I don't have time to blink, much less move. One moment, he's glaring at me from across a safe distance, and in the next, his body is crushed against mine, hard, steely muscles to my softer curves, his big fists twisted in the lapels of my suit jacket. Snatching me up so only the tips of my stilettoes scrape the floor.

Faint echoes of alarm blare in my head, my chest, quiver in my belly. But they're nearly suffocated by the razor-sharp, greedy edge of anticipation slowly piercing me, slicing deep. Seeping dirty excitement into my bloodstream.

This is us. This has always been us, if I'm being repulsively, yet starkly, honest.

Hatred denying lust. Revulsion masking fascination. Resentment justifying shame.

Asad Prince has always been easy to loathe.

And easier to crave.

I cover his fist, grabbing at his clenched fingers, attempting to wrench them away from me. But this is more than a struggle to free myself from his grip. It's a futile struggle to escape the truth.

Disgust races across Asad's face, and then he releases me so fast, I stumble backward, my heels almost slipping out from underneath me. I quickly steady myself, but there's nothing I can do for the erratic racing of my pulse, the frantic pounding of my heart . . . the slick, hungry ache of my pussy.

"I swear to God, for someone so fucking smart, you don't see a muthafuckin' thing. The world doesn't revolve around you, ma, and you don't corner the market on tragedy and loss," he says, voice so cold, so flat, I almost wish he'd shout at me, read me for filth. But this . . . this emptiness has a dread yawning wide behind my sternum, and I don't know how to close it. How to fill it.

"Asad—" I whisper.

"Nah, for once, shut the fuck up and listen." His words are a slap in the mouth, and they sting. I taste phantom blood on my tongue. Shameful blood, and I don't even know why. Asad takes a step forward, silver eyes dark, big body drawn tight, and for the very first time in thirteen long years, I see him as . . . breakable. "I can tell you the details of how Kimberly Jacobs Cross died. The time, date, the cause. It's all I've heard from you. All I've heard from Michelle. You hate Michelle for coming in and trying to replace her with your father, and Michelle hates your mother for simply existing. And because of that, she's this presence that's never really been gone. Not even a ghost, because they at least pass on at some point, but your mother is as present, as . . . as sentient as if she never left. And in all this fucking tug-of-war, no one has ever mentioned Khalil Amir Prince. He's been forgotten by everyone. Everyone but me."

I stare at him, speechless.

No, that's not exactly true.

Too many words crowd into my head, scramble up the back of my throat. But they're mired in the quicksand of guilt, slowly sucked down as useless and inadequate.

Because even though I've never heard the name of Khalil Amir Prince before, I still know who he is—Asad's father.

Even if the last name didn't give it away, the reverence wrapped around the syllables would've.

"No one seems to give a flying fuck about a man who grew up in the shithole of LA County's foster care system but still put himself through college and an apprenticeship while working two jobs. He built one of the most successful jewelry businesses and an unimpeachable reputation by hours, years, of hard work, perseverance, and integrity. He was a good man, an honest man. A better father. His only fault was falling in love with and marrying a faithless, greedy bitch who only saw him as a stepping stone for more and could never be satisfied with what she had. My father's downfall was refusing to see people—namely, his wife—for who they were and instead for who he wanted them to be. And by the time he did, it was way too fucking late."

Something spasms across his face. That same *something* flickers in his storm-darkened eyes. My stomach hollows, the bottom plummeting into free fall.

No.

I don't realize I must've said it aloud until his eyebrow arches and he slightly turns his head, narrowing his gaze. The look he pins on me is somewhere between sarcastic amusement and incredulity.

"No?" he asks. "You were the recipient of her"—his mouth quirks at the corners—"love often. You don't think she's capable of it?"

He still doesn't come out and explicitly say Michelle's sin—her crime—but he alludes to it, and my mind still can't fully grasp that she . . . that she would . . .

"Your mother is a monster. I've never, nor will I ever, deny that. Still, abuse is one thing. But . . . but . . ." I can't even say it. Can't shove the word off my tongue.

"Murder. That's what you seem to be having a hard time saying. Murder. And if you really believe Michelle isn't capable of it to get what she wants, then you haven't been paying attention. Or you're as willfully blind as my father was."

I shake my head, briefly closing my eyes. "It's not—" Shit.

I don't know what to say. *How* to say it. I'm not stunned or desperate for it not to be true for Michelle's sake, but for *his*. I've had courtside season tickets to their relationship over the years. How she dotes on Asad. How she reveres him. How he protects her. For some inexplicable reason, I don't want him to bear the soul-shattering agony of knowing his mother would steal his father from him.

"Think, Ember." His deep, midnight voice is an irresistible lure as he nears me, that gaze still studying me like I'm this peculiar, exotic specimen he needs to figure out. He desires to dissect and expose. And I feel like an experiment, like a frog cut open, splayed, my heart, organs, and soul on display. "This is the woman who brought you a puppy, let you get attached, and fall in love with it. Then six months later, forced you to take it to the pound and get it euthanized. She's the woman who locked you in a wooden chest in the attic for over fifteen hours because you spilled juice on a cloth napkin at lunch, not checking on you once. Not caring if you suffocated. And those are just the highlights. Michelle is sadistic as fuck. And you don't think she's capable of murder?" He laughs, and he's so close, I feel it before hearing it. The puff of air caresses my forehead, and the caustic sound is one that will follow me into my dreams. My nightmares. His mouth twists into a smile that, if a person's delusional, might appear kind. But I'm not as deluded as he likes to call me. He lifts a hand, traces a finger over my temple, down my cheek, to the corner of my lips. He gently taps it. "Baby girl, I didn't think there was any more innocence left in you, but shit, you keep surprising me."

He's taunting me, seeking to get a reaction out of me. And since thirteen years have conditioned me to give him one, he almost succeeds. But even as anger sparks to life deep in my chest, I peer into his eyes. And it's not the glitter of anticipation that smothers the flames; it's the shadows of the foreign, nearly unrecognizable pain behind it. A pain I'm so intimate with I've lain with it, cuddled up to it, cried out to it.

As if the most complicated hypotheses suddenly rearranged itself and became crystal clear, I can easily read him. Asad wants to fight, to release the roiling, twisting emotion inside him. And in this moment, I desire to give that to him. But not as a sparring partner.

Something altogether different.

I'm a creature of reason, of deduction and equations; they make sense in a world of chaos and disorder. But I shove all that I've relied on for so many years as my life raft to the side and sink into the madness of emotion.

Sink to my knees.

Asad goes unnaturally still and doesn't make a move to stop

or encourage me as I settle my palms on his powerful thighs. Nerves riot in my stomach, battling against a burning insecurity. Heat creeps up my neck and pours into my face, but it's not from arousal. No, its sole source is embarrassment, self-consciousness. Just last night, I was a virgin—that includes my mouth.

Goddamn. This is what happens when I'm impulsive. When I allow emotion to run me. I should've thought this through. I don't fucking know wha—

A calloused hand cups my chin in a hard but incongruently gentle grip, tipping my head back. Just that simple, but so fucking complex, touch quiets the frenzy of thoughts ripping through my head. It ignites another flurry of anxiety, but this isn't steeped in uncertainty and self-doubt. No, this originates from a wholly different, darker source.

His expression is neutral, damn near aloof. But again . . . those eyes. The traces of pain remain, as does the predatory glitter. But the latter has shifted from a cruel anticipation to a hungry one. Without removing his unblinking, steady gaze from mine, he sweeps a thumb across both of my lips. Once. Twice. A third time. I don't need to see the skin on the pad to know it's stained with my dark red lipstick or to look into a mirror to know he's made a mess of me.

Both have my pussy seizing like she's stroking out.

I don't drop my head as I move my hands from his thighs to the thin leather belt encircling his waist. Fingers that have performed highly delicate experiments are suddenly clumsy and uncoordinated as they undo the buckle and the closure on his suit pants.

But I manage and pull down his zipper. Anticipation, nerves, and desire barrel through me, and though this dick has rearranged my insides, I'm still nervous as hell about sliding it in my mouth. But this is for Asad, about him, not me. Wrapping my fingers around his long, thick dick, I palm it, instantly thinking back to how it felt shoving deep within me, and I pant against his skin. Wanting that again, but settling for this. A whimper nearly escapes me.

"You're . . . beautiful," I whisper, risking a glance up at him and feeling scorched by the heat staring back down at me. "I'm going to . . ."

Lowering my head, I drag my lips up his length, graze my lips over the precum-dampened tip, and roll my tongue over and around it, sucking at the small slit. His taste, so musky, unfamiliar, and so *him*. The singular flavor send my taste buds dancing, and I can't contain my hum of pleasure. He hisses above me, and when I glance up at him, a frown darkens his face as he glares down at me.

Embarrassment singes my throat and face because I obviously did something wrong. I start to withdraw, but he palms the back of my head and pushes me back down on his dick. The tip penetrates my lips and, reflexively, I suck on it.

He grunts then brushes the backs of his fingers over my cheek. The gentle caress and the swollen head in my mouth is a juxtaposition that sends heat and something . . . softer through me.

"You good, ma," he murmurs. "The only thing you did wrong was almost drag this nut out of me too early."

A warm rush of pride eliminates the burn of humiliation, and I eagerly lower my head and take more of him. My mouth is as much of a virgin at this as my pussy was last night. Uncertain and drawing on what I've seen in porn, I go with instinct and, hollowing my cheeks, suck on him. Sucking, licking, kissing. I have no idea what I'm doing for real, but none of that matters. Soon, I'm lost in the feel of his hard, throbbing dick pumping in and out of my mouth. I'm fascinate with the veins trailing his length like a road map. Popping him out of my mouth, I follow those delineated lines with my tongue, learning them before inhaling him again. With one hand pressed to his thigh, I fist the almost brutish bottom half that I can't take, pumping it.

His groan has my nipples beading, stomach clenching and pussy wetting up my panties. The sound is agony and lust, and a direct result of me pleasuring him. I'm not ashamed of the same rush of pride swelling inside me. This beautiful, powerful, lethal man, who incites respect and fear in so many people, shudders in pleasure because of me.

"Open your mouth, Ember. Wider," Asad grinds out while slowly pulling his dick free.

Another hiss escapes him as his length glides over my tongue. I obey that rough demand, stretching my mouth so wide the corners pinch. His fingers sweep over my hair then grip the thick strands. He gently removes my hand from the other half of his dick and replaces it with his own. He taps the tip, wet with my saliva, on my bottom lip, teasing me. Every muscle in my body stiffens in anticipation. My breath comes out in heavy pants, but lust prevents any shame, any embarrassment.

"Stay just like that. Flatten your tongue," he orders, and glides his dick back inside me, filling me. I instinctively close my lips around him, but he shakes his head. "Nah, baby girl. Keep that mouth open for me."

My jaws tingle, but I acquiesce. And my reward is Asad gently but firmly fucking my face. I whimper, my sex completely soaked and aching. Gripping the backs of his thighs, I dig my fingernails into his pants-covered muscles, holding on to steady myself in the filthy winds of this storm I've thrown myself into. He continues to take my mouth, and with each thrust, he claims more and more of me, his fist retreating farther and farther on his throbbing flesh. When his tip grazes the back of my throat, I gag and he withdraws, the head resting on my cheek.

I try to swallow and wipe away the saliva pooling in my mouth and dripping down my chin.

"Don't do that." He cuffs my wrist and pushes it away. "You don't know how gorgeous you are, kneeling here with your mouth stuffed full of my dick. Giving me sloppy head like a good girl. Nah, don't wipe your mouth. Give me all of that." He guides his damp length toward me, pausing on my bottom lip. "Spit on it." I blink up at him in confusion, but his hooded eyes don't waver. "Spit on it, ma."

Hesitantly, I lean back a little and spit on his dick. Without breaking visual contact with me, he strokes his flesh, grunting with each pump of his fist. I'm captivated, burning hot watching him handle himself so roughly, twisting and jerking the hard, wide length.

With a rumble in his throat, he buries himself in my mouth again, not easing me into this fucking. It's wild, dirty, and, yes, sloppy. Saliva seeps from the sides of my pursed lips, slides down my chin. And I don't care. Not when he's breaking me in with each thrust and grind.

When he touches the opening to my throat, and I, once again, gag, he soothes me. Softly caressing the length of my neck, he croons, "Relax your throat, Ember. Relax and breathe deep."

I force myself to obey even though my eyes sting and jaws ache. Anxiety spears through me, but I trust him. In *this*, I trust him not to hurt or take advantage of me. I follow his instructions, and he slips into my throat. My muscles reflexively constrict, but I close my eyes and deliberately breathe through my nose. His long, tortured moan is the perfect praise. Asad cradles my head and, murmuring how good I'm doing, presses back inside and eases farther into my throat. Tears prick my eyes, but the feel of him penetrating me in another way, and the lust stamped on his face, has me shaking with the arousal and heat coursing through me. I'm swamped in it, ready to cave for it.

"Gotdamn, baby girl." His fingers press harder into my face, and his teeth sink into his bottom lip. "You trying to snatch this nut outta me. You and this fucking mouth gon' be my downfall."

I briefly pause at his words—words I don't even know if he's aware he uttered. But they touch something deeper than my pussy. What that is, I don't want to analyze. Not here. Not now. Maybe never.

I go wild on his dick, attempting to shove his declaration out of my head. Bobbing up and down his length, maybe trying to push him toward release. Maybe trying to show him I'm his equal in more ways than one. I'm definitely trying to comfort him, and I don't even know what to do with that, so I focus only on the sex. Only on the sex.

He fucks me with an abandon that leaves me breathless and so damn hot. Each hard stroke brands his dick on my mouth, my tongue, my throat. And I don't resist. No, I want more of it. More of him.

Withdrawing far enough to drag in air through my nose, I take him again. Deeper. His thighs clench hard under my nails, his breath is a harsh melody in the room. My name is a sacred yet dirty prayer on his lips. He lowers a hand and wraps it around my throat, gives it a gentle squeeze.

"Fuck, I'm cumming." He growls the warning, his hips punching forward harder, more insistent. "Where you want this nut, baby girl?"

Reaching up, I remove his hand from my cheek and move it to the back of my head. Silently telling him to give it to me.

"Ember. Dammit." He groans, thrusting faster and harder. Gripping his hips, I hold on, bracing myself.

He releases a low roar as the first splash of his seed hits my tongue; his eyes, hooded and gleaming, meet mine. They refuse to release me. Not as I swallow him down. Not as the last tremor ripples through him.

On a strangled groan, he yanks me to my feet. "Open your mouth. Let me see," he hoarsely demands, lust savagely stamped on his features.

Even though I'm new to this, I understand what he requests of me. And I don't hesitate to give it to him. Stretching my mouth wide, I extend my tongue and show him how I swallowed all of his nut like the good, obedient girl I am. The one I become with him. Only with him.

Does that scare me?

God, yes.

Is my mouth watering to have his dick possess it, pound it, desecrate it again?

Oh God, yes.

With a growl, Asad grabs my arms, yanks me to my feet, and slams his mouth to mine. His tongue thrusts between my lips, and I shamelessly offer him mine, letting him taste his nut. He doesn't shy away from it. No, just the opposite. Asad sucks on my tongue, lapping at it as if the combined flavor of me and him is a heady chaser. Creed and cedarwood have my head gone. The hungry moan he direct deposits into me got me more lit than the strongest weed. The echo of his dark, hoarse praise has me ready to drop to my knees and swallow him down all over again.

Because the impulse surges within me so hard, so bright, it threatens to eclipse every need, every thought, I step back. That's such a coward's way of describing it.

I tear away from him, imbibing large gulps of cleansing, mind-clearing air. I must look unhinged to him, sucking in air as if my head just broke above water and my lungs are aching from lack of oxygen. Turning my back, I press my fingertips to my ravaged, sensitive mouth with its ruined lipstick, then trail them lower to the tender throat that is no longer virgin territory. We'd been physically intimate as two people could possibly be, with a dead body in the room no less. But allowing him to see how much he affected me seems too vulnerable. It would be granting him an advantage over me that would lead to me crawling on the floor to him like a dog.

The part that terrifies me more than that image?

That I might willingly put myself down there for him.

Viciously shaking my head of the horrifying thought and vision, I turn back around to face him, and his eyes are narrowed on me. Words as corrosive as the acid burning the back of my throat sear my tongue, but before I can utter them, Asad does the unthinkable. The most profane, terrible thing he's done to me so far.

He closes the gap between us, grasps my upper arms in an implacable grip, and tugs me forward . . .

And presses the softest kiss to my forehead.

"Thank you," he murmurs, lips moving against my skin.

If the gentle caress didn't rock me to the core, those two words from *this man* do. Just minutes ago, I believed the pulse of his dick, the rumbled growl of my name as he came down my throat, had weakened me.

But no.

The combination of a nearly chaste touch and humble words of gratitude nearly wreck me.

And when he steps back and releases me, I almost stumble, unanchored, reeling from the punch, the impact that leaves me confused and needy. Hungry for just one more of those kisses that I had no idea my affection-deprived soul cried out for until this very moment.

Shit.

Shit.

This man is going to break me. He's going to break me in ways even his mother never accomplished and leave me scattered, bleeding, and in pieces.

Fuck him. Fuck *him*.

And fuck me because I'm going to let him.

Mentally crab-walking away from the terror of that premonition, I lift my head, meeting Asad's steady gaze and praying mine doesn't betray the confusion and panic playing hide-and-seek in my mind.

"Thanking me for head?" My lips twist into a sardonic half smile even as I mentally envision the quickest, easiest escape path out of this room. "That has to be a new one for you." I shrug. "Given my inexperience, it was amateurish at best, but—"

"Don't do that." The sharpness of his words doesn't match his low, quiet tone. I still nearly flinch as if he'd shouted it. God, I almost wish he had. "Don't insult me, and don't belittle yourself. And don't pretend that I'm not perceptive enough to understand what you did—and why you did it. You believe there's been nothing but hate and pain between us for over a decade. And that could be true. But it's also true that no one knows you better than me. And no one on this earth knows me more than you."

A shudder races through me at that ominous-sounding proclamation, and denial is hot on its heels.

My lips part to tell him that's some bullshit. But the objection won't come.

The lie refuses to leave my tongue.

He reaches out, rubs the roughened pad of his thumb over my bottom lip in a firm caress that brands his fingerprint into my flesh.

"You knew what I needed, and you gave it to me. You and this pretty"—he presses hard against my lip, my teeth grinding into the tender flesh, a reminder of how hard pleasure and pain ride for each other—"ruin you call a mouth. A blind, foolish man would think with his dick and assume you just couldn't wait to get you a taste. But when it comes to you, I've never been blind or foolish. Nah, you've been my dedicated field of study for years. And you got on those knees to either distract me or comfort me. And since both of us know you'd never admit to the latter, we'll go with the first. So." He gives my bottom lip another firm pass, then drops his arm. "You have my gratitude, no matter how uncomfortable it makes you."

Once more, the denial becomes mired in my throat. I don't want his gratitude, his . . . his unfamiliar softness. It has my survival instinct kicking me in the ribs, and screaming, *Fuck fighting. Run!*

But my feet are glued to the floor, and I'm stuck, trapped in uncertainty and doubt.

And curiosity.

But when it comes to you, I've never been blind or stupid. Nah, you've been my dedicated field of study for years.

What did he mean? Because if it'd been any other man, it would almost sound like he was obsessed with me. But this isn't any other man. This is Asad Prince, my childhood bully, my tormentor, my enemy. My fiancé. The only obsession we've shared is hatred.

And now a burning, bottomless hunger that even now stretches and yawns low in my belly, even though his cum just filled it moments ago.

I take a step back from him.

And immediately recognize my mistake.

His silver eyes narrow, and his chin lowers as if he scents the tangy, acidic flavor of dread emanating from my pores.

My phone vibrates against my hip, and relief washes over me in a heavy deluge. Without breaking eye contact with Asad, I reach into my suit pocket and remove the cell, touch the screen, and lift it to my ear. I don't bother looking because I don't give a fuck.

"Yes."

"Ember," Perla says, and tension snaps into my body. She knows I'm in a meeting and wouldn't call unless it was vitally important. "When you have a minute."

Code for *Get your ass here now*.

"Noted." Ending the call and slipping the phone back into my pocket, I give Asad an insincere, small smile. "Are we done here? I'm needed back in the lab."

"Everything good?" he asks, those too-perceptive eyes roaming over my face as if attempting to ferret out the truth.

This is me though. I earn W-2s in ain't-shit-here-to-see face.

"Of course. Are we done?"

He closely studies me for several more seconds, then slowly nods. "Yeah, we're done, Ember."

Not waiting for him to change his mind, I turn on my heel and stride toward the door.

"Don't you want to know why she killed him?"

His voice rings out across the conference room just as my fingers close around the knob. I freeze. My mind screams at me to move my ass. That I'm almost home-free and to get the fuck up out of this room with its emotional and physical carnage. But apparently, my body votes against my self-interest, because I remain at that door, waiting. Hanging on the silence weighted down with expectation.

No, with anticipation.

I remain silent, but no words are needed. My presence and refusal to escape the room speak loudly enough.

"Turn around, Ember. Turn around and look at me if you want to indulge in my trauma porn."

I don't manage to fully control my flinch at his bald accusation, yet I still do as he orders. And as I face him, the sarcasm drenching his voice also twists his lush mouth. But even that mocking thing of a smile doesn't reach his eyes. No, they're blank canvases of gray sleet and ice. Opaque, muddy, and . . . nothing.

My fingers remain curled around the doorknob, much like a shipwreck victim clinging to the shattered debris of a mast. It's keeping me grounded, afloat. Protecting me from diving into unchartered waters and swimming toward this suddenly unfamiliar . . . *vulnerable* stranger to wrap my arms around him. Comfort him.

Lunacy. That is the urge to cross the room and touch him. Absolute lunacy.

"Ask me." His demand is nearly mangled by the low growl of his voice. "Ask me what you want to know."

No, don't give in. Don't surrender another inch. There's been too many intimacies exchanged between us. My sanity can't afford another one. Too bad my curiosity hasn't received the menu. That bitch is shameless.

And apparently, so am I.

"Why did she kill him?" I murmur. "Only tell me if you want to, Asad. Only if you *need* to."

Emotion flickers in his gaze, but it's there and gone before I can decipher it, hidden behind that wall.

"If I need to?" He softly chuckles and shakes his head.

I almost tell him never mind; more than anyone, I understand the cost of allowing someone behind those barbed, guarded walls. Of wondering if you just handed your enemy a loaded gun with armor-piercing ammo.

Almost.

Because there's this secret, hungry, *clawing* thing inside me that craves more of him. And it has nothing to do with his dick.

In all the years he's been in my life, Asad has never understood the concept of personal space. Who am I kidding? He's never given a fuck. And he doesn't switch up on me now.

He stalks forward, his long, powerful legs aggressively eating up the distance until his big body towers over mine. It doesn't escape me that only with him do I feel delicate, fragile . . . wanted.

And that kind of power is chains forged in titanium.

"Yeah, Ember, I need to. I need you to listen. You gon' give that to me, ma?" That roughened-silk voice steals the breath from my lungs, but I nod. His lips momentarily flatten into a grim line before he dips his chin in response. His head lowers, and when he speaks again, his mouth brushes my ear. "What Michelle wants, she gets. You should know that better than anyone. She set her sights on Marcus, and fucking him behind my father's and your mother's backs wasn't enough. Not when she could be Mrs. Marcus Cross and have access to the lifestyle that came with it."

Shock ripples through me, and I lightly shake my head as if attempting to shake free the low, insistent buzz gathering in my head.

"Marcus was having an affair with Michelle?" I rasp.

"He married her only three months after your mother died. You can't possibly be that naïve, baby girl."

Naïve? No. In denial and clinging to the last tattered vestiges of hope that maybe, just fucking *maybe*, Marcus wasn't as much of a soulless piece of shit as my suspicions whispered? Yeah.

But in seconds, Asad stripped those busted and warped rose-tinted glasses away.

God*damn* him. Godda—I gasp, horror and a sharp agony striking me in the chest so hard my hand releases the doorknob and splays over heart.

"Did he . . . ?" The thought crashes against my skull, loud and angry. But my throat cinches closed around the words. I can't squeeze them past the constriction. I lick my lips and try again. "Did he ki—"

"Did Marcus kill your mother?" Asad raises his head, cocks it as he stares down at me, his dark, thick brows arrowed down over his arctic gaze. "No, not that I'm aware of. Marcus might've been a shit husband who couldn't keep his dick in his pants and didn't know a mu'fucking thing about through sickness and health, but he didn't murder her. But when Michelle became aware of your mother's cancer diagnosis, she became a widow within months. One day, my father was healthy, and the next, he was a walking skeleton throwing up blood and pissing on himself." A smirk rides his mouth, but a gloriously hot fury sears away the ice from before. "The truly fucked-up part? Toward the end, I believe my father knew she was poisoning him. It was in his eyes—this sad, almost resigned knowledge. But instead of saying anything to the doctors, shit, *to me*, he lay in that hospital bed, wasting away. She played the grieving-widow part to perfection. No one suspected. Just me. But she knew I wasn't a threat. She knew I would keep her fucking secret."

"Why did you?" I whisper.

He leans farther back, his arms falling to his sides, his hands sliding into his pants pockets. A long, silent moment passes between us, and it possesses a heavy, thick heartbeat.

"Because she's my mother," he finally says, voice flat, void of emotion. "And if my father didn't say anything to save himself and betray her, I couldn't either."

The logic is fucked-up.

And yet, I get it.

It's why I could hate my father in one breath and still be unable to fully exorcise that part of me that yearned for his approval. Hungered for his love.

"I'm sorry, Asad." My hand lifts seemingly without my permission, but as it hovers over his jacket-covered forearm, I freeze. Staring down at it, I slightly shake my head, then lower it back to my side. "I'm sorry about the loss of your father," I say again.

"It's been thirteen years since my mother's been gone, but the pain, the grief of not just their death but of who you could've been if they'd stayed, never truly leaves, does it? The sense of being cheated of the life you could've led, of . . ." *Being loved.* I swallow, unable to vocalize that too-telling admission. "So yes, I'm sorry that all these years you have been alone in honoring the memory of Khalil Amir Prince. You won't be any longer."

He stares down at me, but his throat works as if he, too, is swallowing down a response.

I shake my head and step to the side. Again. And then again. Placing distance between us. "But what you just shared with me only solidifies my earlier point. When it comes down to it, you'll always choose Michelle. Like you said, she's your mother. I don't have the benefit or grace of trusting you. As you reminded me, it can literally get me killed. And I don't trust you to intervene. So-called fiancée or not."

I don't wait for the ice-cold bite of rage that will surely come in a scathing insult. Instead, I grip the doorknob again, twist it, and pull open the door. My heart pounds in my chest, the rhythm pulsing in my throat, chest, and belly, as I tread down the hall to the elevator. When the doors open, only then do I turn around and glance back toward the conference room door.

But the corridor and the doorway are empty.

And if I'm disappointed that Asad didn't follow me, didn't try to convince me that I was wrong, that I could trust him—that he would choose me before this organization, this family, his mother—well, it's nothing I haven't experienced before.

No one has ever prioritized me.

No one has ever put me first.

Loved me enough.

So I'll do what I always have.

Go to work.

CHAPTER TEN

Asad

"Prince, there's no activity around the perimeter of his house. None at all." Eli's voice echoes in my earbud, low but clear, as if he's sitting next to me in this box van instead of lurking somewhere around the rear of Xavier's Malibu mansion. "Either he's out for the night, or he's one cocky-ass son of a bitch having zero security."

"Neither." I shift on the silver bench and stare out the van's tinted back window at the top of the massive white Mediterranean-style home with its terra-cotta roof, huge windows, and patios through the trees. Parked in a cut a short distance from the house, that's all that's visible to me. From experience, I know those glass walls offer gorgeous ocean views. I hope Xavier carries the memory into the afterlife, 'cause from what I hear, the lakes of fire in hell don't carry the same vibe. "He's in there," I assure Eli. "And yeah, he's bold as fuck, but this ain't 'bout that. That mu'fucka know we coming. As soon as he arrived at the meeting today at the Castle, he knew. I saw that shit in his eyes."

"If that's the case, he should have a gotdamn armada waiting on us," Makeda scoffs. I can't see her from the window of the van where I'm waiting, but I don't need to in order to know she has teams positioned on both sides of the mansion. "Maybe he pulled them inside for the element of surprise."

Maybe. Every instinct whispers Xavier's there, alone. Waiting. On me.

I ain't never been one to disappoint.

"Let's move out," I murmur, shifting off the van's bench and reaching for the handle on one of the doors. I tap the side of my earbud. "Ro? The system down?"

"Done," she affirms from her position in another van farther down the road. "Alarms off and the cameras are on a loop. You're good."

"Bet." I tug down my ski mask and shove the van door open.

Crystal, Murk, and Corey climb out of the van with me, while Dana stays behind the wheel. In our all black, we silently and as one coordinated unit move across the street, sticking to the late-evening shadows. That's one of the great and advantageous qualities about these huge houses on these quiet, set-back roads that are monuments to a person's ego and bank account. No neighbors for fucking miles. Which equals to no witnesses to a crime in progress.

I creep close to the small guard shack with its pointed turret and tiny window, pressing my back to the thick, towering hedge. Crystal slides to the other side of me, her short, slender frame moving with a graceful, deadly ease, and removes a thin, silver wand with a small, circular mirror attached at the end. She extends it just past the corner of the shrubbery, and we glimpse the guard on duty. Instead of being alert and on his shit, he leans his big, thick build back in his chair, his attention glued on whatever's in front of him. Hell, I'm doing Xavier a favor by taking this mu'fucka out. He's a waste of a W-2.

Crystal glances at me, and I nod. Removing my Glock from my hip, I round the hedge, and on quick, noiseless feet, approach the shack and pop the guard twice in the temple through the cracked window.

In minutes, we're running up the long driveway and soon approaching the gurgling stone fountain and shallow front steps. Satisfaction pours through me. The first kill of several tonight, if I'm lucky. I need this—the adrenaline rush, the whistle of excitement rushing through my veins that taking a life brings. In ways, it's cleansing. This shit, I know; it's simple. It's easy for me. And right now, I need simple and easy.

I don't have the benefit or grace of trusting you. As you reminded me, it can literally get me killed.

My jaw clenches as Ember's words from earlier in the day slip through my mind, a stealthy, unwelcome intruder. For hours, that accusation has been attached to me like a parasite, burrowing its way deeper and deeper inside me. It shouldn't bother me. I'm not requiring her fucking trust. I just want her surrender and obedience.

Fucking liar.

Yeah, I am. I'm the filthiest of liars, because I want all of her—crave all of her. Her allegiance, her body, her thoughts, her fucking breath. I'm jealous of anything she attempts to keep from me.

Including her trust.

Shaking my head, I focus on the task at hand. Which is traversing this long-ass driveway to get to a man who finds himself unlucky enough to be my prey for the evening.

"We're at the door," I inform Eli, Makeda, and the others through my headset. Corey, Murk, and Crystal gather with me.

"At the kitchen patio door," Eli says.

"I'm here at the first-floor balcony door," Makeda adds.

"Let's get it. Meet outside his study."

I don't need to give them further instructions or directions. I've been here so many times, it's like a second home to me. And I made sure to send the layout to the team so it would be emblazoned on their minds. We don't have any room for mistakes tonight.

Corey hunkers down in front of the door, removing a small kit from his hoodie pocket. In an impressive number of seconds, the lock softly *snicks* and he twists the knob, pushing the door open.

I step first into the large, shadowed foyer with its high ceiling and ornate chandelier, pausing, listening. Behind me, Crystal, Murk, and Corey fan out, forming a circle around me before they stop, too. I don't hear anything. Not even our own people breaking into the house. Giving them a nod, I carefully close the door and lead the way down the corridor toward the study. Within seconds, Eli, Makeda, and their teams gather on either side of the shut study door.

As if on cue, we all pull our weapons and hold them at our sides. Before I can reach for the knob, Makeda slips in front of me and slowly edges it open. Three members of her team swiftly fall in behind her, forming a shield between me and the shadowed interior of the room.

Irritation flashes through me. I'm not accustomed to standing back and letting others charge into a situation before me. Not used to letting people sacrificing their welfare and safety for me. It's the other way around. That's how I move. But even as that gnawing need to stride into the room and do just that grinds at me, I sublimate it. I could move like that *before*. Before I became head of the Cross organization. Before I became directly responsible for hundreds of people. Before my actions weren't only me but the livelihoods and stability of an entire company and their families.

So yeah, I have to move different.

I still hate the shit.

"Clear, except for our mark," Makeda announces several moments later from inside the study.

My stride is casual as I enter the room, hands tucked into the front pockets of my black cargo pants, but nothing about the rage I've kept carefully banked is *casual*. Peeping Xavier, perched behind his large, gleaming desk, an arrogant smirk curving his mouth, has the valve on that fury slowly turning, the vise loosening. My fingers curl into fists, and it requires every scrap of control I possess not to leap across that mu'fucking desk and rip his fucking head off his shoulders with my bare hands. I want his blood. Literally. Nobody betrays me and lives to tell it.

Xavier won't be the exception.

I could've killed him at the meeting earlier. I could've taken his and Deacon's life at any time between last night and right now. But I want—no, need—answers first. And then I want them to suffer.

"I knew you would be showing up sooner or later, Prince." Xavier's smirk deepens, and his large frame settles back in his chair as he temples his fingers underneath his chin. "Once I heard Demarcus and Carter were dead, I figured it wouldn't be long before you came for me. Have to say, I thought it would be sooner rather than later."

"Sorry to disappoint you, Xavier." I stroll across the room that's as familiar to me as my face and approach his desk. Floor-to-ceiling bookshelves. Leather furniture. A mammoth fireplace. Makeda and her team form a phalanx around me, and I don't need to glance over my shoulder to know Eli and his hittas have moved in behind me. I sink down into the armchair across from him and cross my ankle over my knee. Spreading my arms wide and settling them on the arms of the chair, I meet Xavier's flinty, dark gaze that does a shitty job of concealing his hatred. "I'm here now though. I hope my presence makes up for my tardiness."

He snorts, the haughtiness finally falling from his face, replaced by condescension.

"You always were an arrogant li'l shit, Prince. From day one, walked up in here like you came from Marcus's nut sack. Like this family owed you something. That arrogance was and is misplaced. You haven't earned your stripes, put in enough work. You got bosses, even leaders been here longer, put in more time, more work for Cross, been loyal while your mother was still swallowing your father's kids."

"Soldiers like who? Like you?"

As if he remembers himself, Xavier pulls in a calming breath and lowers his arms and rests them on top of the desk. That taunting smirk returns to his face, but it's a facade, a defense mechanism. And shame on him for letting me glimpse it.

I smile.

"Go 'head and admit it, Xavier. Get that shit off yo' chest. What's that saying? Better to let it out and be ashamed . . ." I snap my finger, looking over at Makeda with a frown.

"Better to let it out and be ashamed than hold it in and bust a vein," she finishes for me with a roll of her eyes.

"Yeah, that's it." I point a finger at her. "'Preciate it."

"Ain't that about shittin' though?" Eli frowns.

"I'm pretty sure it is," Makeda cosigns with a nod.

A chorus of voices rise in agreement, and I shrug. "Okay, damn. It's still appropriate. Just don't do the shit literally. You were saying, Xavier?" I tilt my head. "We're all listening."

"You're so sure of yourself, Prince. Think you're fucking untouchable. When the truth is you're only where you are today thanks to your mother's good back and friendly pussy. You didn't earn a damn thing. You're not family. Just a money-hungry, faithless bitch's wayward cum who took advantage of a man desperate to have a son."

The sound of multiple guns cocking punches the air, but I hold up my hand, preventing them from sending their bullets flying and having Xavier's bitch ass look like a cheese grater.

He doesn't get to go that easy.

Softly chuckling, I tip my chin at Xavier. "Well, damn, from all of that, I can't tell if you got a hard-on for my mother or Marcus. Maybe both."

"Don't fucking play with me, boy—"

"Nah, we ain't doing that." I don't raise my voice, but all traces of humor flee. "Now, you're not walking up out of here, but disrespect me like that one more time and it'll be in pieces. Your sister and that niece you love so much, who're sleeping so well in that pretty house you bought for them over in Brentwood? DeAnn, right? Too bad about that congestive heart failure diagnosis. Do you think waking up next to a suit of your skin will send her into a heart attack? Stroke?" When Xavier's mouth flattens into a grim line, I nod. "Yeah, how 'bout if you keep family out of it, I will, too."

"They don't have nothing to do with—"

"You fucking betrayed me, mu'fucka." I cut him off again, seething. "Betrayed this family when you tried to have me killed. The moment you sent members of *my* organization after me—yeah, *mine*, ho—you entered a murder-suicide pact. Their deaths are on you; you killed them. I'm just the bullet you aimed in their direction. Shit, Xavier. As you pointed out, you've been in this longer than me. So you know how this shit goes. You're so fucking arrogant that you didn't weigh the costs of failure. Didn't consider who would pay the debt along with you if your little plan to take me out didn't work. Well, you're looking the consequences in the eye." I lean forward and smile. "If it's any comfort to you, I'll make it quick. Call it a concession for your many years of service before you became a tender dick bitch incapable of taking a loss."

For a moment, his face sags with the weight of sadness and guilt. Both flash in his dark eyes, turn down the corners of his mouth, and in mere seconds, he appears ten years older. Even the proud carriage of his shoulders droops, and he's broken. But only for a moment. Anger—at me, himself, his failure, all three—mottles his light brown skin, and his eyes narrow on me. He damn near vibrates with his rage, and I drag in a deep breath, swearing I can smell it. Fucking taste it.

And it's gotdamn heady.

"Just get the shit over with, Prince," he snaps, rising from his chair.

"Unh-unh." Makeda waves her SIG at Xavier. "Sitcho ass back down."

He glares at her, probably balking at either a woman talking to him like that or having to take an order from her. Don't matter in the end. 'Cause he sits his ass back down.

"You came here for answers, right?" he continues, leaning forward on his elbows, his attention pinned on me. "That's what you want to know. Why I sent those incompetent mu'fuckas after you?" He laughs, shaking his head. "Fuck, I wish they were alive so I could kill them myself."

"You should've. But then again, if you had the balls to handle your own shit, you wouldn't have been able to be sitting where I am. Since the Cross organization doesn't look too kindly on assassination or treason." I lower my leg, fury and impatience to watch his life drain from his eyes swell inside me, shoving against my sternum with increasing hunger. "And let's be honest. Whatever reason you give me—loyalty to the family, lifelong friendship to Marcus, protecting Cross, blah blah fucking blah—it all comes down to two things. Greed and power. You want to rule, Xavier. And you expected to when Marcus died. Or maybe . . ." I drum my fingers against the arm of the chair. "You got tired of waiting and decided to give him a helping hand to hell."

He blinks, then scowls at me, mouth twisting.

"The fuck you talking about, Prince? You want honesty? Yes, you have no business leading Cross. You're not blood. Not family. Me, Deacon—we've been here beside Marcus since he first stepped into power. We know the workings of this family. We served it, sacrificed for it, bled for it. What did you do? What have you done? Michelle understood Marcus's disappointment that Kimberly couldn't and didn't give him a son. So she preyed on that and gave him you. Her, you, your brother—you're parasites who fed on his need, on this organization, and you're still doing it even after his death. As far as I'm concerned, I was just exterminating our pest problem."

I flick my hand, waving his insults off. "Fuck all that. Is that supposed to move me? And let's just lay the shit out on the table, Xavier. This isn't about blood, about family. Because you knew of Ember's existence all along, the only one person who carries the name Cross now, and it never occurred to you to protect her, bring her into your confidence, to revere her? Nah. This is about greed, power. About you being one bitter-ass bitch because your boy didn't leave you shit but a pat on the head and a wet ass.

What the old saints say? Favor ain't favor. Answer my question. Did you kill Marcus so you could finally get your shot at the top?"

Again, he mugs me as if being a fucking Judas doesn't offend him, but being called a murderer crosses the line.

"What? No! Fuck no. Marcus was murdered? I heard the rumor, but I thought it was just that—rumor." He starts to stand, but after a quick glance in Makeda's direction, he aborts the motion, frustration and rage crowding into his face. "No," he stresses, unflinchingly meeting my gaze. "I didn't have anything to do with Marcus's death. He was my friend. My best friend. I wouldn't have killed him. I swear that on my sister's life."

I believe him. I trust him as much as I do a cop on a traffic stop, but yeah, I believe he didn't have anything to do with killing Marcus. He still gon' die though.

I straighten in the chair, then prop my elbows on my thighs. "But the fact remains, you took a shot at the king, and you missed. You not making it out of here alive, but how you go is on you. I already know Deacon is in on this with you. Tell me who else you're working with, and I'll make it quick. Make me work for the information, and it's gon' be a long night. For you, not me. Because I'ma enjoy the shit."

A grin spreads across Xavier's face, and though I catch a flicker of fear in the older man's eyes, he's not afraid to die. Nothing like a person who's down for the cause and willing to make themselves a martyr.

Course, they're all stoic until that first slice.

"You think I'm going to make this easy for you? The fuck?" He laughs, tipping his head back as if Dave Chappelle is sitting in this mu'fucka instead of me. "You want me to hold your dick for you, too? I waited here for you, remember? Gave you easy access to my house and me. You haven't done shit I didn't invite you to do. Including getting this shit over with. Go 'head, Prince. 'Cause I'm not telling you a fucking thing. We all gotta die, and my family's always known what it is to be in this shit. You'll find out soon enough everything you want to know." That low, raspy chuckle again. "No, hold on. I've changed my mind. I'll give you something. What was it you said? How 'bout I keep family out of it? A little too late for that shit."

The words, uttered with a grimy, irreverent glee, sink into me like claws, injecting shock, suspicion, and a bone-chilling rage. The noxious mixture seeps into my blood, marrow, my fucking DNA. The implication . . .

"The fuck is that supposed to mean?" I growl, slowly straightening, my narrowed gaze pinned on him. "You tryin' to say my family's working with you? That they had something to do with that hit?"

My heart swings at my chest with wild haymakers, the pounding reverberating in my body, echoing in my head. It's so loud, his answer is damn near lost under the primitive rhythm.

Almost.

"Did I say that?" he asks, looking like a wide-mouth-ass bass wearing that fucking grin on his face. "It'd be a shame though if they were. I mean, if you can't trust the ones who're supposed to have your back, then you're fucked. You should—"

I jump to my feet and round the desk, not hearing shit else he has to say. Not even seeing a gotdamn thing but that thick-ass, lyin' tongue.

My hand shoots out, gripping his face tight and squeezing his cheeks together. Ignoring his squawk of surprise and outrage, I swipe my Bugout knife from my pocket. With a quick press of a button on the hilt, the short black blade appears, silent and deadly. In seconds, Xavier's fury morphs to terror, all that shit-talking bravado dying a quick death. Unlike him.

He cuffs my wrists, claws at them, trying to escape my grip and keep the knife away from him. Pleasure—slick, obsidian, and feral—slides through me, weighing down the doubts, the questions whirring in my mind until they're suffocated, extinguished by the sheer joy of the upcoming kill. Even the sting of his short nails in my skin is another dick-hardening sensation, adding to the purity of this moment.

I release him, palm his face, and mush him back against the chair.

"Prince, fuck y—"

He doesn't finish that sentence.

Isn't able to.

Not without a tongue.

His sharp, agonized screams ricochet off the walls. Xavier's hands fly to his mouth, covering it. But they do little to contain the sound. And the shit is sensual. I swallow a groan at the texture of it, the wet, metallic scent of the blood, the gorgeous sight of all that dark crimson running down the sides of his lips and over his chin like tributaries. He's a fucking sensory feast.

I toss his tongue to the desk, and it lands on top of his calendar with a sickening *plop*, then return my attention to him.

"Since you said you ain't telling me shit, you won't need that," I say, tipping my head toward the severed offending muscle. "And you also don't seem to hear or comprehend the consequences of fucking with me, so this can also go."

Quick as a snake, I strike out, slicing his left ear off. Another gargled cry pierces the room as I drop the useless cartilage to the floor right next to his foot. I lean over him, ignoring his tortured writhing and pitiful whimpers.

Getting right up next to the space where his ear used to be, I whisper in the bloody hole, "You should've gone for quick, Xavier."

Then I get back to work.

Hours later, with Xavier's blood still staining my nails and its pungent odor lingering in my nose, I sit in the back of the van several feet away from another dark house.

"Shit, I'm about to be in my fucking feelings," Eli mutters, his irritation coming loud and unfiltered through my earpiece. "No security in sight here either. Did Deacon and Xavier get together and form some sort of pact? I mean, gotdamn, I ain't even get a chance to pinch a mu'fucka tonight."

I snort, dragging a new black hoodie over my bare chest. Unlike my second-in-command, I'm relaxed, my muscles loose, a calm blanketing me like I just took the biggest shot of Patrón to the head or faced the fattest blunt. That's what a good-ass torture session will do for you. Clear your mind, body, and spirit.

"Deacon doesn't have cameras, so you're clear on that." Disgust tinges Ro's voice at his obvious negligence. "Also, the security system is not engaged. I don't know what that means, so move with caution. He has a keyless entry. Let me know when you're at the front door so I can give you the code."

"Got it."

I stamp my feet into a new pair of black Timbs and quickly rearm myself with the weapons I removed when changing out of my clothes covered in Xavier. Moments later, I step out of the van and join Corey, Murk, and Crystal. It's a repeat of the same mission at Xavier's. Same plan. Same execution. In and out.

Deacon's Pacific Palisades house sits even farther back in the cut than Xavier's, which is a benefit to us. The four of us take off up the winding road heavily bordered by forested acreage, which provides better coverage for us, while the rest of my team approach from different angles. Our boots hitting the pavement at a steady clip join the nocturnal sounds of insects and distant traffic. By the time we creep to the front door, it's clear, as Eli warned, that security is nil. If we hadn't already experienced this with Xavier, the absence of a detail would concern me, but like his friend, maybe Deacon decided to roll the red carpet out for us.

More expedient for me.

"I'm here, Ro," I say.

"Hold on, stop." The low yet strident alarm in Makeda's forceful demand halts my hand, leaving it hovering over the keypad.

"What's going on, Makeda?" I ask, unease skittering down my spine.

"What's up?" Eli crackles in my ear at the same time.

"The French doors to the patio on the east side are wide open. Gimme a second." A pause, and the low murmur of voices. Several moments pass before her voice echoes in my ear again. "Same on the other side of the house. Not French doors, but the ground-floor windows are open. I don't trust it."

Yeah. Even with the lack of security, leaving the house vulnerable is suspect as fuck.

Me, Corey, Crystal, and Murk crouch down on either side of the front door, waiting for Makeda's signal to move. Impatience and a little unease crawl through me. This was supposed to be as clean and simple as Xavier's. But it's not shaping up that way, and it's worrisome.

"Can you see anything?" Eli asks.

"Negative," she says. "Too dark."

I glare at the keypad next to the front door, running the information and possibilities through my head. "What do you suggest, Makeda? What's the play?"

"Let me and my teams go in first and clear the house. If it's all good, we'll come to the front door and let you in. And, Eli, on my word, you enter through the mudroom."

"Got it."

Silence beats down our connection for the next ten minutes, and I can't lie. Nerves twist my stomach in knots. Not because I don't have faith in the skills of my enforcer and her teams. Nah, Makeda is the best at what she does. But something . . . call it sixth sense, instinct, or a primal sense of self-preservation . . . call it that warning of family being involved in the attempted hit . . . something crawls over my skin, leaving a slick trail of unease in its wake.

The sound of a lock disengaging interrupts my thoughts, and I stiffen, laser focusing on the front door. It slowly opens, and I draw my weapon, extending it toward the dark space, but Makeda stands in the entrance, wearing an inscrutable expression.

Though she doesn't step back and allow me into the house, I still catch a glimpse of forms darker than the shadowed depths littering the floor behind her like Raid-sprayed roaches. Turning a questioning gaze back to Makeda, I arch an eyebrow.

"They're all dead. Nah, I didn't do it," she adds, answering my next question. Not that I would've cared if she had handled it; that's literally her job. There just hadn't been any report of shots. But this did solve the mystery of the lack of security. Makeda briefly glances over her shoulder before returning her attention back to me. "If I had to guess, it was some kind of gas, maybe carbon monoxide. None of 'em have any signs of violence or injuries. And it would explain why the windows and doors are open."

Finally, she shifts backward, and I step into the palatial foyer that is as familiar to me as my own home—maybe more so. About ten bodies sprawl across the gleaming black marble, and farther down the hall, a pair of booted feet protrude from a room. I don't recognize the faces, but from the black shirts, cargo pants, and weapons riding their hips, I can only assume this is the missing security detail.

"This is some fucked up shit." Corey whistles, moving into the house and standing to the left of me, his hand wrapped around the butt of his rifle. Shock covers his face, brightens his dark eyes. Shock and maybe a little bit of fear. I don't blame him. I have no idea what the fuck we're dealing with. "Like some Jonestown-drink-the-fuckin'-Kool-Aid shit. You think that's what's going on here?"

"No," Makeda flatly says.

I tear my gaze away from the men and women, who almost appear to be sleeping, if not for their unnatural stillness, and look up at Makeda. She crouches next to one of the bodies, a younger guy with cornrows and piercings dotting his face.

"Why do you say that?" Again, not doubting her, but that "no" was so definite, without any room for argument.

"Because of what else we found," Eli answers for her, striding down the hall from the rear of the house. His face, like my enforcer's, is smooth, clear of emotion. But unlike Makeda's indecipherable gaze, shock glistens in his. "It's Deacon. He's in his library."

I don't waste any more time talking. Stalking forward, I circle the bodies and head for the library. Within moments, I approach the cracked door and, without hesitation, push it open.

At first, it's déjà vu.

Deacon, perched behind his wide, imposing desk like a king.

But then, stepping farther into the room, I realize that's where the similarities end. Because Xavier had been alive. Deacon is dead as fuck.

"Gotdamn," Crystal breathes, drawing to an abrupt halt next to me.

Yeah.

I walk closer and closer until the edge of Deacon's desk presses against the front of my thighs. This close, the sight doesn't change. Doesn't become less gruesome.

I flinch at the black, empty holes that remain where his eyes used to be. His tongue, bloated and heavily veined, hangs outside of his mouth. Dark red, sticky fluid trails from nose and over his swollen lips. Deep, raw scratches—damn near gouges—crisscross his throat. And a glance down at his curled fingers on top of the desk reveal bloodstained nails.

This wasn't an easy death. And it for damn sure wasn't natural. I'm used to death, but this . . . this is on another level. I search inside me for some kind of sympathy for the man who I once respected. A little sympathy for the torture he must've endured.

Yeah, nothing. Fuck him.

The longer I stare at what used to be Deacon, the looser my chest grows. The lighter I feel. The harder it is to control the amusement swirling deep in my stomach and rising for my throat.

"What the fuck happened here?" Corey murmurs.

I briefly glance over my shoulder, meeting his confused glance before skimming over the faces of the others who've crowded into the library.

"What happened?" I repeat, dragging my attention from the carnage that couldn't have been wreaked by a gun or knife. The burned-out eyes? The marks on that bloated tongue? Chemical. Returning my gaze to the corpse of my enemy, I smile. "My muthafuckin' wife."

CHAPTER ELEVEN

Ember

"What the fuck am I doing here?"

The gorgeous, cavernous room with the huge, elegant sleigh bed, step-down sitting area, large fireplace, and floor-to-ceiling windows doesn't reply to me. Neither do the beautiful French doors or huge armoire that looks like any moment it will invite me to "Be Our Guest." Not for the first time, I slowly turn, taking in my new surroundings. My new home for the next few years.

Asad's home.

Huffing out a laugh that sounds abrasive and slightly macabre to my own ears, I cross the room on bare feet to the glass balcony doors. One hard push on the handles and they give way under my palms. The cool night air immediately wraps around me, it and the chilled stone under my feet causing a shiver to race through me. But I still don't return to the guest room until I have to move yet again, four weeks from now. This time, down the hall to the master suite, to share with my future husband.

Folding my arms on top of the thick railing, I stare at the stunning view of towering trees and the dark. In the distance, mountains rise to the sky, and I bet they're absolutely gorgeous at sunrise. The breathtaking beauty is lost on me though. Because I'm still confused on how I ended up here weeks ahead of schedule. And I'm pissed about it. A text. A goddamn text. He upended my security, my stability with a text. Didn't even have enough respect to call and ask me, discuss this with me. The worst part? Here I am. Right where he wants me.

Shit. I need a fucking blunt, because I swear, I'm about to crash out.

I lean forward, pressing my arms into the railing as if the cool stone can ground me. Can somehow siphon some of the chaotic emotion whirling and screaming inside me.

In the last few days, I've had my immediate future changed. Been blackmailed into marriage. Forced to remain in a company—a fucking "family"—that has barely acknowledged me, and when it did, brought me nothing but pain and sorrow. It's taken, taken, taken and given nothing in return. Yes, I negotiated better terms for myself, but it didn't change my circumstances. It didn't liberate me from soon being Mrs. Asad Prince and chained to this organization when I was so close to freedom, the taste of it had my belly grumbling in hunger.

But even those negotiations apparently don't mean shit when it comes to the desires of the men in this family. I have four weeks to acclimate myself to this . . . sentence. Four weeks to retain my sovereignty. Four weeks of limited independence apart from Asad.

On a whim, he stole that, too. Demanded I move into his house, be up under his thumb.

My ol' bitch of a frenemy, anger, eddies in my chest, and the familiar flush of heat spreads like a virus over my skin, racing up my throat and pouring into my face. My palms and fingertips tingle, and I swallow hard to pop my ears, to clear them of the thick pressure bearing down on them.

Closing my eyes, I deeply inhale, hold it, then exhale. Then I begin my grounding technique, moving through it at a deliberate pace. By the time my eyes open once more, the worst of the warning signs of an imminent explosion have calmed.

"*Fuck*," I whisper, pressing my forefinger and thumb to my forehead and massaging it.

I don't need to be on anyone's couch to recognize what brought this on. Fear. Feeling out of control . . . powerless. Asad once accused me of being afraid to live with him again. It amazes me how he can be so damn obtuse in some things, but terrifyingly perceptive in others. Hell yes, I'm scared of living with him again. And not just for the reasons I gave him, although they're very valid. We don't have the best track record of living under the same roof. Not only was he my tormentor but he abetted and aided my main abuser. Still . . .

Now, there's an even more lethal one. One that horrifies me more. 'Cause if I'm being one hundred percent down 'n' dirty truthful, I don't believe Asad will physically hurt me. Will he lock me in another closet, chain me to another chair for hours? No. The threat he presents now is much more hazardous. He won't bruise my body but my spirit, my confidence . . . my very sense of self is at risk. Asad Prince has the power to strip me bare and leave me shuddering naked in the cold. Vulnerable. Exposed. Unprotected.

And unmitigated fool that I am? I'll give him the shears to cut away the layers.

"Jesus."

"Oh, ma, it's much too late to call on Him."

I whip around, pounding heart lodged in my throat, pulse crashing under my skin. The anger and unease churning inside me morphs, sliding into something hotter, fiercer, rawer. I could almost hate myself that all it takes is the sensual midnight tenor of Asad's voice. Only requires the sight of him leaning against the open balcony doorway, arms crossed, gray eyes hooded. If it wouldn't betray my weakness—my pussy's weakness—when it comes to him, I would close my eyes, block him out. But that would be like me turning my back on a ravenous lion on the hunt.

That would be destruction.

Mine.

And I've already compromised too much already. If I'm not

careful, I see myself slipping more and more away into the shadow of him. The all-consuming heat of him. And there won't be anything left of me but ash.

Mimicking him, I cross my arms and tilt my head.

"You're in the wrong room," I remind him, voice cold, flat. Revealing nothing of the storm battering me.

"Jesus . . . God . . . You already know they're not listening to you, right, Ember?" His gaze, glittering like jewels, sweeps over me, heating my skin as if it's the sun itself kissing it. I curl my fingers into my palms to keep from trailing the tips over my exposed throat, arms, and upper chest. But short of slapping my hand over his mouth to shut him up, there's nothing I can do about that sinful voice. "You know what the difference between you and me?" He pushes off the doorway and stalks across the balcony, approaching me. My breath catches in my throat as a shiver trips down my spine at the sight of his hooded, molten gaze, the small smirk and that intimidating stride. "I don't try to hide what I am. People look at me, and know they got life fucked-up if they try me. They look in my eyes and see nothing. Not remorse, not regret, not mercy. And I like that shit."

He draws to a halt in front of me and, without releasing me from his visual entrapment, he lifts a hand and cuffs the front of my throat. It's not gentle; he's ensuring I feel him, feel his intent. But his grip isn't bruising either . . . yet.

My breath snags in my throat, and I still, waiting for that first punch of fear. But it must be off somewhere getting drunk off its ass because fear doesn't make an appearance. Lust does. Like there's a shimmering thread that connects his hand to my clit, a dirty, grinding lust twists its way up my stomach to my chest and then winds back down between my legs. I clench my thighs against the wet, terrible, and *delicious* ache.

He chuckles, and it's as mean as his grip on my neck. And my pussy quivers, spilling moisture onto my panties, making a mess.

"No one sees you coming though. No one guesses that underneath your ice-bitch demeanor, ol'-lady suits, and many degrees, there's a killer as brutal, as depraved and heartless, as me."

Warmth at his praise sweeps over my skin, sinking lower into tendon and bone. Pride balloons behind my rib cage, and I feel *seen*.

Except for . . .

"I don't wear old-lady suits."

The cruel slant of his mouth deepens. His hold on my neck tightens.

And my pussy volunteers herself as tribute.

"They're cover, just like everything else about you is, so no one guesses the real you." He lowers his head so his mouth barely brushes against mine in a dick tease. I taste the bourbon he must've drunk either before arriving here or on the way to the guest room. My head swims, intoxicated by him even as my belly spasms in hunger for a sip. "You've been bad, ma. What have you been up to tonight?" he damn near purrs. "And before you think to lie to me"—he squeezes my throat—"I'm like God. I already know the answer to the question I'm asking."

He knows.

He knows.

I hike my chin up as far as his hand allows.

"What have I been up to besides moving into your house when we agreed I wouldn't have to for another month?" I arch an eyebrow and lean my head forward until our lips play patty-cake. "Moving."

Admit muthafucking nothing.

He slowly dips his head in a mocking nod.

"Is that what we're doing?" His lips stretch into the first genuine smile I've ever witnessed on his face. And both dread and excitement carve out a bottomless hole in my belly. And when he opens that beautiful, corrupt mouth over mine, gliding his wicked tongue over my bottom lip before sucking on it so hard my pussy twinges in sympathetic pain, lust and an instantiable, shameful need rushes in. A whimper escapes me, and before another wave of embarrassment can wash over me, his lewd groan nearly drowns the sound out. "Good. I was hoping you'd go there. 'Cause I for damn sure didn't want to go easy on you."

He thrusts his tongue between my lips, taking immediate control of my mouth, of this kiss. It's wet, nasty, wild. And I adore every teasing suck, every long, luxurious lick. He just took my virginity twenty-four hours earlier, but already he's made me crave him. He's branded himself on my senses, my skin, my damn bones. Definitely my pussy.

I'm sure there are reasons I should say, "Hold on. This is too fast and will only complicate things between us." Reasons like our convoluted past, the extortion masking as an engagement. And those are just a few very good, very valid reasons. But as he sucks on my bottom lip, then my chin, scraping his teeth over my jaw, nothing matters except him not stopping. Except this searing, addictive pleasure that will chain me to him tighter than any contract.

Goddamn.

Who would've ever suspected Asad Prince could kiss like he was in love? Like he created it and sex in the first seven days of earth's molding.

With a deep moan, I surrender to him. Don't protest when he slightly bends, picks me up like I'm a size four instead of a fourteen on a good, pre-period day, and carries me to his bed. Asad stokes my arousal, my passion, with a humiliating ease.

And as he lays me down on the mattress, I shamelessly spread my thighs wider, wrap my legs around his waist, inviting him to press his weight on top of me. Smother me with it. He accepts that silent invite and covers me, one hand planted near my ear and the other circling my neck, squeezing until I whimper from the constriction that should be frightening but instead sends a bolt of electricity, of excitement, straight to my clit.

Boldly, lewdly, I rub my pussy up and down the thick, wide length of his dick. Digging my nails into his back, I arch into the decadent caress, breath catching at the electric friction against my clit. Pleasure spirals out from every limb, every cell, and I twist under him, hungry, restless.

"Come on, ma. Wet my pussy up. Get her good and messy so I have something to clean up."

Gotdamn, his *mouth*. It's a sensory-overload switch, and blinking up into his molten-hot eyes and lust-roughened face, I press my head against the mattress and bow until my back no longer touches the bed, rolling my hips, grunting at the bump of his dick and glide of his thick length over pajama-covered pussy and clit.

Oh my God, I pant. I need a PowerPoint and three-page, double-spaced essay on why this is so fucking *good*.

Asad pushes off me, taking his beautiful, blessed dick with him. I mewl an objection, but when he scoots backward to jerk my pajamas and panties down my legs, then pulls my top over my head, I quickly shut up. This is only my second time completely bare with another person, and vestiges of modesty creep in, and my hands move of their own volition toward my breasts and pussy.

"Don't make me tie you up, baby girl," he warns, lightly popping my hands and shoving them away. "Give me a reason. Shit, I might do it anyway." He leans down and without any warning sucks my nipple into the hot depths of his mouth, his tongue mercilessly lashing the tip.

"Fuck, that's pretty," he whispers, his gaze flicking upward to my face before returning to study his handiwork. Cupping my other breast, he gives it the same treatment, working it over while his thumb rubs and circles my damp flesh. When he lifts his head again, pride and lust stamps his features, curls his mouth with a brutal carnality. "Yeah, so fucking pretty. Never doubt how beautiful you are, baby girl. No one compares to you like this."

My pussy and heart clench at his growled words. I lift an arm, skimming and, after a brief hesitation, cupping his face, sweeping my thumb over his cheekbone. Under his gaze, I don't doubt his praise, just crave more of it along with his special brand of pleasure. Turning his head, he presses his sensual lips to my palm, then sinks his teeth into the heel, causing my belly to go concave.

"You gon' let me eat, Ember?" He doesn't wait for me to answer but shimmies down my body, trailing kisses over my belly, hip, and finally my inner thigh. "I'm so hungry. I can still taste you from last night." He tongues the sensitive skin just above my mound, and I wiggle, widening my thighs, needing a hotter, dirtier touch. "Oh yeah, ma. I'm taking that as a yes. Open wider." I spread my legs more. "Wider." I open them until I can feel the strain in my muscles. "So good, baby girl. I'm not leaving here until I'm full."

For a moment, he closes his eyes, and his deep inhale both embarrasses and turns me on. There doesn't seem to be anything that is too far, too much for Asad. As if there's nothing about my body, my pussy he doesn't enjoy. Since I've had to mostly build my own self-esteem and have my own emotional back, his expressions, his words, his obvious hunger . . . they heal something in me I didn't know was cracked and a little fractured. It's scary how much power I know I could so easily give him.

Terrifying.

His fingers tightening on my thighs drags my attention back to his breath tickling my bare folds. Wedging his shoulder under my thigh, he dives face-first into me.

Fuck. Fuckfuckfuck.

Maybe I chant this aloud, or maybe it's deafening in my head. I can't really understand the jumbled scream that escapes me, so it could go either way. But when his tongue strokes through my bottom lips, coherent thought splits like a damn atom. He laps at my clit, flicking it before returning to the heart of my pussy, and tongue fucks her. I can *feel* the moisture seeping out of me, and he literally sips from my pussy, claiming each drop.

I writhe under him, scraping his shoulders and neck, surely leaving a stinging trail of marks that will decorate his skin tomorrow. I buck under his mouth, in this moment, unsure if running or staying is the correct option. If they *are* options. With a feral groan, Asad clamps firm fingers down on my hip, holding me in place while he plunges two fingers inside me. Even though he broke me in last night, the fit is still tight, still a little uncomfortable. But I'll rip my own tongue out before telling him to stop. My pussy says what I can't, ordering him not to stop, to stay, with every squeeze and quiver around his fingers.

Maybe he's bilingual in pussy speak because he obeys the demand, going harder, plunging deeper as his tongue coils around my clit. I shake my head back and forth, losing my senses, a veil of black closing in on me. And still he doesn't let up. He alternates between long, decadent sweeps over my flesh to almost punishing thrusts to my core.

Twisting his wrist, he corkscrews his fingers high into my pussy, treating her to grinding thrust after thrust, his knuckles smacking my swollen lips and creating a lascivious soundtrack for our fucking. My muscles quiver, stomach clenches, and without warning, spasms erupt inside me, catching me by surprise. My cry rips free, and I surrender to the cataclysmic pleasure tearing me apart.

"You were created to nut for me," Asad rasps, giving my pussy one last lick before pulling free and rolling off the bed.

Within seconds, he strips naked, and I stare, in awe, at his beautiful, big body. Wide chest and shoulders, ridged abdomen, powerful thighs, and even pretty feet. And that dick. A work of art. I worshipped it earlier today, and it's worthy of every praise.

Like a sexy beast, Asad crawls back on the bed, hair slightly fuzzy, beard messy with my juice, and mouth glistening. His muscles contract with every movement, and he's the epitome of sexuality and grace. In this moment, I'm jealous of every woman who's been able to see him like this. I want to hunt them down, and removing their eyes wouldn't be enough. Only a lobotomy would do so they forget the pleasure he's brought them, the rough silk of his touch, the possessive brand of his dick.

I'm sick, a little depraved. And this is what his dick has rendered me to.

"I need inside you, ma," he murmurs, not asking but telling me.

I still nod and reach for him, welcoming him with spread arms and legs.

He crawls up my body, covering me. Cupping the nape of my neck, he lowers his head and captures my mouth. Wet, feverish, needy. I taste myself on his tongue, and instead of recoiling from the fresh yet musky flavor, I angle my head and thrust my tongue deeper, lapping at his lips, beard, craving more of *us* in my mouth.

Gripping my waist, he steadies me, then with a sensual roll of his hips, he buries his length deep in my pussy. Like the first time we did this, he has to put in work to get inside me.

"You know what I need, ma," he breathes against my mouth, his hooded eyes hot, fevered. "Let me in. You did it last night. Take this dick like a big girl. Like a mu'fuckin' queen."

I moan, sinking my teeth into my bottom lip, and deliberately relax my body. And shortly after, he slides balls-deep in one final thrust. He stills, kissing me like he can't stand for us to not breathe the same air, and the intimacy of that kiss pricks my eyes. No one has ever kissed me with such passion. Made me feel so wanted, like I was their lifeline. Because Asad doesn't simply kiss with his mouth. It's with his body. With small caresses to my nose, cheek, hairline. It's murmured words of praise. It's the brush of his body as if suffering even one second away from me is anathema to him.

That further cracks me open. Threatens to send everything spilling out in a chaotic, emotional mess.

"Asad. More. Please move and give me more," I plead.

Bending his head, he sucks on my neck and slowly withdraws . . . then slams back inside. I gasp, my pussy quivering at the rough, hard thrust. I claw at his arms, shoulders, ass, anywhere I can touch, grip. Pleasure whistles through me, and I hike my legs higher, spread them wider, offering all of my pussy up to him.

He takes full advantage, pounding into me, and I feel him all in my stomach. Shit, I breathe this dick.

Asad leans back, and his hand dips between us, saturating his fingers in my wet. God yes. I tremble, hovering on that edge, ready to crash out. But then, without pausing in delivering long death strokes to my pussy, he shoves my legs back, curling me up so my thighs press into my stomach.

"Asad," I whimper, but he shushes me, and I scratch at his arms. Ignoring me, he trails his damp fingertips over my spread-open pussy and lower to my asshole. *"Asad."*

"You can take it, ma." He presses a fingertip to my hole, not entering, just teasing with the threat of it. I stiffen, feminine anxiety and a little fear swirling and clenching my belly. "Unh-unh. Don't do that. Relax and trust me, Ember."

He slows his thrust, and instead of hard plunges, he switches to a slow, dirty grind, circling his hips, and each roll brushes my clit, ratcheting my arousal until I'm leaking. And those fingers are steadily circling, steadily pressing.

Then, as his dick rocks into me, his finger breaches the tight circle. Fire races through me, and I squeeze my eyes closed, crying out at the flash of pain. As quickly as it burned bright, the pain ebbs, settling into a burn. And a fullness that's weird, but no longer painful.

"Gotdamn, you should see yourself. Pussy and ass stuffed. No going back, Ember." My eyes jerk open at the dark, nearly ominous tone. His silver gaze bores deep into mine. "You let someone else touch you, I'll kill him and make you watch. Don't try me, Ember. This pussy is too good, and I'm too loose. I'll crash out behind both of you."

Being overfull steals any words I would've uttered. I should be afraid at his words, at the serious tone. But it's not fear shivering under the overwhelming lust.

It's . . . comfort.

Peace.

Security.

Jesus. What's wrong with me? What's wrong with both of us?

He doesn't give me time to wonder as he gently but firmly fucks my ass. Between his dick and his fingers, I'm spiraling into new territory, and a sob rips free of my throat.

"Unh-hunh," he grunts, never stopping his sensual assault on my body and senses. "I feel that little pussy fluttering, getting ready to nut for me."

One moment, he's shoving me toward that precipice, and then in the next, he slows. I claw at his shoulders.

"Asad, *move*," I whine.

"I got you, baby girl. But you have to do something for me, first."

"*Anything*. Just, please . . ." I try to fuck him back, but the position won't allow it. He holds all the control, and I'm almost feral with lust and pleasure.

"Did you go to Deacon's tonight?" Another sob rips free as he flexes his finger in my ass, sending a bolt of lightning through me. "Did you?"

"Yes, shit, yes, I did," I confess. "Please, finish."

"Not yet, ma." He circles his hips, and his dick hits a spot that has me arching as high as his hold will allow. My whole body shudders as pleasure ripples through me, and more juice seeps out of me, wetting both of us up. "Why? Why did you go there?"

I didn't intend on talking about this, on even confessing the truth. But with that orgasm right on the horizon, pride abandons me without even the dignity of a wave goodbye.

"Because he fucked with you. He hurt you. I made him pay for it." I dig my fingernails in his wrists, scratching at them. "Now, *fuck me*."

"Look at me, Ember." I open eyes I hadn't realized had closed and meet that bright gaze. "Thank you."

Tomorrow, this moment will seem too vulnerable, too fraught with . . . something I'd rather not acknowledge. But right now, I don't care. Not when I'm half out of my mind.

"Come get this nut, ma. Come for me."

As if his permission was all I needed, I detonate. Explode. Hell, implode. My screams fill my head as I careen into oblivion. He pounds me into the flames, granting my body no mercy, no quarter. And as I tumble into the waiting darkness with arms wide open, I send up a silent prayer that he never does. That he will always want me with this abandon. This need. This hunger. Because I fear I will always need him.

CHAPTER TWELVE

Ember

I open the bathroom door and steam billows out into the bedroom as if heralding my arrival. Tightening the belt of my black silk robe, I glance at the sleigh bed and the twisted sheets hanging halfway off the mattress like they're white-girl wasted. The heavy musk of sex still lingers in the room—unlike the man who delivered teeth-jarring back shots to me a half hour earlier. Our fluids, a mixture of sweat and cum, form haphazard puddles on the light blue, five-hundred-count Egyptian cotton, marking the spots we fucked like X's on a treasure map. I don't know where he went after into the bathroom, but either he's going to change the sheets in here or I'm getting appointed another room. But one thing's for certain, two things for sure, I'm not sleeping in nobody's wet spot. His or mine.

Trekking over to one of the suitcases I packed, I remove several smaller bags. One contains my hygiene products. Perching on the cream-colored chaise lounge, I take my time smoothing shea body butter over my skin. Am I using my normal moisturizing routine to stall facing Asad again after letting him lick and suck on every part of me between my forehead, ass, and toes? Yes. Is it foolish to want to avoid facing him after he's seen, touched, and been inside just about every hole in my body? Definitely. But embarrassment and forced proximity isn't a good enough reason for neglected, dry-ass skin.

Twenty minutes later, I emerge from the bathroom once more, skin hydrated, hair tucked into a messy bun, teeth brushed. A sweep of the area reveals he still hasn't returned from wherever he disappeared to when I escaped to the bathroom for a shower. And I do mean escape. I swear to God, that man tried to assassinate me with the dick. No lie, I damn near had to crawl out of that bed, and if Asad had reached for me again, I would've killed him in self-defense. It would've held up in any court, too. Even now my muscles gripe at being bent and contorted into positions that my nut-dizzy pussy might've consented to, but not me.

Sighing, I pick up the second bag I removed from my suitcase and head for the balcony. I push open the French doors, allowing the night air, stamped with the salty, fresh scent of the ocean, inside the room. Inhaling deeply, I head for the small love seat and glass coffee table, the stone cool underneath my bare feet.

"Took you long enough. I was beginning to think I'd have to come in there and get you."

"Shit." I jerk around, heart slap-boxing my ribs. Splaying my fingers over my chest, I glare at Asad—or rather his shadowed, long, big body reclining on the oversized club chair sitting in a dark corner of the balcony. "Goddamn. Was that necessary?" I snap, breath still breaking in short bursts over my parted lips.

"Your head should always be on the swivel, ma."

A second later, soft, golden light floods the contained area, beaming from the small, elegant sconce above his head. I notice a wall switch just above his head and shake mine. He couldn't have done that when he first came out here? I suck my teeth. Dramatic ass.

He shifts in the chair, and like the tide responds to the lure of the moon, my gaze follows the motion, taking in his wide, bare chest, brutally sculpted abs, the black-and-gray basketball shorts hanging indecently low and exposing the tops of carved hips and long, powerful legs. Shit, even his feet are big, masculine, and pretty. I return my scrutiny to his face and find his low-lidded eyes on me, his face relaxed. I don't think I've ever seen him . . . relaxed. It's a good, delicious look on him, though it doesn't dampen the danger that sits on him like the lotion I just rubbed on my body. God. The man is perfect in every way, and like the dickmatized bitch that I am, I fell for that perfection. Fell for that beauty and damned myself.

Eve would be proud as fuck.

Turning away from him, I continue to the love seat and sink down to the cushions. Ignoring Asad, I pull out the contents of my bag and set them on the table—my rolling tray, grinder, flavored rolling papers, lighter, a jar of my favorite hybrid blend of weed. The routine of preparing my blunt lends a calm that seeps into me, and for a moment, I'm able to tune out Asad's magnetic presence.

Lie.

I'm able to dampen the intensity of it. But him rising from the chair, crossing the space, and dropping right next to me, his thick thigh brushing mine, dials it back up until I'm vibrating with tension and nerves.

Still, even with that penetrating, weighty stare on me, my fingers don't falter, nor do my movements slow. This is straight muscle memory, and the monotony of it, soothing. Within minutes, I have the blunt lit and am lifting it to my lips, pulling from it. The sweet, fruity yet herbal flavor fills my mouth and lungs, and I close my eyes, leaning against the back of the couch. Hard, long fingers pluck the blunt from mine as I exhale, and I turn my head to watch Asad take a hit off it. The end glows red, the fragrant smoke curling from his parted lips a gut punch of lust. I've never seen him in this environment—in the security of his own home, half-naked, smoking and relaxed. Well, relaxed for him. It's unfamiliar. Disconcerting.

Sexy as fuck.

And . . . nice.

Jesus. I need to be more lit than I am if I'm having those thoughts.

"Puff, puff, pass, muthafucka," I say, flicking my fingers in a "gimme" motion. "Greedy ass."

One moment, I'm waiting to get my blunt back, and in the

next, I'm straddling Asad's lap, my pussy high-fiving his dick again through his shorts and the thin panties I'm wearing under my robe. A wave of heat barrels through me at the contact, and I manage to catch my gasp before it escapes. I wish I could say the same for my body. That traitorous bitch hums as if happy I've made him my personal throne.

I'm strung tight, which is sacrilegious considering this perfect blend of weed. But the intimacy of this position, with us face-to-face, body to body, dick to pussy. I'm out of my realm, unprepared, and . . . unsettled. One of his big hands cups my hip, and the weight of it grounds me, ordering me not to flee. Because God knows, I'm considering it. Jumping off him and hightailing it back to the guest room with my drugs and little bit of guard left.

"Here." He passes me the spliff, and I accept it, puffing on it and exhaling. "You created that blend yourself?"

"Mm-hmm." I squint at him, taking another hit, letting it spread through me and loosen my muscles.

"It's good. I usually don't care for the flavored shit—especially anything sweet. But that"—he nods at me—"it's good."

"I know."

The corner of his mouth twitches.

"When I was in your apartment, I noticed you got a whole-ass collection. If it was anyone else, I'd think they were—"

He tilts his head, studies me. When he lifts a hand toward my face, I expect him to cup it or my chin, touch my mouth, or even slide his thumb in between my lips as he's done several times tonight. But this is Asad; he doesn't do the expected. Instead, he traces a gentle path over my forehead, down the slope of my nose, and then under my eye. Thank God I'm sitting. This caress, which smacks of a tenderness I didn't know he was capable of—particularly toward me—has my knees weak, my stomach twisting. A part of me, that scared, uncertain part of me that fears his newfound control of my body, longs to rear back and crawl away from him in horror. But the other part . . . that other part . . . fuck.

As if he senses the conflict brewing deep inside me, Asad shifts his hand from my face to the back of my neck, gripping it, holding me in place. Preventing me from retreating, from running.

"Snooping is beneath you." I squint at him, teasing but also—not. "Didn't your mama ever tell you if go looking for shit, you'll find it? Oh wait." I pop up a finger. "This is Michelle we're talking about. Never mind. She wasn't into parenting or lessons."

"Nah, baby girl. Distractions won't work on me." He squeezes my neck, sending a blast of heat soaring straight to my middle. It's a damn shame how much I enjoy this man's hands on me. Lust flares in his eyes, telegraphing he doesn't miss my reaction to him. "When did all that start? I knew you smoked, but what you got in your house? It looks like a fucking dispensary."

I mug him. "I know the drug lord isn't coming for me over some weed. The audacity."

His hand slaps the curve of my ass, and the sharp sting radiates from the spot and down between my legs. Arousal flares like an SOS to my brain and heart. Get the fuck up and out.

I remain perched on his thighs, pussy wetting up his basketball shorts.

"Answer me. Why the fascination with weed?"

Shrugging, I lift the blunt to my lips once more and after a moment, release smoke along with my answer.

"It . . . helps." I stare into his unwavering silver eyes, and though it is madness and a betrayal of every sense of self-preservation I possess, I let him in. And pray he doesn't wield this against me later. Here, in the dark, with his big, hard body under me like a foundation I've always secretly yearned for, I take a chance. A risk. "I stopped taking the meds for my IED."

He frowns, both hands cupping my hips and squeezing. Hard. "The fuck, Ember? Why?"

"Because I couldn't deal with the way they made me feel. Thickheaded, sometimes like a zombie. No, I refused to have something control me like that anymore." I shake my head. "I had to put up with that for years because I didn't have a choice; the doctors didn't listen to me when I told them about the side effects, and Marcus only cared about what they had to say. For too long, I felt invisible, voiceless, and disempowered in my own mental health. When I finally was able to take the reins, I made the best choices for me. And yes, that's weed because it calms me—and shit, I like it—but there's also therapy, yoga, and the grounding techniques I've learned." I twist around and sit the blunt on the rolling tray. "Speaking of that, how did you know about the 5-4-3-2-1 technique?"

The question has plagued me since the moment he helped me through my last episode. There's no way he should be aware of it, unless . . . I narrow my eyes on him.

"As soon as you were diagnosed, I read up on it," he admits, voice void of inflection. "And I asked your therapist about coping mechanisms so I would know what to do if you were ever triggered in front of me."

"You . . . you did what?" Shock is a sucker punch to my soul, and I gape at him, breathless. "Wait . . . What?"

"It was clear Marcus didn't give a fuck. Somebody in that house had to."

"Somebody in that house had to," I slowly repeat. His stoic expression doesn't change, not even when I chuckle. "Are you dead ass right now? You muthafuckas are part of my trauma that led to me having IED. It was bad enough I was a young girl who'd just lost her mother and was stuck with a father who couldn't wait for gotdamn rigor mortis to hit before he brought another woman in the house. But then I was subjected to fucking sadists instead of a family." I laugh again, but the vise around my chest renders it little more than a huff. I lift my leg up, ready to climb off him. "Let me the hell up out of here before I—"

"You're not going no-fucking-where," he growls, his hands clamping down on me—one on my hip, the other returning to the nape of my neck. "You got me fucked-up."

He pins me to him, dragging me forward until our noses

nearly bump. To prevent myself from falling against his body, my hands fly up, and I slap them against his wide, bare chest. Five minutes earlier, I would've probably acted on the heat from his skin that sends tingles up my arms and down to my chest. But now, the flare of desire only dials up my simmering anger until it licks my skin.

"Get your hands off me," I snap.

"No." He shakes me, and it's hard enough to rattle my teeth if I weren't clenching them. "For once, shut the fuck up and listen. Say it again," he grinds out, eyes hooded and gleaming with . . . Shit, I don't know.

Rage, yes.

That's easy.

But there's more. On anyone else, I would say pain. Or even sorrow. But this is Asad. Asad Prince, my stepbrother, my tormentor, the merciless head of the Cross organization. He's not "anyone else."

"You're so fucking blind, Ember."

"Why do you keep calling me that?" I suck my teeth, pushing back against his hand on my neck to insert space between our faces.

But that's futile. His hold is a shackle, and in this moment, I'm his unwilling prisoner.

"What did I say?" he snarls, lip curling. "Shut the fuck up. My turn to talk." His jeweled stare roams over my face, down to the deep V of my robe, which widened in our small struggle. The wedge exposes the smooth expanse of skin between my breasts and the plump inner curves. But when his eyes lift to meet mine, arousal doesn't burn in the depths; that same indecipherable, knotted mixture of emotion that I can't quite untangle glitters there. "You know the problem with making victimhood your whole identity? You become too comfortable with it. Walking around this bitch like Linus carrying your trauma like it's a mu'fucking blanket that you'll crash the fuck out over if anyone dares try and take it. By this time, you've invested so many years and so much effort in being a victim, you might as well be collecting social security for the shit. Did the people in your life fail to protect you? Did they fuck you over? Did they treat you like the opps instead of family? Yeah, yeah, and hell yeah. But you've let it taint how you move, who you are, and how you deal with the world. And it's fuck everyone who doesn't agree with cosigning your version of the past or present."

"Shut up. I don't want to hear this," I whisper, squeezing my eyes closed, trembling on his lap.

His words pelt me like darts, breaking skin, sinking into tissue and bone. The . . . rancid truth of them screams in my head so loud, I fist my hands on his chest to keep me from slamming them over my ears and rocking like a child.

"You gon' hear me, Ember, because no one in your life gave a gotdamn to give you the brutal, ugly truth before. You're so consumed with how you've been wronged, you don't stop to consider or recognize who you've caused harm to, baby." I choke on a half whimper, half objection. "Nah, I'm not talking about people like Deacon or Carter or those pieces of shit you experiment on. I mean the ones you've hurt by refusing to let anyone past that no-man's-land you call a heart. Even your lab rats only get so far past the gate, and you care for them. Instead of trusting people, taking a chance, and believing that maybe, just fucking maybe, they'll like the real Ember Cross you try so hard to protect, you choose to retreat behind your pain, your trauma, your grief. You're more at home with them and in the past than in that fortress you built for yourself."

He shifts a hand from my nape to my chin, pinching it tight and tilting my head down so I have no choice but to stare into his eyes. Can he see the screams in mine? It's possible, because he gently sweeps a thumb across the skin just under my bottom lip.

"Everybody isn't a potential enemy out to get you, baby girl. Including me." His voice lowers, deepens, as if he's about to impart some great secret. Asad sits up straighter, gently pulling me closer into his body, and my breasts brush his chest. "Close your eyes again."

My mind screams, No, go to hell, but my lids are already lowering, obeying him.

I'm tired of fighting, so, so tempted to accept the haven that his body offers.

"Think back. When you were twelve, I locked you in my closet. Kept you there for hours. Was I doing it to bully you, or because Michelle was in a foul-ass mood and was on the hunt for the one person in the house who had become her favorite chew toy? When you were fourteen, I tied you to a chair and blasted music so loud it felt like torture. Was it? Or could it be I didn't want you to hear Michelle and Marcus arguing because she was trying to get rid of you? Or catch when that mu'fucka said you were staying because all Cross children had to remain with their parents until they reached majority. But he promised to send you away as soon as you graduated high school. Could it be I wanted to save you from hearing what a weak, dickless bitch your father was?"

My lips part, but no sound emerges. It's lodged in my throat, trapped. Which might be a good thing. If it escaped, I'm not sure if it'd be a scream of fury or a sob of grief. Maybe an unintelligible, messy blend of both.

On the blank wall of my mind, I'm viewing what he's describing, and for the first time, the perspective of the scenes is different. I'm viewing them through an alternative lens. And that view . . . Again, my lips move but there's nothing.

"When you were sixteen, I drove you miles from the house, made you get out and walk home. Was I being an asshole, or was I making sure you were nowhere near that mu'fucka because Michelle had invited guests over and planned you to be the entertainment. In what capacity—I don't know. But I for damn sure wasn't trying to wait around and find out. But never at one moment during that night were you by yourself. I followed behind you. When you were seventeen, Michelle had all of your mother's clothes, furniture, and jewelry she left you brought out to the backyard and burned in a big-ass bonfire. I held you down and made you watch. Or did I hold you so you wouldn't be alone while my mother destroyed the last ties to yours?"

"Why?" I rasp.

I don't need to elaborate; if the tilt of his head is any indication, he understands what's left unsaid. And thank God, because I'm not able to squeeze anything else except for that one, tired word past my constricted throat.

He leans forward. Allows that silver gaze to touch every inch of my face before meeting mine again.

"At the time, with the little power I had and understanding Michelle like no one else, I did what I could to shield you from her and not make you even more of a target. Because if she guessed the truth, you might've been buried right beside your mother."

I shake my head. "What truth?"

His hands abandon my neck and hip to smooth up my arms, over my shoulders, and around my neck, his thumbs tipping my chin up. This time, it's very easy to decode the emotion swirling in his eyes, stamping his face.

A fierce, cold determination.

"You're mine. You've always been. Mine to protect. Mine to keep. *Mine.*"

His mouth crashes over mine, and with a whimper, I open up for him. Maybe it was the growled possession carved into his tone or the fact no one had ever claimed me before—that no one had ever made me feel *claimable*—but lust flared like a struck match, burning away the shock and confusion from his earlier confessions. In minutes, he'd changed aspects of my worldview, my life, that I'd been certain about for years. It'd been my truth. And he'd substituted it for his. I didn't know how to deal with it in this moment. Didn't know if I wanted to. Only thing I possess one hundred percent clarity about is this relentless hunger for him. And I'm going to allow him to consume me with it.

"We made you," he murmurs against my mouth. "Torture by torture. Insult by insult. Neglect by neglect. We made you."

I'm shaking my head before he even finishes the sentence.

"*I* made me. In spite of all of you, I made me. You don't get to take credit. None of you do."

I brace myself for his response, stiffen against the inevitable lashing out. It's in the molten gleam of his eyes, rapid beating of his pulse at the base of his throat. But I don't move. I don't flinch. I don't rescind my words. I just . . . brace. Expecting the worst.

I don't expect a beautiful smile.

Or the pride that seems to emanate from it.

"Nah, we don't. You did this shit. Now own it from a place of strength and not weakness. You're nobody's victim, Ember. Just a fucking . . . miracle."

A miracle.

No, a *fucking* miracle.

As if my whole body—my whole damn soul—loosens in the same moment, a sob rips free from my throat. It feels like it originates from a place deeper though. A place that I've refused to let people in or touch in years. Thirteen, to be exact.

I start to shake, almost violently. Long, hard, *protective* arms band around me, and I sink into the safety of them. Asad becomes my shelter in this emotional storm. He anchors me.

And I trust that he will keep me afloat.

Because he's been doing it for years.

I lift my face, wet, probably swollen from tears, to his and take his mouth this time. I slide my tongue between his lips, tangle it with his, suck on him. At the sound of his rich, luxurious groan, pride roars through me like a lion, riding shotgun next to lust and a wild, nearly feral joy that is alien as it is freeing.

With hurried, frantic movement, I claw at the waistband of his shorts, tugging it back and pulling his dick out. My fist closes around his already thick and long flesh, and his hips punch up into my sloppy, uncoordinated stroke. There's nothing graceful about me pushing aside the seat of my panties. Nothing skilled about me notching his slick, wide head at the opening of my pussy.

I crush my mouth to his, and our tongues tangle, tasting each other. Tasting *us*.

Though I've been here before, I still hold my breath. Waiting. Shivering. Savoring that first thrust. The first moment of penetration. The first stretch and burn. Raising an arm above me, I grip my own hair, tugging as I sink down his dick.

"*Oh God*," I breathe, arching tight as the pleasure careens through me like lightning.

Asad cups my breast, holds me captive as he fucks me from underneath with deep, grinding thrusts. I'm open for him, vulnerable, and though I should hate it, fight it, I don't. Instead, I indulge in it, letting him control it and just receive. Knowing he'll take care of me.

And *God*, does he take care of me.

His fingers toy with my nipples, tugging, tweaking, stroking. Drawing passion out of me, damn near marking it on my skin. With each stroke, he stirs my lust higher, hotter. His dick brands my pussy, possessing it, beating it out the frame and shaping it so only he will ever be enough for me. Ever fill me. Ever satisfy me. And that thought both thrills and terrifies me.

I palm his chest and lean back, twisting my torso around so I can pick up the still-lit blunt. Grabbing it and turning back to Asad, I meet his molten gaze as I puff on it, and the end glows red. I squint at him through the haze of smoke, and his hooded gaze meets mine. Lust tightens his features, and his thrusts slow, becoming a hard, filthy grind. A shudder runs through me, and I close my eyes, glorifying in every tight circle of his pelvis against my clit.

My breath rushes out of me, a whimper escaping me. I lift the blunt to my mouth again and drag in a long inhale full of the fragrant smoke. Without breaking our visual connection, I lean forward and raise the hand on his chest higher until I'm pinching his chin and pressing down. Silently demanding he open his mouth. Asad doesn't hesitate, and I lean forward, pressing my mouth to his, and shotgunning him. He greedily accepts the smoke I blow into him, shoving his tongue past my parted lips, chasing the last of the weed, lapping at the roof of my mouth. Sucking it off my tongue.

"Give me another one," he roughly demands.

I obey, repeating the action. While I shotgun him again, I lower my arm and bow my head, trailing my fingers over my chest and belly until my tips stroke the place where we're connected. Fire races through my veins as I circle my clit, playing with myself, shuddering under my touch and his possession. I shift and bring my other hand down, tracing my folds, sliding it over his hard flesh as it drives in and out of me. We—his precum and my moisture—coat my fingers, and I rub it into the skin of my lower stomach, as if I can somehow mark myself. Crazy, wild. But that's what he does to me. Makes me want the impossible.

Trembling, I return the blunt to the table, continuing the sensual torment.

"Gotdamn, Ember. Gotdamn, baby girl," he grinds out, pressing a hot, open-mouthed kiss under my ear. "Get there. Get us there."

His fingers slide over my hip, then tangle with mine. We both strum my clit, working me in tandem. In perfect synchronicity. Pleasure, so sharp, so loud and bright, vibrates within me. Crackles along my skin like electricity over exposed nerves. My hips buck against our joined touch, turning me into a willing captive to his dick, our fingers.

"Asad," I rasp, my voice serrated by raw lust. "Please. I need . . . Oh God." I groan, shaking. "I just *need*." I'm not above begging. I want to be *ended* by this lust.

"Hold on to me," he rumbles, and not waiting for me to comply, he cuffs my wrist and draws my arms up and around his neck. "Hold on, and don't let go."

I can't tell if he's referring to now or ever. And I don't question it.

And that is foolish.

Gripping his hair, I turn myself over to him completely. And as he fucks me, as I fuck him right back, I break. Crack and explode into pieces. And even then, it's not enough.

And I'm just aware enough to be scared by that.

CHAPTER THIRTEEN

Asad

"Well, I guess I should thank you for making time to see your mother today."

I stare at Michelle as she strides across my office, the cloying perfume of her passive aggressiveness preceding her. Glancing away from her, I nod at Mars, my executive assistant, silently ordering her to close the door behind her. After a hard, narrowed look at my mother's back that she probably doesn't think I catch, the beautiful, plus-size woman with her halo of red natural curls returns the gesture and quietly exits the room.

"It's only eight in the morning, Michelle. A little early to be on the rampage and terrorizing the staff, isn't it?" I tap my pen on the desktop as she gracefully perches on the chair in front of my desk and crosses her legs. "We'll need to make this quick since you don't have an appointment and I have a meeting in thirty minutes."

When Michelle called asking to see me, I'd been wrapped around Ember. For the first time in, well, ever, I'd overslept and had been contemplating not coming in to work, which I'd never done. But that's what Ember did to me—changed me. Made me operate different. Put someone else's needs other than my own first. For years, my sole goal was to inherit Cross and claim Ember. All the years of planning and scheming had finally earned out. And while lying there, arms full of the woman who'd been my obsession for longer than I care to admit, I finally felt . . . whole. And hopeful that all the fighting was coming to an end. Now I could be the one who started living. Nah, everything isn't solved between us, but last night was the move in the right direction.

Then Michelle hit my line, and here I am instead of fucking my soon-to-be wife.

Whatever this is had better be important and not the same ol' bullshit. Because Michelle can complain, she can threaten, but I'm not letting Ember go. There's nothing she can do about it.

She stares at me, her fingernails tip-tapping on the arm of the chair the only sound in the heavy silence. I almost smirk, but instead sink back into my leather chair. The silent treatment is an old game, a tired one. She must've forgotten who she's dealing with though. I like the quiet. I thrive in it. And Michelle Prince ceased to intimidate me a long time ago.

"I saw on the news that Deacon and Xavier are dead. The only details they've released are that the deaths were particularly brutal and appear to be targeted. You don't think it would've been wiser to be less . . . splashy?"

Locking my fingers over top of my abdomen, I cock my head.

"I have no idea what you're talking about since I haven't seen the news this morning. It's a damn shame about Deacon and Xavier though. A real damn shame."

She mugs me, but I return it with another stare. Fuck what she thought. I don't know what Marcus handled shit with her, but damn if I'm discussing confidential Cross business with my mother. And keeping it a hundred? I don't put it past her to walk up in this bitch wired up. Loyalty was never one of Michelle's virtues or burdens.

Just ask my father.

"Really, Prince?" she scoffs, brushing an invisible wrinkle from the razor-sharp crease of her pants. "Is that what we're doing? It's bad enough that you're going against every principle Marcus taught you and all of his wishes about the survival of Cross by inviting Ember"—she practically growls her name, the disgust dripping from her tone—"into family business, but you cut your brother out of it. Like last night. Why wouldn't you have him by your side? I bet you took your new *second*. And that other bitch you promoted. But not Kareem. How do you justify that?"

"I don't." I shrug and fall back against my chair. Drumming my fingers on the arm, I tilt my head. "Because once again, I don't know what you're referring to. But, hypothetically, if I had handled a contract for the fashion house and Eli or Makeda accompanied me, it would've made perfect sense since both are part of my security. Also, hypothetically, brother or not, if he's not qualified or experienced enough to handle whatever business I'm on, then it is what it is. I'on know, Michelle. It feels like I'm having a sense of déjà vu, as if we discussed this very same thing before. But that can't be true because we both know how I hate repeating myself."

Her face hardens with fury, and that shit doesn't move me. There was a time long ago—when my father was alive—when her approval meant everything to me. When I breathed to please her and witness that beautiful smile spread across her face.

Those days are long gone. She killed that impressionable, blindly loyal boy with the same doses of poison she administered to my father.

Michelle created the monster before her lie by lie, betrayal by betrayal, murder by murder.

"I'm your mother, Prince." She states the obvious after another long beat of silence.

I nod. "Yes."

"You wouldn't be sitting behind that desk if not for me. You wouldn't have this life if not for me. This position, the power, the influence—all me."

"Okay."

I don't do that arguing bullshit. Yeah, she fucked Marcus, brought me into his house and to his attention. She got my foot in the door. But I also paid with a dead father and a lost childhood. She doesn't get accolades as Mother of the Fucking Year.

"Wow," she sneers, shaking her head. "Ember must have a

fucking water park between her legs for you to be so quick to turn on your mother."

I lean forward, frowning. "Did you really come here first thing in the morning to discuss my stepsister's pussy?"

She releases a low, angry chuckle, dipping her chin and staring at the floor for a moment. When she lifts her head, the anger is gone, replaced by a calm, smooth mask. I trust the anger more. At least it's honest. This . . . this hides secrets and intent.

"If you wouldn't mind indulging me just a few minutes longer, I would appreciate it if you would come with me to the executive conference room. I have something important to show you."

"To show me?" Suspicion creeps over me, the sense of unease billowing until it fills my stomach like a boulder. Part of me wants to tell her, no, I don't have the time or the desire to play into whatever shit she's on. But the bigger, more cautious side knows *not* discovering what she's up to isn't even an option. That would be like allowing a snake in your house and then staying up all night wondering when it would strike.

"Yes, please." She gives me a tight-lipped smile.

"Yeah, Michelle. Give me a second. I'll be right behind you."

"Thank you, Asad." We stare at each other, her face revealing nothing but that phony-ass curve of her lips, before she finally stands and exits my office.

The door barely closes behind her when I pick up my private cell and tap a contact in my favorites. Keeping my attention on the door my mother just left out of, I wait for the person on the other end of the line to pick up.

"Wassup?" Eli answers.

"What's your location?" I pull open the desk drawer and remove my SIG Sauer, leaning forward to tuck it behind me at the small of my back.

With the two in my shoulder holster, that's a total of three guns and the knife in my ankle strap. It's a shame that I'm preparing to meet my mother strapped. But then again, my mother *is* Michelle.

"Me and Makeda are gonna pull up in about eight minutes. We're headed to see you."

"Do me a favor. Make it five minutes." I rise from my chair and grab my suit jacket from the back of it. "I need both of y'all up on the executive floor. Michelle might be on some bullshit, and just in case something goes down, I need you two nearby. I'm supposed to be meeting her in the conference room."

"Bet."

We hang up, and five minutes later, I walk out of my office and pass Mars's desk. She's not behind the big, curved piece of furniture, but I pause in front of it and write her a note, letting her know of my destination.

As I set the memo on top of her keyboard, the elevator doors slide open, and Eli and Makeda step out. Makeda hikes her chin up at me, expression reserved, stoic, while Eli wears a fierce frown.

"Ready?" I ask them.

"Yeah, let's get this over with." Eli grunts and turns to walk ahead of me, and Makeda falls in place beside me.

"No clue what this is about?" she asks, her gaze steadily sweeping the empty hall.

"No. She came to my office, complaining as usual, then asked for this. It could be anything."

"Ain't that the truth," she mutters.

Eli draws to a halt in front of the closed conference room entrance. Closed blinds stretch across the room's long window as well as the top half of the door. He glances over his shoulder at me, nods, then grabs the handle and slowly pushes the door open.

His big frame blocks my immediate view. Anticipation, unease, and impatience trickle through me, and as soon as Eli steps inside and to my right, I enter.

The fuck is going on here?

Michelle waits for me in the room that's a mirror image of the one we all just gathered in yesterday several floors down.

She stands in the exact same place I did, at the head of the long glass table, and also like yesterday, she's not alone. Not as many people are crowded around the table, but I recognize each and every one.

Kareem. Naoki Sato. Don Amato. Malcom Sutter, Marcus's old enforcer. And several other street bosses appointed under Marcus, not me.

Rage consumes me. Fucking becomes me. It pours through me in a torrential slide, and I can barely see the room past the crimson bath.

This bitch set me up. This fucking bitch. Set. Me. Up.

She can't hide her self-satisfied smirk or the victorious gleam in her eyes. I glance at Kareem, who sits in the chair next to her, and he can't even meet my gaze. Don Amato and Naoki Sato, who sit next to each other on the right side of the table, calmly stare back at me, their aloof faces revealing nothing. Malcolm and the other street bosses can't hide their reluctance to be here. It's in the slope of their shoulders, the slight bowing of their heads.

"Well, this is unexpected. And more than a little Machiavellian." I gesture to Eli and Makeda, silently ordering them to wait by the door. They nod, and then I walk to the front of the room, my gaze not moving from Michelle's, hoping she sees just how much she fucked up in my eyes. I don't know if she's the "family" Xavier spoke of, but she's for damn sure my enemy now. I stop in front of her. "Move."

That smile falters and she remains still, but when she blinks, staring up at me, and realizes I'm not joking, she scowls and peers around me. As if any of them will help her before I can snap her lying-ass neck.

"Asad, you can't—"

"I said *move*." I lean down until my face hovers directly above hers. "If you believe I'm about to attend this shit while you stand here and run it like you got my balls in your pocket right next to Marcus's, you done lost your fucking mind. But I have no issue helping you find that mu'fucka." I straighten. Smile. "Now move."

She flinches, and her swallow is damn near audible. But she moves. And doesn't stop until she's perched on a chair at the other end of the table.

"Now that we've straightened that shit out"—I slowly lower onto the chair—"why don't we get on with why I'm here."

Don Amato leans forward, setting his clasped hands on the tabletop. "I'm sorry, but I was under the impression that you requested I be here. Me and Naoki both." He looks at the head of the Yakuza seated to his left. "Isn't that what you mentioned?"

Naoki glances from Amato to me. "That's correct. But it sounds like you are as much in the dark as we are." He shifts his gaze to Michelle, who, wisely, doesn't meet his perusal.

"I won't keep any of you long." Michelle forces a strained smile, ignoring the two family heads' comments. Another wise move. It's one thing to trick me; shit, I'm her son. But to lie to the head of the Yakuza and Italian mob? This bitch is loose. "And, son, I apologize for just springing this meeting on you like this. I didn't have a lot of time when I found out this information."

"Is that right?" I prop my elbows on the chair's arms and rest my chin on my templed hands. "Yet you found time to call everyone here, but someone couldn't get to me. Makes sense." Her lips part as if about to reply, but then pop closed. But her eyes definitely tell me to get fucked. "How about we get on with it since I have a busy schedule and I'm sure everyone else here does, too. You cool, Kareem?"

My brother nods, nerves flashing across his face before he smooths his expression out.

"Yes, Asad. Everything's good."

"Good, good." I rub my hand over my beard. "Glad you got the phone call, too."

Malcolm side eyes one of the Cross soldiers, and the latter clears his throat. I could give a gotdamn about anyone's comfort in here.

"Kareem, can you hand your brother the laptop, please?" Michelle waves a hand, and as Kareem removes a computer from his briefcase, she smiles at me. And it's sneaky, avaricious. "I was forwarded intel that I couldn't, in good conscience, hold to myself." She rises from her chair and pauses, loving the audience she has. "As you all know, I lost my husband recently, and I was even more devastated to learn he was murdered."

Neither Amato nor Naoki appear taken aback by this info, their faces remaining stoic. I'm not shocked that they're aware. Just like I have my resources, they have theirs as well. Still . . .

I swallow a bitter chuckle. Michelle talking about Cross business so freely in front of people who aren't members of the organization is another strike and betrayal. One I could've never seen coming. I've never seriously considered killing my mother before, but apparently, this is a day of firsts.

Because anyone else wouldn't even still be standing.

"My hurt was compounded when I discovered this evidence about who's responsible for Marcus's death. Kareem." She addresses my brother, but she's looking at me, and that dirty glee shines in her eyes.

Dread twists in my stomach, and acid churns there before racing toward my chest. Only strength of will keeps my arm at my side and not rubbing the burning, painful spot. I don't need to glance down at the laptop screen Kareem turns and angles so I and everyone else in the room can watch.

It's the video from Marcus's building.

It's the video of Ember.

Somehow she located it, and fucking checkmate.

I lower my gaze to the laptop, confirming my suspicion. The lobby of Marcus's building and Ember, hooded and silent, will walk through those revolving doors in any moment.

My mind whirs as the video plays. Just from the reactions around the room—the fury darkening Malcolm's face, the whispered "What the fuck?" from the other soldiers, the crime family heads' reserved but gleaming stares—it's obvious this won't just go away. I can't sweep this under the rug again. And this was Michelle's plan all along.

Well fucking played.

I lean back in my chair, fisting my hands on my thighs. As if feeling their scrutiny on me from the back of the room, I look up, meeting Eli's and Makeda's gazes. Eli subtly shakes his head, and Makeda glares at the back of Michelle's head as if she's envisioning holding her gun to it and pulling the trigger.

Kareem leans forward, tapping the keyboard. Initially, no one speaks, but that doesn't last long. Michelle flattens her hands on the table and leans forward.

"I apologize for the subterfuge, but not only am I a widow who loved her husband, I'm also a mother who's willing to do whatever it requires to protect her son and family from being used by a conniving, murderous whore."

"Watch that shit, Michelle. Don't let that mouth write a check that I'm willing to cash," I warn, flipping my jacket back and revealing my holstered guns.

"Are you seriously sitting here threatening your own mother?" Malcolm snaps. "Especially when she just showed us irrefutable proof of your *fiancée* murdering your stepfather?"

I slowly turn my head, silently staring Marcus's former enforcer down. By the nature of his former position, he's about violence, retribution, protection. So I get his anger, but I'm not Marcus. I'm something altogether different.

"Yes, I did threaten her, and I can easily include you in that group if you don't watch who you're coming at. You might want to take that fucking bass out your voice when talking to me."

Malcolm's face tightens, and next to him, the other three soldiers stir in their seats. One of them, a dark-skinned, middle-aged man with graying dreads, squeezes Malcolm's shoulder.

"We're all upset, understandably, and I'm sure Malcolm didn't mean any disrespect," he says. I think his name is Greg. "But with all respect, this video answers who killed Marcus. What other reason would Ember have to be there that night? Why didn't we see her come back into the camera's frame? And as a scientist who designs drugs for Cross, she, more than anyone, would not only be able to gain access to Marcus but also be able to shoot him up." He sighs, holding his hands up, palms out. "The evidence is damning and clear. So it just leaves us one question. Prince, what do you plan to do about that?"

"That? Meaning my fiancée?" I arch an eyebrow, deliberately not addressing every valid and truthful argument he made. Fear for Ember lodges between my ribs, threatening to snap them in half.

Michelle laughs, and it's caustic, bitter. "You cannot be serious. You're still claiming that bi—"

"You got one more time." I cut my eyes at Michelle. "We're going to talk about this video, but if you can't stop calling her out her name, then sit there and don't say shit. When you disrespect her, you disrespect me. And we both know I don't handle that well. So the decision is yours. Choose wisely."

We engage in a visual war, humiliation flickering over her face, in her eyes.

"Fine," she snaps. "But the point is Ember killed Marcus, the head of this organization. It's the worst and most unforgivable sin to commit. Not to mention, only other bosses can sanction the taking of a life of another boss. So she broke not only the rule of the Cross family, which is punishable by death, but also the biggest one in our world. A life for a life."

And this right here is why she invited these particular witnesses. Marcus's enforcer, who would gladly avenge his death. Greg and other soldiers to attest to the crime. Don Amato and Naoki to verify the cardinal law in the underworld was broken.

She's outmaneuvered me.

Hatred for my mother seethes beneath my skin, poisoning my blood until it seems to replace it. Most mothers would protect their sons, support them, seek to help them in any way they could. But not Michelle Prince Cross. She walked in here with one goal—to undermine me, to embarrass me, and to trap me. Her loathing for Ember weighs more than her love for me. And when it comes down to the choice between revenge and abuse or the love of her son . . . there is no choice.

After years of watching her operate, after seeing how she betrayed, destroyed, and eventually killed my dad, I shouldn't be surprised by her actions. And yet, I sit here with a hole in my chest, slowly bleeding out at her final betrayal.

"Where did you get this?" I ask Michelle, flicking a hand toward the laptop.

"It's real, if that's what you're trying to imply."

I scrub a hand down my face. "I'm not taking your word for it. I'll have it authenticated myself."

I already had. Ro had verified that the recording hadn't been altered or somehow deep-faked before she sent me the original. But I needed to buy time, to plant doubt, to somehow, fucking somehow, save Ember from an imminent execution at my mother's urging.

"How long will it take to have that done?" Naoki asks.

I search his face for any hint of condemnation, of rage, but it's as unreadable as always.

"Not long. I have a tech who can handle it," I reply.

He nods and stands. "Let me know when it's done and the results. Until then, I have a meeting I need to attend."

Don Amato follows suit, rising and rebuttoning his suit jacket. "Same. I'll be waiting to hear the verdict. From you," he pointedly states, pinning a flat, menacing stare on Michelle. "We'll talk soon, Prince."

I don't say anything as the two men leave, probably fed the fuck up with our infighting and the messy way this entire meeting went down. Damn sure annoyed with Michelle. It isn't often I'm embarrassed, but watching the don and oyabun exit the conference room, it singes my face, neck, and chest. This bullshit is an indictment of my leadership. Just a couple of days ago, they'd been praising me, and now . . . Shit, now they undoubtedly view me as incapable of handling shit in my own house.

Shifting my focus back to my mother, I've never so desperately wanted to treat a person like a random bitch on the street and choke her out.

"You've let whatever . . . fascination you have with this girl blind you," Michelle says to me after the door closes behind the two men. Her voice softens, turns placating.

As if that's going to work on me.

"Mom, please." Kareem holds up a hand, wincing before giving me a sympathetic but firm look. "She might be going about it in an . . . unusual way, but Mom has a point. As much as I don't want to believe Ember is capable of murdering her own father, there's proof that she was there, in Marcus's building, headed in the direction of his apartment the night he died. Did she tell you she was there?"

"No."

A gloating smile stretches across Michelle's face as she crosses her arms over her chest.

"Of course she didn't. I mean, why would she? There was no reason for her to be there that night . . . except for one. And if she would kill her own father, what would she do to you? What *has* she done to get to you? Maybe Deacon and Xavier weren't working alone. Maybe they had help. Inside help. We all know they resented Marcus choosing you as his heir. Someone who supposedly wasn't family—who wasn't a Cross. Could be they intended to install a Cross by blood as the head. Not many people would be able to turn down the seduction of finally being in power. Especially when a person believes their inheritance was stolen from them. Is it so far-fetched to believe they would come for the perceived thief?"

"No one could've convinced me that Xavier or Deacon would've ever betrayed this family or Marcus. But now that we know they have, Michelle's point holds merit." Malcolm looks from her to me, straightening in his chair and leaning forward, pounding a fist on the table. "If they went to the drastic length of trying you, they were also capable of working with Ember and killing two birds with one stone. Especially since it was common knowledge he'd chosen you as his heir apparent."

"I don't know," Kareem interjects with a frown. "That's a bit of a reach."

I'm not buying it either. Besides, I've already had this conversation with Eli and Makeda. Yeah, Ember killed Marcus, but I can't help but believe it was for her own personal reasons, not to be installed as the one true Cross. Not when she's too ready and willing to walk away from all this shit.

But that doesn't mean family wasn't involved, as Xavier warned.

What was it you said? How 'bout I keep family out of it? A little too late for that shit.

Xavier's taunt spins in my head, and I side eye Michelle. Today showed me that she's more than capable of being a traitor. Of risking it all to gain what she wants. Power. Revenge.

The only thing keeping me from latching fully on to the idea of Michelle being that mastermind working with Xavier and Deacon is she can't rule. Not as a woman, and not as simply Marcus's wife. Hell, Ember would have more of a chance than Michelle would.

But now, I'm widening my circle on who could be involved. He said "family." That could realistically be anyone in this organization.

I'm still not ruling out Michelle though. And I can't discount Ember.

After last night? After our connection and what we shared? After she admitted to killing Deacon for me, because of me? No. No one could convince me that she still wanted me dead. But the hit was made *before* then. When she loathed everything about me.

Shit. I splay my hands wide on top of the table in order not to ground the heels into my eyes. I silently, viciously curse. Exhibiting any sign of emotion, of weakness, might as well be handing her bullets to load a Glock. And my mother, of all people, isn't afraid to use it.

"Prince," Kareem says, gently closing the laptop. "I get it. This is a hard decision. If you need time . . ."

"No." Michelle slashes a hand through the air with a small growl. "Time? For what? She played all of us. No one—not Marcus, not Asad, or you—believed me, but I always told you Ember isn't as innocent as she likes to portray. After watching her father prefer you all these years . . . watching him groom you to take over the business and family, she decided to take what she knew Marcus wouldn't willingly leave her. Unfortunately, her father didn't find out in time how much of a snake his daughter was, but thank God we have. We need to act. Now. An eye for an eye. It's fair, and everyone in this organization would agree. As the head of Cross, it's your duty to do what's right."

I'm so tired of hearing her fucking mouth. The more she talks, the more I'm not looking down on matricide.

"I agree with Michelle," Malcolm states. He looks at Greg.

Slowly, the other man nods. "I have to agree, Prince."

The other soldiers murmur their agreement, and my throat feels as if every one of their words is like a shovel of dirt being thrown on top of me, burying me alive.

Anger coalesces in the pit of my stomach, hardening, a tumor I fear is incapable of being excised. Why didn't Ember say something about killing Marcus? At least say something to me, grant me some way to try and protect her. By staying silent—and in turn forcing me to remain silent—we're both fucked.

And now, I might have to kill her.

"Thanks for the information. I'll handle it." I push back my chair and stand, indicating this bullshit meeting is over.

But Michelle being Michelle refuses to let it go. Her thin eyebrows arrow down into a frown. "What do you mean, you'll handle it? In what way?"

I inhale. Exhale.

Yeah, fuck it.

Grabbing my Glock from my shoulder holster, I set the gun down on the table and stare unblinking at my mother. I'll give credit to her; she doesn't hightail it out of here. But she can't hide that flinch or the tremble in her hand as she lifts it to the base of her throat.

No doubt, she's probably choking on the words she wants to hurl at me, but wisely, she swallows that shit down. Right now isn't the moment to test me. I'll forget she pushed me out her pussy and treat her like the cold-blooded bitch who murdered her own husband to get to the top.

"Fine." She forces a smile that's as real as her eighteen-inch buss down. "If you don't mind, I'd appreciate you keeping me posted on the steps you decide to take. This is my family, too, after all."

I nod, and she turns and leaves the conference coom, leaving behind traces of her signature perfume and not one damn hint of the peace I'd walked into this office with this morning.

"I'll follow after her and make sure she's okay. And isn't out there causing more shit." Kareem's attempt at levity falls flat, but I appreciate the effort. And unlike his mother, I appreciate the loyalty to me he displayed today. After he rises to his feet, I pull him into a hard, brief hug. Shock wavers over his face, but it's quickly replaced by a small smile. "I'll call you later."

"We trust you'll make the best and appropriate decision," Malcolm says, also standing and striding over, arm outstretched. I clasp his hand, and he gives it a firm squeeze. "I'll be waiting to hear from you."

The other ol' head soldiers approach to shake my hand and they, too, exit, leaving just me, Eli, and Makeda. They held their own counsel the whole meeting, but now I look toward them for any advice.

Eli crosses his arms over his chest. "Your mother screwed you."

I slam a fist down on the conference table.

"Fuck."

"You sure about this?"

I glance at Makeda before the elevator doors open on a soft

hiss and step inside, she and Eli following me. Once the doors close, I lean forward and stare into a concealed retina scanner. It flashes green, and only then do I remove my keys and insert one into a slot below the numbers panel. The elevator gives a tiny, soft jerk and then starts to descend toward the basement.

"I'm sure I don't have much of a choice," I reply to Makeda's question.

"I just don't like it." She hikes an eyebrow. "Okay, we know the video is legit because Ro verified it. But Michelle doesn't, and she doesn't give a fuck. And I really would like to find out how she came by the video in the first place. How long has she had it? And why is she showing it to you just now? Nope." She shakes her head. "Something in the milk ain't clean on this one."

"You think I haven't asked myself the same questions?" I stare at the sealed elevator doors. "But none of those answers matter now, and even if we had them, it won't change what needs to be done."

Eli glances at Makeda with a shake of his head.

"No one here believes Michelle gives a fuck about avenging Marcus's death or that she even has any real love for him. This whole thing leaves a bad taste in my mouth because it feels like we're being used as puppets and she's the fucking puppeteer. But the truth is, none of that shit matters. Ember's crime isn't killing Marcus, it's Michelle finding out. Now there's no other course of action. If Prince doesn't go forward with this, he appears weak and disloyal in front of not just all Cross members but the criminal underworld. No one would trust him as a leader. And that invites chaos and instability. Is one person's life bigger than the good of the entire organization or all those in it?" Eli shakes his head. "Nah. Ember's left him with no choice, just like he said."

I don't say anything after Eli, and neither does Makeda. We continue the ride to the basement in silence, each of us lost in our own thoughts.

Anger, grief, and a sickening, heavy resolve sit on my chest like an albatross, and I can barely breathe past it. It's been hours since Michelle ambushed me in that conference room, and I haven't inhaled a deep breath since. As much as I tried to figure out how to not end up here, there was no escape. Everything Eli said is true. No one person is bigger than the family, just as Michelle depended on. I'm cornered like a rat and feeling as dirty and fucked as one, too.

My personal desires and feelings didn't matter when I made the calls to Don Amato, Naoki, Malcolm, and the others earlier this afternoon.

And they don't fucking matter now as I'm about to step off this elevator and head to kill Ember.

Slamming a fist against the wall, I embrace the ripple of pain. Savor it. Better this physical ache than the one tearing at me with greedy, bloody hands. For the first time since my father died, I started to hope. I began to believe that I could have something unspoiled. That maybe, just maybe, I could have something—someone—just for me. Only for me.

But my need, my obsession, blinded me to the truth I've never been able to escape.

Hope is a figment of imagination for saints, children, and idiots.

I ain't none of those.

The elevator stops, and the doors slide open. We step off onto the floor very few people are aware of. The subterranean basement is located several feet below Ember's lab, completely soundproof and secret. The first room, with its cement floor and walls, runs the length of the building. It stands empty except for a folding chair next to a reinforced steel door. In seconds, I'm in front of it, submitting to another retina scan and pulling open the door.

Several people turn to look at me as I enter. Corey, Crystal, Murk, and several other top soldiers. Kareem, posted up against the back wall, arms crossed, hooks his chin up in greeting. Unlike the first room, this one looks exactly like what it is—a torture chamber. Plastic sheets cover half of the floor. Steel beams run along the ceiling, and hooks extend down from them. Steel wheeled trays line one wall, an array of tools neatly laid across the tops. A long coil of hose lies in the far back corner, ready to be turned on to wash away blood from the cement floor.

The room is set up, ready and prepped for a guest of honor.

And, as I step farther into the room, my current one sits on a chair, arms and feet bound.

Ember raises her head.

Irrational fury consumes me in a murderous, crimson haze as I meet her steady, calm gaze and blank expression. As I note the damage done to her face. That rage washes over me, and for a moment, my body trembles with the effort to not pull my gun and empty the clip into every person in this room. I close my eyes. Inhale. Hold the breath, desperately attempting to regain any scraps of control. Only after I've counted to ten twice do I lift my lids. But the moment my gaze lands on Ember again, the thin, tenuous reins on my rage quickly unravel and snap.

"Who did it?" I ask, voice calm. Deadly fucking calm. When no answers me, I tear my focus from her and scan the room. The only people safe in this room are Makeda and Eli since they've been with me. Everyone else, including my brother, is fair game. "Who put their hands on her?"

No one speaks up, and I stalk closer to Ember, studying the busted lip crusted with blood at the corner of her mouth and the bruise already darkening her cheek. My palm itches with the need to cup her face, tilt her head back to see if any other injuries mar her skin. But derision suddenly riding her mouth warns me I'd end up missing some digits if I tried it. She's bound to the chair, but her stiff frame and taut shoulders scream with the same bloody rage that runs through me.

"Who. The. Fuck. Hit. Her?" I grind out.

After several more moments of a tense, weighted silence, I slowly pivot, reaching for my Glock at the small of my back. Everybody can get it.

"Me. I did." Ransom, a soldier who's been with the Cross organization for at least five years, speaks up. He holds his hands up, palms out, but throws a mug in Ember's direction. "The order that came down was to bring her in by any means necessary. She hit me first and tried to run, so I had to do what I had to do. I mean, she's a traitor. She killed Marcus and that's why we're bringing her down here in the first place, so I didn't think it mattered. My bad, Prince."

"Your bad?" I chuckle, shaking my head. "Your bad, huh?"

"Yeah, I—"

I snatch my gun out and stop whatever bullshit he's about to say with a bullet to the eye. His body jerks, dropping backward. His skull cracks against the floor with a loud thud. Not satisfied with the shot to the eye or the TBI from that fall, I stride over to him and pump four more bullets into him—one to each hand he used to touch her, one to his mouth for speaking that stupid-ass shit, and the last to the forehead for fucking thinking.

Is the anger still eating at me in big, gulping flames logical? Especially since if Ember doesn't give me the information I'm seeking, I'll do worse with the instruments waiting on the tray? No, but I don't give a flying fuck. No one touches her but me.

Mine.

Even despite the circumstances, the word shimmers in my head. Again, the shit is irrational considering I'm here to carry out the only punishment her actions demand. But I don't give a fuck. I'm the leader of Cross. I introduced her as my fiancée. No one gets to touch her but me. Even if it's to snuff out her life in retribution for the one she took.

Shit.

Why hadn't she told me? Trusted me? Maybe, just fucking maybe, we could've avoided this together. But her silence and my position have placed us here, in an untenable situation that has only one outcome.

Another blast of anger sears me from the inside out—at her, at myself, at Michelle, at this fucking family.

Gotdammit.

I retrace my path and approach her, not stopping until the toes of my shoes bump the pointed ones of her stilettoes. Staring down at her, I could hate her. I almost do. She makes me weak—she *is* my weakness. And I can't afford to let everyone know it.

"You've been lying to me, Ember," I growl.

"I don't know what you're talking about." She tips her head back, nothing—not rage, fear, guilt—reflected in her face. Only her eyes order me to go fuck myself. I lied. There's the rage, the confusion. The hurt.

You could've been honest with me. Fucking come to me before deciding to kill Marcus. The words slam against my skull like bloodied, bruised fists. Shit, I would've done it for her if she'd asked.

"You don't know what I'm talking about?" I shift closer, curl my fingers around the back of the chair, and lean down over her. Close enough that I glimpse the green striations in her eyes but far enough away that she can't exact any damage to my face. "Nothing jogs that big, beautiful brain of yours? You can remember formulas to engineer complex compounds but not what that pretty mouth has been lying about for weeks? No, ma. I ain't buying it."

Instead of shrinking away from me, she leans forward as far as the zip cuffs binding her to the arms and legs of the chair will allow.

"I speak English, Spanish, French, and Mandarin, but not riddles. Say what you mean."

"Look where you are, ma. You sure you want to talk shit right now?"

"Prince, man, that's your girl. Maybe you should take a beat—"

My head jerks in Kareem's direction. "Right now, she's a possible traitor and threat. If you don't have the stomach for this, get out. Now. But don't fucking interrupt me again. We good?"

Kareem shoves off the wall and returns my stare, but after several long seconds, he nods. "We're good."

No one else moves to interrupt or speak on Ember's behalf, although Makeda rolls her lips as if she's trapping an objection behind her teeth. She crosses her arms, widening her stance as she scans the others, disgust saturating her face.

"Now." I return my attention to her. "You ready to tell me the truth, or do you need some incentive?"

Eli wheels one of the trays over, stopping at the edge of the plastic sheet, and Ember's gaze flicks in that direction. Panic widens her eyes, but she still mugs me.

Gotdamn.

She's going to make me hurt her.

"I'm a traitor and a threat now?" She scoffs. "Just this morning, I was an asset to this organization and a fiancée. That went left quick."

"You got jokes."

"No, I got no fucking clue why I'm here."

I push off the chair, straightening and removing my cell from the inner pocket of my suit jacket. It doesn't take me long to pull up the video I sent myself from Michelle's laptop and hold the phone up in front of Ember.

For the next ten minutes, silence fills the room as we watch her watch the security tape. A myriad of emotions marches across her face. Shock. Anger. Resolve.

Guilt.

My gut clenches hard around nothing, and I grip the phone hard. Either that or hurl it across the room to shatter against the concrete wall. Or go kick a fucking hole in that wall. Anything to release this fucking pain. If I caught that flicker of guilt, then everyone else in this room did, too. Ember has sealed her own fate.

Sealed ours.

And that's a good part of my rage. Her actions ruined us before we could even fully begin. I get the why—God knows I get the why—but her recklessness, her carelessness has stolen something from me.

Stolen her.

And that makes her crime fucking unforgivable.

"I didn't kill Marcus," she fervently says as I lower the phone.

I study her face and chuckle, the sound dry, disbelieving as that flash of guilt flickers in my mind again. Part of me hungers to claw it out of my head, but I can't.

"What were you doing there, Ember?"

"I went to see him."

I wait for her to continue, to add to that obvious-as-fuck statement. When she doesn't, I huff out a dry laugh and hunker down in front of her.

"Careful, baby girl," I murmur. "Be real careful how you choose to move next. You about to fuck around, but I'ma help you find out. Now"—I lower a knee onto the floor and lean closer to her, peering into her eyes and letting her glimpse the pain she's courting by being evasive with me—"what were you doing there at Marcus's apartment building?"

"I didn't kill him," she reiterates, jerking at the bindings on her wrists. With a frustrated growl, she sucks her teeth. "Marcus was a piece-of-shit human being and an even shittier father, but I. Didn't. Kill. Him."

"Then why did you go there, Ember?" Makeda asks as gently as I've ever heard from her. Ever. Uncrossing her arms, she steps forward into Ember's line of sight. "That apartment was well-known as his ho pad. Why would you go there to see him?"

Ember's head jerks toward Makeda, but she doesn't answer. Instead, she looks at her for a long moment but eventually shifts her attention back to me. And I decipher the answer in her eyes.

Michelle.

It'd been years since Ember had willingly stepped foot in her childhood home, and she for damn sure wouldn't seek out Marcus in that house where Michelle lurked, exerting influence.

"I said all I'm going to. If you don't believe me, then you better get on with what you have planned. But the answer isn't going to change."

Rising, I'm almost rocked back on my heels by the blast of heat surging through me. She thinks this is a game? Thinks we're playing fucking show-and-tell? She's in a torture chamber, and in this moment, with all these people here prepared and eager to witness her death, she isn't better than Deacon or Xavier. Nah, she's worse. To them, she killed not just the head of Cross but her own father. To them, she's worse than any traitor.

"Were you working with Deacon and Xavier?"

Unbidden, an image of Deacon's body invades my mind. Just last night, she confessed she'd done that for me. Because he'd hurt me. But could it have been for an alternative reason? After all, dead men can't talk . . .

She recoils in shock . . . or flinches in guilt.

"What?" She frowns, and what sounds like genuine offense and hurt echoes in her voice. "Are you serious right now? You believe I . . ." She trails off, but I pick it up for her.

"You killed Deacon before we could get to him." I tilt my head. "Was it because you didn't want him speaking to me? You afraid of what he had to tell me?"

Disgust darkens her expression, and the shit leaves me winded.

With my back to the rest of the people in the room, I risk briefly closing my eyes. Risk that momentary sign of vulnerability. I believe her. I believe she didn't have anything to do with Deacon or Xavier. Or the attempt on my life. Even with all signs pointing to the exact opposite. And yet, it won't change a mu'fucking thing. Except my loathing for myself. I won't ever be able to wash the stink of that clean.

"Fuck you," she coldly snarls.

The blow of it, of the hatred drenching those two words, has my body aching but I step back and away from her. I don't try to smother the pain. Nah, I bask in it, fucking roll in it. Because what kind of man abandons the woman he . . . the woman he claimed for his own to this fate? I'm no better than Michelle, killing my father for a come up.

I almost bolt to the far corner to hurl the nonexistent contents of my stomach.

Instead, I backpedal toward the tray. Only when I reach it do I break our visual connection, and I scope out all my choices of tools, running my fingers along the scalpel, pliers, ice pick . . . I eventually pick up the pliers.

"Prince," Eli murmurs, moving to my side and speaking low enough for just me to hear. "Be sure this is what you want to do. There's no coming back from it."

I ignore his warning and walk back over to Ember, and she defiantly watches me. Her cold demeanor doesn't change. Even when her gaze dips to the pliers, she doesn't plead, doesn't sweat, doesn't flinch. I admire her for that.

"Prince," Kareem calls out, but I ignore him, too.

Gripping her slender pointer finger between the pliers, I apply pressure. Blood sluggishly starts to pool as the blade bites into her skin.

Still . . . No movement. No confession.

Her jaw clenches, a tiny muscle ticking along the edge. Moisture glazes her eyes but not one tear falls.

I apply more pressure.

A small, muted sound crawls out of her, but it's immediately silenced as if she deliberately cut it off, refusing to give me that satisfaction, although her shoulders hunch slightly forward and a very fine tremble races through her.

Bile rushes in my stomach, races like a gold medalist for the back of my throat, the acid burning my esophagus. *Do it. Fucking do it. Make an example out of her. Show every person here,* show her*, that you're not weak. That she's not your weakness.*

More pressure . . .

Gotdammit. Fuck.

I release my grip on the pliers and damn near lurch back a step.

"Everybody out," I growl. No one moves, and I whip around, gaze landing on each one of them. They stare at me, eyes wide, mouths open like I've lost my shit. And I have. "I said, get. The fuck. Out."

One of the soldiers looses a sharp bark of laughter, spreading his arms wide. "What the hell? You gotta be fucking kiddin—"

I whip out my gun again and aim it in his direction. His mouth snaps closed, and he holds his hands up, palms out in surrender.

"You want to finish that?" He shakes his head, but I don't lower my weapon. "Like I said, get out."

In seconds, the room empties, the heavy door slamming shut and leaving only me and Ember inside. Disgusted with myself, her, and this fucked-up situation, I drop the pliers, and they hit the ground with a *clank* that seems deafening in the tomb-like quiet.

Dragging both hands over my braids, I stalk over to the second tray and grab a white towel before returning to Ember. She doesn't snatch her hand away from me while I tightly wrap her injured finger. She doesn't look at me when I kneel down in front of her, briefly pressing my forehead to her hand before lifting my head.

"Look at me." She keeps her gaze fixed straight ahead. "Ember, look at me." A full minute passes before she lowers her head. "Why were you there that night?"

She stares at me, her eyes blank, freezing chips of amber. She's not going to tell me. And I don't blame her.

And I'm still not going to kill her. I refuse to become Michelle.

Is one person's life bigger than the good of the entire organization or all those in it? That's what Eli had asked Makeda in the elevator on the way down here.

Then, my answer was no. Shit, until seconds ago, it remained no.

But now?

Yes. Gotdammit. Yes. Her life is bigger, more important. And if I have to replace hers for mine, then so be it. Mine is forfeit because I'm not killing her.

I sigh, standing to my feet—

"To see him. I was there to see him. I didn't lie." She grimaces. "I didn't just plan to make my exit strategy from Cross after Marcus died. It'd been in the works for months, over a year. I was walking away the very next day, and I couldn't wait to be free of Cross and HoC. And Marcus. I didn't need any of his money, because God knew he wasn't going to offer me any. Not my inheritance, not any percentage of the profits from HEA or Glass Slipper. But none of that mattered because I had my own source of income." A small smile ghosts across her face, there and gone. "I've designed another drug—Fairy Dust. Once it's complete, get ready, 'cause it's going to give yours competition."

"Why're you telling me this now?"

Not 'cause she trusts me. We've both destroyed those tentative tethers and salted the fucking earth. She might've went low, but I went to hell.

I became Marcus.

I placed the company, someone else's word, a whole fucking organization of people above her. I had the opportunity to choose her, put her first, and I failed.

So no, this isn't about trust because we no longer have that, thanks to me.

Which makes why she's telling me about a new drug she created, knowing I could use the info against her, even more confusing. I could come for it and her since this Fairy Dust is technically Cross property because she designed it while working for the family. The safe bet would've been to keep me in the dark about what she got going on. But she chose not to. And she chose not to when I had her bound to a chair in a torture chamber.

Why?

"So you'll understand that I had nothing to lose and everything to gain by walking away from all this shit on that night. Autonomy. An identity. Freedom. And that's why I went to see Marcus. To let him know I was out, that he wouldn't get to use and hide me anymore like his dirty little bastard secret. I wanted to see his face when I told him all the shit was on him now. That he would no longer get to prosper and benefit from my knowledge and hard work while pretending I didn't exist." For the first time, emotion starts to leak through her icy demeanor. Her soft mouth trembles before she firms it and there's a sheen in her eyes. Then she closes them, blocking me out. "But." She swallows hard, then rasps, "I wanted to see if there would be regret. More than anything, I longed to see that. Then I . . ." She reopens her eyes, and the agony there damn near steals my breath. "I hoped he would ask me to stay. Tell me he needed me for once in both of our lives."

Her harsh breath bounces off the walls of the chamber, the sound labored, heavy.

The pain in her gaze echoes in my chest, and if I could somehow use the scalpel over on that tray to remove that ache of loneliness and rejection, I would become one of those mu'fuckas off *Grey's Anatomy*.

"Anyway, he didn't answer. And I called his name when I got there, but . . . Standard operating procedure. He didn't even bother answering the door when I knocked. Either he was too busy fucking to talk to me, or he sat in that ho pad and just didn't want to see me. That muthafucka couldn't even give me the courtesy of goodbye. So I left. But I was too humiliated to go back through the lobby just in case someone saw me go up. They couldn't have known that I'd been rejected *again* by my father, but I felt the stink of it, the taint all over me. I left by the stairs and out the side entrance."

"That's why we didn't see you leave on the video."

"Yes."

"Why didn't you just tell me that, baby girl? Why did you hide all of this from me? Why didn't you come to me?"

She blinks, and though the sheen of moisture glistens in her eyes, so does the glint of steel.

"Because I didn't want to be seen as a pathetic ass who, after twenty-plus years, is still running after Daddy's love and approval." She inhales a deep breath and looks me right in the eye, her gaze unwavering. "And don't call me *baby girl*. You don't get that privilege anymore. You don't get the privilege of *me* anymore. Now either get on with killing me or let me the fuck go."

No.

The denial roars in my head, and it's all I hear, all I feel. Panic surges and pulses within me like an electrical current. Pushing past it, I inhale a deep breath and bend to pick up the pliers. Quickly, I snap the zip ties, and she stands, rubbing her wrists.

"You're not. You're staying with me."

"The fuck I am." She cups her injured hand and mugs me. "You must be high on my good shit if you think I will go anywhere with you. *I trusted you*. Against everything I knew about you, against all the evidence of who you are, I still *trusted you*. I won't make that mistake again. And I don't lay up in the same house as people who I wouldn't turn my back on. I'm going home. You can try to stop me, but then you're going to have to finish what you started."

That panic flares bright and hot again, and I'm ten seconds from being on her, knocking her out and throwing her ass over my shoulder, and not stopping until she's locked in the bedroom I assigned her.

But it wasn't her who broke trust.

No, she didn't tell me about being at Marcus's apartment building, but I also didn't go to her after that bullshit Michelle arranged and ask what was up. I had the opportunity to choose her, to trust her, but instead, I let her down, like her father.

From the time Marcus brought Michelle, me, and Kareem home, he chose Michelle over Ember. Every time he turned a blind eye to the abuse, he chose Michelle over Ember. Every time he didn't acknowledge Ember as his daughter but claimed me as his son, Marcus chose Michelle.

And when I was willing to sacrifice her for a legacy that didn't mean shit without the one person whose blood made that shit possible, made it legitimate and powerful, I chose Michelle.

I chose myself.

A wild, uncontainable pain howls in my head, slams against my chest. It sends me reeling back and away from her. From the raw, unfiltered truth of my greed, my cowardice. My weakness.

Ember isn't my weakness. My fear is.

I could've trusted her. Trusted what I knew about her, who I know her to be. I could've believed in what I'd glimpsed in her face, her eyes last night as she rode my dick. Lust and pleasure, yes, but . . .

Affection.

Acceptance.

Trust.

Instead, I chose to ignore what was right in front of my eyes. Instead, I chose to betray her. And acknowledging all of this, admitting that I'm a selfish, cowardly piece of shit, I still can't let her go.

I still refuse to let her go.

"I'll give you this week," I concede, nodding although my body damn near shudders with the force of my objection to this. "Don't make me come for you, Ember."

She looks me up and down, the *fuck you* written on her face. In permanent marker.

"And don't threaten me. This isn't going to end how you think it is," she warns, moving past me at a slow but deliberate shuffle, holding the bloodstained towel to her hand and cradling both against her chest. "You'll let my supervisor know I'll be out of work for the next few days. My fucking hand hurts because a bitch-ass muthafucka took a pair of pliers to my finger."

Shame coats me in a filthy grime. She reaches the door, and I call her name.

"Our engagement ball is in seven days," I say to her taut back. "You will be there."

If possible, her spine goes even straighter. After a pause, she opens the door with her uninjured hand and walks out. No backward glance. No words. No . . .

Nothing.

I stare at that empty doorway, but it doesn't make her turn around or reappear. And fear encroaches deep inside me. Fear, revulsion, and grief.

Instead of Ember, Eli and Kareem move into the entrance.

"Hey, is everything good? I just saw Ember leave. I'm assuming she explained why she was at Marcus's and what happened?" Kareem frowns, glancing from me to the door.

Eli studies me in his silent way, his expression stoic and . . . sympathetic.

This room that had seemed so large seems to shrink, pressing in on me. Not answering Kareem, I stalk forward, passing him.

"Prince? You good?" Eli murmurs as I move past him.

"Fine. Get someone in here to clean up." Ransom's body is still sprawled out on the floor with Ember's blood.

I want all traces of tonight gone.

If only erasing it from my head was that fucking easy.

CHAPTER FOURTEEN

Ember

"I can't lie. After working in this lab for the past week, it's going to be real hard returning to that small one at the Castle," Jaq says, walking into the laboratory at my house.

They're not lying. Yes, the timeline for leaving Cross had been pushed back, but that didn't stop me from having my home lab completed. With state-of-the-art equipment and much more space, it's a scientist's fantasy. It's everything the secret lab is except grander, bigger. More workstations, better technology and lighting, more cages. More subjects.

It's a dream lab. And it's become my safe harbor this past week away from HoC.

Away from Asad.

The all-too-familiar wave of anger swells within me, and all I have to do is glance down at my forefinger and the bandage on it to remember why I'm so fucking *furious*.

And betrayed.

And hurt.

No, not going down that mental pitted and cracked path today. Especially when I finally have good news. Triumph flares in my chest, a rush of adrenaline quick on its heels.

I smile at Jaq from my perch on a stool at the first station. "We were waiting on you."

They strip out of their jacket and grab their lab coat off a nearby hook. "Well, I've been sleeping here two nights in a row. If I didn't go home and let Bennie look at my face, you would've had to let me claim homestead on one of those nice apartments." They weren't lying. We'd all met Bennie, their girlfriend of two years. She was beautiful, fun, and extra as fuck. I had to take her in carefully measured doses. But Jaq worshipped the ground she walked on, so that's all that matters. "Where're Perla and Gus-Gus?"

"I told your aggravating ass to stop calling me that," Gus grumbles, emerging from the outer door with Perla in front of him.

His hand rests on the small of her back, and his big frame hovers over her. I tilt my head. His stance is protective like a—

"You two fucking?" Jaq bluntly asks.

I snort as Perla blushes and Gus glares at them.

"Jaq," Gus growls.

"What? What'd I do?" They shrug. "We're here to care for our intrepid leader while she's hurt. You're the ones doing the nasty beast with two backs in your employer's house. That *has* to violate some human resource rule."

This time, I can't contain my laughter, and despite her glowing cheeks, Perla grins. Gus crosses his arms over his chest and aims a dark scowl at Jaq.

I can't lie. Having them here with me has kept me grounded, sane. Has helped battle back the sadness. Being the wrongly tortured fiancée of the boss has its perks. I shot Asad a text telling him they were on vacation until future notice, and he okayed it. I guess guilt will get you all kinds of shit.

"Okay, okay. I'm claiming culpable deniability. As far as I know, HoC doesn't have a fraternization clause, but I need to deny any knowledge in case they do. But"—I arch an eyebrow, fighting back a smirk—"just know I'm going over all my furniture with a black light after you leave, and I will send y'all nasty asses a cleaning bill."

Perla snickers, then Jaq lets out a hoot of laughter.

"You got that, now can we get to work?" Gus scowls.

"Sure." I wave them toward the door leading to the secondary lab holding our subjects. Another thing I love about this new space. We have the main area with separate showers, centrifuges, eight stations complete with their own sinks, tubes, microscopes, and any other equipment we use on a daily. And we also have a separate room for housing the subjects. No more being crammed together in one space. We have privacy to conduct our experiments. And don't have to listen to all that whining.

As the door closes behind Gus, I lead them over to the subject in the chair.

"Subject three. Test group," I begin, picking up my tablet from the small desk. Maneuvering to the file that holds its data, I double tap, opening it. Satisfied, I walk over to the chair and stand in front of it. "Before you three arrived, I took its vitals, and temperature is 99.3 degrees, blood pressure 130 over 90. Heart rate 110. A 24 BPM." I scan the subject, and it stares back at me, glossy eyes wide. The fear and uncertainty there is like a heated, sensual touch across my skin. With anticipation crackling in my veins like a hit of my own drug, I pass the device to Perla, who stands closest to me. "Take notes, please," I say, removing a light from my lab coat pocket. Clicking it on, I shift closer to the subject and shine the beam into one eye then the other. "Pupils slightly dilated. Relaxed jaw and neck. The neck of its gown exhibits signs of perspiration, but only around the collar. Recording now at 8:16 a.m. that the drug was administered—" I pause and turn so I'm looking at my assistants. "At 9:00 p.m. the previous evening."

Their gasps and exclamations of "What?" and "Are you serious?" elicit a huge smile that feels foreign on my face. I chuckle and shake my head as Jaq grabs the tablet from Perla and devours the data on the screen as if it's their last meal.

"From the vitals, slightly elevated BP, heart and respiratory rates, and temperature, the drug is still having a physiological effect. *Eleven hours later.* Holy shit," Jaq breathes.

"Vomiting? Hallucinations?" Gus raps out, gaze glued to the screen over Jaq's shoulder.

"None. Not once. And check the last lab results." I wait for them to click through to the file, but I can't hold my excitement. "The urine and blood samples are completely clean. And it hasn't even come completely down from Fairy Dust yet," I brag.

"Holy shit," Jaq repeats.

Perla's head pops up, and a grin stretches across her face and lights up her eyes behind her glasses. "You did it. You really did it."

"*We* did it," I correct her.

All three smile at me, and I return it, thankful for them. And not just their hard and tireless work but their loyalty, their friendship. For so many years, I didn't have any of those—wasn't allowed to by Marcus or Michelle. Which makes Jaq, Gus, and Perla's presence in my life even more special.

"Of course, we need to run more tests for both groups and with different variables, but I think we can cautiously celebrate. Fairy Dust is a success. And I couldn't have done it without you three." They shake their heads and start to object, but I hold up a hand. "It's true. So that makes this drug yours as much as it's mine. I don't know if I've made it clear before, but over at the Castle, we might be employer, employees. But we stopped being that a long while ago. We're partners. Which means, once Fairy Dust is perfected and ready to be distributed, we will split the proceeds four equal ways. As partners should."

Shock saturates their expressions, and they glance at one another. Even Jaq is speechless.

"Ember, are you sure?" Perla hesitantly asks. "I mean, we're employees—"

"This doesn't belong to Cross; it never has. This"—I sweep an arm, indicating the entire lab—"is ours. So yes, I'm sure. I mean, we have a long way to go before we start to see profit, but believe me, when this hits the streets . . . Freedom," I murmur.

"Well, shit, I'm not going to try and convince you otherwise," Jaq announces, clapping their hands once, then rubbing them together. I laugh. "The thought alone of paying off my student loans has me ready to get to work now. Cross pays me nicely, but a PhD doesn't come cheap." They frown, lowering their arms. "Oh wait, that's right. Are you working today? You have that ball tonight—your engagement party on steroids. Hulk Hogan steroids. The steroids he refuses to admit he was jacked up on, steroids." They scan me up and down. "Are you spending the day getting pampered for it?"

I barely smother my snort. "Yeah, no." I dip my chin toward the strapped-in subject. "Gus, could you move it back to its cage?"

He moves to handle that, but Perla and Jaq continue to frown at me.

"What do you mean, 'yeah, no'?" Perla asks. "You can't mean you're not going?"

"That's exactly what I mean," I say, taking the tablet from her and walking back to the counter.

Fuck that ball. And fuck that engagement party. A fake-ass engagement that doesn't mean shit except three more years of confinement in a gilded cage. There isn't shit to celebrate. And I refuse to be threatened into attending. Because it's fuck Asad forever.

My gaze drops to my stitched and bandaged finger. It's not the wound that causes me to wake up late in the night and stare at the ceiling, pain radiating throughout my body. It's not even the bruise to my face or the healing split lip.

No, it's the memory of being bound to that chair with strangers and Kareem watching me with those cold, dead eyes. It's the hot anger, fierce joy, and satisfaction that had buoyed me in that torture chamber as I waited for Asad's arrival. I just knew when he walked into that room, he would go to war and drop bodies on my behalf for being handled so disrespectfully. I knew he would ride in like that fabled prince in fairy tales to free me and repay insult for insult.

So no, it's not physical pain that tortures me in those dark, lonely hours. It's the agony and grief that had sliced through me after his arrival when I realized he wasn't there to have my back. He was the knife in it.

I can't get past it. I can't forgive it.

Because for the first time since my mother died, he made me trust. He made me *want* to trust. Made me . . . hope. And he killed it as surely as he murdered the soldier who punched me in the face when I refused to docilely accept my own kidnapping.

That crime—the crime of hope—is punishable by a life sentence.

Asad Prince can go fuck himself.

"Forgive me if I overstep, Ember, but with you being here this past week and not at the lab, I'm assuming something happened between you and Asad," Perla hesitantly says. "With you nursing your injured hand, we didn't want to pry, but . . ."

"But your hand is on the mend, so what she's so delicately trying to say is, it's obvious he pissed you off, and it must've been pretty bad for you to say fuck even the pretense of going into work and focusing on your own project," Jaq adds.

"I don't think she was trying to say exactly *that*, but neither one of them are wrong." Gus returns from storing the subject and leans back against the counter.

"You're not wrong." On reflex, I cradle my injured hand to my chest. "But there's more going on here that I can't really get into—"

"Oh, we already figured that out once you turned up engaged to the human version of Thanos." Jaq snorts. "And we're not asking for the details, but since I've just been elevated to partner status, I'm going to say it. You would be making a mistake not going to that ball."

"Is that right?"

I don't see how they came to that conclusion, but then again, none of them have all the details. Or the nightmares of the man they'd come to trust and believe in trying to break them.

"Hear me out, and don't slip anything toxic into my afternoon smoothie." They point a warning finger at me. "I'm not asking any more questions because, frankly, I don't want the answers, but your finger was fine when you left out of the Castle a week ago. Then we showed up here to work and you had a busted finger. So by the power of deduction, I'm guessing your lovers' quarrel involved that. So all's I'm saying is, it would be a miscalculation and sign of weakness on your part to not go. You need to go to that thing and show him and everyone there—including that heffa mother of his—what a bad bitch you are."

Jaq doesn't have the details—is missing torture, near death, and murder—but they have the gist of the situation.

The last time Asad—and maybe, more importantly, the members of the Cross organization—had seen me, I'd been strapped to a chair, under interrogation, and then walked out of that basement, bloodied and hurt.

I'd been weakened.

I'd been humiliated.

But . . . I'm not ready to see them again. Not ready to look all of them in the eye knowing they saw me at my weakest. Knowing they've probably told others that Asad thinks so fucking little of Marcus's daughter, his new fiancée, that he damn near cut off her finger while accusing her of being the worst kind of traitor. Knowing they probably believe I *am* that traitor. Usually, I don't give a fuck about people's opinions of me, but having to spy the disdain and suspicion in their eyes—the unwarranted and unfounded disdain and suspicion . . .

I'm not ready to see that ho Michelle. It didn't take a lot of digging to figure out she was behind the video. Stepping into that ballroom and facing her glee, the gotdamn triumph? She wounded me through her worst and most effective weapon—her son.

I'm not ready to see *him* again. When I told him I needed space, I meant it. Other than that text about Gus, Perla, and Jaq, I haven't reached out to him. And I've blocked his contact so he can't contact me. And I can't be tempted to call or text him. The pain is too fresh, the hurt, the humiliation too close to the surface. I'm not ready to look into all that dangerous, deceptive beauty and accept that I'd fallen for it like a naïve-ass bitch who should've known better. Somewhere, Maya Angelou's sucking her teeth at me because Asad has shown me over and over exactly who he is, but I chose not to believe it.

Consider me baptized and saved because I'm a believer now.

"You're not wrong, but I'm good," I say to Jaq, entering the code for the door and exiting into the main lab. "Besides, I didn't bother buying a dress or any of that. And it's a little too late to go shopping."

Perla scoffs, waving a hand. "As far as excuses go, that's a pitiful one. Especially since Jaq and I kind of foresaw this and have a stylist on standby ready to arrive with several gowns, shoes, and other accessories for you to choose from."

I blink, lips parted.

"You have what?" I blink again. Because . . . what? They made all these plans, went to all of this trouble, for me? Love for them blooms inside me, even though I still have zero intention of going to this farce. "When?"

"Bennie." Jaq shrugs. "She does too much way too often, but bae comes through with this kind of shit. She knows *everybody*."

"And my sister should be here in about"—Gus glances down at his Grand Seiko watch—"an hour and a half to do your nails and feet. She's also bringing a friend who does hair." I frown, and he shrugs. "She owns a nail shop, and when I told her I'd pay triple her regular price, she agreed to make a house call."

"Gotdamn. If that's the family discount, just treat me like a regular-degular customer." Jaq winces.

"She's about her business first, so I can't be mad at her." Gus hikes up an eyebrow. "So, you're fully taken care of, literally, from head to toe. Are you going?"

I sigh, pinching the bridge of my nose. "Look, I appreciate all of this. And you. I appreciate you for arranging all of this for me. But, why is this so important to you? What does it matter if I go to this thing or not? C'mon, we all know this ball is less about my engagement and more about House of Cross business and flaunting its wealth and connections. I'm just a sideshow."

And I was tired of being other people's entertainment. Their joke.

To the man whose one job was to love me, protect me, nurture me, he only used me. First, for an heir. And when I bombed that assignment by being born a woman, then later for his wealth and gain. But not before turning me over to the tender mercies of his wife.

My pain, my torture was her favorite pastime. And her son continued the hobby last night after he made me believe he'd once been my savior instead of my tormentor.

So no, I'm not tired. I'm fucking exhausted. Of being their punch line. Their toy. Their scapegoat.

"It matters because they don't want you there," Perla quietly says. "Ember, since we've been working here, you've made it a point not to mention anything family related. But we're not ignorant or blind. We've all witnessed how the employees here act toward you when they come in contact and how they behave toward Prince, Kareem, or Michelle. Either they're incredibly disrespectful or they have no clue who you are—Marcus Cross's daughter. We witnessed that for ourselves at the funeral. You weren't allowed to sit with the family but with us, as if you were just someone who received a paycheck and didn't possess half of that man's DNA." Perla's voice trembles with fury, and it's such a juxtaposition with her sweet, bespectacled pixie appearance that in other circumstances, it would've been funny.

But she's enraged on my behalf, and there's nothing humorous about that. There's nothing amusing about someone loving you.

I squeeze my eyes closed against the embarrassing sting of tears. Against the burn in my heart that goes a little way to exorcising the hurt.

"I can't speak for Prince," she continues, "but all of us here know Michelle doesn't want you anywhere near there, and everyone else doesn't think you belong. *That's* why you need to go. To show that cunt and those privileged one-percenters that not only do you belong at the table but you *own* that muthafuckin' table."

Well. Damn.

"And go be on your ratchet bald-headed ho shit to make Mr. Asad Prince pay for whatever fuckup he committed and rub in his face what he's been missing," Jaq cosigns.

"Please don't be on your ratchet bald-headed ho shit." Gus sighs. "But everything else, hell yeah."

I look at the circle—no. *My* circle. I look at my circle of support and smile.

At my courage in physical form. If they believe I can do this, that I should do this, then damn, maybe it's about time I start believing in myself.

"Fuck it. I'll go."

"Miss Ma'am, you are giving." Bennie steps back, a grin stretching her full, glossed lips. "I knew this dress was the one as soon as Sheri pulled it." Without glancing away from me, she bumps fists with the statuesque redhead with the ebony skin and lush curves. "Great job, friend."

"Of course. You know I don't do anything but win," Sheri gloats. "But she's not wrong, boo. You are wearing this dress, and it looks even better than I envisioned. And I can admit when I'm wrong. I thought those glass shoes were giving *P-Valley*, but they work. They really bring the look together."

I turn and take in my reflection in the tall cheval mirror. And I'm . . . in awe. One would expect the daughter of a fashion mogul and the head of a billionaire drug empire to be blasé about gorgeous evening wear. But one would be dead-ass wrong. This is my first. As is this ball. I've never been to a formal occasion that called for a gown or jewelry. Not a dance. Not a gala.

How pathetic is it that I'm twenty-five years old and am attending my first prom?

Shaking my head, I stare at myself. The black mermaid-style

dress fits my curves like the proverbial glove, gliding over each one like a level-ten clinger lover. The sweetheart neckline draws eyes to my generous breasts and the tiered bottom of the dress flares from my knees in a glorious display of silken obsidian feathers. I twist to the side, and the straps wrap over my shoulders and under my arms, leaving my entire back bare down to the small of it. The light of the room bounces off the black sequins covering the entire dress, and it's almost as if I glow and burn with a dark fire with each movement. Only the toe of my glass stiletto peeps from underneath the feathered hem—an identical replica of my mother's wedding shoes that I had designed years ago but have never worn.

Black polish and tiny diamonds decorate my nails and toenails, and my blond hair brushes my shoulders in a ruthlessly straight sheet. A part down the middle has the strands framing my face, emphasizing the flawless beat the makeup artist applied. Diamonds dangle from my ears and circle my throat and wrist.

I'm beautiful.

Sadness trickles through me, and I blink against the sting in my eyes. A memory of my mother sitting at the vanity in her bedroom, putting on her makeup, preparing for a night out with Marcus, floats in front of my eyes. She'd loved dressing up. Loved getting her dark blond hair styled and her nails done. Kimberly Cross would've probably been standing here, dabbing at her eyes, delighted and proud to see me looking just like her.

She should've been here. God, I wish she were.

Inhaling deeply, I turn back around and give Bennie and Sheri another smile—tremulous but genuine.

"Thank you both." The words seem inadequate for the gift they've given me. I'm walking into the lion's den tonight, and they've clothed me in impenetrable, gorgeous armor.

Maybe they read the immensity of what I'm unable to express because Sheri grins widely and Bennie crosses the short space separating us and pulls me into a short but tight embrace.

"You're welcome," she says, releasing me. "Now you know if

we didn't come correct, Jaq would be all over my ass. And not in a way I'd enjoy."

Sheri snickers and I scrunch up my nose, but then laugh.

A knock sounds on the door before it opens seconds later. Jaq appears in the gap. Their eyes widen, further gassing me up.

"Gotdamn, Ember."

"Right?" Bennie bumps Sheri's shoulder. "Bad bitch walking."

"That man is going to crash out behind you," Jaq says, shaking their head as if they're sympathetic. "I almost feel sorry for him."

Perla slips by Jaq with a snort. "Not. He deserves all of this"—she sweeps a hand up and down my body—"coming for him. And I, for one, am utterly delighted."

"That part." Bennie points a finger at Perla.

Chuckling both at their girl-power moment and to cover my nerves, I walk over to the dresser and grab my matching clutch purse. Moments later, I exit the apartment and descend the stairs with my entourage behind me. More than ever, I feel like I'm headed to prom with family seeing me off. All that's missing is an overprotective fath—

"Sam." I jerk to a stop at the bottom of the steps, splaying my fingers wide over my chest and thudding heart. I'm staring at my godfather, outfitted in a tuxedo, but I'm still not comprehending that he's here. And *why* he's here. "What are you doing here?"

He moves from beside Gus and approaches me, a wistful smile curving his mouth. Sadness flickers in his eyes, and in that instant, I know he's thinking about my mother.

"You look just like her," he whispers, confirming my suspicion. Taking my hand in his, he guides me off the last step and presses the backs of my fingers to his cheek. "Ember, sweetheart, you're beautiful, and Kim would be so proud."

"Thanks, Sam. I really appreciate that. I needed to hear that," I murmur.

I step into him, wrapping my arms around him and hugging

him tight. And when his arms close around me, it's almost like receiving a hug from my mom.

"Anytime, Em." Clearing his throat, he steps back and blinks fast, then clears his throat again. "I have something for you. I hope you don't mind?" he asks, stepping closer and reaching behind my neck.

He pauses, giving me the opportunity to object, but I don't. Nodding, he removes the necklace I'm wearing and passes it to Gus. Then he reaches inside his coat and removes another one. I nearly gasp at its loveliness. The choker is comprised of brilliant diamonds and emeralds, and looks like something that belongs behind a glass case in a museum, not around my throat.

"It's your mother's," he says, moving behind me and placing it around my neck. Astonishment, love, and threads of sadness well inside me, and with trembling fingers, I brush a caress over the jewelry. "Before she died, Kim asked me to put this aside for you. She left it up to me to choose the occasion, but she was adamant about it being a happy or meaningful one. Your father gifted her this on the night of their engagement, so I thought it was fitting." He circles me once more to stand in front of me. His dark eyes glisten, and admiration and love shine through the unshed tears. "Perfect."

"Thank you, Sam," I rasp. Yes, the jewelry originally came from Marcus, but that doesn't diminish the beauty and power of the gift. She thought of me, loved me. And once more, it's as if my mother is standing here with me.

"You're welcome." He picks up my hand, pats it, then loops my arm through his. He turns me toward the front door. "To answer your question about why I'm here, I'm escorting my goddaughter to the ball. Your carriage awaits, sweetheart."

Confusion still swirls inside of me, because how did he know to come here? Who contacted him? But one glance at Gus, Perla, and Jaq standing next to the open front door wearing big, goofy smiles, their arms around each other, and those questions are answered. They have really come through for me, and even with all my degrees and years of education, there aren't enough words to thank them or express how much their generosity and affection have meant to me.

Guiding me out the door, Sam leads me down the steps, but I draw up short again at the sight of the vehicle parked in the driveway. Shock has me damn near weaving on my glass stiletto heels.

The mint-green Aston Martin Valkyrie Spider sits there like a monarch of automobiles. It should with a four-million-dollar price tag. Oh no . . . wait. I drag my gaze from it to Sam.

"Sam, you didn't . . . That's not . . . You can't . . ."

He gives a low laugh, gently tugging me toward the vehicle. "Yes, I did buy the Valkyrie Spider a month ago but had no intention of ever taking it on the road. But when Gus called and informed me that you didn't have an escort to your own engagement ball, I figured there wasn't an occasion more momentous than this one or a passenger more important than tonight and you. So tonight, this is your carriage to the ball." He bows and sweeps his arm out with a broad smile.

His smile is contagious, and I move forward, still stunned over the turn this evening—this entire day—has taken.

Once I'm settled inside, Sam rounds the hood and climbs in. When he starts the car, the engine purrs and he looks over at me, beaming like an eleven-year-old boy who just found his new toy. It's endearing and amusing—and thinking back, I don't think I've ever seen Sam this carefree. Not even when Mom was alive. But then again, how can you be carefree when you're in love with your best friend's wife?

"Did you ever tell her?" I ask Sam as we coast down the PCH toward the main street. The night sky, though clouded by smog, is still beautiful, as is the ocean stretching out on the other side of us, its salty, fresh scent its own perfume.

He glances over at me, eyebrows hiked high. "I'm sorry?"

"Did you ever tell Mom that you loved her?"

Silence fills the interior, almost drowning out the old-school R&B playing on the radio.

"No," he finally says, and I'm grateful that he didn't play in my face by pretending he didn't know what I was talking about. "No, I never did."

"Why not? You were Marcus's friend; you had to be aware he wasn't faithful. And you were around them as a couple enough to also know that they weren't happy. At least Mom wasn't. Even as a kid, I could tell that, so I can't imagine how you'd miss it. Why didn't you tell her and give her the happiness she deserved? Even if it was the last couple of years of her life?"

There's a long pause, and once more I'm left wondering if he's going to reply. Finally, he sighs, and the exhale is weighty with . . . something. Everything.

"For one reason—your mother loved Marcus. Until her last breath, she loved him. But if she'd given me one clue, one iota of a sign that her love had lessened, I would've confessed it all and taken my chance. Kim"—he shakes his head, and I catch the small quirk at the corner of his mouth—"she was unique, special. And not just because of her beauty. She was kind, sincere, honest, generous, loyal to a fault. Once she loved someone, it would take an act of God for her to abandon them. And though Marcus wasn't God, he did give you to her. And for that, she would always remain indebted to him. Would always love him."

"And he took advantage of that love."

"At times he did, yes." Sam stares straight ahead out the windshield. His jaw clenches even as he easily handles the car. "But, in his own way, he loved her, too. He fucked around on her, and there's a part of me that didn't forgive him for that all the way up to his death. I couldn't forgive him for squandering the most perfect, precious gift. Couldn't trust him, to a degree, after that. But still . . . he loved her right up to the end. He wouldn't never have left her, no matter how many other women he had on the side."

"That doesn't make him some hero."

"No, it doesn't. It makes him complicated, imperfect, an idiot, and my best friend. Which is another reason I didn't confess the truth to Kim. It would've destroyed my friendship with Marcus."

I nod, even though I don't agree with everything he's said. It doesn't make a man complicated when he cheats on his sick wife or ignores his only daughter. It just makes him selfish and faithless. And unable—or unwilling—to control his dick.

"Why're you asking me all of this? Does it have anything to do with why I'm escorting you to your engagement party instead of your fiancé?"

"I didn't ask you to do it," I point out rather harshly.

Bitterness coats my tongue, and I try to temper my reaction, but the anger resides too close to the surface. Pain still bubbles beneath my skin. Resentment at even the word *fiancé* claws at my stomach like a wild thing. Fiancés don't throw each other to the wolves.

Fiancés protect each other. Trust each other.

Love . . . each other.

None of that applies here.

"Don't get defensive, Em." He reaches out and pats my thigh. "I'm just asking. Did something happen with Prince?"

"We're fine." I could tell him the truth, but Sam works for Asad now. And while I believe he would say "fuck Asad" if he had to choose between us, I don't want to put him in that position.

"He's not your father, Em," he quietly says after several moments. "This whole engagement took me by surprise, and at first, he is not who I would've chosen for you, but after some thought, he's a good choice. A good man. He'll protect you, go toe to toe against Michelle for you. He'd burn all this down for you. I've seen how he watches you. Hold on in there, Em. I think it'll be worth it in the end."

I nod and look out the window, not replying. I love Sam and respect his opinion—I love him—but his best friend was my father. He's blinded in some respects when it comes to questionable people. Neither he nor I can be lauded for having great taste in people. His best friend was a trash-ass daddy who valued wealth and power over his own flesh and blood.

My husband-to-be blackmailed me into an engagement by threatening my friends' lives, and then when I finally, finally lowered my guard and allowed him into a place no one had ever claimed access to, he tortured me in front of his buddies.

No, we're all good on opinions other than my own over here.

A half hour later, we pull up to the Ebell on Wilshire Boulevard. LA traffic whizzes by us in a cacophony of loud engines, music, and laughter. Do I find it ironic and humorous that House of Cross, a company founded and owned by a patriarchal crime family, is hosting its extravagant ball at an iconic building that's basically a monument to women empowerment? Why yes, yes, I do.

Sam exits the Valkyrie Spider, and I can't contain my chuckle at the valet's wide eyes and slacked mouth. Whatever Sam says to him has his mouth snapping shut. If I had to guess, I'd assume a threat to his life to not get even a thumbprint on the paint. The valet vigorously nods as Sam hands him the keys, then rounds the front of the vehicle and opens the passenger door. He holds his hand out to me and helps me out.

The nerves in my belly twist and writhe. This is it. This is happening.

Sam and I make our way to the Lounge, which is a misnomer. It's not a small, shadowed room. Instead, we enter a cavernous yet packed space with soaring, beamed ceilings, floor-to-ceiling arched windows, gleaming hardwood floors, gorgeous chandeliers with lit candles. We stand at the top of an elegant, luxurious staircase at the mezzanine level where more partygoers gather on balconies to watch the festivities below. It's a blur of color, light, and people. Oh so many people.

"Ready, sweetheart?" Sam whispers.

I nod, and as we begin to descend, the noise level in the area lowers. Heads from the mezzanine turn our way and faces below tip back, their attention focused on us.

And almost out of thin air, Asad appears at the bottom of the staircase. We halt; even if I wanted to move, I'm unable to. My muscles refuse to cooperate as I stare at my fiancé for the first time in a week.

And God, I'm not ready. I'm not ready for the sight of him.

He steps out of my darkest, weakest, dirtiest dream—or nightmare—with all that black hair smoothed up into a neat knot at the top of his head. His thick beard is shaped up, the edges razor-sharp. It surrounds the mouth that has wrecked me, introduced me to a pleasure that surely God never intended his people to know this side of heaven. Those beautiful, all-too-perceptive silver eyes sweep over me, from my straightened, dark blond strands to my glass-encased toes. When his gaze lifts to mine, his is guarded . . . but I still glimpse the flare of heat there. And an answering flame sparks deep and low in my stomach. This is what he does to me. This is who and what I am to him. A reaction to his action. The effect to his cause.

I briefly close my eyes, but they don't stay shut. It's as if they open on their own to soak in the rest of him. The spread of his shoulders and chest underneath the perfectly tailored black tuxedo jacket and white dress shirt. The edges of black-and-gray ink peek above the collars, and neither the formal wear nor the bow tie can harness the sexual charisma or wildness he literally wears in his skin. The black pants skim over his trim waist and powerful, thick thighs, and I fidget, squeezing mine together, seeking to assuage the near-painful ache pulsing in my pussy. It's been a week since he's touched me, since I've inhaled his decadent scent, since he's stretched my walls. Since I've screamed his name so loud, so hard, it leaves my throat raw.

I foolishly believed a week's distance would dampen his impact, his power on me. If "I can show you better than I can tell you" were a person . . .

"Sam, if you don't mind, I'll escort my fiancée from here," Asad says, his tone not seeking permission but informing him.

He may be speaking to my godfather, but his gaze doesn't leave me. Those eyes search mine, as if seeking for the objection or argument he expects me to throw his way. If we weren't in front of most of the fashion industry's royalty and business world, I just might. But . . . I wouldn't embarrass him like that. Even if he wouldn't afford me the same courtesy when he damn near cut off one of my fingers.

"I do mind, but all fathers have to give up their daughters someday," Sam says with a wry smile. He kisses my temple and squeezes my arm before treading down the stairs.

"You look . . . stunning, Ember," he quietly says. His arm lifts, his hand hovering near my cheek, but then he blinks and lowers it. Part of me is thankful because I don't know what his touch would do to me, how it would shake me. But the other half? It already misses something that it didn't have.

"Thank you." I part my lips to say something else—anything else to dispel this awkward cocoon we've found ourselves in while the world moves on below us. But I'm at a loss. There's so much I want to say that it all crowds into my head like a BOGO sale, but only "thank you" slips free.

Then he lifts my hand and brushes his lips across my bandaged finger.

A gasp escapes me before I can trap it. The noise silences. And it's just the two of us in a ballroom full of people. No, it's three of us. Him, me, and this thick, tangled mess of . . . emotion that I'm afraid to unravel. Afraid to touch at all . . .

"Let me guess," I say, voice even, cool, removing my hand from his grasp and ignoring the tremble. "You're sorry and you'll never do it again."

He stares at me, and it takes a will straight from the ancestors not to look away.

"Not that way, I won't."

The threat and promise linger between us as he leads me down the stairs at his side. They settle into my chest and lower, between my thighs, and *goddamn*, there *must* be something fundamentally wrong with me.

I want to forgive him. Want to sink into his arms and turn back the clock to the last night we were together on the balcony, in his bed. But that block of ice right between my rib cage won't allow me to make that move. Won't permit me to do something as foolish as easily believe in his words again. I'm torn in two, confused, ashamed because I should hate him, but *God*, I want him.

Crave what that night prematurely promised.

The sensation of all eyes on us has me wanting to swipe at my exposed skin. After so many years of existing in the shadows, being thrust into the spotlight is surreal and disconcerting. And doing so on Asad's arm only deepens the oddity of it all.

The crowd parts for us—for him—like he's carrying a stick and they're a roaring sea. The display of reverence and fear only sharpens the ache in my pussy and damn the cut of this dress that doesn't allow underwear. Wet dampens my inner thighs, and I swallow a groan. A week without him and minutes in his presence has transformed me into a walking, breathing nerve ending. One that's seconds from pulsing in orgasm with just the slightest touch.

He did this to me.

He introduced me to pleasure, to lust, to fucking.

And now I'm in its thrall. Its submissive.

As if on cue, the live band set up on a raised dais at the far end of the room start playing a stylized version of "You" by Jesse Powell, and Asad ushers me to the middle of the ballroom and takes me into his arms. There isn't even room for daylight between our bodies. And if I didn't know it before, I'm clued in now that Asad gives zero fucks about propriety. Not when he cuffs my wrists and lifts my arms around his neck, then smooths his big palms down my arms, over my ribs and hips, and presses them to the bare space just above where my dress begins again. Several of his fingers rest right on the upper swell of my ass.

His head lowers over mine, those carnal lips capable of such devastation brushing against my temple, the top of my ear, my hair. He surrounds me—his big, hard body, strong arms, fresh, woodsy musk. And for the first time in days, my heart calms. My soul is at rest. I can breathe fully, with full lung capacity.

I close my eyes, fighting against the truth even as I press my lips to the hollow of his throat. My mind might war against this . . . visceral connection. But my body, the most primal part of me, has accepted what it's struggling against.

He isn't letting me go.

And I . . . I don't know if I want him to lose me.

Oh God. *Oh God*. Those thoughts are more dangerous than the man holding me so close right now.

"I missed you." I shiver at both his lips caressing my ear and the quietly spoken words. "And not just the grip of that perfect pussy you took away from me. Or the pretty-ass fuck faces you make. Or how your breath catches just before you cum all over my dick." One hand stays at the small of my back while the other travels up my spine, tapping each disc as if they're keys on a piano, and he's playing our special song.

Shut up, my mind, my soul rails. *Shut up, shut up. You don't mean it. You can't and hurt me. You can't and allow other people witness my pain, my emotional nakedness and vulnerability. You can't and have put me in a place of ridicule.*

But my body, my silly, foolish body, and that equally silly and useless organ beating behind my sternum don't listen to common sense. Won't let us be safe.

They want us to dive off the cliff into troubled waters named Asad Prince.

"I miss how your body seeks me out in the middle of the night as if even subconsciously, you need to be up under me. I miss how your mouth tightens just a little bit when you're trying not to smile. Or how the vein on the side of your throat throbs when I piss you off. I miss how your hair curls up right along your temple and forehead when you sweat." He presses a kiss right at the edge of my hairline. "I just miss you, ma."

I don't reply—I *can't* reply. Asad has never spoken to me like this before. I didn't know he was capable. The scared, leery side of me doesn't want to believe him, wants to dismiss him and his words as him trying to fuck. But the other side . . .

That other side is going to be my destruction.

The song ends, and other couples move onto the floor surrounding us. After one more dance, Asad leads me off, and relief pours through me. I need the distance and space of the social hell laid out before me. At least then I won't be pressed up against him, confused and needy.

The next thirty minutes or so pass with a blur of introductions to people currying favor with him. He presents me as his fiancée and Marcus's daughter, never hiding my identity. And that frigid, silver gaze never fails to dare someone to ask an intrusive question. Which no one does. Apparently, they all value their lives more than some tea.

"Hello, Ember. We haven't seen you in a few days."

I excuse myself from a conversation with one of the designers of a couture house and her husband to face Michelle. My old friend rage simmers in my belly, swirling and working its way up my chest wall. I inhale a deep breath and force my muscles to relax.

You can't crash out. Not here. You can't kick the bitch in her pussy.

Life is so fucking unfair. People come up to you on that good bullshit, but the minute you try and match energy, you're the bad person. They shouldn't get to be protected by manners when they have none.

Good thing I don't believe in that shit. I'm old-school. You show out on me in public, I show out on you in public.

"Yes, it's been a very peaceful, stress-free week, thank you." I offer Michelle an ingenuine smile—while brushing my hair back off my shoulders with my middle finger.

Her condescending smile slips, and her eyes narrow, the hate she's never tried to hide for me shining bright. Her attention dips to the hand holding my glass of white wine. More specifically my bandaged finger. When a mock sympathetic expression replaces the flash of anger, I know what time it's about to be.

Beside me, Asad stiffens, the hand on my elbow tightening

almost to the point of pain. I look over at him, and he gives the tall, gray-haired man he's speaking with a firm nod and then turns toward me, obviously not giving a fuck that the other man was still talking. The cold, menacing mask that drops over his face kick-starts a stampede of nerves down my spine.

"Oh, honey. What happened?" Michelle tilts her head and tsks. "Did you hurt yourself? That looks pretty nasty. You have to be more careful out here."

I chuckle, and Asad subtly shifts, placing himself between me and his mother.

Like a shield. That was . . . unexpected. And though I can fight my own battles, welcome it. I stare at the wide expanse of his back, stunned, shaken. He really just knight-in-shining-armored me.

My chest constricts, and a low, quivering sigh escapes me.

No one, not even Sam with his best intentions, has ever stood in the gap for me.

No one except Asad.

"Michelle," he growls. "Fuck you doing here? Your invite was rescinded."

"No." Clearing my throat, I hold up a hand, letting it hover over his back before tentatively setting it just below his shoulder blade. Stepping to the side of him, I press my shoulder to his. "Your mother was just expressing her concern over my injury. And I appreciate it. To answer your question, Michelle, no, I didn't hurt myself. This"—I switch the glass to my other hand and hold up my bandaged one—"is what happens when people don't know how to mind the business that pays them and have nothing else to do in their pathetic, miserable li'l lives but to be a shit stirrer. But luckily, or rather unluckily depending on who's doing the telling, my fuck-around-and-find-out spirit is strong. So." I wink at her. "Be safe out there."

A gasp echoes from in back of me, and apparently the people Asad had been in conversation with didn't leave fast enough and got them an impromptu show.

Shock slacks her facial features, and she shoots a look at Asad, but if she expected him to jump to her defense, his silence shouts just the opposite. That's right. Cleave, muthafucka. Your son believes in cleaving.

"Asad?" Michelle snaps, mugging him. "Are you really going to just stand there and let this bi—"

"I will call security on your ass right now, and open the door and hoist a toast as they throw you outta here," he warns her, his voice calm but holding a steely thread that she would be suicidal to ignore. "Now I don't know how you got in, but you better start practicing your best apologies, because if my fiancée decides your presence is disturbing her feng shui, you're out."

Holy shit. My pulse thuds in my ears, races in my veins. My choice? He's really choosing me before his mother?

Another first.

No one has ever prioritized me above Michelle. I swallow and turn my head, briefly squeezing my eyes shut. *You cannot cry. You cannot cry. Bennie will beat your ass.*

But given that I'm being championed like some princess at a real-life ball, I think she might forgive me.

"Are you serious right now?" Michelle's head jerks back, and she glares at him.

"Yeah." Tipping his head down, he arches an eyebrow. "Baby girl? Your call. She stay or go?"

Before I can answer, Michelle looses a soft, undignified squawk of outrage, but then it transitions to an abrupt laugh. "Oh, I see where this is headed. Forget that she probably murd—"

He moves so fast, it's a fucking blur, and *holy shit*.

"I see you one of those 'give a muthafucka an inch, they take a gotdamn mile' bitches, huh?" Asad murmurs, his voice possessing an almost curious tone.

But it's that calm, inquisitive note that makes the hard, punishing grip on his mother's cheeks all the more ominous. Michelle's eyes bulge, her lips purse under his implacable hold, and her hands flutter around his wrists. And Asad . . . He doesn't appear angry or bothered. Like manhandling his mother is just something on the hors d'oeuvre menu along with the stuffed salmon bites.

Around us, murmurs and soft exclamations rise, and more than one person is noticing this exchange. I peek around his big body, and more than a few guests nudge each other, whisper behind raised hands or subtly point. But *all* are looking in this direction.

"Asad." I touch the back of his shoulder, but it doesn't seem to faze him at all.

"I've warned you about playing with me. Thinking I won't do you dirty because you pushed me out that ran-through pussy is where you got me fucked up. Now this my last time. Shut the fuck up if you want to stay here, and heed Ember's warning about finding something safe to do. And that doesn't include being around me or talking shit to her. Besides"—he bends his head and says this close to her ear so only the three of us can hear—"we both know the only murdering bitch standing here is you." He abruptly releases her, and she stumbles back several unsteady steps on her heels. Whipping out a handkerchief from his jacket pocket, he wipes his fingers on it without removing his hooded gaze from his mother. "Now, Ember, she staying? Yeah or nah?"

I swallow, a little disturbed but a whole lot turned on.

And awed. And humbled.

I peer at Michelle. "She can stay."

"The announcement about our engagement is at midnight. You might want to fix your face if you intend on staying."

Like, literally fix her face. Her formerly flawless makeup looks like somebody has . . . well . . . jacked her up.

Michelle's chest rises up and down on quick, loud pants. Humiliation, fear, and fury stain her face and gleam in her eyes. I have zero doubts if she could kill her son right now and get away with it, she would. That anger carries a sharp, deadly cold edge, and without realizing it, I take a step toward Asad, the surge of protectiveness propelling me forward. Her gaze shifts to me, and her eyes darken more. But in the next second, her expression clears, all traces of emotion gone as if the altercation with Asad never happened. A strained but cool smile curves her lips, and she dips her head.

"You're right. Now isn't the time or place for this discussion. If you'll excuse me." Head held high, she leaves, the nosy-ass crowd swallowing her up.

Stage whispers and loud murmurs pepper the air, but as Asad turns around to face me, he doesn't seem to give a flying fuck that these people witnessed him yoke his mama up. His *I don't give a fuck*ness is both worrisome and hot as fuck. Worrisome, because if he ever tries that with me, I'm with the shit, too. We would be like a hurricane, fucking everything up in our path. And hot as fuck, because in a world where lies are a universal currency, that kind of brutal honesty where everyone can get it, with no respect of persons, is addictive.

I can no longer deny that Asad has fast become an addiction for me. Like I'm one of the fiends hitting a drug supplied by Cross, I crave a hit of him.

But fear holds me back. Fear of losing myself. Fear of him turning into Marcus and me becoming my mother. Fear of being . . . nothing to him.

"What the fuck just happened here?" Sam hisses, joining us, his furious scrutiny landing on us before scanning the partygoers. As if suddenly remembering they have something else to do, they disperse, leaving the three of us in relative privacy. "I heard about a commotion and then your mother just flew past me. Without her broomstick. What the hell is going on?"

Before Asad or I can reply, Kareem stalks up to our small group, a fierce scowl marring his handsome face.

"I just bumped into Mom, Asad, and she looked terrible. She told me to ask you what happened. What the fuck? Did something go down with her?"

"Yeah." He arches an eyebrow. "Me."

"Prince, are you okay?" Aryn appears next to Kareem and lays a hand on Asad's forearm and the other on his chest.

The fuck? There's no stopping the killing fury surging like a raging tide. Where did she come from? And why is she touching Asad as if she has the right? The ho was at the dinner, so she understands who I am to him.

"Here's where you got me fucked up." I reach over, wrapping my fingers around the ones splayed over his chest, and squeeze. Then bend them back. She gasps and tries to snatch her arm away, but I continue to arch those fingers back until one of them snaps. One down, three more to go. "Maybe no one ever taught you to keep your hands to yourself. Allow me."

"Ember," Kareem gently says, settling his hand on my bare back and covering my fingers with his. I instinctively cringe from his touch. "Let her go, sweetheart. People are looking."

"Get your hands off her," Asad snaps at his brother, and the menace infused in those five words has both him and me dropping our arms to our sides. "Get the bitch you came here with and leave my woman to me."

"Prince—" Aryn whines.

"Okay, okay." Sam steps forward, glancing around with a frown darkening his expression. "This is a fucking sideshow, and we're not here for that. Kareem, take your"—he sneers—"*date* and go get a drink. Prince and Ember, there are a few people who I'd like you to meet," he says, playing peacemaker and directing everyone to their respective corners.

After a hard, enigmatic look at his older brother, Kareem cups Aryn's elbow and leads her away, getting swallowed up by the crowd. The question of why in the hell he's here with his brother's ex–fuck buddy gets lost in the buzz that grows louder and louder in my head. This—his emotional confessional, Michelle, Kareem, Aryn—it's too much, and I need a moment.

"Excuse me for a second. I need to use the bathroom."

"I can take you—"

"No." I shake my head, interrupting Asad, and hold up a hand for added emphasis. "I'm fine. I'll be right back."

"Em . . ."

"I'm good, Sam."

Not waiting for any further argument from either of them, I wind my way through the thick throng of partygoers, offering polite, meaningless smiles to people but not stopping to talk. Some of them I just met while on Asad's arm and others I've never seen before in life, and they only want to speak because of my connection to him. My patience level has hit zero fucks given, and if I don't get to a people-free area, I might scream.

Finally, I push through the entrance and into the airy hall and farther still, out onto the courtyard. The cool night breeze greets me, and I gulp it down like it's red, sweet, and fermented grapes instead of air. I tilt my head back, closing my eyes, and allow the relative quiet, compared to the ballroom, to wash over me. But it's not enough.

Needing more space, more distance, I walk deeper into the shadows, past the gurgling fountain and under the opposite walkway. Once I prop a shoulder against the cool stone column, I exhale and relax. All I need are a few minutes away from all the noise—from the drama—and I'll be okay to return and continue this circus of an evening.

The whole evening—the fairy-tale makeover, Sam, Michelle, and Asad's display of heroism that leaves me breathless and confused—has me reeling and almost overwhelmed. Right now, I'm warring with myself. Stand my ground and resist making another mistake that will land me with my heart torn in pieces? Or take a chance and trust Asad again? Trust that maybe he'll let me fall . . . but not by myself.

I'm not ready to make that decision.

No.

I'm scared to make that decision.

"Ember."

Sighing, I open my eyes and glance at Kareem, leaning against one of the columns. Irritation flashes inside me like dry lightning. So much for those few minutes of solitude.

"Kareem, I don't mean to be rude, but I came out here for a few moments of bullshit-free silence. So, if you don't mind . . ."

The corner of his mouth quirks, and he slides his hands in the front pockets of his tuxedo pants. The moonlight casts half of his face in sharp relief, and for a second, he reminds me of that guy from the Batman cartoon. The one whose face is split in two—one half fucked and the other normal. I don't know why that image pops in my head right now, but I can't shake it.

I straighten, stepping away from the column.

"I'm sorry. The last thing I want to do is intrude, but I saw you walk out of there"—he jerks his chin in the direction of the ballroom—"and wanted to make sure you're okay. You looked a little upset."

I wave a hand. "I'm good. I just needed some air."

"And you're not one for all the drama. And between Asad and my mother, we're nothing but drama," he drawls.

It's on the tip of my tongue to agree, but . . . speaking on Asad behind his back, even if it's to his brother, feels shady and disloyal. Now Michelle, fuck her.

"It's fine," I say, wanting to end this line of conversation. Well, wanting to end the conversation, period. I ventured out here for peace and quiet. Kareem is preventing me from having both.

"Is it though?"

"Is it what?"

"Is it fine?" He tilts his head, and his scrutiny roams over my face. "Because you can be honest with me, Ember. You're safe with me."

I frown, genuinely confused. "Kareem, what're you talking about?" And why are you still here forcing me to have a conversation when I clearly said I'm good and I just want to be alone?

He looks down at my bandaged hand and nods toward it. "I tried to talk him out of picking you up. Mom showed me the same video, but I couldn't believe you would kill Marcus. There had to be some kind of explanation. But we both know my voice holds little weight around here—especially with Prince. So I couldn't stop him. And I'm so sorry you were hurt."

I cradle the hand with the injured finger in my other, holding them both to my stomach.

"You're wrong," I correct him. He stares at me, and I shrug a shoulder, uncomfortable at this line of discussion. Why can't he leave it and me alone? Like. I. Asked. "I could've killed Marcus. I just didn't. And trust, if it had been me, the manner of death wouldn't have been as pedestrian as a drug overdose."

He chuckles, and irritation flashes inside me, hot and bright. "I stand corrected. And you're right. We're all capable of committing things. It's the decision of whether or not to act that separates us from others." He takes a step forward, and it requires everything in me not to retreat. I'm not scared of Kareem. But unease frog-marches down my back. It increases when his voice takes on this faraway quality, as if he's no longer talking to me but himself. "That's what connects you and me. People tend to overlook us, underestimate us. Marcus did it for years with you. Asad and Mom do it with me. It's a blessing and a curse."

"Kareem." I lift a hand toward him, and it hovers just over his forearm. But that unease screams louder inside me, and I lower it. "Are you okay?"

"Hmm?" He gives his head a small, sharp jerk and smiles. The unease deepens, burrowing beneath my skin, sinking in my stomach. "Yes, fine. Sorry. Like I was saying, I'm sorry about your hand. If someone really cares for you, they wouldn't be able to hurt you like that. Or continue to humiliate you by playing in your face. I get your . . . relationship isn't conventional, but—"

"Hold up, hold up." It's me who steps forward this time. I circle my hand in a rewind motion. "Run that back, please. What're you talking about, he continues to humiliate me and play in my face?"

"Ember." Kareem's heavy sigh is as fake as the sympathy he's trying to emit. The shaft of moonlight hitting the upper side of his face reveals the delighted gleam in his eyes. For the first time since we met, when he was thirteen and I was twelve, the resemblance between him and Michelle is uncanny. And unnerving. Because I'm outside, relatively alone with the offspring of a snake. "I came here tonight with Aryn, but do you really think she's for me?" He tsks. "Prince had me bring her as my date so he can access her. She's here *for him*, not me."

His words land on my body, blow after blow, kick after kick. They leave me breathless, aching. Is this true? It could be. Asad and Aryn had history. And if I'd learned anything in the last week, it's that Asad is highly sexual. If he wasn't getting pussy from me . . . My hand splays over my heart, and each lungful of air I take hurts like flesh scraping over jagged glass at just the thought of him putting his mouth on someone else, touching someone else, sliding inside someone else . . . giving them what I'd, at some point, started to consider mine.

"I don't say this to hurt you," Kareem continues, his voice clear despite the pounding of my heartbeat in my ears. "But you've been lied to and used long enough. Another thing we have in common. Prince doesn't deserve your dedication or loyalty. And Cross doesn't deserve your brilliance or service. You're better—meant for better and much bigger things—than my brother and the organization your father didn't even see you worthy enough to lead."

I stare at Kareem, seeing him, really fucking seeing him for maybe the first time. Glimpsing the animosity and jealousy of his brother. Catching the ambition and avarice he's no longer bothering to hide now that he thinks he has an ally in me. A malleable, weak ally he can manipulate and twist.

It's then that my head clears of the noise, confusion, and doubt. Asad might be a cold-blooded, merciless, and murderous asshole, but he's an honest one. He's never lied to me; to the contrary, he's been brutally, even uncomfortably, honest. So having his brother bring his ex-slide to the ball? No, that's not Asad. And if I hadn't let my own doubts supersede my common sense,

I would've immediately rejected that accusation. Kareem played on my insecurities, and I allowed him to momentarily get into my head. The question is, why go through the effort? What does Kareem want from me?

I don't give a fuck.

And I have no desire to be out here alone with him any longer.

"I should get back inside. I'm sure your brother or Sam are looking for me by now," I say, descending the short flight of stairs and heading toward the archway.

"Ember . . ."

"See you in there, Kareem." I lift a hand, wiggling my fingers and walking away as fast as the tight fit of my dress will allow.

He sighs. "I can't let you do that."

Frustration joins my annoyance, and it flares so bright inside me it should light up this fucking courtyard. I hold up my hand, giving him the same one-fingered salute I gave his mother not so long ago.

"Can't let me do—"

Pain explodes in the back of my skull. A burst of light behind my eyelids blinds me.

Then . . . nothing.

Asad

Standing near the bottom of the staircase, I lean an elbow on the curved newel post and murmur a noncommittal reply to the CEO of a prominent and prestigious hedge fund who approached me ten minutes ago with his COO. This isn't a friendly greeting from two guests attending my ball and wanting to shoot the shit. It took a little time, but they eventually started their pitch of why they were a great company to invest my money. I stare at them, allowing them to get the whole spiel out, and apparently, they take that as positive sign.

But they must now know about me. How thorough and distrustful I am.

I had every person attending tonight investigated before an

invitation was even issued. From their childhood pet's name to the brand of toothpaste they use, I'm aware of everything about them. Including things they hide.

Which is why I'm not taking shit these two men are saying to me. Because I know that their hedge fund is in serious trouble due to the CEO playing make-it-rain with clients' money, and his boy, the COO, covering up his theft.

"We would love to schedule a meeting with you, Mr. Prince," Brian Warrington, the CEO, says, wearing a smile so wide I can see his wisdom teeth in the back of his mouth. The silver hair, glasses, sharp yet handsome features, and perfectly tailored Italian suit give the air of a wealthy, successful businessman. But his tanned skin is giving tropical vacation on someone else's dime. "At your convenience, we would like to go more into depth of our services and portfolios."

I lift my glass of D'USSÉ and take a sip, switching my gaze between Brian and the COO whose name I didn't bother to catch.

"I'm going to have to decline." Straightening, I tuck my hand in my pants pocket, never removing from the men in front of me. With his slim, damn near fragile build, dull brown hair, and shifty eyes, he's probably used to being overlooked.

"Mr. Prince, if you would give us a chance to—"

I shake my head and take another sip of the cognac.

"Nah. I'm actually saving your life by declining your offer. 'Cause you fuck around with my money and it comes up missing, you gon' need to paint lamb's blood over your door because I'm coming for you, your firstborn, and first cousin. Everybody can get it behind stealing from me."

Brian blinks. Then blinks again. When he sees I'm not smiling or laughing, he swallows so hard his Adam's apple scales his throat before bobbing back down. He clears his throat, and parts his lips to say something else to me, but I'm done here.

Patting his shoulder, I stride past him, heading for the other side of the ballroom in the direction I last saw Ember before she left for the bathroom. Unease creeps through me as I slowly scan the large space and don't find her among the guests. The fuck she doing in that bathroom? It shouldn't take—I glance down at my watch—fifteen minutes to go and return. I narrow my eyes, surveying the room again as that unease crouching behind my rib cage expands, breathes into a dread that wraps around each rib like a poisonous, clingy vine. Something's not right. It's not right . . .

"Prince." A large hand claps down on my shoulder, much like how I did Brian. I turn around and Eli studies me for a moment, a frown wrinkling his forehead. "It's 11:53. You and Ember should be heading to the stage for the midnight engagement announcement."

"She's not in here." I shake my head. "She went to the bathroom fifteen minutes ago, and I don't think she returned because she's not in this room." Dragging a hand over my mouth and beard, I inhale a breath, trying to calm my racing heart. "I'm about to check the bathroom—"

"Nah." Eli squeezes my shoulder then steps back. "I'll go check it out. You stay here just in case she returns."

"Yeah, okay." I nod, turning to scan the room one more time. Praying to God that I just missed her the previous two times.

"Be back."

I make my way through the throngs of partygoers, not pausing to reply when my name's called by various people. Sam stands near the black marble bar, flirting with the bartender while holding a tumbler of liquor in his hand.

"Sam."

I hate to break up whatever he has going on, especially since I think getting a good nut would loosen him up, but Ember and her whereabouts are my top priority right now.

He turns around at the sound of his name, still wearing the smile he'd been giving the bartender. But my expression must convey the growing anxiety that's been clawing at me with razor-sharp, bloody talons because the smile fades, replaced by a stoic mask.

"What's wrong?" he bluntly asks, reaching behind him to set his drink on the bar top.

"Ember. Have you seen her?" My fingers flex and straighten, flex and straighten.

Sam goes unnaturally still, and he studies me for several long minutes as if he's searching my face for the reason behind my question.

Finally, he inhales a deep breath then slowly releases it.

"Why are you asking me that, Prince? What's happened to my goddaughter?" His voice is quiet, low, but the ominous tone would have made a lesser man quake in his Ferragamos.

Not me though. Fear settles in my chest and gut like squatters in an abandoned building, and it's for Ember, not Sam.

"She went to the bathroom almost twenty minutes ago, and she hasn't returned. I have a bad feeling about this, Sam," I lowly admit.

"Maybe she became sick. Or is just taking a moment to decompress. She isn't a people person, and it could be this ball became overwhelming for her . . ."

He trails off, and I can practically hear the desperation in his tone as he grasps at straws. Shit, I can't lie. I'm clinging to that same hope with cold, trembling hands. Sam rubs his jaw as he inspects the thick crowd. The second his shoulders drop, I know he's come to the same conclusion. She's gone.

Out the corner of my eye, I catch Eli as he reenters the ballroom. Spotting me, he hurries over, pushing a path through anyone in his way. He appears . . . grim. His mouth is flattened, eyes hooded, and before he even closes in on me and Sam, I already know what he's going to tell me.

Acidic bile churns in my stomach, and my chest burns. White noise fills my head, the cheerful sounds in the room fading away. I'm damn near deafened by the rush howling in my ears.

Yet . . . Yet, when Eli says, "She's not in the bathroom. I searched the entire area and couldn't locate her anywhere," I hear him loud and clear. His words are amplified until they threaten to burst my eardrums.

Panic crouches at the edge of my dark fear, ready and hungry to swamp me in its suffocating, blinding grip. But I can't afford to give in to the almost sensual temptation to fucking lose it. I have to find Ember. It was my job to protect her, keep her. And I've failed.

The weight of that guilt is breathtaking and damn near crippling.

"Where is your mother?" Sam snaps, even as he searches the room again.

"She's right there in front of the second window," Eli answers for me.

Michelle holds court, surrounded by a circle of women and several men, laughing and chatting away like a queen with her loyal subjects.

"Wait." I stalk forward several steps, my hands fisting at the sides of my thighs. "Where's Kareem?"

The three of us silently go over the guests again, and *fuck*.

"He's not here," Eli growls.

"We need to find his ass." I don't wait for them as I pivot and stride for the exit. Urgency and blind rage consume me. It could be a coincidence that Kareem is absent the same time as Ember, but every nerve in my body screams that it's not.

Eli barks out orders to the Cross security team, ordering them to search the building and all the grounds to find Ember and Kareem via his commlink. Sam keeps stride with me as we push through the doors and step onto the courtyard. The soft, almost cheerful bubbling of the fountain is incongruent to the panic pounding in my ears and flooding through me. Matter of fact, the moonlit beauty of the arches, flowers, lush grass, and shadowed alcoves is an affront to the ugliness of my suspicions and rage roiling inside me.

I round the fountain, peering into the darkened stairs behind the stone columns.

"Nothing," I murmur. "Fucking no—"

The moonlight hits something in the grass, and it glimmers. Breaking into a run, I reach the object in seconds and pick it up.

A shoe. A lone glass shoe.

Ember's shoe.

CHAPTER FIFTEEN

Ember

The fuck?

I shift on my bed, groaning. My head is *killing* me. What the hell did I drink at that ball, and how much? Gingerly, I roll over, but instead of sinking into my comfortable mattress, my elbow hits a hard-ass surface, propelling another groan from me.

I repeat, the fuck?

Sitting up with my eyes squeezed closed against the terrible pounding in my skull, I press my palms to my forehead. But the pain isn't emanating from the front of my head but the back. Teeth sunk into my bottom lip, I move my hand and encounter a tender lump right above the base of my skull. I probe it, and another blast of pain damn near sends me into a fetal position and my stomach soaring for my throat. I swallow back bile and breathe in and out. In and out. In and out until the worst of it passes.

What the hell happened? Was I in a car accident? Am I in a hospital? That would explain the hard-as-bricks bed.

Slowly, I peel my eyelids open and . . .

Not a hospital.

A cage. I'm sitting on the floor of a muthafuckin' cage.

As if just the sight of my jail unlocks the steel door in my mind, the memories flood in, worsening the ache and nausea.

The ball. The courtyard. Talking with Kareem. Feeling uneasy with the conversation and leaving. Then . . . nothing.

That muthafucka hit me. And apparently kidnapped me.

A huff of laughter escapes me as I stare out at the ordinary-looking den, with a regular desk, boring leather couch, a couple of chairs, and a scratched coffee table, that stretches out beyond the black bars of the cage. The irony isn't lost on me. I'm the one usually on the other side, but now I'm the subject, imprisoned, waiting for God knows what.

Son of a bitch.

I bow my head, the weight of my predicament pressing down on me. What the fuck does Kareem want with me? And does Asad even know that I'm gone? How long have I been locked . . . where here is?

This can't be the end for me. There's too much for me to do. Too much for me to say.

"What the fuck do you have going on, Kareem? You had one job. One damn job, and you fucked that up."

My head snaps up at the familiar voice, and I instantly regret the abrupt motion. The explosion of agony has me swaying, and I allow it to take me back to the floor of the cage. I curl in on myself, body half twisted to face the door as it opens and reveals Michelle, wearing the same dress from the ball, stalking into the room behind her son. Her steps are agitated, jerky, a contradiction to her elegant appearance.

Rage fills me, battling back the pain, shooting adrenaline through my veins and clearing my head. These two? I should've guessed it, but I didn't. This bitch tried to have me killed by execution. Of course she's in on my kidnapping.

"Plans changed, Mom," Kareem says, casually striding into the room and over to his side bar. Still wearing his dress shirt and pants, he doesn't appear like someone who just committed about four felonies. He grabs a decanter and pours a couple of fingers of alcohol into a tumbler. "I changed the plans. You wanted me to take out Asad so you could take over—"

"That's not true! I wanted this for *you*, Kareem. So *you* could run House of Cross and the Cross organization."

I almost gasp, nearly giving away I'm not asleep. The hell? What did I just hear? She and Kareem are plotting on Asad, not me? They're the ones who're working with Xavier and Deacon? My heart slams against my chest, causing an echo chamber in my head.

"Bullshit." He chuckles and takes a sip from his glass. Who is this person? The Kareem I know has never stood up to his mother, has always been obsequious. *This* Kareem is a stranger. And apparently, not just to me either, judging by the jerk of Michelle's chin. "You want me to take over Cross because you think I'm easier to manipulate. Since women can't sit on the throne, you'll do second best—rule through me. There's no way in hell you could do that with Prince. C'mon, Mom, give me some credit."

Michelle doesn't reply, but the heaving of her chest and clenched fists is reply enough. Shit, even I know he isn't wrong. Asad checks her every time she steps out of line. He can't be run or managed.

It's starting to make sense now. It's starting to make a terrible sense. The anger coursing through me has me seeing red, and I don't need to close my eyes to envision their deaths. Their painful, slow deaths.

They took from me.

I don't need to hear them say the words to confirm what I already know.

They're responsible for murdering Marcus.

As shitty as he was, they stole my father from me. Maybe more importantly, they stole the chance I had to make peace with him. To reconcile who we were to each other, whatever that would've been. Father, daughter. Employee, employer. Or nothing. But it was *our choice*. Not theirs. Now, I'll never know what we could've had. I'll never know if . . .

They took from me.

And now they nearly took Asad, too. For what? Power. Money. Greed.

They can't have anything else from me.

Now I'ma take every fucking thing from them.

Even if we all die right here in this dusty-ass den.

Carefully, slowly, so not to draw their notice, I inch my shoe off and reach for it. While they continue to go back and forth, I quickly screw the heel off, removing a needle inserted on the inside of it. Who knew my own special design would come in handy so soon? Time isn't my bitch, so I stick the needle, cap on, against my breast and twist the heel back on the shoe.

"You're an ungrateful shit, Kareem," Michelle fumes, jabbing a finger at him. "I did all this for you. Arranged all of this *for you*. Do you really think Deacon or Xavier would've entertained working for us if not for me? No, they respected me, not you. I got that videotape from Marcus's building. I arranged for that whore to overdose him. What have you done except play the pathetic sycophant fool for Prince? What are you without me? What do you really think you're going to do without me to tell you how to wipe your own ass?" she sneers. "You're nothing."

"Shut the fuck up," he shouts, hurling the tumbler at the wall. Michelle jumps as glass splinters and alcohol decorate the wallpaper near her head. I don't manage to control my flinch. Gotdamn. Thank God they're too embroiled in each other's mess to notice. "Just shut the fuck up for once. All we've ever heard is what you've done for us. What you sacrifice. I'm sick of it. We weren't born to be your fucking pawns. Shit, we didn't ask to be fucking born. Did you ever stop and think for once that Prince didn't give you a position in his inner circle at Cross because he knows he can't trust you? I mean, why would he?" Kareem starts laughing, and the deranged note sends chills racing over my skin. He's unraveling. And Michelle is too arrogant to realize it. "He knows what you're capable of. You murdered our father for a come up. Why wouldn't you take him out for one?"

"Shut up!" Michelle screams. "That's a lie! Don't you ever say that again."

Kareem laughs again and grabs a bottle off the bar but is careful not to turn, giving Michelle his back. Smart guy.

"You keep telling yourself that," he taunts, pouring another glass of alcohol. "But here's what's going to happen. Fuck Cross. I'm tired of standing in the shadow of my big brother. Even in this plan, I'm second best to you. So fuck him and fuck you. I'm taking the key to all this shit"—he turns toward the cage, and I quickly shut my eyes, going so still, I stop breathing—"*her*, and leaving. I have a plane ready to leave in ninety minutes, fueled up and headed to Europe. I'm going to start my own empire. And the only reason I have someone on Prince to kill him is because I don't feel like looking over my shoulder for the rest of my life. So congratulations, Mom. You'll still get what you want. Prince, dead. Though what you can do with that and a crumbling kingdom with no king, I don't know. And don't give a fuck."

"You can't possibly believe you'll get away with this," Michelle says, a note of desperation creeping into her voice beneath the fury as she spreads her arms wide.

"Get away with it? Shit, it's done. You already said it. I'm the pathetic sycophant brother. Who would suspect me of trying to kill him or kidnap his fiancée? I don't have it in me."

I lift my lids to see him set his glass on the bar and approach Michelle. I stiffen, expecting him to choke her, kill her . . . anything but plant a kiss on her cheek. Grinning, he turns and walks toward the cage.

My heart kicks against my rib cage, attempting to execute a jailbreak, but I deliberately force my body to relax, trying not to give him any reason to suspect I've awakened. *Patience. Be patient*. Clearing my mind, I focus on his every movement, planning mine. It's two against one. But one at a time.

I cautiously roll over, moaning as if I'm just waking up. Kareem, standing at the cell door, smiles at me, and I want to burn the shit off his face with hydrofluoric acid. Give that muthafucka a facelift.

"Ember, you're awake." He winces when I touch the back of my head, and the genuine concern in his expression has my belly clenching against the nauseous churning. "I'm sorry about that, but I needed to incapacitate you fast. Don't worry though. I have painkillers for the headache you no doubt have."

I don't say anything, just stare at him. What am I supposed to say? Thank you? The fuck?

He doesn't seem to need a response from me though. Nodding and giving me a sympathetic glance, he unlocks the cage door and steps inside. Reaching into his front suit pocket, he removes a knife. A second later, the blade flicks free.

"Sorry about this, but we have a plane to catch, and I can't afford any trouble out of you." Bending down, he cuffs my upper arm with the hand free of the knife, and helps me to my feet, steadying me when I pretend to stumble. Out of my peripheral vision, Michelle glares at us, her hands clenching and releasing in a spasmodic rhythm. While he's focused on playing the gentleman, I finger the cap on the syringe off and hold it, needle down, between my fingers, hidden at my side. "If you come quietly, I won't have to hurt you again," he says, guiding me from the cell. "I have clothes for you to—*fuck*!"

He screams, hand clutching his neck where the syringe protrudes from it. Eyes wide, he snatches it free—oh, but it's much too late for that. I back away, satisfaction and grim delight burning through me as he falls to his knees, limbs jerking, body convulsing.

"Bitch, what did you do?" Michelle cries, running to her son and falling to her knees beside his body. She attempts to turn him over, yelling his name, but his eyes roll into the back of his head and he goes unnaturally still. "What did you do?" she screams again, running her hands over Kareem's body.

"Botulism toxin. Well, my altered form of it. Instead of hours or days, he's experiencing paralysis of his body now, in seconds. And respiratory failure won't be too long now. Basically, he's suffocating in his own body. But he can still hear you for the next couple of minutes. So, Kareem"—I tilt my head even though he can't move to see me—"bye, bitch."

The labored rattle of his breath signals his imminent death, and I don't turn to run for the door. I don't try to escape. I should, but I'm too hungry to witness the death throes, his final, pitiful moments on this earth. Then I want to send his dirty-ass cunt of a mother after him.

Slowly backpedaling, I split my attention between them and searching the room for any item I can use as a weapon.

"I'm going to kill you," Michelle thickly whispers, running a hand over Kareem's back. "I'm going to do what I should've done the moment your father introduced your ass to me. Put you down like the little whore you are."

Before I can charge her, Michelle jumps to her feet and darts across the short distance to the credenza against the wall. She snatches open a drawer and pulls a gun out, pointing it at me.

Fuck.

I didn't think about her having a weapon.

Fear should prickle my skin, flood my nervous system. But it doesn't. A calm descends on me—calm, and a resolve that this may be it but she won't be able to get away with murder. Asad won't let her. And that is more than enough for me.

Asad.

A wave of grief hits me. Grief and regret. Of what could've been. Of things left unsaid. Of fears not conquered.

Of love not professed.

"Put it down, Michelle," the low, midnight voice comes from behind me, and I almost sink to the floor.

Not with relief. Not all of relief. There's joy. There's fierce triumph.

There's an even fiercer, obsessive, all-consuming love.

Asad came for me.

He *fucking* came for me.

"Prince." The gun trembles slightly in Michelle's hand as she rushes toward me. Cursing, Asad moves at the same time, but she grabs my shoulder and spins me around, jerking me in front of her. "Wha-what're you doing here?" Not waiting for his reply, she retreats, tugging me with her. "She killed your brother, Prince. I have to shoot her. For him. She can't live, and she killed my baby."

"Cut the shit," Prince growls, moving farther into the room, his own weapon trained on her. "I know everything. Next time, choose a better partner than my fuckboy brother. He kept everything on his computer—every email, transaction, text. Once I knew where to look, it was all right there. Including the messages between you two." He shakes his head, and underneath the rage burning in his molten gaze, pain lurks there. A hurt that causes a corresponding ache in my chest. This is his mother, and his brother lies dead on the floor. At my hands. "Xavier mentioned family being involved. But I swear, even with how you did my father, I for some reason didn't conceive you'd do me the same way. So much for that maternal instinct. It's over, Michelle. You're not walking out of here. Let Ember go."

"Ember. Fucking Ember," she snarls in my ear, her fingernails digging into my bare shoulder. Hate and fear jumble together. Hatred for this woman who harms everything she touches. Including her sons. And fear because she's about to steal one more thing from me. My future. "That's all you care about. All you've ever cared about. You think I didn't notice how you were with her when you were younger? It's how I kept you in line. As long as she was around and under my thumb, so were you. But she's not your mother, *I am*. I should have your loyalty. Your love. Fuck her. Fuck her mother. And fuck you if—"

A shot rings out, and the heat of the bullet sears me. Behind me, Michelle stiffens, her grip reflexively tightening on me, but I jerk away in time to see her body tumble to the floor. A neat bullet hole pierces her forehead, and she stares up at me, sightless, lifeless.

I whip around, and Asad lowers his Glock, his gray gaze fixed on me. Scanning over me.

"I'm fine," I rasp.

"C'mere."

"You came for me," I whisper.

"C'mere, Ember."

"You chose me."

His hard expression softens. "Come here, ma."

On a broken cry, I'm moving before I acknowledge it, and I'm flying across the room. I'm running to my safety. My protector. My home.

Before I reach him, Asad crashes into me, his arms closing around me so tight, my ribs faintly protest, but I shut that down because this is what I need. How I need to be held by him. If I could, I'd crawl inside his skin and pay rent to stay.

He's mine. Because I've chosen him, too.

"I'll always come for you, Ember. Love won't let me do anything else."

"You love me?" I ask, cupping his face, sweeping my thumbs over his stark cheekbones. Aside from Sam and my mother, no one has loved me. Has ever said those words to me.

He shakes his head, gently cradling the back of mine. Making a soft, soothing sound when I wince at the bump there.

"To be a genius, sometimes I question your IQ. Yeah, baby girl, I love you." He captures my mouth in a filthy kiss that's all tongue, teeth, and moans. He doesn't seem to care that he's pledging his love for me over his mother's and brother's dead bodies, and shit, neither do I. "Let me hear it."

I don't need to ask what he means, nor do I make him wait.

"I love you, Asad Prince."

Epilogue

ONE MONTH LATER

Asad

"Look at this simple ho, sleeping all good like she ain't violated." Mugging Aryn, Ember lifts her booted foot onto the mattress and jostles up it. When Aryn, bonnet on and makeup-free, continues to sleep like a baby, Ember lowers her leg, reaches over, and pops my ex–jump off in the back of the head. "Wake up, ho."

I snort, standing on the other side of the darkened bedroom, arms crossed. Sure, it's two in the morning, and true, we broke into her town house. But damn, is she fucking Rip Van Winkle? I glance down at the lit face of my watch. I'm giving her twenty more seconds before I pull that pillow out from under her head and smash it over her face. I bet she wakes the fuck up then when she can't breathe.

That's not needed though. The smack to the head—which, fucking *ouch*—does the trick. With a gasp, Aryn jackknifes up, rubbing her scalp through her silk cap. The confusion abruptly evaporates from her face when she finally notices Ember standing next to the bed and me on the other, dressed in all black.

She licks her lips, the whites of her eyes bright in the dark. "What the . . . What're you . . . Prince—"

"Aht, aht." Ember cuts her off, leaning over so they're face-to-face. "Don't talk to him. That's why you're in this position now."

"Wh-what p-position?" she stutters, shaking her head and holding her hands up, palms out.

Ember smiles, and it's all teeth. And it's nothing nice. Aryn actually flinches.

"Fucked. And not how you're used to."

I move, coming to stand at the foot of the large sleigh bed with its mountain of pillows, and pin her with a steady look.

"What did I tell you to do if you and my dick were ever in the same room again?" I ask her.

She whimpers, fear damn near streaming out of her pores. It's one of my favorite scents. Her lips part, but then she glances at Ember.

"Go ahead. Answer him." She grants her permission.

"To exit it."

I nod. "Right. And I warned you what would happen if you didn't. Now, when you showed up at the ball, I was there. And so was my dick. Not only did you not exit, but you put your hands on me. My wife took exception to that."

"Wife?" She frowns. "I thought she was your fiancée—"

"Hey." Ember snaps her fingers in front of her face. "See, you worried about the wrong shit. I'm his wife now. We made it official. Now pay attention."

"Anyway, like I was saying." I lift a foot to the end of the bed and prop my forearm across my knee. "My wife took exception to that, so being the good husband I am, I'm giving her a belated wedding gift. Ma?"

"Thank you, baby." Ember reaches into the pocket of her cargo pants and removes a syringe. At the sight of it, Aryn squeals and scrambles off the bed. Or tries to. I'm already on her, holding her down. In seconds, Ember has the needle sliding into Aryn's neck and injecting whatever new thing she's created into her bloodstream. "There you go."

I release Aryn and step back. We both stand there, watching as her body jerks, eyes roll back, and foam bubbles at her lips. It's over in seconds.

"A shame. Such a promising career cut short by drugs and a friendly pussy."

I bark out a laugh and, gripping the front of her throat, drag Ember close for a kiss. That I can have this, have her so freely without any lies or hidden agendas, still has happiness and peace surging inside me a month after we eloped. Ember Cross Prince is mine. She rules House of Cross and the Cross organization beside me as my equal, no longer in the shadows, no longer in silence.

And I wouldn't have it any other way.

"Have you ever fucked her in this bed?" Ember frowns up at me, the fingernails digging into my skin a threat.

My head jerks up and I mug her. "Hell no. Hotel rooms. I didn't do house calls."

Snickering, she glances at the bed and Aryn's corpse sprawled on it. Stepping out of my embrace, she climbs onto the mattress, snatches her shirt off, and throws it over the side of the bed. With a grunt, she shoves and shoves at Aryn's body until it rolls off the bed and hits the floor.

Well. Gotdamn.

A bark of laughter escapes me, and I stare at her, shocked. Ember grins, and when she crooks a finger at me, I'm already moving toward her, peeling off my shirt. This woman might be more deviant than me. And fuck, I love that for me.

Because she's my equal.

She's mine.

Acknowledgments

First and foremost, I have to give honor and gratitude to God, my heavenly Father. None of this would be possible without Him. He has kept me physically, mentally, and emotionally through the most difficult of times, and I am blessed. Thank you, Father, for never leaving nor forsaking me. I love You.

Thank you to Gary. Not only have you been incredibly long-suffering but you are patient, loving, selfless, and steady. When I say you've been my safe harbor in a storm, I mean that. Thank you for loving and lifting me up through the good and the bad.

Thank you to Kenya Goree-Bell. I thank you for that one a.m. text, for your beautiful brain, and for being an endless source of encouragement and faith. I'm truly blessed to be able to call you friend.

To Juliette Cross. I adore you! And thank you for your kindness, your lovely spirit, and your generosity of time and creativity. Not only are you my publishing sister, but you are my friend. And I count myself lucky.

To Mara Delgado Sanchez. I could spend a whole page listing all the reasons why I'm grateful for you. Not only for helping me to make this book stronger and one I'm even more in love with but also for your infinite patience and kindness. You have no idea how much your "YOU GOT THIS!" messages encouraged me. You've been my editor and support, and I just appreciate you.

Thank you to my agent, Rachel Brooks. Oh my gosh, where do I start? There's sooo much to say, but I don't have the space. So I'll say thank you being my advocate, my defender, my cheerleader, and my advisor. Your compassion and understanding are gifts to me, and I do not take them for granted. You are a blessing—and deliverer of reality checks. LOL!

Finally, thank you to my amazing readers! Those who have been rocking with me since 2009 and my newest ones. I adore all of you. Thank you for taking a risk and following me into this new genre and world. And loving it. That means the world and I'm so grateful for your continued support.

About the Author

Sean Evans of Sean Evans Photography

USA Today bestselling author Naima Simone loves writing sizzling romances with heart, a touch of humor, and snark. Her books have been featured in *The Washington Post* and *Entertainment Weekly* and are described as balancing "crackling, electric love scenes with exquisitely rendered characters caught in emotional turmoil."

She is wife to Superman—or his non-Kryptonian, less bulletproof equivalent—and mother to the most awesome kids ever. They all live in wonderful, sometimes domestically challenged bliss in the Southern United States.